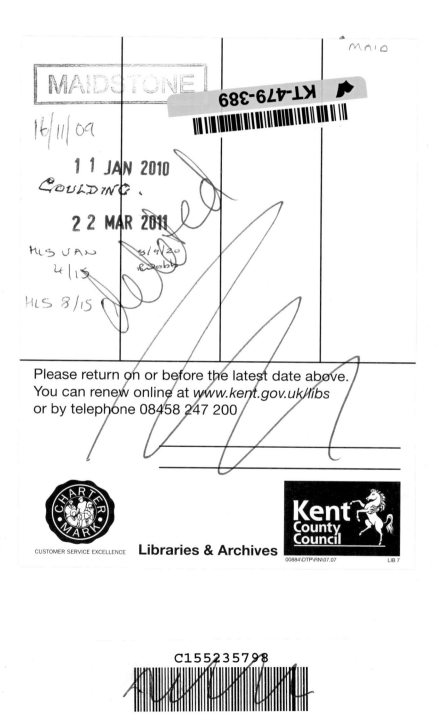

THE GARDEN

Holders Hope, Herefordshire. The roots of a great garden are laid in the long summer of the Edwardian age. Grown from a woman's desperate need to hold on to beauty, created by a man who plants his love for her, hated by a husband it humiliates and imprisons – the garden grows around a secret. Two families are bound up with the garden, three children meet in it, and after some of the most turbulent years of Britain's history it is a young man from the twenty-first century who will finally solve its mystery and brings a hope of its re-birth.

THE GARDEN

THE GARDEN

by

Gillian Linscott

Magna Large Print Books
Long Preston, North Yorkshire,
BD23 4ND, England.

British Library Cataloguing in Publication Data.

Linscott, Gillian
    The garden.

    A catalogue record of this book is
    available from the British Library

    ISBN   0-7505-1999-1

First published in Great Britain in 2002 by Allison & Busby Limited

Copyright © 2002 by Gillian Linscott

Cover illustration © Anthony Monaghan

The right of Gillian Linscott to be identified as the author of this work
has been asserted by her in accordance with the Copyright, Designs
and Patents Act, 1988

Published in Large Print 2003 by arrangement with
Allison & Busby Ltd.

Magna Large Print is an imprint of Library Magna Books Ltd.

Printed and bound in Great Britain by
T.J. (International) Ltd., Cornwall, PL28 8RW

Acknowledgements

The author would like to thank the following for their invaluable and patient help. The staff of the Royal Horticultural Society's Lindley Library and advisory service; Herefordshire Libraries Services; South Wales Miners' Library, University of Wales, Swansea; Treorchy Library local history collection; Cardiff Central Library; Rhondda Heritage Park; Cheltenham Ladies' College Archive; Museum of British Road Transport, Coventry. Also warm thanks to Peter Austerfield, for his knowledge of old apple varieties, Jennie Guille for hers of trees and plants and Anne Ellis for Welsh dialogue.

For Susan Solomon

1

Around midday, with the sun warm on his bare back and a halo of midges round him, Colin found three more finger joints. They were in his sieve, along with two stones, a brown shard of broken teapot and pieces of dried up bulrush stem. The sieve was lying in a green plastic wheelbarrow, half full of riddled loam as dark and rich as chocolate cake. It had taken longer than usual to get the wheelbarrow half full because he'd been working slowly in the heat, hypnotised by the sievefuls of swirling leafy loam that seemed to move to a rhythm of their own, even though he was aware of the lengthening and contracting of his arm muscles. Several times he'd stopped work altogether, leaning on his spade in what would have once been the middle of the pond with his sandals sinking into the loam and the feel of it cool between his toes, thinking and looking out over the nettles and burdock to the blue ridge that was the border with Wales. Sometimes he thought about the garden. Sometimes about Kim, when she'd leave and how much it might hurt. Now and then he wondered when the next bones would turn up. Yesterday there'd been four of them – all fingers he thought. The day before something chunkier

13

that might have been a wrist joint. Only the first lot a week ago had surprised him and that was because six came up in one spadeful still in finger formation, lying next to each other as if bone and cartilage had melted away.

'Kim will want a picture.'

Everything, she'd said. Anything new, as soon as you find it. If he'd shouted she'd have come with the camera that was round her neck almost every waking moment. Only he hadn't shouted. He was no zoologist but from the first there wasn't a doubt in his mind that the bones were human. Too big for chimpanzee and besides what would a chimp be doing in Herefordshire? In the end he'd wrapped them in one of the paper bags that supermarkets supplied for putting mushrooms in but he found useful for collecting seeds, and tucked them in the pocket of his shorts. That evening, in his own tent, he'd transferred them to a plastic lidded box he'd brought for plant samples. Even then, it had struck him that he might need a bigger box before he finished.

Now, with this latest three, it didn't even occur to him to call Kim. The decision had been taken and to explain the growing collection in the samples box would have meant questions. Why hadn't he told her before? What were they going to do? And the question of what to do would mean expulsion from Eden. Thrown out of the garden by the angel with the flaming sword in the shape of police, coroners, archaeologists. He was quite clear that all human remains, however old, had to be reported. Whether his bones had been a

14

deserter from a Roman legion, a medieval plague victim or a drunk Victorian poacher who'd fallen into the pond and drowned, somebody would have a claim to them. But what would happen if he carried his story and his box into the nearest police station? For a start, he didn't even know where the nearest police station was. Probably Hereford in one direction, Abergavenny the other side of the Welsh border in the other.

'Where did you find these bones, sir?'

'Holders Hope. Big house, closed up and nobody living there for a long time by the look of it. The garden's pretty well ruined, only you can still see some of it, steps, the structure ... then there are just three photographs in an old gardening magazine.'

'You own it, sir?'

'Good God no. I'm just working there, trying to see if it's revivable.'

'Employed by the owners?'

'Not employed by anybody. I don't even know who the owners are.'

They were breaking the law, he and Kim, though where was the justice in that when he was giving, not taking? Working through the long June daylight hours, twelve, fourteen hours a day, sometimes digging, cutting and carrying, sometimes measuring, recording, sketching, sometimes just sitting there waiting for an almost dead garden to show some sign of life, like waiting by a patient in a coma.

'Dead?,' Kim had echoed, the first evening, when they were standing on the overgrown terrace with the blank and shuttered house behind them, looking down to the valley and a bend of the little river glinting gold in the sunset. 'You call that dead?'

Acres of competing vegetable life heaved below their feet. The terrace walls had fallen away in places. Brambles rampaging up the gaps over fallen blocks of sandstone met wild clematis swinging down. A rose with floppy pale pink flowers occasionally fought its way out of the tangle. Red valerian clung to the ragged edges of the terrace along with rank yellow flowers of ragwort, each plant alive with caterpillars banded horizontally in orange and black. An elder bush had pushed between the stones of the terrace wall, grown upwards till the top of it was level with their knees then broken into a mass of creamy flowers, wafting a smell that felt sharp in the nose and throat. Halfway down to the river, birch trunks stabbed up through the brambles in thin silver streaks, contrasting with clumps of holly that looked shiny and near black in the horizontal light. On the other side of the birches was a glimpse of dark water, surrounded by bushes. Beyond that, bracken, foxgloves and meadowsweet surged down towards the river.

'Dead as a garden.' Colin said. 'A garden dies when you can't find any sign left of the person who made it.'

'Nothing left of anyone, is there?' She was wearing a white shift dress, no camera for once. Her feet were thin and pale in sandals that were no more than beaded thongs. He felt in his bones that she must be cold, longed to put his jacket round her shoulders but knew how she might go

16

as tense as an angry cat at any clumsy contact.

'Except I've got this feeling that somehow it's not quite dead. If I can look at it for a few days – listen to it.'

'Listen?'

'Sort of listen.'

If he could have explained it to her, he would. Not just listening with ears. Listening with fingers, fingers crumbling soil, stroking along a branch as they were now aching to stroke along her arm. Listening with eyes for rhythms of plants, water courses, pathways. Listening with the part of his mind that came alive and picked up signals from gardens. He looked down, trying to find something that would make her understand.

'There, for instance.'

There were steps curving down from the terrace into the mass of greenery as if into a swimming pool, almost hidden in a tangle of small bushes and convolvulus. Near what was probably the foot of them a tangle of rusted iron hoops stuck out from the weeds with a grey-brown trunk writhing over them. He'd meant her to look at the curve of the steps, but as he spoke he saw there was more than that and felt a rising excitement as if, already, the garden knew he was there and was on his wavelength, communicating.

'I think, I really think it might have been a wisteria tunnel.'

He saw the puzzlement in her eyes and tried to explain, words tripping over each other.

'They'd train the wisteria over the hoops to make a tunnel just high enough to walk through,

17

and the flowers would hang down inside. Can you imagine, you'd go down those steps into this tunnel lined with lilac coloured flowers, then you'd come out at the end of it with the whole view of the valley and the hills in front of you?'

Hills, in some lights, the same colour as the wisteria flowers. Or white under the first snow of winter, framed in twisted bare branches. If Cordell had thought of that he was a master designer, far more than the mere plant collector in the reference books. Kim moved suddenly. He felt her bare arm brushing against his jacket and the coldness of it seemed to get through the material and come straight in contact with his hot skin. He turned towards her and her hand darted inside his shirt, rubbing against his chest. Her mouth opened and his tongue found its way inside. Later, sitting side by side in the dusk, listening to the beep-beep call of a little owl hunting over the river fields, she pointed to flowerets from the elder bush that had stuck themselves to her pubic hair and laughed as he picked them off one by one with his tongue.

2

March 1907

The journey from Hereford station to the house took most of a March afternoon. The three vehicles crawled between hedges whipped bare by the wind, wheels carving red slices of mud from faded grass verges when the steering wavered. The private omnibus Mrs Allegri had hired went first, drawn by a bay and dapple grey cob. The faded brown and yellow paintwork, the badly matched horses, hadn't improved Leon Allegri's temper.

'For God's sake, Isa, I didn't know we were joining a circus.'

She hadn't replied, intent on settling Petra onto one of the long leather covered benches. The child, nine years old, travelled badly. The cold she'd caught in London had got worse, her nose streaming, the eyes that followed her father's every move red-rimmed. On the journey Leon smoked cigar after cigar, lounging on the bench, long legs stretched out and the look of an elegant martyr on his face. When the driver tried to persuade his team to turn off the main road into the lane that led to Holders Hope, the grey was willing enough, but the bay was young and had taken a dislike to something in the hedge. Behind them, the governess cart waited its turn, carrying

19

the maid Jane and the more delicate luggage. The tougher luggage, crates of provisions, books, bedding, was piled in a dog cart behind the governess cart. The dog cart driver had decided that it was going to be a long wait and was letting his horse crop the unrewarding grass beside the road.

Marius, fourteen years old but looking older, with his father's Italian good looks, opened a window and leaned out, shouting advice to the driver.

'Hit her. Don't just crack it. Really lam into her.'

He stood up but found his way blocked by his father's legs angled across the carriage.

'Excuse me please, Father.'

'Sit down, Marius. Your mother's paying him God knows what to get us there, so let him damned well earn it.'

His voice was deep, beautiful and bored. But Marius sensed the anger under the pose of boredom and moved back sulkily to his seat.

'Soon be there,' Isabelle comforted, smiling at Marius. He didn't respond, but Leon took it as the match for the explosion he'd been keeping in store since they'd left Chelsea.

'Soon be where, for God's sake? The back of beyond. If you wanted to drag us on holiday at this time of year, that's your privilege. Why a god-forsaken place where it's even wetter and colder than London?'

'I do own it, after all.'

'You have tenants in. Are we supposed to share with them?'

The driver shouted. The carriage gave a lurch and tilted sideways. Petra whimpered and burrowed her face in her mother's sleeve.

'No, we're not going to share with them. I bought out the lease.'

'You did what?'

He stared, his uninvolved pose gone. 'You bought out nearly a year's lease?'

The carriage lurched again, straightened, began to move forward. She had to raise her voice to be heard over the creaking of springs and harness.

'We're living here.'

'You've gone mad.' Then, to Marius, who was staring at Isabella, mirroring his father's unbelieving expression, 'Your poor mother's gone mad.'

She looked away from them as if she hadn't heard and pushed back Petra's grey felt hat to stroke her hot forehead. The governess cart and the dog cart followed them up the lane towards the house.

The butler sent to tell the housekeeper when he spotted the top of the carriage above the hedge, giving her time to warn the kitchen and inspect the two maids for cleanliness. The butler, Rees, was Liverpool born, a small grey-haired man in his fifties who had served most of his life as a purser on passenger boats. Mrs Morgan, the housekeeper, was from Cardiff, young for the post in her late twenties, come to it after being widowed. They'd got on well enough with tenants and had been disconcerted to find their lives turned upside down in a matter of weeks by a flurry of telegrams and letters from Chelsea. As

21

they waited on the front door steps Rees asked, 'What's she like, Mrs Allegri?'

He'd come with the tenants and never met the family.

'Beautiful.' Mrs Morgan said the word like something holy.

'Fancies herself?'

'Not like that. She's no trouble. Only beautiful.'

In Rees's experience, women weren't usually so reverent about beauty in others.

'Well, he's a painter so I suppose she would be.'

The grey and bay heads and the coachman on the box were in sight now above the hedges. Rees noticed something else and cursed.

'Those kids of Thomas's poking their noses in.'

She looked in the same direction. The field on the far side of the lane rose steeply to a little hillock. Three small figures were standing on it, two boys close together and a girl a little apart, hatless, her long dark hair blowing in the wind.

'They're doing no harm,' she said.

'Ragamuffins.'

Evan, who was eight, wanted to run down to the hedge and see the carriage from close to but Trefor, four years older, held him back.

'Keep some dignity, boy.'

'What's dignity?'

'All you've bloody got.'

Megan took no notice of them, staring at the slow-moving carriage as if she expected to face an examination on every detail of it. The low sun was shining on the windows of the carriage, making them as opaque as metal plates. However she turned her head or screwed up her eyes she couldn't see anything inside, not a curl of hair or a tilt of hat brim. The carriage was turning off the lane and into the gateway, going carefully between the stone pillars topped with globes of pink sandstone. Megan shrugged her shoulders and began walking down the other side of the hill towards the Thomas's cottage. Evan was going to follow her, but Trefor caught his hand and turned him round again to look at the carriage.

'Take a proper look, boy. You're seeing the enemy.'

The coachman was having trouble getting the bay to stand, so Rees had to open the door at the back of the carriage. He expected the gentleman to get out first and help his wife down, but what he got was a child swaddled in shawls with a red nose and sad grey eyes, practically pushed into his arms. Mrs Morgan hurried forward to take the child, giving him a chance to attend to the next person. A woman in her mid-thirties, face shadowed by a wide-brimmed grey hat with a travelling veil, pinned up at one side. Her hair was fair, almost silver-fair in the last of the sunlight, her complexion pale with a greyish tint from tiredness and mauve circles under her eyes.

'Nothing special,' he thought, feeling cheated. He said, 'Mrs Allegri, we're all very pleased to welcome you back.'

She put out her hand and smiled at him and his stomach turned over. Her eyes were the colour of the Mediterranean on a fine day and it seemed as if she'd somehow made that happen for him, like an entertainer pulling a coloured slide across in a

23

magic lantern show.

'You must be Mr Rees. Thank you so much.'

Her voice was low, warming. Her hand touched his briefly, went away again. A shutter came over the magic lantern and she was just a tired woman again. Mrs Morgan, guiding the child up the steps, looked back and felt a personal sense of loss and betrayal. Looks gone, poor thing. Thought she might have hung on to them a bit longer, with her advantages. The child coughed, reminding her where her concern should be.

'Soon have you warm, Miss Petra love.'

It was as if she was comforting the child for her mother's loss.

Rees, in the courtyard, had a small crisis on his hands. Clearly, he should escort Mrs Allegri up the steps and into the house. On the other hand, there were still family in the vehicle. He breathed a sigh of relief when a pair of legs in light coloured trousers and slim-fitting brown leather boots came into view.

'Mr Allegri, it's a pleasure to...'

But the face under the hat brim as the figure straightened up, couldn't be Mr Allegri, not unless Mrs Allegri had gone in for cradle-snatching. It was as smooth as a peach with an expression like royalty on a visit.

'Marius Allegri.'

Emphasis on the first name. The son. Fourteen coming on forty.

Isabelle said, 'Go in and get warm, Marius.'

At least she spoke to him as a child and he did as she said, though in no hurry, sauntering up the steps and looking round as if to check that nobody had pinched a few pillars from the portico since he'd last been there.

'Was Mr Allegri detained in town, ma'am?'

A voice came from inside the carriage.

'Send me out a pot of coffee and a large brandy.'

'Mr Allegri is joking, Rees. Please have coffee and brandy sent to the studio.'

'Yes ma'am.'

He hurried up the steps, worried that his first meeting with the family had gone nowhere near as well as he'd planned. Both horses were fidgeting now in the cold wind and the carriage was grinding slowly forwards on its brown and yellow wheels. Allegri continued sitting as he'd been for the whole journey, legs stretched out, neat beard jutting.

'You'll have to come in, Leon.'

'I am not coming in. I'm going back to the station.'

'The last train will be gone.'

'Just get them to send me out a flask of brandy and some more rugs.'

'You'll have to come in for them.'

'Can't you even control your servants now?'

'Yes. That's why you'll have to come in for them.'

She turned away and walked up the steps. He gave her plenty of time to get inside and stepped down on the gravel, shuddering at the cold and damp. As he passed the driver on the box he said, 'Wait there, I'll be back in a minute.'

The driver waited, got down to light the lamps, got up again and waited some more. After a while

25

the butler came out.

'Mrs Allegri says you can go.'

''e said I were to wait.'

'You go.'

The carriage turned out onto the lane, headlamps throwing wavering patches of light on bare hedges as it went.

Petra was up in her pink and cream bedroom with the curtains drawn, being fed warm bread and milk by one of the resident maids, Susan, who was good with children. A blazing fire reflected off the swan's neck curves of the brass fender and the glass of the pictures round the wall. She knew without turning that the picture on the wall behind her was the Good Shepherd and that his sheep looked like bewildered spaniels, that the one on the opposite wall was Florence. Her mother had promised to take her there one day when she was old enough, because Florence was in Italy and Italy was where Papa's family came from. She lay back in the chair by the fire, half asleep, and let the warm little cushions of bread slide comfortingly down her sore throat, lulled by Susan's words that she hardly understood because of the accent but knew to be kindly. At nine she knew she was far too old to be fed by anybody, but she was ill after all, and that gave her the excuse to be five years old again, as if the last four years hadn't existed. Or not all of the four years. Just the last few months since it had happened. Whatever it was. They wouldn't tell her, or perhaps they might have told her if she'd asked only she didn't know how to ask because she didn't know what it was.

She moved her head, coming unwillingly towards full wakefulness.

'Had enough, my love?,' Susan asked, spoon poised.

She shook her head, opened her mouth to accept the spoonful, letting herself be lulled.

'But after all, if *she* can't be extravagant with coal, who can?'

Mina Morgan was in her own territory, the housekeeper's room, with Rees present at her invitation in the respite between the arrival of the family and dinner. She wanted them to agree on an approach to Mrs Allegri as soon as possible about the necessity of getting more staff. Part of the problem was fires. As she'd pointed out to Rees, there were eleven of them, one in each of the four family bedrooms, one each in the drawing-room, small sitting-room, dining-room, butler's room, the room where they were sitting and the big hungry range in the kitchen.

'That's ten,' he'd said.

'I know it's eleven. What have I forgotten? Oh yes, the studio.'

'Don't forget the studi-o-o.'

He drew out the word, and they laughed. Turning the morning room into a studio had been one of the biggest problems of the last few hectic weeks, wallpapers and blinds, tables, easels and a drawing board sent in almost daily loads from Hereford or even Cardiff, letters of instruction from Mrs Allegri arriving almost as frequently in the minutest detail. They were to be sure the blinds rolled right up to the top of the windows.

Every inch of light was precious. A crate of six new patent lamps, with easily adjustable wicks, was to be sent from Birmingham. It had all been faithfully carried out, so the studio-o-o made eleven rooms with fires, all of them needing coal scuttles refilled, hearths swept, ash carried. With the rest of the household work, that amounted to more than Susan, Mary and the other Mary from the village could do, even if Jane from London had been willing to help out, and she'd already made it perfectly clear that she was a lady's maid, so no fires or cleaning. Rees agreed that an approach must be made. He agreed too that the supply of coal was at least no problem. The Rhondda valleys with their fifty collieries were only a few hill ranges away from Holders Hope and three of those collieries were entirely owned by Mrs Allegri.

Allegri stared at the fire in the small drawing-room, foot on the fender, a smell of scorching leather rising from his boots. In spite of the heat he was still wearing his outdoor coat. Isabella sat in an armless chair upholstered in blue damask, watching him as he drained his second glass of brandy.

'I'll write to you from town, Isa. There are things we must discuss.'

He picked up his hat. She stood up.

'I want to show you something first. A surprise.'

'You've given me enough surprises for one day.'

'Please.'

He shrugged. 'It had better not take long. The circus wagon's waiting.'

She opened the door into what had been the

28

morning room, stood back to let him go first and watched as he took a few steps inside.

'What's all this for?'

The tone of his voice told her that she'd failed. She said to his back, 'Your studio.'

'I've got a studio in London.'

In spite of her care, it didn't have the feeling of a studio. The new easel, the table with boxes of paints, brushes and bottles of linseed from his usual suppliers, the blank canvases stacked against the wall were like things marooned by accident.

'You've got one here now.'

At least he registered the care she'd taken, because his voice and the look he gave her were more sad than angry.

'Isa, what could there possibly be here for me to paint?'

She looked back at him for a long time, face as blank as one of the canvases. Then she put her hands over her eyes and turned away.

'Oh God, what have I said now?'

'Nothing. Nothing.'

Genuinely puzzled, he started walking round the room and stopped in front of a picture on the wall opposite the windows.

'What's that doing here?'

A portrait of a woman, young and fair-haired, standing in an open doorway to a garden, the vivid blue of her eyes picked up in the ribbons on her dress and the flowers behind her. It seemed to glow with a light of its own, independent of the sooty lamps.

'I had it sent down from London two weeks

29

ago. You never noticed it had gone.'

'It's yours after all. Up to you where you put it.'

She nodded and walked out of the studio, through the drawing-room to the hall.

'I'll go up and see that the children are all right.'

'Say goodnight to them for me. I'll write.'

He opened the front door for himself. At the bottom of the steps a driver and a boy were unloading the last of the things from the dog cart. Allegri put his hat on, walked to the bottom of the steps and yelled into the darkness, 'Hey, I'm ready now.' The dog cart driver looked at him, puzzled.

''E's gone back to 'ereford an 'our ago, sir.'

'But I told him to wait.'

Isabelle's voice drifted down quietly from the top of the steps. 'And I told him to go.'

He sprang up the steps as if he intended to attack her. She didn't move.

'How am I going to get back? Tell me that? How am I going to get back?'

There was panic in his voice. The dog cart man said helpfully, from the bottom of the steps, 'I'll be going back meself when we've got this lot out, sir.'

There was straw on the floor from the packing cases, hard plank seats without upholstery. Without saying anything Leon went back up the steps, past Isabelle and into the house.

3

Will Thomas came from shutting the hens in, one small pale egg cradled in his big hand, a black and white terrier scuttling after him.

His wife Bathsheba was standing at the range, stirring a big black saucepan. The heat from the range blasted up at his wind-chilled face and roused a faint smell of chicken-shit from his corduroy trousers and old tweed jacket. He held out his hand, offering the egg to her.

'Only the one?'

'Not properly started yet, they haven't. It'll make a little batter pudding anyhow.'

He unlatched the meat safe in the corner and put the small egg carefully in a cracked willow pattern tureen.

'Hello, Megan love. Enjoy your walk?'

'Cold, it was.'

Megan was setting the table for supper, laying spoons and forks on the faded oilcloth in five place settings, by the light of an oil lamp that hung over the table. The arrival of the nephews and niece had strained all the resources of the cottage to their limits, including cutlery. There were soup spoons for Will and Trefor, old dessert spoons with the edges worn thin for Bathsheba and Megan, but Evan as the youngest had to make do with a jam spoon with an enamel crest of Weston Super Mare on the top and most of the plating worn away from the bowl.

Bathsheba said, still stirring, 'They saw them arriving.'

'What did they look like, Meg?'

'Dunnow, couldn't see anything.'

'How do you know it were them, then?'

He spoke in the coaxing tone he used with his animals, willing her to look at him and smile. Megan smiling was one of the prettiest things he'd ever seen. But she seemed preoccupied, as if putting forks parallel to spoons needed a lot of attention.

'You'll need to go up and see her, Will, see what she wants doing about the garden,' Bathsheba said.

He nodded, not looking happy about it.

'Then there's the bit of field.'

'Three ponies don't eat much.'

'Four with the foal.'

'He don't eat anything. He's got his ma's milk.'

'Put the plates out, Megan, and call the boys down.'

There wasn't much room between the range and the table but Megan moved neatly. Will watched her ankles and the start of the curve of her calf under the blue wool skirt and sighed.

'Trefor, Evan. Supper's ready.'

She hardly needed to raise her voice because the boys' cubbyhole wasn't much higher than her head when she stood on the living room floor. They came clattering down in their nailed boots, Evan in a rush and Trefor more slowly, and went to their places at the table. Bathsheba ladled out a stew of potatoes, leeks and turnips, flavoured by ham bone. The shreds of ham that had boiled away from the bone went into Will's plate. The bone, cooked to blue-white cleanliness with no more than a dab of fat and a smell clinging to it, was put aside on the dresser to cool for the dog.

They ate quickly and in silence. When the plates were empty Megan stacked them up and carried them out to the scullery. While she was out of the room, Bathsheba said to Will, 'If you're up there tomorrow, try and get a word with Mrs Morgan. All the extra work, might be a chance there for Megan.'

Will nodded sadly, thinking of the smile and ankles moving around rooms that weren't his own.

'What do you mean?'

Will and Bathsheba stared at Trefor. At twelve his voice was breaking and the four words had happened to come out in the gruff, grown-up tone that made it seem as if another person had arrived suddenly in the room. He was looking gruff too, a quiff of dark hair falling over one eye, scowl on his face. It had disturbed Will when the three children first arrived that Trefor seemed sullen, but Bathsheba had said not to mind, some faces were made like that and there was the worrying about his mother too. But even making allowances, he looked angry now. Bathsheba didn't take offence and answered as if he really were grown-up.

'A chance for her to go into service.'

'No.'

'I'm not saying she could go straight into upstairs work. You wouldn't expect it, her not

33

knowing anything. But if we can get her a little job in the kitchen and she gives satisfaction, there's no telling...'

'No.' No making allowances this time. The boy was angry, insolent. 'Megan's not going to sir and madam anybody.'

Evan sucked the last of the salty stew taste off his spoon, looking at his brother with big, curious eyes. Bathsheba waited for her husband to remind Trefor about manners, but as with most things he reacted slowly and had hardly opened his mouth before Megan was back in the room.

'What's he saying about me, Auntie Bath?'

'We were talking about getting a situation for you up at the house. Your brother's taken it on himself to say no.'

'A situation?'

'Working, like.'

'For her? For the lady?'

She was pleased, curious. Trefor said, 'You don't want to...' But his voice let him down, skidding back to little boy's. Megan looked at him with the authority of a fifteen-year-old sister over a brother of twelve and he went quiet. Will hardly ever argued with Bathsheba, but he looked at the girl standing so eager and pretty in the lamplight and tried a protest.

'They'll be needing her at home, after...'

After their mother was dead. Although nothing had been said to them, the three children knew why they were with their aunt and uncle. Back home in Treorchy in the Rhondda their mother, Will's sister-in-law, was lying day and night by the fire in the parlour, coughing her lungs out.

Bathsheba said: 'There's Sarah at home. They won't need both the girls.'

Sarah, at sixteen, was nursing her mother and cooking and washing for her father who came off shift at the pit and scrubbed in a zinc bath in the outhouse until his skin was raw, trying to get off the smell of coal dust that made his wife's coughing worse.

Megan said, trying out the idea, 'Not go home, you're saying?'

Evan was sucking at the spoon so hard his mouth felt metallic. Tears ran slowly down his face, saltier than the stew.

Bathsheba said to Will, 'Look what you've done now. You've made the boy cry.'

Will's broad shoulders slumped. Small guilts for things done or undone nagged at him most of the time and words seemed to be the worst, which was why he used as few of them as he could. Bathsheba put her arm round Evan's shoulders. Of the three children who'd come to them when she'd given up hope of having her own, she loved Evan best, a child still, with a child's willingness to be made happy. He leaned against her, burrowing his damp face against her breast and she rocked him backwards and forwards.

Megan said, 'He's tired. He needs his bed.'

'Yes.'

Reluctantly Bathsheba stood him up and guided him to the foot of the stairs.

'He'll want the candle,' Trefor said, back to his usual politeness now. He picked up the enamel candle holder from the hearth, took a three inch candle stub from his breeches pocket and held it to the fire to light. Upstairs in the boys' cubbyhole Evan was sitting on the mattress of sacking stuffed with hay while Bathsheba knelt to unlace his boots by the light coming from downstairs through the cracks between the floorboards. Trefor put down his candle on the floor throwing the shadows of the three of them over the packing case walls.

'Don't you bother, Aunt Bath, I'll see to him.'

Reluctantly she got to her feet, kissed Evan on the hair parting like somebody stealing and went downstairs, drawing the curtain across their door space as she went. Without saying anything Trefor undressed his brother down to his shirt, socks and underpants, waited while he settled on the mattress then tucked the grey scratchy blanket round him. Then he pulled a pamphlet out from under his own side of the mattress, moved the candle holder to keep the light off Evan and onto the pages and started reading in a low voice the only thing he knew to give consolation to himself and his brother: *Why Are The Many Poor?*

The son of an owner of ironworks is now in the House of Lords; he has a fine town house and two or three country mansions; his children are brought up in ease and luxury.

Evan, drifting to sleep, asked 'Do they have jam roly-poly every day?' Trefor read on, the words so familiar that he hardly needed to look at the page in the wavering candlelight.

But where are the children of those whose work made the fortune? They toil from morning to night for

36

a bare living as their fathers did before them.

Downstairs, Bathsheba heard the chanting voice but not the words and smiled. 'Bless him, he's reading his brother a fairy story.'

The time approaches when capital can be made public property, no longer at the disposal of the few but owned by the community for the benefit of all. You can help to do this; without you it cannot be done.

Evan was asleep, curled on his side with one hand flat on the pillow. Trefor tucked the pamphlet back under his side of the bed and blew out the candle.

4

Mr and Mrs Allegri stood side by side on the terrace, well wrapped against the March cold. She was wearing a violet wool cape with the hood drawn up round her face. He was in his travelling clothes of the day before, including the broad-brimmed black hat. Behind them the windows at the back of the house, facing south east, caught occasional glints of sun when the clouds blew aside, but there was no warmth in it yet. The house was built of the local pink sandstone that looked warm in the sun but the colour of condemned meat when wet. It had rained in the night. The house's straight classical outlines contrasted with a setting that was all curves – curve of the wooded hill above, curves of the little river running through the meadows below where black cattle were grazing. Beyond the river the ground rose up to the ridge that divided them from Wales. The lower slopes were separated into small pasture fields surrounded by high hedges. Above the fields a dry stone wall cut a wavering line across the hillside, and on the far side of the wall dead bracken, brown and damp. After a long time, Leon spoke.

'I doubt if there's a more dismal outlook in the whole of Europe.'

Isabelle knew he wanted an argument, but couldn't help defending the place her father had bought. He'd walked her hand in hand round the estate when she was no older than Petra, glowing with pride, mining engineer to country gentleman in one generation, all his own efforts.

'It's beautiful in summer.'

'Beautiful is people. There isn't a single person within twenty miles of here who's been outside the British Isles, or tasted wine, or heard a symphony orchestra, or doesn't think Velazquez's some kind of cattle drench.'

'Leon, you can't know that.'

In spite of everything, he could still make her laugh when he went off on one of his tirades and the laughter made her feel warm inside, like a little orgasm. He knew that because she'd told him once, lying sated and happy on a bed in Italy with white curtains blowing in the breeze from the lake. She wished now she hadn't told him.

'I'm not staying here, Isa.'

'So where are you going?'

'Home to Chelsea, of course.'

'I shouldn't. You'll find the decorators in.'

'Isa dear, is all this drama simply so that you can have the house redecorated?'

'Not entirely. The tenants insisted.'

He put a hand to his head. He couldn't help being theatrical but he was truly puzzled.

'But you bought the tenants out.'

'That was the tenants here. I'm talking about the tenants who're taking the Chelsea house.'

'What?'

'I've let it, Leon. An American couple. He's attached to the embassy.'

'How long?'

'Six months initially, with an option to extend if it suits them.'

In the past, her business sense had enchanted him. It went piquantly with her fair and fragile beauty, like Titania with a machete.

He said bitterly, 'You don't waste time, do you?'

'You knew that.'

She was capable of hesitating minutes long over which peach to take from a bowl, then deciding to off-load a parcel of railway shares that were performing disappointingly with a speed that rocked the men who thought they were her financial advisers. The Chelsea house was her own, a gift from the old man when Marius was born.

'I shall stay at my club.'

'Will they let you?'

It was his own fault that she knew about the unpaid bills. He'd taken to leaving them casually about the house in the hope that she'd settle them. She hadn't taken the hint. He turned away from the view, trying urgently to make her

39

understand before this thing set like plaster of Paris round him.

'Isa, it's people I paint. And you'll go mad shut up here with the children.'

'I was going mad in London. Have you any idea what it's like, every time you go out, to dinner, to the theatre, knowing that people are looking at you, talking about you, pitying you?'

He sighed and turned away. 'That again.'

'No, not that again. It's not going to happen again. That's why I'm staying here.'

'But what will you do here? Church-going? Soup to the peasants?'

'I'm going to make a garden.'

He made a derisive noise. 'Like that?'

Below the terrace a bank of pale tussocky grass with a few clumps of daffodil leaves stretched down to a path where couch grass fought its way through thin gravel. Iron railings protected it from the sheep grazing in the field downslope. A circular bed had been cut out in the middle of the bank. The pinkish brown soil was bare, apart from a straggle of groundsel and couch grass.

'Anything but that. Something beautiful.'

Beauty had been the engine that drove her life, that made things happen to her. Until a few months ago, it had been her own beauty. Now that beauty wasn't working any more. It had ceased to function like the motor cars she saw sometimes beside the road, helpless drivers explaining that this rod or that shaft had gone.

'And my place in this? Gardener's boy? Five shillings a week for my pains?'

'You have a home here. You know that.'

40

He had five shillings and threepence in the pocket of his trousers, nineteen pounds and ten shillings in his wallet up in the dressing room. Nineteen pounds fifteen shillings and threepence would get him back to London, pay a few months' rent on some squalid garret. He could tout for a commission or two. Say five hundred guineas in his hand by the start of summer then – Italy. His bones ached for heat, for sun that didn't ration itself by half hours, for red wine pouring out of spigots, not doled by butlers out of bottles. But the prospect of poverty in London's grudging spring was more than he could face and after what had happened the class of men who could pay several hundred guineas for a portrait wouldn't leave him alone in a studio with their wives and daughters. Isabelle saw his shoulders sag and knew, with heart sinking, that she'd won. It had been in her mind that he might even now do a miracle and turn back the clock for both of them.

'This garden – can I guess the identity of the gardener's boy?'

'I thought I might ask Philip Cordell for some suggestions.'

He turned and smiled coldly at her.

'What a very good idea.'

Petra, waking late and watching from her first floor window, saw them walking into the house together and felt tentatively happy because they were back at their real home and her father was there.

5

Philip Cordell sat by a crate in a darkened room in Alexandria and prayed, 'Let it live.' Then he thought about the sea voyage through the spring heat of the Mediterranean, between the Pillars of Hercules and up the rough Atlantic to the Channel, and added, 'But not too much. Not yet.'

He was dealing with a kind of vegetable sky rocket. Inside the crate, which he'd had made at great trouble and expense at Mombasa, was a ball of long dark green leaves about five feet in diameter. Four more of them were curled in similar crates against the wall. 'Cordell's cabbages' were what his travelling companion, Henry White, called them but then Henry only cared about the journey, not the plants. Lobelias, Philip had told him. Wollaston's lobelia, Lobelia wollastonii. Not possible, Henry had said firmly, poking at a plant with his stick as if it might be provoked to bite him. He didn't know much about flowers but he knew lobelias from his mother's garden. Little fiddly blue things at the front of borders, six inches tall at most, whereas these monsters... That conversation had gone on in the very centre of Africa, thirteen thousand feet up in the Mountains of the Moon when the two of them and their porters were surrounded by great towering flower spikes three times their own height, shaggy as goat skins at the tip where the buds hadn't opened, hazed lower down with small flowers of a brilliant sky blue. Little green birds were darting in and out of the flowers, looking no bigger than bumble-bees in proportion to the insane, totally unreasonable size of the plants. Philip had got Henry to stand alongside the tallest spike with a porter on his shoulders holding up their tape measure on the tip of the longest stick they could find and recorded it at one inch over twenty feet from hairy tip to ground. He wrote it down in his notebook, along with the circumference, time of day, surrounding vegetation, altitude, humidity, like the good plantsman he was, but all the time he'd been in a daze of wonder and unbelief. Whenever you thought you'd reached the outer limits of the things plants could do there was always a surprise ready to spill out of an Alpine scree slope or swing down from a tree in a rain forest or in this case sit there just below the snowline of a mountain practically on the Equator, waiting a few thousand years for a party to come along and see the joke. While they were measuring he'd felt pure childish laughter twitching at his diaphragm and at last it had spilled out so that he couldn't stop. Henry had stared at him for a while, obviously concerned that he was suffering the effects of exhaustion or altitude, then he'd started laughing too.

'See what you mean, old boy. They are a bit … well, a bit hard to live up to.'

Then they were both of them laughing

43

uncontrollably, surrounded by a grove of giant vegetable phalluses and the porters were laughing too, pointing to the plants, gesturing to show they understood. Their laughter whirled up to the snowy summits, out over the long green reaches of Africa under their feet, scaring the birds away. But although Philip had started the laughter and enjoyed the joke as much as any of them, it hadn't been what he'd meant at all. His own private laughter had been a delight at the whole unlikeliness of the things. The thought that came into his mind was something on the lines of, 'If they can be like that – anything's possible.' But he couldn't have explained what he meant to himself, let alone to Henry, so he was happy enough that they all thought he was laughing at the shape of the plants.

They'd calmed down and got back to the serious business of plant collecting, which was what Philip did for a living. Usually it was a matter of bringing back seeds, bulbs and dried specimens but one of his clients in Cornwall had heard about the giant lobelias from a report of an earlier expedition sent out by the British Museum and had a rich man's impatience. He desperately wanted them in his garden and had commissioned Philip to bring some back alive. Not in their full twenty foot glory. Even a rich man knew that was impractical. What he wanted was the younger rosette-like plants that would launch their rockets only when safely planted in Cornish soil. The trouble was that nobody knew what lit the fuse, what combination of heat and cold, light and dark, would start the growing process. Philip had chosen specimens that looked a long way from rocketing and on the dragging journey to the coast, with each plant in its ball of black earth slung between two porters, he'd fussed over them like a hen with eggs, only in this case anxious that the life force shouldn't be doing its work yet. All the way from Mombasa by cargo ship up the Indian Ocean they'd slept peacefully in the hold. From the Gulf of Aden, through the baking heat of the Red Sea and the Suez Canal, he'd thought that the leaves of two of them were beginning to draw back from the centre and spread, but it must have been his imagination because when they arrived at Alexandria and he booked a separate room for them next to his own at the hotel, they were still curled in on themselves, protecting and hiding their explosive hearts. Cordell's cabbages.

A knock on the door. Henry's cheerful voice.

'You in there, Cordell?' He walked in, wrinkling his nose against the damp earth smell. 'Wishing them bon voyage are you?'

They went next door and Henry waited while Philip sponged himself and changed into evening clothes that still felt unfamiliar after months of travelling. They were going for the night out on the town that they'd promised themselves while wet and shivering on the mountain or wakeful with insect bites in camps in the rain forest. A few drinks on the terrace, a good dinner then a stroll to a place Henry knew where the girls all claimed to come from Paris and might not all be lying.

45

Henry worked as a military attache at the embassy in Cairo, so knew his way around. While Philip buttoned his shirt and tied his tie Henry went on teasing him about the plants.

'I suppose you've booked them a first class salon.'

'Naturally. Outside cabin and personal waiter.'

In fact, the giant lobelias would be making the next stage of their journey in the hold of a British cargo ship whose first mate, providentially, was a devoted botanist. Philip had already provided him with three pages of instructions on their care and the impatient millionaire would be waiting at Dover with his chauffeur, head gardener and motor car, to rush them to their new home. The plan was to load them at dawn to save exposing them to Egyptian light and heat. Philip and Henry sauntered down to the terrace. It was the time of evening when the warm air off the desert with its whiff of camel or donkey and sweetly rotting fruit from the market met the salt breeze coming from the harbour. They decided to start the evening properly by sharing a bottle of champagne.

'Thanks Henry. Here's to journeys.'

'And to homecomings.'

Philip gave him a glance, but drank.

Henry said: 'Why not go home with your cabbages? You've seen them this far. Might as well see it to the end.'

'I've told you. I want to be in Erzurum for the irises next month and drop in and talk to Siehe on the way through Turkey about the new finds.'

'The irises will wait, won't they?'

46

'That's exactly what they won't do.'

Irises of the oncocyclus group, the most beautiful of the whole complicated species in Philip's eyes. Almost as odd in their way as the giant lobelias, though so much smaller. Not patient flowers. Even the look of them, with the huge delicate petals poised on top of their short stems, reminded him of butterflies ready to take off. He felt sometimes he needed a net, not a trowel, to take them. Their almost infinite variety of colour and marking – combinations of whites and purples, browns, maroons, yellows and greens in veins and blobs and blotches – seemed nature's joke to drive botanists and collectors mad. They grew in high stony places, often flowering just after the snows went, and the blooms didn't last long. A day or two late and you might miss something that would never be seen again. Although regretting the coming parting with the lobelias, Philip was already aching to be walking up to a pass in the Pontic Mountains, heart thumping at what might be poised to fly away on the other side.

'How long is it since you were home, Cordell?'

He thought about it.

'Two years.'

'More than that, isn't it?'

'Coming up three. I don't know.'

To know for sure he'd have to count back and he'd stopped himself doing that. He changed the subject. They finished the champagne, strolled in to dinner, strolled out some time later, relaxed and pleased with life and themselves. As they were on their way across the hotel foyer the

47

porter gave Philip three letters from his pigeon hole. He stuffed them into his pocket and didn't look at them until the early hours of the morning, when he was on a couch in a room of the place Henry knew, with one of the girls who might be from Paris lying naked against his chest, pretending to sleep. Some men liked to think they'd made a girl sleep from satiation. Philip knew the girl knew this, knew too that she was pretending, but didn't mind. Carefully, so as not to give her the trouble of acting an awakening, he reached for his jacket and looked at the letters under the dim light of one oil lamp still burning. All from England. One from a botanical garden, one from a shipping line. The handwriting on the front of the third made him catch his breath and make a sudden movement, so that the girl had to open her eyes after all.

'Mon cheri...'

But he wasn't listening, didn't even feel the dutiful hand against his thigh. He read.

My Dear,
We are at HH. Leon is unforgivable at last. I want to make something beautiful with what's left of my life. I need you to help me.
Please write and let me know when you will be back in England. Petra sends her love and wants to know if you have found a flower to name after her yet.

The signature was simply an ornate capital I.

Before it got light, two horse-drawn vehicles left

48

the hotel for the docks. One carried Philip, who was sitting tensely on the edge of his seat and Henry, who was puzzled and hung-over. The other lumbered behind them, weighed down with five large crates covered with damp sacking. The ship sailed two hours later with Philip waving from the deck and Henry, still hung-over and still puzzled at the sudden change of plan, returning his wave across a widening gap of water.

6

From John Waterer and Sons Ltd, Bagshot, Surrey to Mrs L. Allegri, Holders Hope, Herefordshire. 17 March 1907.

Madam,
I have today forwarded per rails goods train to Hereford Station plants as listed according to your esteemed order. Hoping they will arrive safely and prove satisfactory. I am, Madam, your obedt. servt.

  3 **Ilex aurea Golden Queen** 5s each 15s
  3 **Ilex Silver Queen** ditto 15s
  6 **Guelder roses** 2s each 12s
  6 **Sweet briar** 1s6d each 9s
10 **Andromeda floribunda** 2s each £1 00
10 **Scarlet dogwood** 1s6d each 15s
  3 **Wisteria sinensis** 2s each 6s

1 **young Weeping Purple Beech**   10s6d
20 **Rosemary** 6d each 10s
20 **Lavender** 1s each £1 00
20 **Santolina** 9d each 15s
  2 **Double White Cherry** 5s each 10s
  1 dozen **Rhododendron myrtifolium**   £1 4s
Rhododendron named varieties
  2 **Sappho** 5s each 10s
  2 **Duchess of Connaught** ditto 10s
  2 **Alexander Adie** ditto 10s
  2 **William Ewart Gladstone** ditto 10s

Total £11-1s-6d

Isabelle Allegri, Holders Hope, Herefordshire to
Philip Cordell, Lupus Street, London. 9 April
1907.

My Dear,
I am so very glad to know you are back. Your note
from Dover came by the same post as your letter
from Gibraltar. Please finish your business in
London as soon as you can and come here. Your
room is ready and the children are so looking
forward to seeing you. Could you be here by the
weekend, do you think? If you'll let me know
when you're arriving, I'll see you're met. I have
already bought quantities of plants from Waterer
(list enclosed.) I've ordered no roses yet, but
shall do so this week. We must have swathes of
roses.
　　Yours affectionately

　　　　　　　　　　　　　　　　　Isa

Philip Cordell to Isabelle Allegri. 11 April 1907.
(Thursday)

Dearest Isa Floribunda,
Listen to me. STOP IT. You will oblige your
devoted and most obedient friend by taking that
catalogue down to the furthest point of your
garden, placing it under the largest rock you can
conveniently handle and leaving it there until I
arrive.
My dear, you are smothering me with cherries,
ambushing me with andromedas, impaling me
on ilex. No wonder the purple beech is weeping.
I'm sure it is from sheer bewilderment.
Oh my girl of little patience, this is not the way
one makes a garden, any more than one makes a
picture by squeezing every tube to hand onto
canvas. I shall explain when I come, which I hope
will be this Saturday provided I can finish with
the boring men in offices tomorrow. Don't worry
about having me met. I'll arrive when I arrive.
My love to the children. I have a snakeskin for
Marius and something that once belonged to an
Egyptian queen for Petra.
    Yours in anticipation
                                        Philip

7

April 1907

'Eleven pounds, one shilling and sixpence.'

Mrs Downs, the cook, ripped the waxy brown skin off a boiled ham like a woman taking vengeance. The sleeves of her flannel blouse were rolled up the elbow, showing forearms latticed with silver burn scars. At the other end of the long table Mary from the village and Megan were slicing cabbages into big enamelled colanders.

'All the way from Surrey, as if there weren't enough plants here. Eleven pounds, one shilling and sixpence.'

'If she's got the money, after all.'

Mary was always more cheerful than seemed reasonable for a woman with five children at home and a husband reputed to spend every penny she earned at The Sun. Megan said nothing. Three weeks as a kitchen maid, on trial for a month to see if she gave satisfaction, had taught her that it was her hands that were wanted, not her opinions.

'If I had her money, I'd be doing a lot more with it than that.'

'What would you do then?'

'Keep my husband happier, for one thing.'

Mrs Downs took a sharp knife and slashed diagonal cuts across the glistening white fat of the ham, turned it and slashed the opposite way, making diamond shapes.

'He's a very nice gentleman, Mr Allegri, for a foreigner.'

'He's no more foreign than you are. Mrs Morgan says he was born in London.'

'It's not a London name, is it?'

'His father was an Eye-tie.'

'Still, he's a very nice gentleman.'

'Meg, you watching that saucepan, girl? Don't you let it stick, now.'

Megan went on slicing cabbage slowly. Two days ago, just before lunch, she'd been sent up to the dining room with a jug of lemonade that had been forgotten and bumped into Mr Allegri coming out. A few drops of the lemonade had spilt over his beautifully polished boots.

'Megan, don't you go day-dreaming. If you let that saucepan burn I'll have it stopped out of your wages.'

Megan registered Mrs Downs' voice and jumped for the big range, scattering bits of cabbage. The heat blasting out of it meant that when you were close enough to stir your whole body came out in a sweat. The handle of the iron saucepan burnt her fingers.

'Ow.'

'You should learn to be more careful. Use the cloth and bring it over here.'

No sympathy you got. She found a cloth and carried the saucepan over for inspection. Mrs Downs stirred the brown syrupy liquid and tasted, added a pinch of mustard powder, stirred and tasted again and was satisfied. She poured

53

the contents of the saucepan over the ham and a smell of brown sugar and spices filled the kitchen. Megan watched as the white fat turned a rich amber colour but her mind was still two days away.

'You clumsy little...' he'd said. Then he looked at her properly and she saw his eyes change. 'Who are you, then?'

'Megan, sir.'

'Why haven't I seen you before Megan?'

'I work in the kitchen, sir.'

A properly trained servant who knew her place wouldn't have looked him in the eye when she said it, but at home in Treorchy you looked straight at people and spoke up for yourself.

'Well, Megan from the kitchen, what are we going to do about this?'

He looked down at the toe of his boot and up at her again.

'Come on.'

He went back into the dining room. She followed. There were starched linen napkins by each place, folded like boat sails. He grabbed one, shook it out and gave it to her, then put his foot up on the damasked seat of a dining chair.

'Clean it off then.'

The way he said it sounded kind enough, but there was something about his smile that made her feel hot and awkward.

'With ... with this, sir?'

He nodded. She put down the jug of lemonade, knelt and dabbed. There were no more than three or four drops of lemonade on his boot, smaller than raindrops. When they were gone she

54

looked up and found his eyes on her as if she'd been carrying out some minor, potentially painful operation on his foot.

'Thank you, Megan. We'll say no more about it.'

She'd gone back to the kitchen, scared but a little excited. Afterwards Mrs Morgan the housekeeper made a row about the creased napkin on the floor. Megan said nothing and supposed he hadn't either.

'Don't just stand there staring, girl. Go and get the cloves. Little stone jar, middle shelf, third from the right. Then you'd better clear up that cabbage you've been throwing all over the floor.'

Staff lunch was at half-past two, in a narrow room next to the kitchen. They ate at a long table with Rees sitting at one end of it and Mrs Morgan at the other. Megan, as the most junior member of staff, had to serve the rest of them – what was left of the ham after upstairs had finished with it, plenty of potatoes, more than enough cabbage. After lunch they all disappeared to their own duties, leaving Megan on her own in the kitchen with the washing up from family and staff lunches combined. Lug big saucepan of water over from the range and pour it into the sink, add handful of soda and scrapings from a tablet of hard green soap. Wash glasses first, then side plates and soup bowls. Scrape dinner plates into the pig bucket under the sink. But then a pile of dirty plates waiting on the draining board to be scraped tipped over, taking gobs of fat, cabbage and parsley sauce into the washing up

55

water, landing on a glass she'd left in there by mistake and splintering it.

'Bloody things.'

Aunt Bathsheba would have made her wash her mouth out with the green kitchen soap, but she was on her own. She scooped broken glass out of the sink, gashing her hand so that blood and greasy water ran together. She grabbed a tea towel to stop the bleeding, nearly crying with anger.

'Oh bloody, bloody things.'

'A very appropriate expression, if I may say so, Megan.'

She gasped and spun round. Mr Allegri was standing in the doorway and, from his expression, he'd been watching and listening for some time. Even she, inexperienced in the ways of households, knew gentlemen had no business at the scullery door.

'What are you doing here, then?'

He laughed, unoffended.

'I've come for some salt and some soda.'

Something in the way he was looking at her made her mind go scrambled.

He came over to the stoneware jar on the draining board.

'I daresay that's soda, isn't it, Megan? So what are we going to put it in?'

When she didn't answer he ranged round the kitchen and found a milk can on a shelf. 'This should do. Hold it steady while I pour.'

She held the can and watched as the crystals clattered into it. 'Salt now. Where do you keep it?'

She looked over to the table. Mrs Downs kept a jar of it to hand all the time.

'Yes, I think that will do.'

There was a flat straw bag hanging from a hook on the wall. He took it down and put the can of soda crystals and jar of salt inside. His eyes met hers, then went to the pig bucket.

'Thank you, Megan. We'll say no more about it.'

Just as he'd said two days ago with the lemonade. Only this time something else happened. As he turned to go he took a quick step towards her, lifted up her injured hand and kissed it. More than kissed it, sucked it as if drinking in the blood and fat, eyes on her face all the time. Then he put her hand down quite gently by her side, and went. When Mrs Downs came back she looked in the stoneware jar and said Megan was using far too much soda. At this rate she'd have the patterns off the plates and the skin off her hands. And did she plan to get that washing up done this side of dinner time or did she have some other idea? Megan took the scolding submissively, holding the side of her hand to her lips, breathing in a smell that was nothing to do with blood or ham fat. He smelt good, like spices in a pudding, candle wax and cigar smoke. He smelt of Christmas.

Isabelle was in her dressing room, which was also doing duty as a schoolroom. Marius would be starting at Eton in the autumn, but a tutor would have to be engaged to get his Latin and mathematics up to standard. Petra could be taught at home for the while. Isabelle was doing her best, with the scraps she could understand from her son's text books, while Marius sulkily copied a map of the United States, with rivers and main cities.

'*Puella* – girl – that's you darling. *Puella pulchra est.* The girl is pretty.'

Petra echoed '*Puella pulchra est*' knowing it wasn't her. Her cold had gone but left a persistent sinus infection that made her face puffy and a sore on her lip.

'Now, it's different with the boy. *Puer*, remember? *Puer pulcher est.*'

'Why isn't it *pulchus*, like *longus*?'

Isabelle gave Marius an appealing look, but he wouldn't respond.

'I don't know, darling. It's just the way it is. Say after me, *Puer...*'

'Isa.' Leon's voice, urgently from outside the door. 'Isa, can we talk?'

She went out. He was leaning against the wall of the corridor, smoking a cigar.

'Can you let me have some money?'

'What for?'

He closed his eyes.

'What for? I've spent all my pocket money, have I? I'm not even allowed a shilling for tipping the boy who posts letters for me?'

'Will five pounds do?'

'It will have to, if that's all I'm allowed.'

'Wait there.'

He heard the inside door close as she went through to her bedroom. She was back in a few minutes with a note. Leon put it in his pocket without thanking her or looking at it, turned to go.

'What's that on your sleeve?'

The question was no more than an excuse for keeping him there a minute longer, still hoping for something better.

'Dirt, I suppose, from living in the middle of a farmyard.'

'Did I tell you, Philip's written? He hopes to get here on Saturday.'

He turned and walked away. Back in the schoolroom, she tried the news on Petra.

'That nice Mr Cordell who went to Africa is coming to stay this weekend. He says he's bringing you something that belonged to an Egyptian queen.'

Marius looked up from his map. 'Did he steal it, then?'

His face and tone were exactly like his father's. Isabelle closed her eyes for a moment then fought back as best she could.

'Mississippi, darling, all double. And don't forget Chicago.'

Petra had hardly taken in what her mother said. She was listening to her father's steps going away along the corridor.

The return of the family to the big house had changed the rhythm of things at the Thomas's cottage, especially in the evening. No point now for Bathsheba in planning supper so that they were all five of them sitting round the table when the hands on the old clock's yellowed face were at six. Megan didn't get back until dinner at the house had been served and washed up, bone-weary. Will came home later too, now that there were the plants to look after. Often, as the light faded in the cottage, he and Megan would be sitting over the meal Bathsheba had kept warm for them, Megan too tired for food, sick of the sight and smell of it all day, Will ravenous himself but more concerned with tempting her to eat something. As Trefor and Evan couldn't be expected to wait so long Bathsheba gave them their suppers at six, calling them in from the fields. Evan would arrive at a run from the orchard or the paddock, merry as a cricket. Trefor was another thing altogether. He'd come reluctantly from some corner where he'd been reading or brooding, looking thinner and unhappier by the day. He'd help when there was something to be done round the cottage or with the hens. He was strong for a twelve-year-old in spite of his thinness and worked with the seriousness and concentration of a grown man. He'd mended the pump that brought their water up from the well and chopped enough wood to take them through most of next winter, but always as if his mind was somewhere else – somewhere that made him angry. That evening, when Megan and Will sat over their late supper, Trefor was by the window, reading his book in the last of the daylight and Bathsheba was hovering by the table. She was always eager for news from the big house.

'What did they have for dinner today, then?'

'Fish and leg of lamb with caper sauce. Mrs Downs took on because there were lumps in the sauce. My fault for not stirring, she said.'

It would have been the time for Megan to tell her aunt, if she ever intended to, about the odd behaviour of Mr Allegri.

'Such a funny thing. There I was washing up the lunch things and in came Mr Allegri wanting washing soda and salt.'

But she didn't say it, thinking of his lips on her hand. So instead she chose a subject that seemed less trouble.

'They were talking about Mrs Allegri's plants and how much they cost. More than eleven pounds, it was. Eleven pounds one and six.'

'On plants? That woman spent eight weeks' wages on plants.'

Trefor was on his feet. His book had gone thumping to the floor.

Megan said scornfully, 'She doesn't have to worry about wages.'

'Nearly eight weeks' wages for my father it is...'

'Well, he's my father too...'

'Eight hours a day underground on his knees in cold stinking water, breathing bloody coal dust...'

Bathsheba, shocked, said 'Language, Trefor, language.'

'...and wondering when the roof will collapse on him because the bloody capitalist owners are too mean to pay a few bob extra for new props.'

'Will, make him stop talking like that.'

Bathsheba had her hands over her ears, tears trickling down her cheeks. Evan, kneeling on the floor with a handful of marbles, was staring up at his brother, open-mouthed. Will looked miserable and at a loss, as he always did in quarrels. Only

Megan ignored her brother and concentrated on cutting herself a slice of bread, very thin the way Mrs Downs had taught her.

Will said, 'You shouldn't use words like that in front of your aunt and your sister, Trefor.'

'I'm sorry, Auntie Bath.' He turned and glared at his sister, 'But she makes me that angry, so full of herself now they've made her a skivvy.'

'Skivvy yourself.' Megan flickered her tongue out at him, quick as an adder's. He took a step as if he was going to hit her, then turned and rushed outside again.

'Having to take a lot of walks up the path, he is,' Megan said calmly.

Up the path to the privy, she meant, and you weren't supposed to refer to it at mealtimes, but Bathsheba was too dismayed to pick her up on it.

Petra dozed uneasily in her pink and cream bedroom. The darkness pressed in, smothering her. She got out of bed and knelt on the window seat to pull back the heavy velvet curtains. It was dark outside too and moonless, but at first it seemed a thinner, less threatening dark. She wrapped her dressing gown round her, curled up on the window seat and dozed then woke again. There was an eye glaring up at her from the terrace – or where she knew the terrace must be though she couldn't see it in the dark. It glowed like an ember in the fire. Two red eyes would have been bad, but one was worse, a monster. She'd been reading about wolves in Russia and knew with certainty that the thing down there was an enormous one-eyed wolf – a wolf the size of a donkey. For a minute the eye went away and she breathed again. Then it was back, first a long way off on the far side of the terrace, then prowling towards her, brighter and brighter. She screamed again and kept on screaming.

'Darling, what *is* the matter?'

Isabelle came running, barefoot in her white nightdress, hair loose. Petra rushed at her and clung.

'The eye. There's an eye.'

'Where darling? Show me.'

Petra dragged her to the window, pointed down at the terrace.

'There's nothing there, my love. You've had a nightmare.'

'It will come back.'

'It won't, I promise you.'

She tried to guide Petra back to bed, but the child went rigid under her hand.

'There. Look, there it is.'

For a moment Isabelle went tense too, then she laughed.

'Oh my poor love, it's only your father.'

'No!'

'Yes it is. He's out there on the terrace, smoking a cigar. That's what you can see, just his cigar.'

Petra let herself be guided back to bed. Isabelle lit a nightlight and sat beside her, stroking her hair, until she went to sleep. Back in her own room, Isabelle stood at the window looking out. The red ember was still on its slow patrol, along the terrace and back, along and back. As she watched it, she felt scared too.

8

The railway line from London to Hereford did a trick that always caught Philip by surprise. After running more or less straight through the plum blossom and market gardens of the Vale of Evesham it made a curve like the blade of a sickle round the spires of Worcester, over the wide Severn and opened up a different view entirely. The Malvern Hills rose up from the river plain with an abruptness that made them seem higher than they were, with scattered villas clinging to the sides of them and their treeless tops bare as upturned basins against a blue sky. On the other side of them was Herefordshire and Isa. Philip had spent most of the two hours of the journey so far standing in the corridor. He'd taken a first class ticket (feeling rich, for once, because the millionaire had been delighted with the giant lobelias and paid his fee without argument) so could have sat in comfort but he was too restless. Besides, even in first class there were other passengers who might have been disconcerted at his need to laugh out loud occasionally. Partly it was because, after Africa and Egypt, the green and succulent tidiness of England in April seemed both endearing and ridiculous, like a basket of puppies. Mainly because, still unbelievably, Isa had sent for him at last. On the platform at Hereford station the porters waiting by the doors of the first class carriages turned away in contempt as he hoisted his battered pack on his shoulder, picked up the bag and strode along the platform like a man with an appointment to keep. Negotiating with cabmen or carters was too commonplace for his mood. On an impulse he asked the ticket collector, 'Is there a bicycle shop?' Within half an hour of getting off the train he'd paid six pounds twelve shillings for a Rudge-Whitworth Crescent Light Roadster complete with pump, spanner and oil can, lashed his bag to the back and was out of the city, skimming southwestwards along a road that gleamed silver in the sunshine.

'There's a man on a bicycle coming up here,' Rees said, looking out of the window. 'Must be a tourer got lost.'

It was mid afternoon. He and Mrs Morgan were in the dining room on the first floor checking the table because tonight was to be a proper formal dinner at half-past seven. Mrs Allegri had insisted on doing the table decorations herself, primroses and budding twigs from the birch trees tucked into nests of moss. The effect against the dark wood of the table was pretty but she'd left little bits of moss and twig scattered all over the place. Rees swept them with a soft brush into a miniature lacquered dustpan.

'So have we settled about waiting at table tonight?'

'I'll do it, with Mary.'

He raised his eyebrows. Waiting shouldn't be housekeeper's work.

'What about the new girl?'

65

'Megan's not quite ready yet. She can carry things up and Mary and I will take them at the door.'

She couldn't explain to him that she felt uneasy, because it wouldn't be fair to the girl who so far was well above the usual run of kitchen maids. But her housekeeper's instinct told her that in some way Megan might be trouble. It was something in those big brown eyes when she looked at you – not insolence at all, but a hint that she was keeping part of her mind to herself and you had no business there. Mrs Morgan crossed to the window, gasped.

'It's not a tourer at all. It's Mr Cordell.'

They'd talked about Philip Cordell in the privacy of the housekeeper's room. Mrs Morgan had been with the family three years ago, before he went away, and Rees had to be told what was being said back then. It was a matter of professional necessity, not gossip.

'You go down and meet him, Mr Rees. I'll pop up and tell Mrs Allegri he's on the way and let Mrs Downs know tea will be wanted.'

Isabelle turned away from the window, heart thumping, feeling sick. 'Petra, Marius.'

Petra had been drawing in the schoolroom. She came running in, nose smudged with mauve pastel. Isabelle dipped a clean hanky in the waterglass, rubbed.

'You're getting it in my eye, Mummy.'

'Hold still, then.' Isabelle's hands were shaking. 'Where's your brother?'

'Outside somewhere. What's wrong?'

66

'Nothing's wrong. Mr Cordell's arriving. We're going down to meet him.'

'Do I have to?'

'Of course you do, darling. Remember how much you used to like him.'

Three years was a world away. She remembered stories about lions and elephants, a winter evening when he'd put on a shadow show for her on the nursery wall using his hands and a handkerchief in the light of a lamp to make rabbits, butterflies, a giraffe.

A knock at the door and Mrs Morgan's voice.

'Mr Cordell's coming up the lane, ma'am.'

'Thank you. We'll be straight down.'

'Do you want me to go and look for Marius, Mummy?'

'No. Stay with me.'

The last fifty yards of lane were so rutted that even Philip couldn't cycle them. He pushed the machine through the gateway at exactly the moment that Marius came sauntering out from somewhere, hands in pockets, staring up at the house. At first glance Philip took him for his father. It seemed impossible that a boy he remembered at ten or eleven years old could have grown up so fast.

'Good journey, Cordell?'

Last time they'd met it had been 'Uncle Philip' – although uncle was only an honorary title. Philip had been expecting much the same thing and nearly dropped the bicycle in his hurry to shake Marius's offered hand.

'Very good, thank you. How are you?'

'I daresay Mama's on her way down.'

Philip looked up the steps and there was Isabelle, hand in hand with Petra. A surge of love and protectiveness came over him. He laid the bike down on the gravel and bounded up the steps, pack still on his back.

Marius mouthed silently to the sky, 'Like a Gypsy pedlar.'

Isabelle put out her hand to him. 'Oh I'm so glad. So glad.'

He took the hand, ready to let go of it after the first squeeze, but she almost dragged him inside, laughing and chattering like a child. '...cycled all the way from Hereford ... should have let us meet you ... must be so thirsty ... so good to...'

Petra, gripped by her other hand, was pulled in after them, not saying a word.

Philip's room was at the side of the house, overlooking the hazel copse and the little water-fall. He washed in cold moss-smelling water from the pitcher, changed his shirt and collar and took three little tissue wrapped packages from the bag. Isabelle and the two children were waiting for him downstairs by the table of tea things.

'Don't worry, Mary, we'll serve ourselves.'

Isabelle poured tea for him, cut a thick slice of rich tea cake, still chattering away. 'You must be so hungry. I told Mrs Morgan we must make it strong for you. I remembered you like your tea strong.'

Strong or weak, he'd never cared. Somehow, in the past, it had entered their mythology that he liked his tea strong and that's how it would stay.

68

For the whole weekend or the whole what? She hadn't said. Her eyes were bluer than ever, her skin paler than he remembered. The strain about the way she talked and moved went to his heart. He wanted to grab her and hold her, make her stop talking, tell her it was going to be all right, whatever it was.

'More tea cake? It's bara brith, really, one of Mrs Downs' specialities.'

He declined more, produced the little packages from his pocket. Isabelle's had been carefully chosen in a Cairo bazaar to be no more than a handsome present to a woman from a travelling family friend, a silver filigree necklace set with small turquoises.

'It's beautiful. Hook it up for me, Petra darling.'

With Petra busy with the clasp and Marius undoing his present she could at least risk a proper look at Philip. Their eyes met and she went quiet at last.

'Thank you, Cordell. Very interesting.'

Marius was watching them, his present only half unwrapped lying on the table beside him. Philip had been proud of the moulted python skin, a perfect specimen nearly six feet long. Remembering his own enthusiasms as a boy he'd thought it would be just the thing for Marius – only Marius wasn't a boy any more. Maybe he should have brought him a box of cigars instead.

'Are you going to undo yours, Petra?'

Almost reluctantly she unwrapped the tissue paper layer by layer. An ivory scarab, mounted in modern gold on a gold chain. It had cost Philip two hours of bargaining and twice as much as

Isabelle's necklace.

'Thank you, Uncle Philip.' There was no enthusiasm in her voice.

The door opened. Leon Allegri paused in the doorway as if surprised to find Philip there.

'Ah, Cordell. So glad you could make it. No, don't get up.'

He was wearing white flannels, a stained blue velvet jacket that smelt of cigars. For a man usually immaculate in dress it could hardly have been a more pointed comment on the status of his guest. Isabelle jumped up, offered him tea.

'Oh, for God's sake don't fuss. After fifteen years you should know I never drink it.'

'Sometimes you do.'

He didn't answer and settled himself deeply into an easy chair facing Philip.

'Back from your travels, then? I'm sure that must be a great relief to Isabelle.'

His eyes fixed on Philip's crotch then travelled slowly up to his face, enjoying his anger and embarrassment. Isabelle's knuckles went to her mouth and it took all her force of will to drag them away and speak.

'If Philip's had enough tea, I thought of showing him the plants.'

'Do, by all means. You won't need me, will you?'

Isabelle and Philip walked along the terrace towards the side beds where Will had heeled in the plants, with Marius and Petra some way behind. Petra had the scarab clasped in her hand.

'Let's see it, then?'

Marius seldom bothered to speak to her, but

when he did his word was law. She gave it to him. He looked at the hieroglyphics engraved on the flat side and gave it back to her.

'What is it, Marius?'

'It's a kind of beetle. It comes from an old tomb.'

She stared at him, distressed and big-eyed.

'Is that what the writing says?'

'It says...' He paused, to give himself time to invent something. 'It says if it's stolen from the tomb and given to somebody, that person will die within a year.'

'No.'

She screamed and flung it away from her.

Marius laughed and strolled back to the house.

Isabelle heard the scream and turned to see the two children together.

'Is she all right?' Philip said.

'I expect Marius is teasing her with his snake skin. I do wish he wouldn't.'

But Petra was clearly in no danger and they were near the plants now. Will had gone to much trouble, clearing an abandoned vegetable patch of weeds, digging them in as they arrived with labels carefully in place. He was there now, hoeing round some lavender bushes. Philip had met Will on earlier visits and liked him. They shook hands and Will's creased face broke into a beaming smile.

'Good to see you back, sir. I've been looking after them as best I could.'

Isabelle took his arm and guided him along the rows, trees first. The guelder roses, dogwoods

71

and double cherries were already putting out buds and should have been in position weeks ago, but at least they were excellent specimens as was only to be expected from Waterers. The buds on the weeping purple beech were still tight and cone shaped, but would a chalk-loving beech be happy in clay? He began, as he always did with plants, to stroke them, look at them with his head on one side as if interrogating them about what they needed. Isabelle and Will watched him anxiously.

'Are they all right?' she said.

'They're very fine plants, but...'

He was going to expand on what he'd started telling her in his letter, that it was no use collecting wagonloads of plants until you'd planned your garden, but the disappointment on her face stopped him.

'Very fine plants. We'll find somewhere for them, get some of the trees planted out next week all being well.'

When she took his arm again and they moved on to look at the rhododendrons he could feel that some of the tension had gone out of her.

Then 'Oh. Oh God, what's happened to them?'

There were eight rhododendrons in a row, then a row of andromedas and several rows of lavender, rosemary and santolina. The smaller plants looked as if somebody had used a red hot poker on them. The glossy leaves of the rhododendrons were brown and blotched.

'Oh Will, what's happened? I told you to take such care of them.'

Will stood and stared at the devastation.

'They were all right last night, Mrs Allegri. I'll swear on the Bible they were all right last night.'

'But you must have done something. Didn't you water them?'

Philip drew his arm out from Isabelle's and laid a calming hand on her shoulder.

'This is something worse than not watering, Isa.'

He walked up to a rhododendron, turned a leaf over and sniffed it, dabbed a finger to the soil by the roots and licked it.

'Salt and soda, Isa. Somebody's deliberately watered them with salt and soda.'

'No.'

She gave a gulping sob and buried her face in his shoulder.

'I'm that sorry, Mr Cordell,' Will said, his expression full of guilt and sadness. 'I'd have given the world it hadn't happened.'

'It's not your fault Will. You can't guard them night and day. Isa dearest, don't cry. We can get some more, lots more.'

Tactfully Will looked away, over the scorched plants.

'Given the world, I would.'

9

June 2001

The days Colin liked best were when Kim stayed and worked alongside him. Quite often, she'd find other things to do, like necessary shopping in Abergavenny or Hereford. Sometimes she'd spend hours on the grass outside their tents, sunbathing and talking on her mobile to friends back in London. Some of them were joint friends from the college where they'd met – he studying garden history and design, she photography. Her voice would go harder and brighter when she was on the phone and he'd feel a tug at his heart wondering how much longer she'd choose to stay here with so much going on elsewhere. It was almost miraculous that he'd had her to himself for nearly two weeks. He tried every day to find something new for her. The only thing he couldn't give her was what she'd have liked best – the bones – because of his certainty that it would end everything. Keeping away from the pond site wasn't difficult because almost everywhere you went the garden gave up a new piece of the puzzle. The gazebo, for example. He'd left the last couple of metres of undergrowth intact so that she could be with him when he broke through. He heard her camera shutter clicking behind him as he swung his machete.

'You Tarzan, me Jane,' she said.

A firmer surface under his feet. The machete clanged on iron.

'Want to get it before I clear the creepers?'

Wild clematis mostly, the twisted trunks of it as thick as his wrist. When she'd taken all the photographs she wanted they both started pulling the creepers away to show a circular stone floor, moss covered but undamaged, and a stone bench.

'They'd sit there on summer evenings, looking at the view,' he said.

'Somebody spent a lot of money. Was he a fashionable designer, your Cordell?'

'As far as anybody knows anything about him – which isn't much he was a plant collector not a designer. The Lindley Library can't find any record of any other garden designed by him.'

'Is there family? Cordell's quite an unusual name. They might have kept records. There's probably an internet cafe, in Hereford. I could do a search if you like.'

'No.'

He wanted the garden itself to give him the answers, not have them imposed on it by things from outside.

She shrugged. 'What are you looking at?'

He realised his eyes had gone back to the dried up pond and made himself look away.

'There's a stream under all this somewhere. You can hear it.'

'Probably goes down to where the pond was. Is there much down there?'

He looked at her, alarmed, but she was fiddling

with something on her camera and the question didn't seem pointed.

'Some flagstones. What looks like timbers from an old jetty.'

'Perhaps they dived in naked,' she said. 'Running down and swimming in the dawn.'

He looked at her. 'What made you think of that?'

A shrug. 'Don't know. Old photographs, I suppose.'

The image wouldn't go away. All day as they cut through undergrowth and the severed docks and thistles bled sap and shrivelled in the hot sun the idea was in his mind of pale Edwardian bodies slicing through air into water that wasn't there to catch them any more.

10

April 1907

Isabelle's hand was lying gloveless on the stone balustrade, very white against the weathered stone and yellow lichen, amethyst-coloured veins standing out. Philip's eyes followed the course of the largest, from her wrist to the delta where it joined other veins flowing to the base of the fingers.

'Water courses,' he said. 'They're the skeleton of a garden.'

'Skeleton.' She shivered, although it wasn't far

from midday on a warm April morning.

'All right, not skeleton. Veins, arteries, circulation system. The point is, you can't make a garden against the flow of water. You have to follow it.'

If you followed the vein in the other direction you could see the little surges of her pulse, to the point where it disappeared into the cuff of her blouse halfway between wrist and elbow. The blouse was silk, also amethyst-coloured, a shade darker than her veins. He put his hand on her shoulder, gently, turning her so that she looked where he was pointing. Her skin was cool under the silk.

'You see the way the stream curves.'

In a gentle diagonal across the pasture then, two fields away, into the river at a muddy bay where the sheep went to drink. Some kindly earth movement tens of millions of years ago had turned these ordinary few acres into something that was shouting to him, singing to him, to be taken and completed.

'We want the garden to echo the curves of the water and the hills.'

Or the way her breasts curved under the blouse. His hand pressed harder on her shoulder, asking for a response.

'That little birch wood on the far side of the stream will stay, but it will need thinning and some new planting. I'm not sure yet what we'll have on this side. We have to let the place speak to us, tell us what it wants.'

She said, 'I want a lot of roses.'

'My dear girl, of course you shall have roses. All

77

the roses in the world. Only you've got to get the framework right first – boring things like walls and paths and moving earth around. I don't even know what sort of soil it is yet.'

'Will says it's good soil.'

'That's another thing, it's more than Will can do on his own. Even when we get it established it will take three gardeners at the very least, double that while we're making it.'

'Oh, I think we can manage that.'

'And we'll need a team of men for the paths and walls, and a good carting firm. It won't be easy getting stone and gravel up that lane of yours.'

'I'll write to Mr Gladwyn.' Mr Gladwyn was the manager of her pits. 'There'll be men who can't work underground any more. They'd be glad of the chance.'

She turned to him, smiling. 'There, you didn't think I meant it, did you Philip? You thought it was just a whim.'

'I wasn't sure.'

She smiled, a sudden tender smile.

'You came all the way from Egypt for something that might have been a whim of mine?'

'I'd have come from the ends of the earth.'

She turned and walked a few steps away, letting his hand fall back to his side.

'The servants might be watching. Or the children.'

'You said Leon is unforgivable.'

'Completely.'

He waited, but she said nothing else.

'Let's walk through your garden, then.'

78

He offered his arm to her, very formally, like a man taking a woman he'd just met into dinner. They walked along the edge of the terrace.

'The balustrade will have to go. It cuts the garden off from the house. I'd like to change the whole shape of the terrace to a semi-circle.'

He led her down the steps that went alongside the bank of tussocky grass with its round flower bed, like a pastry cut-out. That pink earth visible between the weeds meant clay soil, probably.

'We'll want to bring in a lot of earth and make it a gentle slope. Good generous shallow steps curving across it, not a narrow stone stairway like this.'

But for the moment he was grateful to the narrow steps for pushing her closer to him. At the bottom of the bank they came to the iron railings on the edge of the sheep pasture.

'If we take this fence away and let the lawn go right down to the stream, we could have a wonderful iris bed, blues, whites, amethyst.'

Like her blouse. Like her veins. The hills across the river would be blue or amethyst in the morning and evening. When he talked about the irises the pressure of her hand on his arm was more than formal.

'Oh yes, a lot of blue. I love blue.'

An easy colour in gardens up to iris time, more difficult in high summer.

'When you're planning a garden, you have to think of when you're going to be there. For instance, if you aren't usually down here until the London season's over, we'd want it at its best in late July and August.'

79

The rhythms of the fashionable world had never played much part in Philip's life, but he knew that for Leon, and therefore for Isabelle, the summer's progress through balls, parties, exhibitions, was a professional necessity.

'I'm staying here, Philip. I want it to be beautiful all the time.'

He started saying that it was a tall order, but from the way she was looking at him he knew he was meant to understand something important, which he didn't.

'Leon's career...?'

'Is over. You haven't heard?'

'Isa, whatever it is, they weren't gossiping about it on the Mountains of the Moon.'

She turned away from him, leaning against the railings and looking out over the sheep pasture.

'You knew what they were saying, though, before you went away. The joke about Allegri's sittings.'

'That his sittings were...'

'Horizontal.'

'He's still in his bad old ways, then?'

'Worse. You know Lady Kloncaid?'

Philip started saying, lightly, that he hadn't had the pleasure. The only members of the aristocracy he acknowledged were the ones with plant collections. But Isabelle wasn't listening. Once she'd got launched on the story she was pouring it out as though the sheep needed to know it for their survival.

'Two daughters, seventeen and nineteen, both came out last season. They brought them out at the same time because they'd all been abroad.

Lord Kloncaid's with the colonial service. The elder girl announced her engagement at Christmas so they asked Leon to paint the three of them together, mother and daughters.'

Philip put out a hand to her, to let her know she could stop if she wanted to, but she went rushing on.

'They must have heard about his reputation. Perhaps that was the attraction as far as the mother was concerned.'

'Isa...'

'It's true, Philip. Some women deliberately asked him to paint them, knowing what people were saying about him. Anyway, if that's what she was expecting she got more than she bargained for.'

There was a vulgarity in the way she said the last few words that he hadn't heard from her before. It was the voice of her father, the self-made man. 'Triple portrait. When it was finished the Kloncaids gave a party to show it off. We were invited of course. I didn't want to go but Leon insisted. Even he couldn't have expected what happened, of course. I acquit him of *that*.'

It took Philip a while to put a name to the buzzing in his head and the hot feeling that was coming over him. Hatred hadn't played much part in his life.

'They had it there on a little platform with a velvet cover over it. Lady Kloncaid unveiled it. It had been ripped to shreds, just shreds. The youngest girl – she'd had a hysterical fit just before the party. Told her father everything.'

'Isa, for heaven's sake, you should have left him.'

'Oh, I threatened to.'

'Don't just threaten, *do* it.'

'He said, if I did, he'd divorce me.'

'He'd divorce *you?*'

'He could you know. It doesn't matter how many years ago it was. He could still divorce me.'

'Let him. Leave him and let him. Do you think I'd mind?'

'Well, I do. The courts, the questions, the newspapers. Think what it would do to the children, especially Marius.'

'Why especially Marius?'

'What the boys at his school would say. They'd know. Everybody would know.'

'So Leon's still here, still living off you.'

She let go of the railings and turned towards him, smiling.

'Leon doesn't even admit he's done anything wrong. He's an artist, remember. Beauty justifies everything. He even said...' There were tears running down her cheeks now.

'He said ... the younger one, the seventeen-year-old, reminded him of me. He said she was as ... as beautiful as I was once.'

She put her head on his shoulder and leaned against him with the whole length of her body. Her trembling vibrated through him. His arm went round her.

'Oh my darling, leave him. Come and live with me. We'll go abroad.'

Her head moved from side to side on his shoulder. A no. When she stopped trembling and could speak, he got a longer answer, but the same one.

'I'm not running off into exile as if I'm the only guilty one. Why should I?'

'To be with me.'

'Oh my darling.' She moved away from him, took his hand and squeezed it. 'I am with you. We're making our garden.'

Bright and businesslike again. He wasn't deceived for a moment, but if that was how she wanted to face this thing, he'd help her. Only the hate that had come into his body wouldn't go away so easily.

She coaxed him. 'Go on telling me. Lots of wonderful irises. What then?'

He opened a narrow gate in the railings, followed her through it into the sheep pasture.

'It's too open. Like this, there's no surprise in it. A garden should be giving you presents all the time, making you find things when you don't expect them.'

Unlikely irises on rock passes, poised to fly away. He wished he could spirit her to the Pontic mountains and show her. But if she wouldn't come, he'd have to work with what was here.

'You remember the little waterfall near the house? We'll have a path coming down to it from the side door through the hazel wood, quite narrow and secret, primroses and wood anemones in early spring.'

'Bluebells?'

'They're later, but we'll make sure there are bluebells somewhere. Then when it turns across the field – lawn as it will be – we'll have a wider path following it along the upper bank, maybe a gazebo somewhere. The question is, what should

83

we do with all that?'

He stopped and turned her to face the long expanse of pasture between house and the river.

'Is that a pond down there by the willows?'

'I don't know.'

'You careless woman, your own property and you don't know.' It was a relief to pretend to tease her again. 'Shall we go and see?'

'In these shoes?'

They were grey leather, with a little heel and a strap buttoned over the instep. She held her foot up to show him. Even now, she couldn't help doing it in a way that showed off the curve of calf and ankle.

'Certainly in those shoes. When did you ever wear sensible ones?'

When they got to the crack willows they found a pond of a kind, but it was a disappointment. Sheep-trampled pink clay surrounded an oval about the size of a living room with a scum of bright green duckweed hiding the water. A willow branch had torn itself away and trailed in the water, still attached to the tree by a few twisted cartilages, pushing up its leaves through the duckweed. Isabelle wrinkled her nose.

'No water lilies.'

'It's too early for them anyway, but no, I don't think so. Did you want water lilies?'

'Yes.'

He stood and considered the unpromising pond. There were after all two gaps in the duckweed, where the stream ran into it and out of it again.

'If seven men with seven spades digged it for

84

half a year...'

'Half a year!'

'Don't you read *Alice* to Petra? A couple of them digging a week should do it. The flow of water through there must be quite slow or the duckweed wouldn't be growing like that. The nymphaea need quiet water. We could tidy up those willows...'

He'd started talking to comfort her, but as he talked the garden was coming alive for him.

'Some water irises. They'd echo the ones higher up by the lawn. Bulrushes and kingcups. Maybe meadowsweet on the far side.'

A flight of broad steps from the top lawn down to the lily pool. A jetty and a little blue boat for pushing out among the lilies on summer evenings. Was there a rambling rose obliging enough to grow from damp ground up willow trees? Some of the Wichuraianas possibly. Alberic Barbier might do it. Dark glossy leaves among the lighter willows. Yellow buds opening to creamy white flowers.

They walked on the damp pink clay around the pond, her shoes leaving little pointed spoor alongside his solid prints, and stopped by the big broken willow. 'Look.'

He caught a flash of electric blue on the other side of the leaves.

'Kingfisher.'

Her face reminded him of children at a pantomime when the fairy godmother flies into the wings, willing her back. He bent his head and kissed her on the open lips. She broke away just long enough to ask something that seemed urgent to her.

'How do they do it? How do they get that colour?' He stared. She said, 'If a bird can be like that, anything's possible, isn't it?'

He pressed her against the willow that leaned out so that they were suspended above the pond, kissing her all down the throat. Her hand came up, tearing open the buttons on her blouse, pulling down the thin chemise under it so that his tongue could play with her nipples. At the end, she slid down the trunk and they ended sitting on ground at the base of the tree, laughing and gasping.

'Oh God, it's been so long.'

He wanted to ask her if that meant she and Leon hadn't made love all the time he'd been away, but just had the sense not to. As they got their clothes back into some sort of order he couldn't help glancing up towards the house. The willows would have screened them. It was all right, this time.

'Look what I've done.'

She was laughing, showing him where she'd torn a ruffle of her blouse in her urgency to unbutton it, exhilarated by her own lust.

'I'm sorry.'

'Don't worry, Leo won't notice. He wouldn't notice if I wore sackcloth.'

All the same, they walked side by side with a little distance between them on the way back up to the house. Philip felt giddy with happiness, ideas crowding.

'A pleasaunce. We'll have an orchard on the other side of the lawn. A miniature orchard like the ones in a medieval book of hours.' Little glowing pictures of lovers walking under apple blossom or picking ripe fruit from impossibly neat trees.

'I want paeonies,' she said. 'They're like water lilies growing on land. We could plant them round the lily pool.'

It was a reminder that making a garden for Isabelle wouldn't be all easy going. She'd caught from Leon something of a painter's way of looking at things and painters were seldom reliable on things botanical.

'Paeonies mostly don't flower at the same time as water lilies. They're late spring and early summer.'

But today he didn't want to disappoint her in the slightest thing. Botany should bow to her.

'We'll have a paeony path, leading people down the garden as the season goes on. Look.'

He stopped walking and pointed up to where the lawn would be, with the stream running across it.

'There'll be the bearded irises there, late May and early June when you're walking on the lawn, looking down at the fruit blossom in your pleasaunce. Where the irises end, there'll be the steps down to the pool with early paeonies at the top of them. We could have some Wittmaniana.' Yellow, almost as pale as primroses with just a touch of sharper lemon that made them glow against the green. As a plant collector, he liked the species plants as they'd been brought in from the wild, like these delicate paeonies, before the hybridisers got to work on them. But the hybridisers had their place too.

'Victor Lemoine's doing some fine things in France with the Wittmanianas. He's got a new early one, yellowish cream, just what we want for the water lily theme. I don't think he's put it on the market yet, but I'll write and beg him for a plant or two.'

'From France?'

Her eyes were shining, catching his excitement.

'Why not? I'm in correspondence with people all over the place.'

People who were always ready to do favours for a good plant hunter. If she wouldn't roam the world with him, he could bring it to her.

'So you'd have your yellow and cream paeonies at the top of the avenue in early June. You'd stroll on down to your pleasaunce and there'd be more paeonies on the way to it, pink and white to go with the apple blossom.'

Paeonia officinalis alba plena, the double white cottage garden paeony. A whole froth of those. Festiva Maxima, great white petals, splashed with red. Pink and white tree paeonies at the back, between the avenue and the fruit trees.

'By late May, the fruit blossom will be past its best and you'll be strolling further down your garden. We'll have some wide beds beside the steps with some of the best of the albiflora hybrids.'

Stephania, deep cream with golden stamens glowing like a candle flame through wax. More gold stamens glinting from the massed pink centre of Aurore. Another new thing he'd heard about of Lemoine's, with petals like feathers on a

88

swan's wing. White and pink and gold for May evenings, with the sun setting late on the hills.

'Then, by late May to early June, you'll be going down to your pool to watch for kingfishers. Maybe we'll have a little semi-circular terrace and a low stone wall to hide the pool from the avenue so that you come on it suddenly. A seat on the terrace and some of the late paeonies like Avalanche and Baroness Schroeder all round you and the first roses coming out.'

'Yes. Oh yes.'

She sighed it in a way that made him want to start making love to her all over again, but they were well within sight of the house now.

'Then, by the time they're over, the first of your water lilies might be flowering.'

His mind was so full of the slow flower-bordered walk from spring to high summer that it was a shock to look round and see only sheep pasture, the railings, a line of reeds. He felt giddy at the work he'd taken on.

'Will you write to your man in France tonight, Philip? Get him to send the paeonies at once. Tell him he can charge as much as he likes.' She added, after a moment, 'Within reason, of course.'

'Lemoine won't charge me. And there's no point in sending for them in a hurry. We can't just plonk them down in a field and you don't plant paeonies until autumn anyway.'

The light died out of her face. She'd always been as easy as a child to make happy or unhappy but he was beginning to see that this latest cruelty of Leon's had made her grab for happiness a desperate one.

'Isa, dearest, I want to do what you want. But plants are more stubborn than mules about what they will and won't do.'

They walked back to the house together, just the right hostess and guest distance between them.

Petra had been sitting on a stone bench on the terrace, drawing on a pad with a clutch of worn down pastels and broken charcoal sticks her father didn't want any more. She'd been doing it for an hour or more, wrapped in her coat and bonnet by Susan so that she didn't catch another cold, working on her landscape. The willows were there in the distance and the birch copse that was so obligingly easy to do in strokes of charcoal. She watched her mother and Mr Cordell walking through the gate in the railings and wondered if they should be in the picture. On the one hand, they were there and she was doing her best to put everything in. On the other hand, she wasn't good at figures yet. The decision made itself when she looked up and saw that her father had come out on the terrace and was standing at the balustrade, looking down. Longing to show him her picture and get his praise, she blew off the loose pastel dust and walked over to him. She had to tug at his jacket before he noticed her, then he spun round, looking furious.

'Daddy, I've done this.'

He took it in his gloved hand, glanced at it and let the hand drop to his side. His eyes were on her mother's head and shoulders as she came up the steps beside the terrace, then her whole body, then Mr Cordell's head. She felt her father's unhappiness, more solid than the flagstones under her feet.

Her mother said, 'We've been right down to the pond.'

Her shoes were caked with brown-pink mud. There were even smears of it on her grey silk stockings. Mr Cordell said, sounding awkward, that he'd better go in and make himself respectable for lunch. There were willow leaves on the sleeve of his tweed jacket. Nobody said anything to him, but he went anyway.

'You'd better get ready for lunch too, Petra darling. Comb your hair and remember to scrub your nails properly. Twenty scrubs each hand.'

Petra went slowly into the house, so as not to catch up with Mr Cordell. Isabelle and Leon stood side by side, not touching.

She said, 'What's that in your hand?'

He looked. 'Only some scribble of Petra's.'

'Poor love, she wants to be an artist like you.'

'Totally without talent. But then what would you expect?'

Isabelle turned away and walked towards the house. He scrumpled the picture in his hand and followed.

11

Thigh-deep in brambles, Colin swung the machete and saw the sun flash on the silver roof of the old Golf driving along the valley road. Kim coming back from Hereford. He'd been watching for her all afternoon because there were things to show her. A length of hemp rope, thick as her wrist or thicker, green with mildew. A line of posts, mostly broken off and overgrown with brambles and the white trumpets of wild convolvulus. The posts and rope ran parallel to the broad flight of steps they'd been uncovering over the past week, but some way back from them as if there might have been a flower border in between. The garden wasn't just dropping hints now. It was talking to him all the time in joined-up language. He tucked the machete under his arm and walked down past the pond and over the field towards their tents. By the time he got there she was unloading supplies, walking barefoot on the grass. He took a carton off her – on the top, a bag of bruised peaches with the scent rising out of them overpoweringly sweet.

'They were selling them off cheap. I've eaten two already.'

Her lips were glazed with peach juice. He craned over the carton and kissed her, inhaling peach and the sweet smell of her sweat. She returned the kiss with lips and tongue, only breaking away when the carton started ripping.

'You'll drop them.'

She'd remembered everything, canisters of camping gas, new batteries for the torches, oil of citronella against the mozzies, a pad of graph paper for his garden plans.

'And these.' Two big polythene boxes with yellow and blue plastic lids. 'They're the longest I could get. Will they do?'

'Fine, thanks.'

In fact, not long enough for the two bits he thought must be leg or arm bones. They'd have to stay as they were, wrapped up in one of his mud-stained T-shirts and stowed along the tent wall. Sometimes when he turned over in the night he felt them digging into him. It was lucky they'd got into the habit of making love in Kim's tent on the grounds that it was less cluttered, otherwise she might have asked questions. He stowed the boxes and graph paper away in his tent. By the time he came out she'd opened two cans of beer and was sitting on the grass.

'Hot in town?'

'Not where I was mostly.'

'Supermarket?'

'Libraries.'

He looked at her face but she was gulping her beer, waiting for him.

'This place?'

'Mm. At least, I started at the library, but they sent me somewhere else. County record office.'

'Did you find out anything?'

It horrified him that she'd been talking to anybody remotely official.

'Not a lot. But they had some old rates records, so they knew who owned it.'

'Who?'

'A woman. Mrs L. Allegri.'

'Nothing else?'

She mistook his relief for disappointment. 'They thought they might be able to turn up some things if I went back. But it's interesting, isn't it, a woman on her own? I wondered if she might have been widowed in the war and had the garden done in memory of him.'

'No. Those photos I showed you, they were taken in 1915 and it was obviously quite a mature garden by then, five years at least, so it must have been laid out well before the war started.'

She looked disappointed and he realised she'd brought him this scrap of information as a present and he'd made things go wrong, as he seemed to do so easily.

'Finish your beer and I'll show you what I've been doing.'

She dived into the tent and came out with the camera round her neck, feet in the tennis shoes, more green than white now from plant stains, that were her only concession to practical footwear. He'd trampled the brambles enough to make a narrow pathway to the steps they'd cleared.

'I think they probably had borders of perennials on both sides of the steps, then swags of climbing roses at the back. Look at this.'

He was staring at a plant with seed pods like green plush candle flames.

'Tree paeony. They live a long time. That could be part of the original planting.'

She wasn't excited by the tree paeony, but then she couldn't do his trick of visualising it in bloom. He picked up the length of mildewed rope.

'I think he slung ropes between the posts and trained roses along.'

'There's another path here.'

She was scuffling at the brambles with the toe of her tennis shoe. A narrower path of flagstones went off at right angles, across where the flowerbeds would have been towards the notional swags of roses.

'I hadn't seen that. It looks as if it goes to where those old apple trees are.'

'Bloody brambles.' She bent to disentangle them from round her shins. 'Some more of your old rope here.'

She backed out, pulling a length of soggy rope after her. They both took hold of it, laughing, and laid it in slack coils on the step. The end of it came with a rush, snicking snake-like out of the brambles.

'Must have cost them a fortune in ... hey, look at this.'

She squatted over it and he watched her, not wanting to move in case he should spill the sudden happiness that had flooded him when they'd been pulling on the rope together, laughing like children. But she'd gone serious.

'What is it?'

'It's burnt.'

He squatted down next to her. The end of the

95

rope was black and charred.

'I suppose somebody put it on a bonfire.'

He said it, but didn't believe it. Bonfires went with tidying up and this garden hadn't been tidied for decades. She must have caught something of his doubt.

'Bit shivery, isn't it?' She stood up, started taking pictures. 'Those posts look as if something's broken them off as well.'

He started saying that the creeping stuff would have dragged them down and snapped them, but when he thought about it he wasn't sure. He waited while she finished photographing, sitting on a step and looking out over the valley. She came and sat beside him.

'I think we should find out more about Mrs Allegri.'

'Why?'

'It would make it more of a story. Look, I've been thinking. I finish my project and you have to go and look for work somewhere, then what?'

'That's months away.'

He didn't want to think about it.

'Weeks. I mean, there's a lot of work to be done here, isn't there? More than you could do yourself. And it would cost tens of thousands. Even hundreds of thousands.'

'Probably.'

'And even if we found the owners, I don't suppose they could afford it.'

'Probably not.'

'So what I'm thinking, if we could find a story behind it then approach one of the gardening programmes...'

'No!' It came out so explosively that the swarm of midges round his head rose up like smoke. 'Some clown in a helicopter, plus squads of people with buzz saws and JCBs who don't know their arses from their auriculas. Let them loose to skin and disembowel whatever's there in five days or five hours or whatever their idiot deadline is, then rush in some Astroturf and a load of plants from the garden centre that'll die in a couple of weeks anyway because they're all wrong for the soil, but that doesn't matter because they've got their programme and it's on to the next place.'

She stared at him. 'I didn't know you could be like that.'

'Like what?'

'So passionate about anything.'

He stared down at her feet on the step he'd cleared, at the jut of her bare ankle bone between the top of the tennis shoe and the bottom of her jeans. He wanted to say that he was passionate about her, that his certainty that she'd leave him drained the warmth out of the sun and the colour out of the grass, only he sensed that would only scare her away sooner.

'I'm sorry.'

'You're quite secretive, aren't you?'

That wasn't how he thought of himself. He was going to protest, then he remembered the plastic boxes and the long bones that prodded his ribs at night and thought it must be true after all.

It was one of the nights when Kim let him stay in her tent after they'd made love. More often than not she liked to sleep alone and he'd walk naked out of her tent in the grass-smelling darkness, piss luxuriously into the hedge then crawl into his own sleeping bag. This time they curled up together under her duvet that she'd insisted on bringing because she hated feeling constricted in a sleeping bag and he kept himself suspended halfway between sleep and waking for the pleasure of feeling her skin against his, hearing her breathing. In the dark, she was the one who got out from under the duvet and wriggled towards the tent opening. When he pressed the knob to illuminate his watch face it said twenty past three.

'OK?'

'Sure. Just going out for a pee.'

He snuggled under the duvet, curling round the warmth she'd left, hearing her moving round outside.

'Colin.' Her voice, urgent from the tent opening. 'Colin, can you come out here?'

When he went out he could see her bare back, pale in the starlight.

'What's wrong?'

'Shh. I've just seen a light up there, in the house.'

When his eyes got used to the dark he could just make out the looming bulk of the shuttered house. No lights.

'Want me to go up and have a look?'

'No. Look, there it is again.'

Up the hill, on what might have been the terrace, a point of white light. Kim gasped and Colin felt the hair on his neck rise, although he knew so small a light couldn't possibly find them from several fields away. Then it disappeared.

Kim was shivering. He dived into his own tent, clicked on his torch to find a big sweater and took it out to her, leaving the torch switched on inside.

'Colin, they'll see it.'

He turned round and saw his orange tent was glowing from the torch like a Halloween pumpkin.

'So what. They're probably a local couple looking for somewhere to make love.'

'All the way up there? Switch it off.'

He did. After the light, the night around them seemed totally black. He made her put his sweater on. She was still staring uphill.

'Kim love, don't worry. They're probably just campers like we are. Or a caretaker checking on the place.'

'At this time of night?'

'Whatever it is, I don't suppose they're interested in us.'

They watched for a while but when there was no further sign of the light, he persuaded her to go in and get warm. She fell asleep still wearing his sweater and he lay awake beside her, not contented now but more worried than he'd admit. He'd been expecting all along that the angel with the flaming sword would come and chase them out of their garden. Perhaps all angels could run to these days was a not particularly powerful battery torch.

12

When Will Thomas had troubles, he took them to the ponies. There were three of them, all retired or invalided out from the pits on the other side of the mountains. Sonny, the old bay, solid and rectangular as a straw bale on his short legs and black feathered fetlocks. Guto, the grey, that you had to remember not to approach for his off side because he'd lost his eye there and after all these years still wasn't used to it and might lash out or snake his neck round and bare his teeth at you, meaning no harm. Pont, the strawberry roan mare who, unexpectedly, in the autumn of her life and the winter of the year had dropped a foal without fuss or warning by the bare hawthorn hedge when there was snow piled up on the east sides of the yellowed grass tussocks and a wind coming through the gap in the hills that would take the skin off your face. That was three months ago but Will had a guilt about the foal that still troubled him. She'd been born just before the children came to live with them. Needing money for pillows, Bathsheba had told him to wring the necks of three of the hens and take them into Abergavenny to sell. He'd tramped the ten miles there with the bodies slung from his belt, warm at first against his thighs, then the mites crawling out from the dulling feathers and over his corduroy trousers as they cooled. He'd come home in the dark, hitching a lift on a cart, carrying a second-hand bolster in stained striped ticking, told Bathsheba it was all he could get for the money the hens had fetched and not to be angry now, so clever with her hands she was, she could make pillows for three out of it, easy. Only it had been a lie and after all these weeks it was still bitter in his mouth. He hadn't got much for the hens, but there'd been change from the bolster and he'd spent it on a sack of oats the mare must have if she was to keep up her strength to feed the foal. He kept the sack in an outhouse, scared as a thief that Bathsheba would find it, and every morning and evening smuggled a small bag of oats down to the paddock under his jacket and fed them to Pont in his cupped hands, fending off Sonny and Guto with voice and elbows. In spite of it, she'd gone as bony as a frozen crow and he'd expected every morning to find the foal dead, but somehow he'd got her through and she'd got the foal through to now, when the new grass was growing and leaves coming out on the hawthorn. He was watching them as they stood under the crab apple tree in the hedge, the foal sucking away, Pont nibbling at fronds of cow parsley, turning now and then to look. She was still pitifully thin, but her eyes had lost the desperate look that had gone to his heart worse than the sharp wind in his face, Still, all right now. No harm done. Only that whenever he passed Megan's bit of a bed, which he had to do to get to his and Bathsheba's bed on the other

101

side of the curtain, he looked at the inadequate bulge of bolster under the big white rectangle of pillow slip and felt guilty.

But that guilt was only a nag at the back of his mind now, pushed there by worse troubles. He gave Pont the crust he'd saved from breakfast, whistled his terrier and walked heavily along the bank of the river, back to the cottage. Bathsheba was in the garden, cutting broccoli with her old black-handled knife, the blade worn to a sickle by years on the sharpening stone. He told the terrier to wait outside and went into the kitchen, a trespasser in his own home into things that weren't a man's business. The line of objects on the windowsill over the stone sink was as unvarying as the outline of the hills. A washing-up mop in a broken-handled mug, its string head grey from months of service, a bar of Sunlight soap in a tin dish, a big stoneware jar, light brown with a chipped dark brown ring round the mouth. It was the jar he was interested in. He moved towards it clumsily, red gobbets of clay from his boots smearing the stone flags. It was reassuringly heavy, two thirds full with greenish-white crystals. He sighed with relief and put it down on the table, reached across to the little cupboard on the wall where Bathsheba kept her baking things, turned the wooden latch. The thing he wanted was at the front of the bottom shelf, a present from Bathsheba's sister when she went to Porthcawl for the week, shaped and painted like a lighthouse with a hole in the top. He put his thumb over the hole and shook. Half full at least, and the amount that was gone not enough for all that damage. He was still shaking it like a child with a rattle, enjoying the relief, when there were steps on the stairs.

'You thinking of baking then, Uncle Will?'

Megan. She was standing there at the bottom of the stairs, looking at him wide-eyed. His thumb slipped and an arc of salt shot out over the scrubbed wood of the table.

'Oh Uncle, bad luck that is.' She scrabbled up a pinch of the salt and threw it over her left shoulder to hit the devil in the eye. 'Not to worry, I'll clear it up.'

She fetched dustpan and brush from beside the fireplace and whisked the salt away, glad to have something to do to hide her embarrassment, hoping her uncle wouldn't ask why she was at home instead of working up at the house. The truth was, the redcoats had caught her unawares. Her period had started suddenly while she was being taught to lay a table and the housekeeper had given her half an hour off to make the usual arrangements with strips of old sheet and safety pins. Aunt Bathsheba had helped her and the sticky female complicity of it made Megan feel awkward seeing a man so soon afterwards, even Uncle Will. It seemed to her that he must be able to smell the iron-meaty whiff of her blood. They were standing there awkwardly, not looking at each other, when Bathsheba walked in with her basket of broccoli.

'Them quists been tearing at it again something terrible. Take the gun out to them you should, then we'd get pigeon pie at least.'

It was an old argument. She knew she'd never

103

get Will to shoot any bird in the nesting season. Behind her back, Megan picked up the lighthouse, put it away in the baking cupboard. Bathsheba heard the door clicking shut, turned.

'What you want in my cupboard? And what's my soda jar doing on the table?'

Megan's expression told Will he'd have to manage this one for himself. 'Checking it, I was, in case we were getting short.'

Bathsheba stared at him. 'You going keggly in the head, Will Thomas, or you think I am? There's pounds of it in the brown bag out in the scullery.'

As usual, something that had seemed simple was all teeth and claws when you went into it. Megan and Will left together and parted at the plank bridge over the stream. As she turned to go up to the house he asked if she knew where Trefor was.

'Out somewhere with Evan, probably.'

Will watched her going up the field, aware that she didn't seem to be moving as easily as usual. He guessed she was being worked too hard and his heart ached as it did for all misused creatures that he could do nothing about. But there was no help for him and the pond was where he ought to be. One of the jobs Cordell wanted him to do was look at the old crack willows and decide how they should be tidied up. 'Nothing too tidy though, Will. We don't want the whole lot pollarded. Just enough to clear the muddle but leave it looking natural, if you see what I mean.' Will hadn't, quite, but he was anxious to please Cordell. He was quite close to the pond, near enough to notice forget-me-nots in flower in the mud and see that the long green leaves were clear open on the willows, when he heard a voice raised.

A high voice, 'No, no, NO. It's mine. Give it to me.' Then a splash, no louder than a pebble going into the water, and the voice rose to a despairing wail 'No-o-o-o-o.'

Will stopped, boots sinking into mud, and Evan came hurtling towards him, head down, still throbbing out 'no-o-o-o-o.' He didn't see Will until he barged into him and when Will put his arms round him, making little 'whoa' sounds like he did to a nervy horse, the boy kicked and struggled to get away. Will just held him tight and went on making calming sounds until what he was holding had turned from a bundle of grief and fury to a sobbing eight-year-old. He walked Evan over to the stream bank, dipped his handkerchief in the water, wiped.

'What's the trouble then, boy?'

'Trefor.'

'What's he done, then? Whatever it was, I don't suppose he meant any harm.'

The two brothers were as close as could be. You couldn't live in the same house with them without seeing that.

'He did, he did, he did. He threw it in the water. Right in the middle of the water.'

'Threw what in the water?'

'My shilling. The shilling Mr Cordell gave me. He took it off me and threw it in the water.'

It took Will a while to absorb two equally surprising things – that Evan should have a shilling and Trefor should deprive him of it.

'When did Mr Cordell give you that then?'

'Yesterday afternoon. He was walking round on his own with a big measuring tape, only the end of it kept moving and he said would I come round with him and hold the end so I did and at the end of it he said thank you and gave me a shilling.'

'And Trefor took it off you? Didn't you offer to share it with him?'

'I did. I said he could have all of it if he wanted. But he wouldn't. He said it was dirty money.'

Will straightened up, his duty miserably clear. 'Where is he now?'

Evan gestured with his head back towards the pond.

'Right, now you go straight home, boy and make yourself useful with Auntie Bath. No need to be telling her about this and upsetting her.'

Will watched him out of sight, then turned towards the pond. There was no problem finding Trefor. He was sitting astride a willow branch that had split and angled down into the pond, watching a pair of blue damselflies mating on the wing. He heard Will's footsteps in the mud and turned, face expressionless. Will settled himself on the same branch lower down, making it groan and dip towards the water.

'Your brother says you've been throwing his money away.'

Trefor looked at him and nodded.

'Why d'you do that then, boy?'

'I told Ma I'd look after him. Promised her.'

'Is that looking after him, throwing his money away?'

106

'I'll give it back to him, I told him. In a year I'll be working. First wage packet I get, I'll pay Evan back double. Two clean shillings for his dirty one.'

'He'd earned it fair.'

'They've made a skivvy of my sister. They're not doing it to Evan.'

'No one's making anybody a skivvy.'

'Aren't they? What do you call it then? What do you call making free people say sir and ma'am and pretend they've got no lives of their own or nothing they want except filling other people's bellies and emptying their chamber pots? What do you call making a little lad that doesn't know any better crawl round making gardens for a spoilt woman not fit to clean my mother's shoes?'

Will sat, open mouthed as the words poured out. Words, those awkward and dangerous things for him, spinning like conjuror's doves round the head of this lad who'd hardly come up to his shoulder standing. The shock of it almost deafened him to what the boy was saying. He caught 'bellies' and 'chamber pots' with a sense that Bathsheba wouldn't allow language like that, and the general idea that Trefor was angry, with still no clear idea about what. At last, when Trefor seemed to have finished, the response he put together was almost humble.

'After all, what harm's been done?'

What he couldn't know was that this flight of words had come almost as much of a surprise to the boy as to him. Since he was not much older than Evan, Trefor had taken to smuggling himself into gatherings that his father avoided as too hot-headed and radical. He'd stand in the shadows at the back of the room and endure hours of half-understood talk about shift rotas or bonus payments for the magic. Sometimes it would be a man he knew, a man who looked as ordinary as anybody else, who laughed in the pub and talked to his father in the street, now up there like a preacher, only a hundred times better, so that the men listening to him murmured sealike, a soft 'yesssss' gathering under what he was saying, carrying him along until his wave of words broke on the shore of a new heaven and a new earth. Now the magic was there for him, like air pumping into a dragonfly's wings when it crawled out of a chrysalis. To Will it confirmed what he'd feared. He sat there shaking his head for a while then:

'Somebody grows them.'

'What?'

Trefor was still absorbed in the magic, hardly knowing or caring what his uncle was saying.

'The plants, I mean. Somebody had to grow them.'

He stared up at the boy, begging him to understand what he couldn't organise the words to say. That somebody had worked to grow the plants and wouldn't want them wasted. Even that the plants themselves had to work to grow and deserved more reward for it than soda and salt. Nothing. No response in eyes that were as dark as the surface of the pond. Will levered himself off the trunk and walked away, less clear than ever what to do about it.

13

'Corpse-flower, that's what the country people call it. They think it grows where a body's buried.'

Philip's cheek was pressed against cold soil, eye squinting sideways into the roots of a hazel bush. Petra stared at him, not understanding. When he beckoned her she came reluctantly.

'See.' He took her woollen gloved hand and pointed it at a thing growing by the base of a bush, so pink and fleshy she thought it was a fat worm.

'Nothing to do with corpses, of course. It's a parasite on hazel roots. Toothwort. *Lathraea squamaria*. A bit like broomrape, but you can tell toothwort because the flowers are all on one side, look.'

She pulled her hand away. Philip got up slowly. He'd always thought he was good with children, but this one who he wanted to please more than any child in the world seemed unhappy all the time she was with him. After breakfast Isabelle had suggested brightly that he and Petra should go round the garden together. She had letters to write about getting men in to do walls and paths. Petra stood stolidly while Susan wrapped her up and walked out with him, no sign of either pleasure or protest. He took her out of the side door into the hazel wood, shortening his steps to hers.

'We'll have flowers for you to see as soon as you come out of the house. Snowdrops and aconites first – you know, little yellow round flowers like lemon sweets. Then masses of primroses.'

There were some primroses there already glowing against dead grass. If he coppiced the hazel thicket to let more light in, there'd be more next year. Beyond the hazels, where the oaks started, white wood anemones and bluebell leaves.

'Then we could have some of those little pink cyclamens for the autumn. Would you like that? *Cyclamen hederifolium.*'

Long ago, homesick at boarding school, he'd got comfort from wandering the woods and downs on his own chanting botanical names. He hoped it might work for her. Spotting the toothwort and remembering how the Latin name of it had seemed to melt in his boy's mouth like a particularly succulent piece of marzipan had been like finding a present to give her. Only it hadn't worked. They walked on side by side to where the hazel wood met the pasture that would become lawn. Maybe swags of wild roses from China there on the boundary – a kind of horticultural joke, yellow flowers where you'd expect the pink of the native dog rose. Cantabrigiensis was lovely but temperamental. Hugonis might do it. Petra plodded beside him, her feet in their brown buttoned boots as plain and serviceable as logs, quite unlike Isabelle's, more fit like his own for long walking. The thought of that made the love and guilt he felt for the child almost unbearable.

110

'Would you like it if we built a little wooden house here? Somewhere for you to come on your own?' She nodded, no more than politely. He suppressed a sigh and walked with her back into the wood towards the little waterfall, humming a song their porters had sung in Africa, day after day the same few dozen bars, endlessly repeated. It was a cheerful song, if monotonous, and he hoped Petra might join in. When they were just above the waterfall he thought she had and felt happy, until he realised that the sound was coming from somewhere below, not from behind him.

'Listen.'

Unmistakeably the same tune above the clatter of the little waterfall, not sung but played on something like a tin whistle. It led them down to where the stream tipped over a ledge of rock.

'Well, the great god Pan himself.'

A flat cap, a pair of muddy battered boots sticking out over the water. The boy Evan sitting looking up at them, a fife to his lips. From beside him Petra let out a laugh that echoed the notes. It was the first childlike sound Philip had heard from her since he arrived.

'Evan Thomas,' he told her. 'Will's nephew.'

They slid down beside the waterfall.

'Hello Mr Cordell. You measuring things?'

Not Pan, now the fife was away from his lips and he was standing, just a thin lad with a Welsh accent, dressed in dark breeches and Norfolk jacket and a yellowed flannel shirt with a celluloid Eton collar, well smeared with mud. Philip guessed he was about Petra's age but in spite of the difference in class he seemed the more confident one. Petra was staring as if she'd never seen him before, which given that she didn't often come out of the house and he'd never been into it was quite likely.

'How do you do that?'

He grinned at her, then played Three Blind Mice, once slowly then fast. Her eyes widened.

'Can I do it?'

Evan looked at Philip, who nodded, wiped the fife on his breeches and handed it to Petra. She took it cautiously, eyes on him all the time, put it to her lips and produced a sound like a bronchitic kitten. Evan laughed in the exaggerated way of boys with girls, rolling on the ground beside the water, collecting more mud on jacket and breeches. She stared at him, between laughing and crying. Philip put a hand on her shoulder.

'It takes practice. I expect Evan will teach you if you ask him nicely.'

'Will you? Will you really?'

Evan looked at Philip. Philip looked back at Evan and, unseen by Petra, made a gesture of putting his hand in his pocket.

'If you want. Hard it is, though. If you're doing it, you have to do it properly.'

Philip watched as the two of them settled themselves back on the rock by the water and went into a contented daze, listening to the birds, the sound of the waterfall, tutorial tootlings from Evan. The smell of ferns and moss was all round them. Petra was the first to pick up the different, spicier smell.

'Papa's coming.'

Delight in her voice, the rest of them forgotten. As she said it Philip too smelt Leon's cigar smoke.

'Papa, we're up here.'

No answer to her. Instead, in Leon's deep voice, 'Are you there, Cordell?'

Leon Allegri came into view, head in a black floppy cap that would have looked ridiculous on most men but suited his buccaneer good looks. His overcoat was fine black wool, faced with astrakhan. He carried an ebony cane with a silver top. He might have been strolling down Piccadilly. Petra ran to him.

'Papa, Evan's teaching me to play the … the…'

She didn't know what it was called, but it didn't matter because he ignored her.

'Cordell. A word?'

Philip nodded, puzzled. The normal routine of their days was based on avoiding exchange of words between them. Leon came downstairs long after Philip had gone out to work on the garden and spent most of the day in the studio. To that extent Isabelle's plan for it had succeeded, only Leon made it clear that he wasn't painting, wasn't thinking of painting, had no intention of picking up a brush as long as she kept him prisoner at Holders Hope. The packs of charcoal sticks lay undisturbed in their drawer, sleek tubes of paint undented, blank canvases turned to the wall.

'Certainly.'

There was a stone flagged path, mossy and overgrown, leading from the waterfall to the terrace. Philip followed Leon down it, thinking the fight was coming at last and probably not a bad thing. Leon stopped by a low stone bench on the corner of the terrace, put a foot up on it and flicked with the end of his cane at a clod of clay in his shoe welt.

'Do you suppose this is the muddiest place in the whole damned universe?'

'I've known muddier.'

'You're welcome to them, then. This bloody English mud, mud, mud, there's no light and shade about it, no movement, it just sits there.'

'It's not bad soil for growing things though.'

'Ah yes, the great garden.' Leon took a case out of his pocket, opened it and offered Philip one of his thin black cigars. Philip refused and Leon took his time lighting up. 'How serious is she about this business, Cordell?'

'Very serious.'

'It's going to cost her a lot of money. Hundreds for the stone alone and that's not counting the labour. I suppose even crocked-up miners have to be paid something.'

'Isabelle seems prepared for that.'

Leon sighed. 'Cordell, I've lived with Isabelle for nearly half her life. I know these enthusiasms of hers. Give her six months and it will be something else – learning the harpsichord, breeding spaniels. All this expense and trouble, all the mud stirred up, gone for nothing.'

'Have you said this to her?'

'Oh, it's no use arguing with Isabelle when she has one of her whims. But if you were to tell her it wouldn't work, soil all wrong, too much rain

114

or somesuch...'

'It would be a lie.'

'Or simply be called away suddenly. You're always trotting off round the globe. Just take yourself off again for a few months.'

'Not unless she says so.'

'There might be advantages in it for you, Cordell.'

'What do you mean?' The hint of market bargaining in his voice made Philip fire up. But Leon still had that superior smile on his face, quite calm.

'Don't start getting moral. It's a bit damned late for that. Let's look at it like reasonable men. So – what do you want? Isabelle. What do I want? To be out of this place and back in London. What does Isabelle want? God knows in the long run, but it seems to be you at the moment. No reason why we can't all three have it.'

'You talk as if...'

'Hear me out. You go off for a few months so that Isabelle gives up the garden nonsense. We go back to London. When we're nicely established, you turn up and take a cosy little flat round the corner with full access rights to the Allegri household.'

'Am I hearing this?'

'I'm only offering you what you've helped yourself to in any case. I daresay the asses' jawbones will wag as usual but they don't bother me and I don't suppose you're setting up as the Archbishop of Canterbury either.'

Philip looked out over the garden, thinking 'Shall I hit him now?' His right fist felt like an

115

iron ball on a chain, ready to swing. Leon went on talking and from the easy tone of his voice seemed to think the thing was a certainty.

'One thing, though. I know her will's still in my favour at the moment and I don't want her altering it. I'd count on you to influence her. If I'm making it easy for you in certain areas, it's only fair you should look after my interests in others.'

'You utter...'

Leon laughed.

'Blackguard? Rotter? You really don't have to worry, Cordell. She's got more than enough to keep us both in comfort.'

The fist swung, made contact with the side of Leon's mouth. Leon's cane clattered down on the flagstones along with his cigar and he slumped on the bench, hand to his mouth.

'Even by your standards that was stupid.'

When he took his hand away a thick trickle of blood was running down his beard from the corner of his mouth, soaking into the blue silk scarf inside his coat collar. He stood, picked up his cane and walked back towards the house. Philip stood watching him then walked heavily back up the path to the waterfall.

With Philip gone, Evan tried conscientiously to show Petra how to form notes on the fife, but her attention wasn't on it and after a while he gave up and played for his own pleasure, making variations on the few bars that he didn't know came from the centre of Africa. After a while she got up and walked a little way down the path until she had a view of the terrace. She saw the two men talking close together, her father tall and upright in his black coat and hat. He was saying something, gesturing with his arm. Mr Cordell was staring at the ground like a boy being rebuked. Then, as she watched, Mr Cordell's position changed. His head came up, he took a step back then, unbelievably, the long black form of her father was falling sideways, collapsing onto the bench. The sound of his cane clattering on the stones seemed to be echoing inside her head. She wanted to go to him but her feet wouldn't move. For what seemed like a long time she thought he was dead. Then he was walking back to the house and Philip was moving too, coming in her direction. She turned and ran in a panic back towards Evan at the pool. He was still sitting on the rock.

'That your dad calling you?'

'No. It's Mr Cordell.'

She felt shivery and full of a sense of shame at what she'd seen. Mr Cordell appeared, face red and trying to smile.

'Hello, Petra. Had a good music lesson?'

She went back to the house with him, keeping at a distance, hands to her sides so that she shouldn't accidentally touch even his jacket. She was so full of anger against him she felt her head would explode but didn't say anything, in case he should hurt her father again.

Upstairs, in Mrs Allegri's bedroom that over-looked the terrace, Mrs Morgan caught Megan standing with a duster in her hand.

'Megan girl, don't stand there day-dreaming.

117

You should have finished in here half an hour ago.'

'Sorry Mrs Morgan.'

Megan followed Mrs Morgan out of the room, head buzzing with what couldn't be said. 'I wasn't day-dreaming and you'd have been standing there too if you'd seen what I'd seen. Mr Cordell clear as daylight, punching Mr Allegri in the face like two lads who'd had a glass too much outside The Star on pay night, only Mr Allegri didn't punch him back.'

That evening, though, she told Auntie Bath who wasn't sure if Megan might be making it up and didn't know whether to hope she was or she wasn't.

14

Holders Hope.
Herefordshire.
8 April 1907.

Mr S.T. Gladwyn.
General Manager,
Penyrheol Colliery, Near Treorchy,
Glamorgan.

From Mrs L. Allegri.

Dear Mr Gladwyn,
I should be grateful if you would recommend ten

or a dozen men who might be employed here for the spring and summer as garden labourers. The work would not be of a skilled nature but would require reasonable physical fitness and a willingness to be adaptable.

The work might suit older men who no longer wish to work underground or young single men who are not yet skilled miners. I should be offering in the region of 4 shillings a day for an eight-hour day including local accommodation and meals all found, and would pay reasonable travelling expenses from Treorchy to here, with one Saturday in three off (on rota) so that the men could return to see their families.

Please make inquiries and let me have your recommendations as soon as possible, as I am anxious to have the work completed by the end of the summer.

Holders Hope.
Herefordshire.
8 April 1907.

To Sir Cuthbert Bailey, Bart.
Melhampton Court,
Gloucestershire.

From Leon Allegri.

Dear Sir Cuthbert,
You may remember that we were introduced at the Royal Academy last year, when you were kind enough to admire my portrait of Lady Fitzrivers in the costume of a Grecian priestess. You mentioned

then that you might like me to paint a portrait of your daughter Imogen on her coming of age this year. As it happens, due to the cancellation of a foreign trip, I have some time unexpectedly available and should be very happy to undertake the commission as soon as you like, either at Melhampton Court or your house in Town.

I should be very grateful indeed if you could let me know at your earliest convenience as a number of other people are anxious for me to undertake commissions, but naturally I should wish to give yours priority.

Melhampton Court,
Gloucestershire.

10 April 1907.

Sir Cuthbert Bailey acknowledges receipt of Mr Allegri's letter of 8 inst. but wishes to inform him that he has made other arrangements for his daughter's portrait.

Holders Hope.
Herefordshire.
1 April 1907.
To Anthony Black.
Geography Dept. Manchester University.
From: Philip Cordell

Dear Anthony,
I'm glad my amateur notes on the geology of the Mountains of the Moon were of some use. This is an appeal for help. Do you know of any simple

books on surveying and land work for beginners? I've got myself into a position of constructing a garden for somebody I want very much to please. And – don't laugh I beg you – within a matter of days I'm supposed to be supervising a team of Welsh miners turned construction men who will instantly see through me for the tyro I am.

I'm a long way from any bookshops, so if there are any such books I'd be very grateful indeed if you could order them for me and have the bill sent to me at the above address. But for pity's sake make them simple. While they're about it, could you also ask them to send *Alice in Wonderland* and *Through the Looking Glass?*

Penyrheol Colliery.
Near Treorchy,
Glamorgan.
15 April 1907.

From Mr S.T. Gladwyn.

To Mrs L. Allegri.

Dear Mrs Allegri,
Further to your esteemed letter of 8th inst, I append a list of twelve men and boys whom I could entirely recommend for the work you have in mind, who are willing to take up employment from now to the end of August on the terms you set out.

All are prepared to start work next week, subject to transport and accommodation being arranged. If you are agreeable, I shall inform them and could make travel arrangements by rail to Hereford or Abergavenny, whichever is more convenient.

Holders Hope,
Bloodymuddyshire.
5 May 1907.

To: Daniel Feveril.
Oakley Street,
Chelsea.

Dan,
Do not on any account visit. I'd as soon have my friends see me picking oakum in Wormwood Scrubs. In any case, the countryside is not pleasant in May. Three days out of five it rains and a kind of wild gardening man whom Isabelle has acquired is ripping up the fields into a mud plain, aided and abetted by a platoon of decayed miners she's imported and lodged at the dump that passes for the village inn. Needless to say, there's nothing drinkable at the inn. My claret has to come all the way from Hereford and by the time the local incompetents that pass for carters have got it up the ruts in the lane it's so cloudy from sediment that it isn't halfway drinkable for a week and never gets back in good heart. As for company, apart from Isabelle there's nobody but the kids. The girl sniffs all the time and the boy sulks because he wants to be back in London showing at least a modicum of his father's good taste.

Dan, dear man, rather than thinking of visiting me in this prison-house, help me get out of it. I realise that the hypocritical haute bourgeoisie who pass for upper classes in this country are still pretending that I'm a pariah. (Give them until about Ascot time to come round.) For the sake of escaping from here I'm willing to take a temporary step down and condescend to immortalise the daughters of rich and ambitious grocers, rail millionaires or candlestick-makers-to-His-Majesty – provided of course that they are not hideous beyond reason. A brace of grocers' daughters, say, then I've enough in my pocket to spend the end of the summer and maybe all of next winter in Italy.

I'm half sick with longing for warmth. For some reason, my mind keeps going to a village on a hilltop we stopped at on our honeymoon tour just on the Italian side of the Alps. Earlier in the year than this, but the air already smelling warm and the whole village such a froth of pink blossom – almond? cherry? God knows – that it looked as if it could float off like a balloon into the sky and Isabelle laughing like a child, the most loving beautiful creature in the world. Sixteen years ago, perhaps a third of my adult life-span gone. Now she sits there with her garden catalogues and account books and looks at me the way a hotel manager looks at a guest when the bill's unpaid. Never marry, Dan. It lets in mortality.

Leon

Oakley Street.
14 May 1907.

To: His Mudship Leon Allegri.
Holders Hope,
Herefordshire.

Dear Allegri,
In haste – just off to Daly's.

Sorry to hear you so out of spirits. Have been testing the ice as per your valued instructions, but so far no takers. Nearest thing I've got to an offer so far is Percy P who thought he might want you to paint his King Charles spaniels but since he owes money all over town (a thou. to his tailor to my certain knowledge) you'd be waiting a long time before you saw any guineas. Would offer you the couch in my studio but it's taken up for foreseeable future by a protege of Tibs. Deepest sympathies re the claret. Stick to brandy. Yours, Dan.

15

July 2001

On the morning after seeing the torch, Kim insisted that she and Colin should go and find out if somebody was squatting in the house. They took the route over the fields and through the garden, up the broad stone steps, a jump over the stream beside the wrecked bridge and under what had been the wisteria tunnel to the terrace. The downstairs windows were boarded up with thick chipboard that was itself showing signs of age, bulging out at the edges and patterned with green mould and bird droppings. All the upstairs windows were shuttered and the doors had metal plates screwed over them with the dog-head logo of a security firm. Colin felt nervous and out of place there. He belonged in the garden, not with whatever had happened inside. They walked round the corner of the house and found themselves in an overgrown courtyard. Kim's camera was clicking all the time like some monotonous insect in the background.

Colin said, 'What would squatters be doing so far from anywhere?'

'Some kind of weirdo sect?' Kim was walking around, sizing up pictures.

'Pretty small sect with only one torch. I told you, a couple from the village looking for somewhere quiet.'

'Long way to come for a quick fuck.'

'How do we know it was a quick one?'

There was a low building with big doors on one side of the courtyard. It looked as if it had once been a coach house. One of the doors had come off its top hinge and was sagging forward. Kim walked towards it. He started protesting that it was the garden she was photographing, not the outhouses, but knew it would do no good so waited in the courtyard, staring at buddleia bushes sprouting from crumbling windowsills.

'Colin. Colin, come here.'

Her voice from inside the coach house or whatever it was, scared and urgent. He rushed into the darkness, shouldering the gap between the doors wider to get through. It was dim inside, just one little window. Kim was standing in the middle of the stone-flagged floor.

'Look, I told you.'

Something pale and horizontal with something square and dark on top of it. A camp bed and a folded blanket. Other things beside the bed. When he took a step nearer he saw that one of the things was a rucksack, quite new and expensive looking. Also an old apple box drawn up alongside the bed with a bottle and a book on it. Kim picked up the bottle.

'Jamesons. Half empty.'

'For goodness sake, leave it. It's nothing to do with us.'

'I told you there was somebody up here.'

'Well, whoever it is has got as much right to be here as we have.' He remembered that meant no right at all. 'Let's go.'

'Hold on.' She was looking at the book now. She held it out to him and he screwed up his eyes in the faint light to make out that it was a backpackers' guide to California.

'OK, whoever it is has got a crap sense of direction. Now, can we go please?'

'And an expensive taste in Irish whiskey.'

'That's his business.'

'Or hers.'

'Or hers. Anyway, not ours.'

He got her out into the sunshine and dragged the door back to where it had been, brittle wood at the base of it splintering on gravel. As they scrambled and slid back down through the brambles she said, 'Do you suppose he or she was watching us?'

'I hope not. Now, can we forget it?'

She didn't say anything until they were back in sight of their tents then, 'I've been thinking, I might ask around in the village.'

'About the backpacker? For goodness sake...'

'No, about Mrs Allegri. There's bound to be an oldest inhabitant or a vicar or something.'

He couldn't argue with that and at least it was a distraction from the backpacker. But he still didn't like it. The village, Holdersby, was about a kilometre away from the garden. They'd avoided it and done their shopping and pub-going in Hereford and Abergavenny as part of his tactics for not drawing attention to themselves and so far Kim had accepted it. But she was getting restless. If he tried to stop her she might take flight. Anyway, there was no harm in it – except something in his mind was screaming that yes, yes there was.

16

May 1907

'Silk it is, isn't it?'

There were three of them in the laundry room, Mrs Morgan, Megan Thomas and Jane, Isabelle's maid from London. The air was heavy with warm damp cotton and the metallic reek of the flat irons heated on the kitchen range next door. The other servants hadn't taken to Jane, with her London accent and air of being above the rest of them. Megan, getting no answer, repeated her question.

'Silk?'

Jane nodded reluctantly, intent on working the point of the iron down the edge of an amethyst frill. Mrs Morgan, still bent on Megan's domestic education, said, 'One of Mrs Allegri's blouses. Cool iron for silk you need – cool enough to lick your finger and dab it on.'

'I know. Cotton's spitting, though.'

Jane said, 'It was Mrs Allegri's. It's mine now. I found it in the bottom of the wash basket and said should I mend it? She said not worth it, I could have it.'

'Colour won't suit you.'

'What do you know about it?'

Megan put down her iron, grabbed the blouse off Jane's board and held it against the maid's

128

surprised cheek.

'Too pale you are. It needs someone darker.'

'Megan...' Mrs Morgan protested.

Jane grabbed the blouse back. 'What are you talking about, too pale? She's paler than I am.'

'She's her and you're you.'

Meaning all too clearly that Mrs Allegri had the looks and Jane hadn't.

'Megan, the iron. If it scorches that sheet I'll stop it out of your wages.' Mrs Morgan piled an armful of sheets on the end of Megan's board. 'Now get on with those and not so much argument.'

When the housekeeper had left, Jane and Megan went on ironing in silence apart from the thump of Megan's iron. When Jane had finished and was going towards the door with the blouse over her arm, Megan said, 'How much?'

'I beg your pardon?'

'How much do you want for it?'

Since Jane had walked in with it, the amethyst silk blouse had been calling to Megan so clearly that her head, her whole body was ringing with it.

'You? What would you do with it?'

'How much?'

'More than you've got.'

'How do you know?' Megan was paid six shillings a week. Five shillings of that went to Auntie Bath, who saved it for her and let her have a shilling a week back in her hand. She had two shillings and sixpence in her purse at home. 'Give you half a crown for it.'

Jane laughed. 'It's worth pounds.'

'All right then, half a crown and I'll clean Mrs

Allegri's shoes for you everyday.'

All the servants had heard Jane's moans about shoe cleaning not being work for a lady's maid, especially not all scratched and clotted up with mud from her traipsing round the fields.

'Without telling her?' Nodding towards the kitchen and Mrs Morgan.

'Cross my heart.'

'We'll see then. You clean her shoes to my satisfaction all week, then we'll see.'

Jane gathered up the blouse and swept out with it over her arm.

Mrs Allegri's low heeled shoes in cream-coloured pierced leather, cleaned four times. Mrs Allegri's brogue golfing shoes with leather tassels, cleaned six times. Mrs Allegri's high heeled shoes in green leather with T-strap, cleaned twice. A lot of extra work because of scratches from briars. Mrs Allegri's plain black shoes cleaned once, after they'd dried out. The left one was soaking wet and slimy with sheep droppings, as if she'd been standing up to her ankle in the pond. (She had, not noticing the water creeping up while Philip was kissing her.) At the end of the week Megan presented Jane with two shillings, a sixpenny piece and an ultimatum – keep our bargain or I'll tell Mrs Morgan. The amethyst blouse changed hands.

'But don't you go wearing it anywhere she'll see you.'

Megan carried it home wrapped in a bit of tissue paper she'd found in the laundry room, crackling between the yellowed flannel of her vest and the blue serge of her working blouse. It smelt of lily of the valley and expensive face powder, with a faint beeswax whiff of female sweat. Expensive sweat. Isabelle Allegri's sweat. Jane had mended it carefully but not washed it. Megan ached to feel the silk against her skin but couldn't think how to manage it. The bargain must at all costs be hidden from Auntie Bath who'd be horrified at squandering money that could have fed the family for most of a week, and there was no privacy in the cramped cottage. She tucked it away in her pillow case, alongside the cut-off square of old bolster and sometimes at night would dabble her fingers in the softness, but carefully so that the rustle of tissue shouldn't wake up her aunt and uncle sleeping a few feet away on the other side of the curtain.

It was nine days on, the first really warm Sunday towards the end of May, when she decided that at all costs she must wear it. Her day off. Chapel in the morning, Auntie Bath insisted on that, with Uncle Will awkward in suit and tie on one side of her, Evan with scrubbed face fidgeting on the other. The chapel was more crowded these days and the singing better with most of the imported miners in the back pew. But Megan wasn't interested in mining lads. She wasn't interested in anything except being alone and unwatched. Mutton chops and cabbage in the cottage, washing up with Auntie Bath while Uncle Will dozed in the chair and Trefor read in the corner.

'Going out for a walk, Auntie Bath.'

Evan looked up from the floor where he was rolling marbles around.

'Can I come?'

'No you can't.'

Outside, a day just made for new things. Sky a tight-stretched blue, with a few white clouds over the hills. Even the raw scars and banks of earth where Philip Cordell and the miners had been working were shining silver where the sun caught the damp clay. She'd decided on the grove beside the little pond under the waterfall. She knew it because it was a favourite place of Evan's and she sometimes had to go and fetch him. The birches and hazels were well in leaf now, the place invisible until you were a few steps above or below it on the narrow path by the stream. She walked quickly across the edge of the field below the house, hoping nobody was looking from the dining room window, and into the cover of the hazels.

'Marius, please stop fidgeting and come and have your dessert.'

'I don't want any.'

Isabelle caught Philip's eye and sighed. Sundays at Holders Hope were edgy with no work on the garden to absorb energies. Isabelle hadn't been brought up as a church-goer and Philip from long travelling had lost the habit of Christian Sundays but they deferred, reluctantly, to the conventions of the chapel-lands around them. Sunday lunch was more elaborate than the casual weekday affair and until that day Leon had acknowledged that by joining the family.

132

Today his chair at the end of the table was empty and his absence added to the tension. Petra chewed her food doggedly and hardly responded to Philip's attempts to get her to talk. Marius stayed on just the safe side of insolence towards his mother, but came so close to it that Philip had to bite his lip to stop himself saying something. The boy was modelling his behaviour on his father's and seemed to grow more like him every day. There was even a premature dark fluff on his upper lip and his voice was lowering to a sulky growl.

'At least come and sit down until the rest of us have finished.'

Marius didn't answer. He was staring out of the window as if something interested him.

'I'd rather go outside.'

Sheer perverseness, Philip thought. Marius had shown no more interest than his father in the garden.

'Well, go then.' Isabelle's patience snapped. Marius looked at her, eyebrows raised, swivelled on his toe and walked out.

'Can I go too, Mummy?'

'When you've finished your dessert.'

'I've finished.'

'Where are you going?'

'Mr Thomas says I can go and look at his horses.'

She sounded more cheerful. Mr Thomas and the horses had been cropping up a lot in conversation in the last week or so. It gave Philip a pang that his almost inarticulate gardening man seemed to get more out of the child than he

133

could, with all his care.

'Be sure to wear your hat and gloves, darling.'

Petra nodded, scrambled down from her chair and plodded out. When the two of them were alone Isabelle said, 'Do you know where Leon is?'

'In the studio, I suppose. I haven't seen him since dinner last night.'

'I think he might have gone out.'

From her voice, she might have been talking about a mad relative or some unpredictable animal foisted on them. Philip had never told her about hitting Leon, knowing it would worry her, but it was as if she'd guessed it.

'Yes. Look, love, I've been thinking. Why don't you let him go. Back to London, if that's what he wants.'

'Am I stopping him?'

She was looking tired today. He wanted to kneel down beside her and put his arm round her, but Mary would be in with the coffee any minute.

'You know you are, love. Make him an allowance, enough for the rent of a flat and his brandy and cigars, and he'll be off tomorrow.'

She stared at him. 'You know how he'd behave on his own in London.'

'Yes. Let him. The scandal won't touch you. It will be known you're living apart. If anything, there'll be sympathy for you.'

'Or contempt.'

'Why? Anyway, what would it matter? We'd be here, happy.'

'What about Marius?'

'Oh, Marius will be all right whatever happens.'

Too self-absorbed to care either way. She caught his meaning and resented it.

'Marius is sensitive. Think how miserable he'd be at school if...'

'If what?'

'If he hears people saying his mother pensioned his father off so that she could live with her lover.'

The words came out explosively, too loud. He jumped out of his chair, knelt down beside her and took her hand.

'Isa, it wouldn't be like that.'

'Wouldn't it?'

A knock on the door. He let go of her hand and scrambled to his feet but was still standing awkwardly over her when Mary brought in the coffee.

Megan stood by the pool, breathing fast. Every rustle of a bird in the birch trees made her heart hammer. The amethyst silk was draped over the crook of her left arm as she fumbled with the buttons of her Sunday chapel blouse. Even when all the buttons were undone she stood uncertainly, not ready to shrug it away from her shoulders. She'd never undressed in the open air before. The day felt colder than it had been. She shivered then pulled her right arm free, turning the sleeve inside out in her haste to do it before she changed her mind. When she transferred the amethyst blouse to her bare right arm so that she could pull the Sunday blouse off from her left, the feeling of the silk against the soft skin on the inside on her elbow made her shiver again, this time with pleasure.

135

Until then she'd intended to put the new blouse on over her flannel vest – it being unthinkable to remove that in the open air or anywhere except her bedroom with the sheet and blanket already turned back and waiting. Now she found herself wondering what it would feel like to have silk against her back and shoulders, nothing in between. Her fingers fumbled the yellowed bone buttons at the neck of her vest. One of them popped off and into the pond and the noise of it made her pause and took round. Nothing but the birches shifting in a breeze. She knelt down so that she could lay the silk blouse across her knees, took a deep breath and pulled the vest off over her head.

Marius, behind a birch tree above the pond, felt it like a blow to his chest from a clenched fist. When he'd seen her coming up the meadow it had seemed no more than a diversion on a dull Sunday to track her. He'd noticed that she was unusually good looking for a kitchen maid. Noticed too a quality in her that he called cheek. She didn't seem quite to know her place. Once, when waiting inexpertly at table, she'd dropped a boiled potato splat onto the cloth beside his plate and instead of being ashamed had caught his eye and wrinkled her nose in a way that suggested it should be a joke between them. He was curious about her because in the boredom of his life there wasn't much else to be curious about. After leaving the dining room he'd let himself out by the side door and, guessing she might be making for the waterfall, walked down the path beside the stream so that he could watch her from above. He thought, 'What a cheek, she's going swim in our pond' and thought he might wait until she was in the water and take her clothes away to teach her a lesson. Then she pulled the vest up over her head and the punch hit him. His first confused thought, that she'd taken a mean advantage, turned to something else. Her pale breasts, stretched up as she pulled and the tufts of dark hair under her arms, scared him. Her face, invisible under the flannel, might have been uttering spells because when she pulled the vest off and let it flop down on the ground she didn't look anything like the girl he'd been following. Her lips were apart, breasts rising and falling with the panic of what she was doing, nipples standing out from the cold, garnet-coloured. Part of her dark hair had got untangled from its knot and flopped down over her shoulders. Marius had been dragged around art exhibitions from the time he could toddle and grown blasé about nude nymphs before his age reached double figures but nobody had warned him that a perfectly ordinary girl who dropped potatoes and wrinkled her nose could turn herself into one while you watched. What was worse, nobody had warned him what that could to do him. The punch to the chest that forced a yelp of surprise out of him became a hot pain that spread down to his stomach filling his whole body with an urgent need to move. Half-hearing the yelp over the sound of the waterfall, Megan took it for a bird or animal, but it was enough to alarm her. She grabbed the silk blouse from her knees, forced an arm into it, then the other arm. She was broader across the shoulders than Isabelle. A seam parted with a sound like a kitchen knife being sharpened. She was still kneeling, appalled when Marius scrambled out from the trees.

'That's my mother's blouse.'

His voice grated in his own ears like somebody else's. He hadn't known what he was going to say. Her hands moved, gripping the silk ruffles, drawing them over her breasts, fist against fist.

He said, 'Did you steal it?'

She'd been staring at him, frozen, but now her face was alive again and angry.

'I don't steal things. I paid for it and now it's torn.'

'I … I didn't mean…'

He stammered, face and body burning. She saw his confusion and sensed, though she didn't know how, that she was the more powerful one.

'You were watching me. You made me tear it. Look.' She half turned her back on him, so that the shoulder with the ripped seam was pointing his way. 'Look.'

He took a step towards her, then another, put his hot fingers on the slash of white skin.

'Marius. What the devil are you doing?' The voice, Leon's voice, came from up the path. Marius jumped back. Leon stepped out of the trees and into the clearing, looked at his son and at Megan kneeling on the damp earth. Marius was red in the face and near to tears. Leon took him by the lapel of his jacket.

'You're coming with me. As for you, young woman, wait there until I come back. Don't you

138

dare move.'

He pushed Marius in front of him, up the narrow path between the birches and hazels until the sound of the waterfall was just a murmur and Megan and the pond hidden by trees.

'Stop there. Turn round.'

Marius turned, moist with embarrassment and misery. Leon leaned against a tree, lit a cigar.

'Do you think I'm done for?' Marius stared. It wasn't the question he'd expected. Leon repeated, 'Do you think I'm done for? Ready for the knackers? Five bob wreath then dance on your father's grave.'

'No, of course I...'

'Sir, when you talk to your father. No *sir*.'

It hadn't been that kind of household, but Marius managed an obedient, 'No sir.'

'I should be lecturing you about keeping yourself clean and all the rest of it, but I don't want you to grow up as big a damned hypocrite as the rest of them so I'm being straight with you and I hope you've got the brain to understand it. It's a matter of biology. You know what that is?'

'Yes ... sir.'

'Like lions. That's what my name means. They've taught you what the name is for a group of lions?'

Marius grabbed for a schoolroom memory.

'Pride ... sir.'

'That's right. Why do they call it pride?'

'I don't know.'

'Because that's how it works. The strongest lion, he's pride of the bunch. While he's alive, the younger lions can't go sniffing round the

139

lionesses without getting their throats torn out. Did they teach you that?'

Marius's hand went to his throat. 'I ... can't remember.'

'Well, remember now. When the pride of the bunch starts losing his teeth and his hair, when he can't run and hunt the way he used to, then it's his throat gets torn out. Show me your teeth.' Marius stared at him terrified, eyes wide, lips closed. 'I said, show me your teeth.'

Reluctantly, Marius's lips peeled back. Leon stepped towards him until their faces were almost touching. Marius closed his eyes, turned his head away.

'Right, now look. I said look, boy.' Marius's head came round reluctantly and his eyes opened to see, from a few inches away, his father's teeth bared and gleaming. 'Nothing wrong with them, is there? Still tear a few throats, couldn't they?'

Spittle flecked the boy's face. He wiped it with his jacket sleeve. His father laughed and took a step back.

'You can go now, but just remember that. And don't go whining to your mother. She wouldn't like to think of you dirtying your hands on her kitchen staff.'

He gave Marius a little push, watched him walk unsteadily away up the path then, when he was well out of sight, turned back down it. Megan was still waiting at the pond by the waterfall but she was standing and had her chapel blouse back on.

'I thought I told you not to move. Didn't I? Well, didn't I?'

She looked back at him, some fear in her eyes, but behind it still a sense of the power she'd got from Marius.

'I've got a right to move if I want to.'

His hand came down on her shoulder.

'We'll see about that, shall we?'

17

July 2001

The day after they'd found the backpacker's lair, Colin went to work on what he thought of as Kim's path, the one that led from the broad steps towards the rose ropes. Kim herself was away in the village. He tried to concentrate on what he was doing and forget about her inquiries and the backpacker but they were unsettling him. He found himself glancing up at the house, half expecting to see a shape with a rucksack watching him but there was nobody. Once he had the sensation of being watched from somewhere closer at hand.

He said, 'Look, it's OK, I'm only interested in the garden. We won't bother you if you don't bother us. All right?'

But he was speaking to tangles of goosegrass and convolvulus. Nobody there. Kim's path led towards old apple trees. The trees nearest the path seemed to have been planted too close together, so close that over the years their branches had grown into each other and merged at head height into knots like arthritic knuckles. Towards the end of the afternoon the explanation came to him in that rush of almost sexual warmth he felt when the garden told him something important. As he did sometimes when working alone he talked back to it, or through it to the long gone Philip Cordell who'd made it.

'Another tunnel. Did they call you secretive too?'

In spring, you'd walk along the little path through a tunnel of blossom. In autumn, there'd be ripe apples hanging overhead, offering themselves for the taking with all the hoarded sweetness of a long pre-war summer. He used the machete to clear a narrow path down the middle of the tunnel. It came out to an enclosed orchard with overgrown hedges of hazel and hawthorn. A squirrel scrambled away as the last machete stroke brought him through, setting the bushes swinging. From the look of the place, nobody had set foot there for decades. The apple trees were long neglected, some dead, rising from a sea of brambles, trunks green and scaly, crusted here and there with golden lichen. Higher up, great bunches of mistletoe pushed gold flower clusters and pale lizard-skin leaves out from the apple foliage. He guessed the trees had been planted there for pleasure, not practicality, screened by hedges on three sides and swags of roses on the other. He wanted very much to show it to Kim, make love there. There was one place where you might try it without getting lacerated by brambles, a bank under the hedge on the south facing side. When he stamped and cut his way over to it he found leaves of primrose and wild strawberries, purple flowers of betony, patches of dry sphagnum moss. He brushed rabbit droppings away and lay down experimentally, eyes closed. Very comfortable, except there was a rock or something digging into his calf. He sat up and found it was one of a tumble of small sandstone rocks. He got down on hands and knees. Somebody had gone to the trouble of hollowing out a little cave into the bank, lining it with stone to make a grotto, just big enough for a child to get inside. In an Italian garden you might have expected to find a stone saint or Virgin Mary, but it seemed somehow against the spirit of this place. There were ferns growing at the grotto mouth. He moved them aside carefully, prepared for a holy face or some Edwardian wood nymph, obscurely disappointed in Cordell. And found himself looking at the head and upper body of the White Rabbit. Not just any rabbit. Unmistakeably Alice's 'I'm late, I'm late, I'm late' Rabbit in Wonderland. It had broken just below the paw holding the pocket watch. One of the crazy, down-angled ears was broken too but the face with its comic-desperate expression, the waistcoat and the bow tie, looked as fresh as the day it was carved and so vivid that he couldn't help smiling when he saw it. Nice one, Cordell. Some child comes through the tunnel, goes over to the bank where the real rabbits are, then – surprise – there's the rabbit of all rabbits in his own special burrow. He put the torso back carefully in the ferns, as near as possible to how

143

he'd found it, for Kim to photograph. He searched around for the rabbit's other half without success until he thought of looking inside the grotto. Then he laughed again to find that it had been standing there all the time on its big splayed feet, with its plump stone stomach and the lower triangles of waistcoat. This time he didn't touch it at all, wanting her to see it exactly as it was. By the time he'd found his machete and gone back through the apple tunnel to the main path the sun was well on its way down and his thirst reminded him of the beer cans stashed inside his tent. Kim should be back by now and he had the White Rabbit to offer her. When he was in sight of their tents an odd thought came to him. If the legs and stomach of the White Rabbit were still standing up in the grotto, how come his head and chest were in the ferns?

Kim was sitting on the grass outside their tents. He threw down the machete, knelt beside her and kissed her. She returned the kiss, but without much enthusiasm. She seemed tired and nervy.

'How did you get on then?'

'The vicar was useless. He's moved here from Birmingham and was too busy with the kids' playgroup to give a fuck about local history.'

'His exact words?'

'More or less. The village is mostly weekend cottages or people who commute to Hereford. The pub does three sorts of vodka and grilled goats' cheese and the landlords are a gay couple from Islington.'

'No elderly locals reminiscing over pints?'

144

'No. The only piece of luck was a woman in the post office. She used to have a neighbour whose mother worked as a maid up at the house a long time ago. Only the neighbour's moved away and the woman doesn't know where she's gone. All she had was the name of her daughter who's running a computer training firm in Newport.'

'The maid's granddaughter? Shouldn't think she'd know much, would she?'

'I've got the name of her firm. I might go and see her. It's only about half an hour's drive away.'

He stood up, feeling pleasurably heavy-limbed after the day's work.

'Shall I get us a beer then I'll tell you what I've found today?'

She nodded. He fetched two cans from his tent and opened them, gave one to her and drank half of his at one swallow. She watched him, not drinking.

'Aren't you thirsty?'

'I had one when I got back. I went into your tent for it.'

The way she said it and the expression on her face gave him an idea of what was coming.

'Oh.'

'Yes. I mean, I'm not spying on you. I just knelt on something and it hurt my knee, so naturally I had a look to see what it was, like anybody would.'

'Yes.'

'And I'm not criticising. One guy I knew couldn't get to sleep without two teddy bears and a blue felt donkey, for fuck's sake. It's not that I mind, I just like to know these things. They're

145

human, aren't they?'

'I think so.'

'Think so? Where did you get them?'

He swallowed. 'The pond.'

She put down her can and stared at him. 'What is this?'

'I don't know.' He looked back at her, miserable that things were coming apart and added, apologetically, 'I've found a White Rabbit too.'

18

June 1907

Hereford Queening
Hereford Beefing
Tyler's Kernel
Downton Pippin
Stoke Edith Pippin

An afternoon in June, a few days short of midsummer. The grass was warm and dry at last. Isabelle and Philip were sitting companionably side by side at the top of the bank where the railings had been. He wished he had basketfuls of apples out of season to please her, globes of red, yellow and red-striped green to roll down the new gentle slope of the bank. Instead he was reading their names from the Herefordshire Pomona he'd discovered in the library, old country names that murmured like bees in the sun.

Yellow Ingestrie
Wormsley Pippin
Lord Hindlip
Cowarne Quoining
Hereford Pearmain

'All of them,' she said, half asleep from the sun and contentment. 'We'll have all of them.'

'Not sure you could find all of them now. But we'll do what we can, ma'am.'

Around them and below their feet the garden was taking shape. It still amazed Philip, scared him sometimes, how the airy plans he'd made with Isabelle back at the end of the winter were being transformed into paths and flat places and contours. The miners, quiet men who spoke to each other in Welsh and English, were performing miracles as if they were part of everyday work. The bank they were sitting on had been turned to from a sharp escarpment to a gentle slope, the raw clay already covered over with a pelt of turves. By next spring there'd be primroses growing on it and small pale-petalled wild daffodils. Above them the terrace was still its unreconstructed rectangular shape, but a new path ran down from it to the slide of bare earth that would become a flight of steps leading down between beds of paeonies and roses to the lily pool. The acre of flattened ground to the right of where the paeony steps would be was marked out for the Pleasaunce. Today the men were working with shovels and wheelbarrows, spreading thick layers of red sand over the paths, ready for stone flags. An elderly man passed them with a loaded wheelbarrow.

'Afternoon Mrs Allegri, Mr Cordell.'

'Good afternoon Enoch.'

Philip had lost his fear of the miners. Before they'd arrived he'd wake in cold sweats, men with coal-smeared faces laughing at him in a nightmare because of his ignorance. The nightmare hadn't been entirely wrong. They'd tumbled to his lack of experience in the first half hour of working. The man they'd chosen as their foreman, lame and grizzle-haired Robert Williams, had listened to his suggestions, nodded, then gone on to do the thing his own way. Once in those early days, Philip made the mistake of insisting on something that Williams said wouldn't work. The men had followed his instructions without a word then, at the end of the day when the stream had broken through and was pouring down what should have been a curve in the path, Philip stood there with water over his boots and soaking up to the knees of his corduroys and said to Williams, 'I'm a bloody fool, aren't I?' and Williams, without any of the embarrassment there might have been with an English workman just laughed and all the others started laughing and from then onwards they worked together happily, Williams solving problems before Philip knew he had them.

The other pleasant surprise had been how Isabelle and the men got on. Philip had feared she might be *grande dame*. After all she owned the pits and even the houses they lived in back in the Rhondda. But she surprised him by learning their names before he did, inquiring after their families and their ailments, hounding Mrs Tibbins at the

Sun Inn mercilessly about their dinners, bedding and the quality of their beer. Now she surprised him over again by exchanging a few words with Enoch in Welsh. When Enoch had gone on his way he said, 'I didn't know you could speak it.'

'I can't, no more than a few sentences my father taught me. He learned it so that the men couldn't talk about him behind his back. What's wrong?'

She'd caught an expression of doubt on his face.

'Remembering you're a second generation bloated capitalist.'

'Look.' She waved an arm round the garden, the men working in the sun. 'Do they look like downtrodden masses.'

'Not here, but then I've never been to a coal mine.'

'I'll take you one of these days. They're not slaves. I've got some of the highest paid manual workers in Europe on my pay roll. Six shillings a day a man can earn with bonuses and if the price of coal rises, so does their pay. So you don't have to worry about where the apples come from.'

Her lips were moist, as if really tasting the juice of the apples. He'd have liked to grab her and kiss them but the men were there.

'Strawberries too,' he said. 'Sweet little wild ones.' He imagined himself putting one on the tip of her tongue, watching her eyes. 'And we'll have a special little bank of them for Petra.' Perhaps a White Rabbit in stone keeping watch on her strawberries, a secret within a secret. So far, she hadn't responded to *Alice* but he lived in hope.

149

'Petra's spending a lot of time with the Thomas child,' she said.

'Young Evan. You don't mind that, do you?'

'No. What about the other Thomas nephew, the older one? Could we find work for him in the garden? They could do with the money.'

'Trefor. I offered Will. He seemed a bit awkward about it.'

'I don't think he approves of us.'

'Will?'

'No, the boy. He looks at me.'

'Shows his good taste.'

'Not that way. Oh, never mind. What about pears?'

'Pears for heirs. They grow slowly.'

'Never mind pears then. I want my garden quickly, quickly, quickly.'

He'd read her enough lectures on patience, so just scooped up her hand, planted a quick kiss in the palm and set it down again on the warm grass. They sat contentedly in the sun until Robert Williams appeared.

'Can I have a word with you, Mr Cordell?'

Philip took him down the bank, out of earshot.

'Something wrong?'

'The wheelbarrows and shovels. Somebody's been at them.'

'How?'

'You know we keep them at night in the shed by the house. Someone got in last night and took an axe to them. Three wheelbarrows and half a dozen shovel handles in bits.'

'Why in the world would anybody want to do that?'

'Trying to start a fire. The wood was all charred, and part of the wall. Only whoever it was couldn't have been very good at it. It burned itself out.'

'Have you any idea who?'

'No, I haven't.'

'I'll order some more wheelbarrows, get a lock for the shed and give you the key. I don't think we tell Mrs Allegri about this. Let me know if anything else happens.'

He walked slowly back to her.

'Anything wrong?'

'Nothing important.' He picked up the book, gave her his hand to get up. 'We'll make a list of apples this evening.'

The miners were a disappointment to Trefor. When he first found out from his Uncle Will that twelve men would be arriving from the Rhondda it was like the real world starting again. He missed the rhythms of coal towns, the days and weeks patterned by shift times. He missed the talk of seams and pits that had become as familiar to him as nursery rhymes and chanted themselves in his head as he fell asleep, Glyncoli, Bwllfa and Ynyswen, Abergorchy, Llwynypia, Maerdy. Even more than the coal, he missed the Federation men and their determination that there was a better world to be made, not with shovels and wheelbarrows in this passive English earth but hewed out of the rock of political opposition the way their picks broke the stubborn rock underground. On the Tuesday when the twelve started work on the garden he hung around them – making his uncle hope that the boy was taking an interest in the garden after all – and discovered by the end of the day that they were as good as useless to him, no more interested in serious affairs than the birds in the trees. This gardening gang were in holiday mood, joking and singing with each other, glad to be out in the sun all day doing lighter work than back home. Trefor drew back into himself and his round of jobs for Auntie Bath around the cottage, chopping so much wood that the pile at the back of the cottage reached to the eaves.

For Evan, the arrival of the men was one of the most exciting things that had ever happened to him. It was the music that did it. Some of the things they sang were snatches of songs familiar to him, even bits of hymns, but two of the younger men were different. Thomas Owen, heart broken by a jilt in Porth but getting over it fast and Dai 'Waistcoat' Evans (so named because there were three Dai Evans at Penyrheol Pit and he was a natty dresser) had a passion for music hall. They'd been horrified at first to find how far they'd exiled themselves from the Cardiff halls but consoled themselves by singing the latest things to each other as they worked, getting the others to join in the choruses – except for the two or three who were strict Baptist and didn't approve. Keeping close to them as they worked, occasionally being allowed to lend a hand, Evan got words and music to 'Oh Mr Porter' and 'We All Walked into the Shop' and 'Lily of Laguna' into his head with a speed that impressed them.

After a few days of their company it occurred to him to bring his fife and to tootle along with them. He'd a gift, they said, should be on the halls himself. So Dai Waistcoat and Tom Owen would sing as they worked, occasionally breaking off to perform soft shoe shuffles in their heavy boots, while Evan's fingers surprised him by finding variations on the tunes.

She's ma lady love, she is ma dove, my baby love.
She's no gal for sittin' down to dream,
She's the only queen Laguna knows.
I know she likes me,
I know she likes me,
Because she says so.
She is the lily of Laguna,
She is ma lily and ma rose.

Always, not far away but at a little distance from the men and the boy, there would be Petra, not saying anything, not claiming their notice and not getting it.

Late one afternoon when the men were an established part of village life at Holdersby, Bathsheba sent Evan to The Sun with a basket of peas for their dinner. He'd been told to come straight back but lingered, playing with a puppy in the yard, and was still there when the men came swinging in from work. He watched as they stripped to the waist and took it in turns to sluice themselves at the pump, chatting in Welsh for the pleasure of hearing their own language among strangers. Dai Waistcoat was one of the first washed and with his shirt back on and when he went through to the back room of the pub, Evan

153

followed him. There was an upright piano standing against the wall, keys yellowed, top ringed with beer stains. Dai Waistcoat sat down on the piano stool and ran his brown hands over the keys. His left hand had a long burn scar across it. Then he launched into something Evan had never heard a piano do before, didn't know pianos were *allowed* to do, even that music was allowed to do. First a jangling rhythm thrown off casually with one hand, but the rhythm uneven, like a tipsy man trying to walk straight. Then the parlour between its bulging, rose-papered walls became a whole roomful of notes like flocks of birds gone mad, swooping round each other, almost colliding, swerving away and back, faster and faster so that it seemed as if Dai Waistcoat and the old piano should rise up off the floorboards and start spinning too. Evan had never heard so many notes at once or so fast but the strangest thing was the timing of them, crazy, not predictable like music should be, not like heartbeats. His own heart thumped out of time trying to follow them and the breath went tight in his chest. When the music stopped and Dai Waistcoat relaxed on the piano stool, grinning, hands dangling, Evan wanted to shout at him to go on, on, on until he could make sense of it. Some of the other men had come into the room while he was playing and now started commenting.

'You playing that piano or tormenting it, Dai boy?'

'Send him to America. Like that there, they do.'

'Play something soothing boy, not that fidgeting stuff.'

So Dai played 'The Ash Grove' until Mrs Tibbins called the men to supper and Evan went home up the lane, the notes whirling in his head so that he could hardly answer Auntie Bath when she asked where he'd been all this time.

Next morning, sitting on a pile of cut turves at the top of the bank, Evan tried to get the fife to do the same tricks. He went on worrying at it until he was aware of somebody listening.

'Morning, Mr Cordell.'

He stood up in no great hurry, always at ease with Philip.

'What's that you're playing, Evan?'

Evan ran it through again and Philip listened and tried to place it. It came to him as a London memory – the flat of a friend just returned from New York, packing cases all over the place as they listened to the latest phonograph cylinders he'd brought back.

'Maple Leaf Rag. Where did you hear that?'

Maple meant nothing to Evan and rags were what you cleaned boots with. He waited in case he might be told something more useful, like how you did it. But Philip noticed that Isabelle had come out on the terrace and walked off in a hurry. At the end of the day's work Evan was down at The Sun again, but the men didn't sing or josh each other as they washed under the pump and the lid of the piano stayed closed. Dai Waistcoat and some of the others sat silently in the back room, curtains drawn against the sun.

'No piano today, Evan boy.'

155

'What's happened?'

'Explosion at Ferndale.'

Not one of Mrs Allegri's three pits, but over in the next valley, Rhondda Fach. Not an especially big explosion, four men dead and a dozen badly burned, nothing like the one at National Number 2 pit that had killed 119 miners two years before. It had taken most of the day for news to travel the thirty miles or so from the Rhondda to Holders-by, quickly to Abergavenny by telephone, then very slowly into England by the carrier on a horse and cart round that included the Sun Inn. Old Enoch Pugh had worked at one of the Ferndale Pits in the past, had friends there. He begged Mrs Tibbins, 'What number did he say it was? What number Ferndale pit?' But she didn't know and the carter had gone on his way so Enoch sat twisting his pipe in his fingers, ignoring the drink in front of him. Evan went back up to the cottage, important with adult news and found his brother picking gooseberries in the garden.

'There's men blown up.'

Trefor grabbed him and practically choked out of him the few details he knew. He thought at first it was their own pit, the one where their father worked, but even when he knew it was in the neighbouring valley he was still shaking with shock and anger.

'Four men murdered.'

'They weren't murdered. I told you, they were...'

'Murdered because the owners won't spend a few shillings on safety lamps, because they let men go on working in seams they know are dangerous...'

Evan stood miserably and stared at the gooseberry bushes. His brother was beginning to scare him, colder and more angry with every day away from home. Trefor started walking. He crossed the stream, went across the sheep pastures on the far side then up the side of the steep hill. It was a few days from midsummer, the sun still high, air full of the sound of crickets and cockchafers' wings. He threw himself down in a clearing, in the bracken and pressed a hand and ear against the sheep-nibbled grass, hearing the roar of his own blood, convincing himself that it was the torn rock still vibrating from the explosion under its thin skin of turf. For a long time he lay there thinking himself down into the earth, into the rock, lower down into the coal seams and home. When he did sit up at last he looked down on Holders Hope, the curve of the newly sanded path, the long swathe of red earth that would be the avenue down to the lily pond. If he could have made the hill fall on it all by wishing, he'd have done it. There were two people standing on the terrace, a man and a woman in a pale dress. That woman.

'There's never been an explosion at one of our pits, not in thirty-five years.'

But she'd been nervy since the news came through, snapped at the children, only picked at dinner.

'We were some of the first pits in the Rhondda to insist on safety lamps. I'm paying five hundred a year towards research on firedamp.'

Philip was puzzled by her mood.

'So if nobody's ever been killed in your pits...'

'Not in explosions. When I was small, there were five men killed in a roof fall at the Eastside pit. My father was grief-stricken.'

Embarrassed too, by an inquiry that found the roof might not have fallen if the management hadn't economised by using low quality pit props. She'd seen the records when she inherited the pits. Philip moved closer to comfort her and a letter in his jacket pocket crackled. He hoped she might ask what it was, give him a chance to talk about it. It had arrived two days before from an older plant collector he respected. The collector was putting together a seed-collecting expedition to the Himalayas and wondered whether Cordell would be interested. 'Isa, we're making a lot of progress on your garden.'

'It's the only thing that's keeping me sane, apart from you.'

'We can start the stonework next week. Once that's done we can get your lavender border and some of the waterside plants in, but after that there's not a lot we can do till the autumn.'

Will Thomas would be quite competent to see to the planting of trees provided he left him a plan. She must have caught what he was thinking because her body went stiff and he could feel her heart thumping.

'What do you mean? There's everything to do. All my plants to go in. Oh, my lovely purple beech.' Tears were pouring down her face. He took both her hands.

158

'Isa, darling, what is the matter?'

'I'm afraid.'

'What of?'

'That you'll go away. That you'll get tired of me and go away.'

He sighed, giving up from lungs and mind the anticipation of sharp mountain air, of plants waiting for him on screes and ridges that he wouldn't see.

'Philip, promise me you'll stay until the garden's finished.'

'A garden's never finished.'

'Well then.'

He put his arm round her, not caring too much if anyone saw them from the house.

Trefor walked across the meadow, onto the yielding sand of the new path. The smell of newly exposed earth rose round him into the cooling upper air. The light was almost gone but the two figures were still visible on the terrace, the pale dress standing out like a cold flame.

'Murderess.'

A laugh from somewhere up above him. The flare of a match. Dazzled, he could just make out the shape of a man behind it.

'My dear wife, you mean? You're probably right.'

The glowing end of the match arced through the air, just missing him. A dark figure, seeming enormously tall against the sky, moved away up the slope before Trefor could think of anything to say.

19

An edgy day, thermometer in the low eighties, humidity high, sky blue but thunder grumbling a long way to the east, around the Malvern Hills. Philip sweated inside his open-necked shirt and linen jacket, hurrying to get away from the house unseen. But it was hard to walk fast across the half-demolished terrace, past men working with picks and crowbars, piles of old and new stone slabs. Ton after ton of Pennant sandstone had come by train from the Rhondda to Abergavenny, then on in relays of groaning carts. Now there it was, piled up ready to make the new curved terrace and flights of steps. The stone slabs and blocks from the old terrace wouldn't be wasted. They were going to make a paved area beside the lily pool. Philip had been diffident when he mentioned this idea to the foreman, Robert Williams, thinking of the hard labour it would be for the miners to carry the stone down there. Williams had laughed. You didn't carry stone downhill, you let gravity do the work for you. They organised an earth ramp from the terrace down to the pond with a stout wooden box on wheels and a rope and pulley arrangement. As Philip came near the top of the ramp the box had just been loaded and the men were

160

eager for him to stop and watch. One man got ready to knock a chock away from under the wheel of the truck and two others, hands leather-gloved, kept a firm hold on the rope over the pulley that would control the speed of descent.

'Let her go then, Tom.'

The truck gathered speed down the slope, slowed down over the flat area by the pond and came neatly to rest against an earth bank they'd thrown up as a buffer a few yards from the pond edge.

'Fine, Mr Williams. But don't hurry it. We don't want accidents.'

The men grinned. This was a child's game compared to the way they usually earned their living. Philip walked along the new stone flags of the path between borders of infant lavender bushes. He'd gentled them in with barrow loads of sand to soften the clay and a mulch of leaf mould from the woods. Some were flowering already but it would be two or three years before they matured into a border and they saw whether their planting scheme had worked. Isabelle called it their perspective trick. At the top of the garden near the terrace the lavender flowers would be the most intense dark mauve they could find, shading to normal lavender colour, then white at the very end when the lavender path joined the stream on its meander along the bottom of the lawn. The effect, they hoped, would be to make the curve of the lavender border look even longer, as if fading away into the distance. Philip walked on down to the pool. The earth beside it was flattened and sanded, ready for paving

161

stones. All very much in order, but not beautiful and Isabelle was impatient for beauty. So he'd come to see if the surprise he'd been preparing for her was ready. He went right to the water's edge and crouched down on the cracked and dried out mud. Dark green leaves the size of tea plates floated on the water, rubbery stems poking out with egg-shaped buds, green as good jade. Further out a few of the water lilies had opened, three pink and two white.

The hot afternoon would bring a few more into flower. In the evening before dinner he could walk her down there.

'Your water lilies, milady. As ordered.'

When they'd started he'd told her that she'd have to wait until next year. But he wanted so much to make her happy that he'd hurried nature along for once. He'd become a plant hunter again, not among mountain screes and rocks but in the gardens of Herefordshire gentry who, in return for his expert advice on their horticultural problems, instructed their gardeners to fill barrels with lily roots and leaves for him. He'd drive away in the pony cart borrowed from the Sun Inn, pond water and lily plants sloshing in the back. It had taken several loads, and the complicity of Will and young Evan carrying barrels of lilies across the fields in wheelbarrows, to get this display. He hoped, in the dusk, she'd see it as he could imagine it so clearly in a few years' time – the pond a mass of lilies, dragonflies hovering like humming birds, Petra out there in her little blue boat among the leaves, laughing back at them, happy. There was an awkward little area where the willows ended, just a jumble of bushes with wisps of dead grass caught in them from the winter floods. What that needed was the immense rhubarb-like leaves of *Gunnera manicata*, a joke of a plant designed by the botanical gods for the amazement of children. As he watched, the kingfisher jagged out from the alder opposite, almost touched the water, then up and into another alder out of sight, the heart-stopping, unreasonable colour of it seeming to burn a trail on the air.

'If it can be like that, anything's possible.'

He knew they could do it – he and the garden – give her this hope, this happiness. Tonight.

Petra and Evan sat in the shade of an old apple tree, watching the ponies. Guto and Sonny were standing under another tree, dozing nose to tail. Now and then their tails would give a few slow swishes and whisk the flies out of each other's faces. Pont had taken her foal into a cool patch under a tree in the unkempt hedge. A summer of good grass had filled out the hollows in her flanks, sleeked her strawberry roan coat. The foal, a bay with a cobby head that looked too heavy for the rest of his body, was drinking from her teat, having to fold at the knee because it was already nearly as tall as she was.

'Hedgehogs do that too,' Evan said.

'Do what?'

'Drink the mares' milk.'

Petra thought about it. She admired Evan for his ability to play tunes on the fife and vault onto Sonny's placid back, even more for the mystery of coming from the other side of the hills where

163

the earth exploded, speaking a foreign language as easily as English. She'd asked him to teach her, but he was as niggardly with his Welsh as her brother had been with Latin. English people couldn't do it. Almost everything else they shared. He let her play the fife, though he laughed at her lack of ability. She begged slices of cake from the cook and they ate them in hidden dens up in the woods. Instinctively they treated their friendship as a secret. It would have lessened it if they'd guessed that the adults more or less approved. Isabelle was grateful for anything that got Petra out into the air and put colour into her cheeks. Philip made mental notes that their dens must be respected when the wood was coppiced. Only Will expressed concern to Bathsheba that Mrs Allegri might not like her daughter to associate with the gardener's nephew but Bathsheba said they were only innocent children and time enough to worry about that kind of thing when they grew up.

'They couldn't reach,' Petra said, having thought about the hedgehogs.

'Don't have to. Wait until night-time, they do, when the mares are lying down in the grass.'

She stared, not convinced but unwilling to call him a liar. 'Have you seen them do it?'

'Uncle Will has.'

'If we came and watched, would we see?'

'Should think so.'

They stared at each other, eyes scared but challenging.

'Shall we do it?'

'When?'

'Soon.'
'Tonight?'
'Tonight.'

Isabelle's head ached from the heat as she sat at her desk in the small drawing room, writing business letters. She'd have preferred to be outside but Marius had to be kept at working at his isosceles triangles. She'd started to worry about whether he'd be ready for Eton and had located an Oxford-educated curate a few miles away who was willing to act as tutor. He reported that serious work needed to be done, particularly on mathematics and Latin, if Marius were to do justice to his undoubted intelligence. (What the curate said to his fiancee that evening was that the boy was bright enough but bone idle and he hoped there'd be somebody at Eton with the sense to kick the arrogance out of him.) Marius too had pleaded a headache and Isabelle had relented to the extent of ringing down to the kitchen and ordering a jug of homemade lemonade for them both. A knock on the door and Megan came in with a tray. Isabelle indicated that she could put a glass down on the blotter and Megan poured.

'Thank you, Megan. And a glass for Marius please.'

She went back to her letter to a group of other colliery owners about delays in getting coal down to Cardiff Her father had been fiercely independent, not caring much what others did, but times were changing and the small owners had to make common cause.

'...I agree with you that we should ask for a meeting with the rail directors in Cardiff as soon as possible, but suggest that we should talk first to be clear on what we want from them. I could be in Treorchy...'

It struck her that Megan seemed to be taking a long time to pour Marius's lemonade and go. She looked over towards the window, saw Megan bending over with the jug and caught the last word of an urgent whisper from Marius. It sounded like '...tonight.'

'That will be all, thank you Megan. You can leave the jug on the sideboard.'

When the door closed behind Megan she walked over and took a seat beside Marius at the table.

'What is it now? I thought you wanted me to concentrate.'

'What were you saying to Megan?'

'Nothing.'

'Are you sure?'

He banged the ruler down on the paper, drew an angry line. She supposed every woman with sons and servants had to face it at some time. The important thing was to be firm without giving him cause to quarrel with her.

'Marius, Megan's got her work to do. We mustn't make it more difficult for her in any way.'

He moved the ruler, slashed another pencil line.

'If we have people working for us we're responsible for them, especially when they're young, like Megan is.' How young? Fourteen, fifteen? She'd have to find a reason to ask Mrs

166

Morgan. 'So we should never do anything that takes an unfair advantage of them, put them in a position where they might be doing something wrong.'

Marius put down his pencil at last and looked her full in the face. His expression was so like his father's that her stomach jolted with the shock of it. She stared at him, suddenly on the defensive, knowing that something terrible was coming.

'What do you mean?'

She closed her eyes. Her words came out confused and floundering. 'I mean ... if you were thinking of...' Angry at the way her heart was thumping, she put it bluntly. 'If you were making an arrangement to meet Megan in secret somewhere, that would be very wrong.'

'Oh.' He stared at her for a long time. She stared back, trying to ward off the something terrible by force of will, failing.

'Would it? Have you told my father that as well?'

Holders Hope.
Thursday.

To: Daniel Feveril,
Oakley Street,
Chelsea.

Dear Dan,
If Tibs' little friend is still using the couch in your studio, throw him out. My need is greater. I'm coming to town tomorrow and must have somewhere to lay my head for a day or two.

167

Crisis has come and Juno is thundering. When the storm's over I may get my order of release out of this, but must have a base to negotiate from.

Yours in haste to catch post, Allegri.

Philip said, 'You'll have to let him go.'

He'd walked her up to the shattered oak tree above the wood to get her away from the poisonous atmosphere of the house. She'd gone passively, leaning against him most of the time. Now she was sitting on the fallen trunk looking out to the hills where the sun was setting in a bank of cloud, purple and red like a bruise.

'How will that help?'

'He won't be here to hurt you any more.'

'As long as he lives he'll go on hurting me.'

He was aching with pity but appalled too by her stubbornness.

'You could give him an allowance on condition that he lives abroad. You say he keeps talking about Italy.' No answer. 'Isa, you know if he stays here it will happen again. There'll always be some girl.'

'She's pretty, isn't she?'

The change of tack, the despairing way she said it, took him by surprise.

'Megan? Yes, I suppose she is.'

'More than pretty. Beautiful. It's funny, there she was around the house all day and it simply didn't occur to me. You must have noticed though.'

'About her and Leon? No, I swear...'

'No, not that. Being beautiful.'

'Isa, why should I care a hang whether she's

beautiful or not? I love you.'

Silence.

'She'd better go back home to Wales, hadn't she?' he said. 'Do you want me to have a quiet word with Will Thomas for you?'

'Why should she go? It's not the girl's fault.'

The cloud bank was breaking up into rags of red and purple. Thunder was grumbling in the distance.

'I suppose we should go inside.'

She clamped her palms over her eyes and rocked backwards and forwards on the trunk.

'What am I going to do, Philip? Oh, *what* am I going to do?'

Megan took a long time to realise that the quarrel going on upstairs might have something to do with her. As far as the kitchen was concerned, the crisis developed in terms of disrupted mealtimes. Only Mr Cordell and the two children sitting down to lunch, and he as fidgety as a dog with fleas. Then Jane coming down with the smug look of somebody who knew more than she'd say, demanding a pot of Earl Grey for Mrs Allegri, confined to her room with a headache. Mr Allegri in the studio, ringing for coffee and sandwiches, nothing unusual about that except Mrs Morgan coming into the kitchen to insist that it must be one of the two Marys and not Megan who took them to him. It was at that point the looks started. Looks between Mrs Morgan and Cook, between Cook and the two Marys. Towards the end of the afternoon when dinner preparations were in full swing she knew

169

something was going badly wrong. There were carrots with dinner and she and Mary from the village usually did them together, Megan washing and scraping them at the sink, Mary at the draining board cutting them into rings. If Mary thought a carrot hadn't been scraped properly she'd pretend anger, send it splashing back into the sink for Megan to do again, spattering her with water, both giggling until Cook told them to calm down and get on with it. Today, though, Mary stayed at the far end of the kitchen table making a long business of stringing and slicing beans and didn't start on the carrots until Megan had scraped the whole sinkful of them and moved to other things. By then, the shouting and slamming of doors had started upstairs and Jane, coming in for more tea, unbent enough to admit there was an unholy row going on. She glanced at Megan when she'd said it with a look sharper than raw gooseberries. Just before half past six Megan changed into clean cap and apron, ready for serving dinner but Mrs Morgan said, remote though not unkindly, 'I don't think so this evening, Megan,' then glared at one of the Marys when she laughed. So Megan stayed in the hot kitchen and did the washing up. She understood by now that there was a disaster coming and it involved her. Some monster was up there above the kitchen ceiling, paw raised and claws out, and they'd left a space round her to give it room to bring the paw down on her.

'It's not fair.'

The wail to her own reflection in the darkening window started as a protest that they'd left her to

170

do all the work but before it died away it was more than that. It wasn't fair that she must be passive and silent while other people blamed her and said things about her. The pride of men who risked their lives underground every day, who knew their worth and could look anyone in the eye flared in her own blood. She undid the strings of her wet and greasy apron and dragged it over her head. The cap came with it and she let it fall. Her hair tumbled down over her shoulders, heavy with steam and sweat.

'It's not my fault.'

There were two appointments she was supposed to be keeping in the garden when it got dark, one made by a casual command, the other begged for. She couldn't keep both and a few minutes earlier, with the beast's paw hanging over her, hadn't intended to keep either. Now, with resentment taking over from fear, she decided to leave it to chance which one. She took a deep breath and went out of the back door, past the pigbins and through the latched gate in the wall, into the garden.

Petra lay in her deep feather mattress, watching the last of the daylight reflected in the polished wood of the bed's footboard. Her clothes were draped tidily on the chair beside her, ready for morning, the green and red cotton skirt, green blouse with the ribbon fastening at the neck, vest, knickers and socks.

'I'll put them away for you if you like,' Mrs Morgan had offered, seeing her to bed, but Petra had shook her head and turned her face to the wall. The covers were too heavy, her flannel nightdress hot and sticky and her brain such a lump of misery she couldn't think with it any more. But after a while it did squeeze out something and that was 'hedgehog.' She'd accepted Evan's dare to come at night and watch the hedgehog. The thought of going out alone in the dark scared her so much that she decided it was a kind of spell. If she dared to do it and saw the hedgehog drinking then everything would come right, her mother and father would be happy again, Mr Cordell with his tomb beetles and corpse flowers go away back to Africa. Terrified, she got herself upright and out of her nightdress, pulled on her underwear, fumbled with buttons, hooks and eyes. The journey downstairs and along the passage to the side door was the most terrifying thing she'd ever done. The door was unlocked. She sat down on the bench outside and put on her boots, then stood up and launched herself down the steep path towards the Thomas's cottage. There were rustlings from the hazel bushes, an owl hooting high up in the woods. No moon or stars, only masses of clouds like bunches of black grapes against a stretched white sky.

'If I do this it will be all right. If I do this it will be all right.'

By the time she got to the plank bridge there was just enough light left to see a dark silhouette on the other side. It spoke in Evan's voice.

'Where've you been. I've been waiting.'

'Is the hedgehog there?'

'Not yet. Come on.'

She followed his silhouette along the path towards the paddock. The masses of cloud had joined up now, so that you couldn't tell what was cloud and what was dark.

20

Will Thomas, fearing a downpour, went out to his vegetable garden with a lamp to see no tools had been left in the open. Reassured, he urinated in a leisurely arc into the compost heap, rather than face the earth closet on a warm and humid night. He'd been aware all day of the distant thunder but the rumble that came before he'd finished seemed suddenly much closer and made the arc jerk and waver, pattering onto the rhubarb leaves. He buttoned his flies, picked up the lamp and went inside.

'Where've those boys got to?'

Bathsheba looked up from mending socks.

'Haven't seen anything of Evan since supper. I sent Trefor out to look for him half an hour ago.'

'Storm's getting nearer. Think I'll go out and look for them.'

He went carrying the lamp on the path alongside the stream, the terrier trotting at his heels. As well as the two boys he was keeping an eye out for Megan. Bathsheba said not to worry but she was coming home later and later from the house these evenings, so tired she could hardly talk. He could still hear the thunder but it puzzled him because it had gone distant again, right over Hereford way, nothing like that loud rumble he'd heard in the garden. He came to the plank bridge and shone the lamp up towards the hazel thicket.

'You there, Evan boy?'

He thought he heard rustling, but then there were foxes earths and a badger set in the hazels.

While he was standing there, the screaming came. It was below him and to the right, down towards the pond in the meadow where he'd pollarded the willows. His heart lurched and his spine went cold, but he said to himself, 'Foxes.' Sometimes in the mating season they'd scream at each other like sinners in torment, so that if you didn't know you'd be sure there was a human creature out there being done terrible harm. But foxes made these mating screeches in the frosty nights of March, not August. And these screams were going on and on, tearing the night apart. He left the path and started running towards the sound across grass and newly bared earth. The screams stopped before he'd gone far but it was as if they'd been the signal for the rain to start because suddenly it was pouring down warm and heavy, soaking him within seconds, making turf and bare earth as slippery as ice so that he had to wave his arms to keep upright and the small beam from the lamp wavered uselessly around in the dark, making the panic worse.

'I'm coming boy. Wait there, I'm coming.'

He was sure it must be Evan. But the screams had been a long way off and he'd no hope of being heard. When the lamp beam dashed across a human shape a little way in front of him he felt like shouting with relief.

'That you, Evan?'

He held the lamp steady, the figure came closer, dark hair plastered round a pale face and scared eyes.

'No, Uncle. Trefor.'

'Where's your brother?'

'Isn't... Isn't he back at the house? I don't know.'

Trefor's limbs were trembling. He could hardly get the words out.

'What was that screaming?'

'I ... I don't...'

Will grabbed his hand and the two of them went on together, heading diagonally downhill, peering through the rain that hissed down onto the grass. After a while they tripped over a marking string and found themselves on the long swathe of bare earth that would be the avenue down to the lily pool with the miners' ramp for the stone cart on the far side of it. They went cautiously until Will said 'Listen' and put out a hand to stop Trefor. Something was coming up the path towards them, something dark and rounded. It was making noises audible over the hiss of the rain, jagged, high-pitched retching sounds. When Will let the lamp beam fall on it, it fell to the mud and curled up, but the sounds went on.

'Evan boy, what's up? We're...'

Trefor said, 'It isn't Evan.' He slithered down the slope, bent over the curled shape. 'It's her, the daughter.'

175

Will joined him. 'Well, I'll be... Miss Petra.'

He gave Trefor the lamp, knelt down.

'So where's he? Where's my brother?'

'In a minute. Come on there, Miss Petra love. We'll soon have you...'

The face that reared up at him, screaming, was almost dissolved with terror, a white mass with huge, blank eyes and a gape that shot out such an inhuman blast of sound that Will fell back on his heels, hands over his ears. He recovered, got one arm round her and the other pressing her face against the shoulder of his wet jacket so that she couldn't scream any more, but her whole body was jerking. From the smell, her cotton skirt was wet with urine as well as rain. He manoeuvred her over his shoulder and stood up cautiously.

'Best get her up home. You go in front with the lamp.'

'But where's Evan?'

Then, from somewhere not far below them on the avenue, a small scared voice.

'Trefor? Uncle Will?'

The boy staggered towards them, scared but nowhere near as terrified as the girl, apprehensive of trouble.

'Evan, what have you been doing boy? What's happening?'

Evan came into the light, stared at Petra's soaked back over Will's shoulder and started crying.

'Is ... is she dead?'

'No. Just scared out of her wits. What have you been doing, the two of you?'

'We were ... we were looking for hedgehogs. I

176

lost her then I heard screaming and...'

'Come on, the two of you.'

Trefor took his brother's hand. Their progress was slow, up the slippery avenue with rainwater running down it, feet sliding and Petra letting out another scream every time Will slipped. But her screams were getting weaker through weariness. They'd got to the point where the two paths joined when there was the beam of a more powerful lamp up above them and a shout. Mr Cordell's voice.

'Who's there? What's happening.'

Relieved, Will tried to call up to him that it was all right, the little maid had given herself a scare, that's all. When Cordell came skidding down to join them, Will swung round so that Cordell could see Petra's face, talk to her, but she screamed again, so loudly that it was a wonder her body didn't wrench itself apart and burrowed her face against Will's shoulder as if she wanted to climb inside him. They went on, Cordell first walking backwards with the lamp to show Will the way, Will carrying Petra, the two scared boys behind.

At the top of the steps to the terrace there was a cluster of other lamps waiting. Behind them, under umbrellas, the anxious faces of Mrs Morgan, Mr Rees, Jane, Mary and the cook. When they saw the child on Will's shoulder there was a murmur of concern.

Cordell said, 'She doesn't seem to be hurt. Something scared her.'

He looked round the semi-circle of lamplit

177

faces for the one that mattered, couldn't find her.

'Mrs Morgan, could you go up and get Mrs Allegri, please? Don't scare her. Tell her Petra's all right.'

His eyes were on Will carrying the child across the terrace to the door, with Rees holding a big black umbrella over them. Mrs Morgan was saying something urgent to him, standing close and speaking softly so that the others wouldn't hear. It took him a while to understand what it was.

'...isn't in her room. Mr Rees and I have been looking since we heard the screaming. We didn't like to...'

'Can't find Mrs Allegri?'

His voice was louder and sharper than he'd intended. He spun round and looked at the hissing dark below the terrace.

'For God's sake, she's not out in that, is she?'

Mrs Morgan bit her lip, as if it was her fault. 'I don't know where she is, Mr Cordell. Nobody's seen her since Mary took some fresh tea up to her room and that's two hours ago.'

Philip had to fight an impulse to plunge back down the steps into the dark but the impossibility of searching acres of field and woodland on his own held him back. He went striding across the terrace into the house, Mrs Morgan and the rest following. Inside, Rees and Will with the child were hesitating at the foot of the staircase. Petra had stopped screaming and her eyes were closed, soaked hair hanging down Will's back.

Rees said, 'Should we take her up to her room, Mr Cordell?'

He dragged his mind from Isabelle back to the child, realising that they were all looking to him for directions.

'Yes. Mrs Morgan, will you go up and get her into bed? Get her a warm drink and light a fire in her room. I'll come up in a minute and we'll decide if she needs a doctor.'

The procession of Will, Rees and Mrs Morgan went slowly upstairs, printing wet and muddy footprints on the carpet. Mary and Cook disappeared to the kitchen, leaving only Isabelle's maid Jane, wide-eyed and drinking in the crisis.

'Jane, go and check whether any of Mrs Allegri's outdoor things are missing from the wardrobe. Waterproof cape and so on.'

She yes-sired him and followed the rest upstairs. He couldn't believe that Isabelle would have chosen to go out in the pouring rain unless she'd known that the child might be out there in distress. But if she'd rushed out when she heard the screams, why hadn't any of the rest of them seen her? He stood alone in the hall, dripping rain-water, desperate for action but feeling he was the only person in the household with nothing to do. Mrs Morgan must be given time to get the child dried and into her nightdress before he could go up and see her. He moved aimlessly into the small drawing room. It was dark, rain sluicing down the window onto the terrace. He stood looking out, trying to make his mind calm enough to plan a search for Isabelle. Only three of them to do it, Will, Rees, himself. Four if you counted the elder Thomas boy. Two of them down towards the lily pool, two up through the woods and the shattered oak. Probably around eleven o'clock now, so getting light in five hours or so. Light coming up over Isabelle unconscious in the mud, or crying with pain, leg broken in the woods. What did she think she was doing, going out without him?

A sound in the room behind him. He turned round. Nobody there. The sound again. Not quite a snore, too light for that, more an indrawing of breath.

'Who's there?'

He found the table where the lamp stood, fumbled with the knob that sparked the flint. The sound was coming from a small sofa, turned with its back to the door to face the empty fireplace.

'Isabelle.'

She was lying there in the pale dress she'd been wearing in the afternoon, one hand on her chest, the other drooping over the side, fingers curled. Her feet were in pale leather shoes, unmuddied. Beside her on the table a sherry glass and a bottle of the pills she'd been prescribed for when she couldn't sleep, half full. When he said her name her eyes opened, looked startled, closed again.

'Isabelle, are you all right?'

Her eyes opened again, focusing now and saw the expression on his face. She came fully awake, swung her feet to the floor.

'Philip. What's happened? What's wrong?'

'It's Petra.' She flinched with fear. He cursed his clumsiness. 'She's all right. She was out in the rain and something scared her. I don't know what. Mrs Morgan's putting her to bed.'

'Rain?' She looked at the blank window.

'Pouring. She got soaked to the skin. I've told them to light the fire.'

She got up, swayed, clung to his arm.

'Are you all right, Isa?'

Her eyes followed his to the glass and pill bottle.

'When we came back here, you said I should rest. I couldn't, so I took two of my pills.'

'Only two?'

'Yes. Help me upstairs. Poor little mite, what was she doing out on her own?'

It struck him that he'd perhaps done too much to reassure her. Petra's had a scare. Petra's soaked. Childish things that could be put right with a hot drink and a hug. But anybody who'd heard those screams would know it was something worse than that – that the child had almost disintegrated with fear. He wondered whether he should give some hint of that as he walked beside her up the staircase but hadn't worked out what to say before they came to Petra's door.

'Wait for me.'

She slipped inside and closed the door. He heard the murmur of her voice, then Mrs Morgan's but not Petra's. It was nearly half an hour before she came out, face pale and worried.

'Philip, what on earth was it?'

'I don't know. Doesn't she say?'

'She won't say anything. Where was she?'

'Will Thomas found her on the avenue, not far from the lily pool. It looks as if she'd been out playing with Evan and they got separated. I suppose just being out on her own in the dark...'

'Oh God, I'll never forgive myself. But why weren't you ... why wasn't anybody?'

'Isa, we'll ask all that in the morning. The important thing is what do we do now? Does she need a doctor?'

'I don't think so. Tomorrow, if she's no better. She's had some hot milk. I'm going to sleep in here with her tonight. Mrs Morgan will have a mattress brought in.'

'You need your rest. I suppose I couldn't...?'

She shook her head, then buried her face in his shoulder. He could feel her shaking.

'Oh Philip.'

He put his arm round her. 'It's all right, darling. It will be all right now.'

They had to jump apart when Mrs Morgan put her head round the door. Petra was asking for her mother. Philip gave a last touch to her elbow as she went back inside, then helped Rees carry in a mattress from the spare room. When they put it down on the floor of Petra's room he allowed himself one glance at the child lying motionless, eyes closed and Isa kneeling on the rug beside the bed. Afterwards he poured himself a large scotch from the decanter in the dining room, took it up to his bedroom and got out of his wet clothes at last. He lay awake until long after the rain stopped, thinking of the two of them just across the landing.

It was after midday before anybody in the house missed Leon Allegri and even then it didn't cause great concern. For months he'd been living his own life under the same roof as the rest of the

182

household. Nobody had been surprised when he took no interest in what was happening the night before, assuming he was shut in his studio or upstairs in his rooms. Late in the morning Philip asked Isabelle, 'Seen nothing of Allegri, I suppose?' She shook her head. They were in the small drawing room, looking out down the lane for the doctor's gig. Petra was no better, either sleeping a feverish unhealthy sleep or waking and crying for her mother. She was asleep at the moment with Jane watching, under instructions to call for Isabelle as soon as she woke up.

'If we knew what had frightened her...' Isabelle said. 'Could you talk to Evan?'

'I'll try if you like, but I'll have a word with his uncle first. I've got to go out anyway. Williams has sent a message up to say there's some problem with the stone.'

Down by the lily pond. The last place Philip would have chosen to go to this morning – too full of disappointment.

'Could you go and speak to him now? It might help to know, when the doctor gets here.'

Outside it was a bright, clean-washed day, the heaviness gone from the air, hills so clear you could see the bracken sway as sheep pushed through it. Three buzzards wheeled high overhead, floating out their catlike calls on cloudless sky. The torrential rain didn't seem to have done much damage, only carved a few runnels in the sanded paths that could be made good with a bit of wheelbarrow and spade work. He walked down the wide avenue towards the pool thinking that when the doctor came he'd have no right to talk to him, would have to stay in the background and hear about it later from Isa. For a long time he'd accepted the situation but it couldn't go on like that. Not after yesterday.

In the kitchen there was some surprise that Mr Allegri hadn't rung down for his morning coffee but household routine was still all over the place and there were plenty of other things to think about. Megan Thomas, for instance. She reported for work as usual at eight o'clock, pale and tired but then so was everybody else after being up all night. She stood in the doorway while Cook and the two Marys stared at her then, to cover the silence, Cook told her she'd better be getting on washing the lettuces. She put on her cap and apron and went to the sink without a word. Afterwards Cook and Mrs Morgan had a whispered consultation in the pantry and agreed that for the while things would have to stay as they were. Mrs Morgan couldn't dismiss anybody without the agreement of Mrs Allegri, and she couldn't be asked about such an embarrassing subject while worried out of her mind about the child.

Down by the pool, Will Thomas and Robert Williams were in serious consultation over a pile of scattered stone slabs and the wheeled box lying broken on its side. Williams pointed with the toe of his boot to the earth bank that had been built as a buffer a little way from the edge of the pond, to stop the loaded box overshooting and plunging into the water as it came down the bank. There was a long rectangular dent in the landward side of it.

'Did its job, look. That'll be where the bottom of the box hit, then it turned over and out it all came.'

Paving stones from the old terrace were scattered round them, some broken, with the fresh sandstone gleaming pink against the brown weathered surface like the flesh of salmon through charred skin.

'Hit it with a good bang, it would have.'

Will said, 'I think I heard it.'

Williams raised an eyebrow.

'Out in my vegetable patch, just afore it got dark. Only I thought it was thunder. That's why I came out to look for the lad.'

'Yes, the lad.'

Will looked miserable. 'There's no harm in him.'

Williams looked at the stone slabs scattered round them, then away up the ramp.

'He wouldn't have meant it,' Will pleaded.

'Someone must have knocked that chock out to start it. Did you ask him?'

'I didn't know about it till I got here. But I asked him what he'd been doing last night, yes.'

'What did he say?'

'Just he and Miss Petra were out looking for hedgehogs. They got separated in the dark, then he heard her screaming.'

'She would scream, wouldn't she, if she'd nearly had this lot land on her.'

Will's jaw dropped. 'Evan wouldn't have let that down on the little lass. Like brother and

185

sister, they are.'

'I'm not saying he meant to.'

Will, heavy-hearted, tried to think of what he should say and still hadn't managed it when Mr Cordell came in sight.

Philip's first thought as he saw the pool, was regret at the waste. The water-lilies were performing magnificently, stars of soft pink or white with glowing stamens like candle flames. There it was, the first of his love letters to Isabelle through the garden, and she wasn't there to see it. There'd be other days, nearly as good, but you only got the shock of perfection once and this was it. Then he looked away from the pond at the scattered stone and splintered wood and the two men standing dejected, sighed, and scrambled down to join them. Robert Williams did most of the talking, laying no blame and mentioning no names, but making clear that the men had left the loaded box safely on level ground at the top of the ramp the night before, with a solid metal chock under its front wheel. When Philip asked whether the heavy rain might have washed the chock away, Williams just managed not to treat the question with the contempt it deserved.

'Tropical monsoon wouldn't have done that, sir. Anyway, someone had to unhitch the rope from the pulley at the top and give it a shove, look.'

Philip said, slowly, 'I suppose it could have been the same person who watered the plants with salt and broke up the wheelbarrows.'

Will's heart rose then sank again. If it wasn't one brother, it was the other.

Robert Williams said, 'I hope you're not

thinking any of us would do a thing like that, Mr Cordell.'

'Good heavens, no. Anyway, the plants were harmed before any of you got here.'

Silence while they stared down at the slabs and the trampled ground, then Philip sighed.

'I suppose it explains what scared Petra. If she'd been by the pond when that came crashing down...'

He shivered, feeling sick.

Will said, looking at the ground, 'Nobody would have ... up there in the dark ... he wouldn't know the little lass was down here.'

The other men looked at him. After a while Robert Williams asked how the young lady was.

'Not so good I'm afraid, Williams. That looks as if it might be the doctor's gig now.'

21

'He couldn't find anything organically wrong,' Isabelle said.

They were sitting in the drawing room over untasted cups of tea. 'He said we should keep her in bed for a few days and feed her beef tea and milky things until the fever goes.'

'Did she say anything to him about what scared her?'

'No. She answered him when he asked if her head hurt and so on. At least she's starting to talk again.'

'But nothing about what it was?'

'No. If I ask her, she starts crying.'

She looked close to tears herself, eyes huge, skin almost transparent from a sleepless night.

'I think I might know.'

He told her about the ramp and the cargo of paving stones.

'Poor little mite,' he said. 'Imagine being lost in the dark and hearing that thing rushing down on you. It's a mercy she...' He looked at the expression on her face. 'You don't think it was that?'

She shook her head, from weariness more than denial.

'Philip – the doctor. He noticed her fists were clenched – like this – and he wanted her to open them. She wouldn't at first. He had to pretend to tickle her, then ... then this fell out of her hand. She must have been clutching it all night.'

She opened her own right hand. In the palm of it was a small white disc.

'A button?'

'It's off Leon's blazer. You know, that black and white striped one.'

'Did he give it to Petra?'

'Why would he?'

'So did she take it?'

'When? The last I remember seeing of Leon, yesterday afternoon, he was wearing that blazer.'

'So the button came off and she picked it up?'

'Yes...'

But the way she said it meant 'probably not.'

'Isa...'

'It was torn off. Those threads... It was torn off.' He waited. 'Philip, whatever happened to

188

her last night was to do with him. I know it was.'

'You think he'd deliberately scare a child like that?'

'He'd do anything to hurt us.'

He stood up.

'Philip, where are you going?'

'To ask him.'

Her cry of protest followed him out of the door, across the hall to the studio. He hit the door with his knuckles.

'Allegri.'

No answer. He pushed the door open and walked in. Empty. Lingering smells of coffee, tobacco, stale wine. The portrait of Isabelle, twenty and in love, hung on the wall. It had been given, in harsh strokes of charcoal, a moustache and bats' wings. He slammed the door behind him, ran upstairs and battered on the door of Allegri's dressing room.

'Allegri, damn you.'

No answer. He opened the door and found himself looking into the scared eyes of Mary from the village with a feather duster in her hand.

'Mr Cordell ... I was only ... what's the matter, Mr Cordell?'

He apologised for scaring her, explained unnecessarily that he was looking for Mr Allegri.

'I don't know where he is, sir, but he didn't sleep in his bed last night.'

'What?'

'Made up just the way I left it and the bedpan not used.'

Philip went downstairs, more slowly and heavily than he'd gone up. Something caught his attention on the table by the front door. A letter addressed in Allegri's black spiky handwriting to Daniel Feveril, Oakley Street, Chelsea. He hesitated then picked it up and carried it along the servants' corridor to the housekeeper's room.

'Mrs Morgan, do you know how long this letter has been on the hall table?'

She glanced at it, bit her lip at the implied criticism.

'Since yesterday. The post went early because of Mrs Tibbins' lad going back down to the village. It must have missed it.'

He went back to the drawing room with the letter. Isabelle opened her eyes when he came in.

'He didn't sleep in his bed last night. He left this letter in the hall.'

She took it from him, looked at the address.

'An artist friend of his. I don't like him much.'

'I think we should open it.'

She stared at him then, without argument, ripped the envelope open with the handle of a teaspoon. She seemed to take a long time reading the letter then passed it to him without comment. He read and winced with anger and hurt for her, but her face and voice were calm.

'He's gone then?'

'So it seems. But Petra...'

'If she saw him going, she'd have tried to stop him.'

'She grabs him by the button and he pulls away from her and goes? You think that would be enough to make her like this? What did he say to her? Or do to her?'

'Going would be enough. She worships him,

I'm afraid.' This time it was her turn to look for hurt in his face. 'Philip, I'm sorry.'

'So he's gone? Really gone?'

'So it seems. Poor Petra.' Their eyes went to the little white disc and its wisp of thread. 'We'll make it up to her won't we, Philip? We'll make it up to her?' She took his hand and, for all her tiredness, squeezed it so that that bones crunched. 'Won't we?'

22

July 2001

To his own amazement, Colin won the battle of the bones. At first Kim had been so angry because he'd kept them from her that he expected her to fling her tent and duvet into the back of the car and go. Slowly, sitting cross-legged by the tent flap with the beer can in her hand, she'd got the confession out of him. How he'd found the first of the bones three days after they arrived there and gone on digging in the old pond not because he wanted to find more but ... all right, OK, he supposed he was curious to see if there were more but he'd have been digging there anyway because ... OK, OK, he'd admitted he'd been curious hadn't he? Was that supposed to be such a crime?

'You didn't think what would happen when I found them?'

'No.'

191

'And those long boxes you asked me to get...?'

'Yes. I'm sorry.'

'You know I'd have wanted to photograph them. Why didn't you call me?'

'I was scared.'

'Scared? Of the bones?'

'No. Scared you'd want me to tell the police or somebody. Then they'd have thrown us out.'

'So you'd have lost your garden?'

'Yes. And being here with you.'

She moved her head from side to side, staring down at the beer can. At first he thought it meant she was rejecting him, but perhaps it was puzzlement because after a long silence she stated her terms for staying:

1) Any more bones or anything else peculiar he was to tell her at once and let her photograph them where he found them.

2) Bones to stay in his tent and their supplies of beer, tins of baked beans etc. to be moved into the boot of the car away from them. OK, it wasn't rational, it was just the way she felt.

3) No objections from him if she spent her time from now on finding out more about Mrs L. Allegri and the rest of them.

He'd made only a mild objection to the third one.

'It's probably got nothing to do with them. The bones could have been here centuries before the garden existed.'

'Sure, but the more we know about what happened here, the better.'

He suspected that her idea of a television programme had been revived. Nothing like a bit of death and mystery to bring in the helicopters. Still, his position wasn't strong and he was almost giddy with relief not to have lost her. He'd have agreed to almost anything and managed to look cheerful when he waved her off to Newport the next morning to look for the woman whose grandmother had been a maid.

He spent the day clearing more of the under-growth around the gazebo, a long way from the pond. It was evening by the time she got back and he was already sorting out tins and packets for their evening meal. There was a triumphant look about her that made his heart sink a little in spite of their peace treaty.

'Good day?'

'Not a bad day, anyway. I found the woman with the grandmother. Mid-forties, well dressed. I quite liked her. She couldn't give me long because there were a lot of clients coming in but we had a bit of time to talk in a coffee break.'

'Did she know much?'

'Uh-huh. She said her mother had never got on with her own mother – the maid that is. Mary, she was called, Mary from the village because there were two of them – bloody feudal, as if they hadn't got proper names.'

'Wasted trip?' Trying not to sound hopeful.

'Not exactly. Anyway, my woman's mother moved away, so she only saw her granny a few times when she was a kid. But there were some things she remembered. For one thing, Mrs Allegri was supposed to be very beautiful and she was married to a famous artist.'

'I've never heard of an artist called Allegri.'

193

'You haven't heard of anybody except Van Gogh and Monet.'

'OK, I'm just a gardening clod. But you hadn't either.'

'No, so after I'd seen her I went and looked him up in the library in Newport.'

She took a piece of folded paper out of her jeans pocket and gave it to him. A photocopy of a page in a book, with a paragraph marked in felt tip.

ALLEGRI Leon. (1863 – ?) Portrait painter, born London. Studied London and Paris. As a society portraitist of the late Victorian and Edwardian eras he was exceeded in popularity only by John Singer Sargent (q.v.). Frequent exhibitor at the Royal Academy.

'It explains something, doesn't it? You've been puzzled from the start that there's no record of this man Cordell designing any other gardens. My guess is, it wasn't *Cordell* who designed the garden at all. It was Leon Allegri – for his wife.'

'No.'

The protest slipped out before he could stop it. She stared at him.

'There's ... there's a feeling here,' he said. 'A feeling for plants, the way the land goes, the way things grow.'

'OK, I'm not saying your Cordell didn't do the actual gardening bit. But one thing we do know is that Leon Allegri must have loved the garden very much.'

Her voice had gone softer.

'Why do you say that?'

'Something else the woman in Newport told me. Her mother didn't know much about the place but there was a story she'd heard from her own mother about the way the garden got destroyed.'

'Destroyed?'

'Yes. Remember those burnt ropes, the posts hacked down? You thought it was odd.'

'It could have been a bon...'

'No.' She shook her head. 'It was deliberate.'

'How could it be? Who'd do that to a garden?'

'Miners.'

'What?'

'It was coal miners.'

'There aren't any coal mines in Herefordshire.'

'There were in Wales. There was a strike on in the Welsh coalmines, sometime between the two world wars she thought it must have been, and the miners came over the border and set the garden on fire.'

Stunned, he started asking how you could set a garden on fire, but she was too full of the story to stop.

'And he got killed. Allegri got killed in the garden trying to stop them.'

'No.' For a third time, but sheer bewilderment now. 'She said this? She actually told you this?'

'Well, she wasn't clear on the details because she was just a kid when her mother talked about it and not that interested. But some of it stuck. And you see how much it explains? He gets killed, the garden he made for her gets destroyed so she just turns her back on the place and lets it rot.'

195

'You can't know that.'

'Not the last bit for sure. But I wouldn't want to stay, would you? She stays just long enough to see her husband buried in the remains of his beloved garden...'

'Oh God, no. Anyway you're not allowed to do that, are you?'

'Yes you are. You can bury people anywhere. So she has him buried somewhere in what's left of his garden, by the gazebo perhaps, then over seventy years or so his bones get washed down to where you found them.'

'We can't know that.'

'Not yet, we can't, but then we've only just started. Shan't be long.'

She stood up and went inside her tent. His head felt numb, as if somebody he cared about had died but he hadn't taken it in enough yet to start grieving. Cordell's garden.

'Colin.' She was on her knees by the tent flap. 'Have you been in here?'

'No. Why?'

'The zip's not the way I left it. When I went out I zipped it right down to the ground and pegged it. And my loo roll's been moved. I always leave it by the tent pole and it's over in the corner.'

'Rolls roll.'

'I think the backpacker's been nosing round here.'

'Of course not. He's probably miles away by now.'

'Or she.'

In any case, he or she wasn't miles away. Later, when it was dark, they sat outside the tents and watched the little point of light moving along the terrace.

Kim said in a whisper, although their voices couldn't possibly have carried that far, 'Do you think somebody else is onto the story?'

'Maybe it's your Leon Allegri looking for his lost garden.'

She didn't believe in ghosts, she'd told him that, but her body went stiff. Later, though, she relaxed under the duvet in her tent and they made love as enthusiastically as usual. On her part, he thought, even more than usual, her feet thrashing against the tent lining. The scrape of foot-sole on nylon reminded him of sappy stalks sizzling and popping in a fire. Even afterwards, when she lay quiet and asleep in his arms, he couldn't get the sound out of his head.

23

September 1907

Days as hot as August but with a cool edge to evenings and early mornings that showed frost wasn't far away. Two weeks ago most of the miners had gone, leaving the framework of the garden so firmly laid out that it struck Philip with surprise every morning. The overturned cart of stones and flooded paths that had looked such a disaster on the August morning after the storm, had been nothing to Robert Williams and his team, not worth getting excited about. The spilled flagstones had been picked up and put into their places in the terrace by the lily pool. The young tree trunks that had formed a tripod for the winch gear at the top of the ramp had been carried down and sawed into supports for the wooden jetty out over the water and lily leaves. (No blue rowing boat yet, but the order for it had been given, delivery promised for next spring.) The ramp itself had been levelled and the earth from it used to build up the bank of the stream and keep it to its new course. In the wide borders alongside the steps, newly planted paeonies were hidden under a mulch of shredded leaf mould. At the back of the borders, lines of wooden posts were linked by loops of new hemp rope, sent up in great coils by a puzzled ships' chandler at Cardiff Docks who couldn't work out who'd be mooring boats that size in landlocked Herefordshire. The roses themselves were on order, creamy Adelaide d'Orleans with its smell of primroses, Rosa moschata, the old musk rose, Félicité Perpétue, for its long-lasting foliage that would cover the bare ropes, lilac-pink Gerbe Rose for contrast with all those cream colours, Rambling Rector because Isabelle liked the name. On the hill facing Holders Hope a shepherd was whistling to his dogs, flushing drowsy sheep out of bracken that was still mostly green, with only a few yellowing leaves. The sound carried to the slope where Isabelle and Philip were lying.

'Is he bringing them down for winter?'

Philip asked the question lazily. He'd let himself

198

slide further down the bank so that he could rest his head on her bare shoulder, see through half opened eyes the curve of her breasts and almost translucent pink of her nipples.

'Not for months. Not winter yet.'

'Cold?'

She looked at him and smiled a naughty child's smile, eyes violet blue. He knelt over her, flicking his tongue round her right nipple, holding it between his teeth so that she squirmed against the bank.

'What about the other one, then?'

'You need a man with two mouths, my girl.'

'Only two?'

A minute ago he'd felt played out, languid, but the light in her eyes and the breathless catch in her laughter changed that. After their first lovemaking she'd draped her dress over her stomach and thighs – for warmth as much as modesty – and when his hands went down to pull it away he found hers already there. He clamped his mouth on hers and they rolled together down the bank, landing with her on top, impaling herself on him with a force that made him groan. When they'd finished they lay side by side, glued to each other with sweat. In the four weeks since that night they didn't talk about there'd been a recklessness, a greed about her love-making that excited him but scared him too.

'Not cold now?'

'No.'

As she reached up the bank for chemise, knickers and silk stockings he watched the curve of her ribs under skin as white as the inside of a

William pear. A bank for love to lie and play on. In April there'd be violets, primroses and wild strawberry flowers, strawberries themselves in June, edible jewels for her breasts and his tongue. Then the apple trees, already delivered and waiting with their roots wrapped in damp sacking for Will Thomas to help plant them when he got back from the funeral. Wild Welsh daffodils round the trunks in March, swirls of pink and white apple blossom in May, in October globes of red and gold sweetness, all for her. Her and one other.

'Something I want to show you. For Petra really.'

She followed him, crouched down to look and laughed.

'Where did you get him?'

'I've got a friend who does these things. Do you think she'll like him? I wanted to surprise her.'

What he wanted above all was to get a smile out of the child. Since the night of the storm she'd been going round with an expression as unreadable as a Japanese doll's.

She got up, suddenly serious. 'I'm not sure Petra likes surprises very much.'

The sun was almost down on the hilltops. Six o'clock and already a chill coming into the air. They walked slowly out of the orchard enclosure, across the border to the new broad steps.

'Isa, I've been thinking about us and Petra. I think we should tell her.'

She stopped walking. 'No.'

'Hasn't she got a right to know?'

'Yes, but not now. She's only nine. How could

she understand?'

'Perhaps it's easier at nine.'

She started walking again, not looking at him.

'I thought we'd agreed.'

Never an agreement, only Isa saying 'Not yet' and he not arguing, until now.

'Isa, things have changed. He's gone away.'

'She worships him. I found her in his studio the other day using his paper and charcoal, trying to draw him.'

'Oh.'

'I think it was a kind of magic, trying to get him back.'

He felt as if he'd been punched in the chest, but said nothing until they were over the bridge.

'Has she ever said anything to you about what happened that night?'

'No. I'm not sure the stone cart had anything to do with it. I think she saw him leaving and tried to make him stay.'

'She was terrified, Isa. Practically unconscious with fear.'

'At the thought of him going. She worships him, Philip. I wish she didn't, but it's true.'

'How would she have known he was leaving for good? Was he carrying a bag, I wonder.'

'What's that got to do with anything?'

It was the first time they'd discussed it since the day after Leon's disappearance. 'Because if he had a bag with him that would have shown her he was leaving. Have you checked if any of his luggage or clothes have gone?'

'No. For heaven's sake, Philip. He's gone. That's all there is to it.'

He tried not to get angry himself. 'But it's not, is it? Don't you ask yourself whether he'll come back again?'

'I know Leon. He's gone.'

'That letter, the one he wrote to his friend Feveril in Chelsea...'

'What about it?'

'When I was in London last week, I made a point of going to see Feveril. He's adamant that he didn't see or hear from Leon in August. The last he heard from him was a letter in May, touting for commissions.'

'Of course not. The letter wasn't posted.'

'But Leon couldn't have known it missed the post. He'd told Feveril he was coming to plant himself on him but he never arrived there.' She was walking fast now, brushing impatiently past the border of small lavender bushes. He had to rush at it. 'Another thing I did in London, I went round some of the galleries where he's exhibited. None of them had seen him or knew where he was.'

'Perhaps he's found another woman to keep him.'

'You believe that?' No answer. 'Isa, I want to know if you think Leon's coming back.'

'Why?'

'Isn't it obvious? If he's not coming back, that's desertion.'

'No!'

Desertion by the husband was one of the very few ways a woman could get a divorce. It was that idea she was rejecting. He sighed, knowing that he'd rushed things and it had done him no good.

She hurried up the steps, across the terrace and in through the French windows. He lingered, looking back down the garden to the enclosure that would be their orchard and some lines from Browning came into his head unwanted.

Where the apple reddens
Never pry –
Lest we lose our Edens,
Eve and I.

24

There was no room for cemeteries on the floor of the valley. That was taken up by the collieries and the railway that carried the coal down to the docks at Cardiff. No room for cemeteries either among streets that ran curving up from the valley floor where the miners and their families lived under lines of slate roofs in terraces so steep that if two neighbours stepped out their doors at the same time, the head of the lower one would be more or less on a level with the waist of the next. To get buried, a person had to be carried out of his or her front door to where the terraces ran out high on the hillside and there was space at last for square, neatly walled graveyards like the one where Maud Thomas, thirty-nine years old, was being buried. Just beyond the graveyard the bracken started and there were skylarks singing. Will Thomas heard them above the voice of the minister, Bathsheba crying silently beside him, his eyes on the three children standing on the other side of the grave, alongside their father and their older sister, Sarah. Megan's dark hair was pulled back so tight under her round black hat that it looked close to tearing the skin of her face. Trefor was looking down over the valley Evan clinging to his father's hand, eyes going everywhere for anyone who'd tell him that this was all a mistake, that when they went back down to the eleventh house up from the valley in the terrace just behind the minister's shoulder, his mother would be there stirring something in the kitchen with the worn wooden spoon she used to let him lick clean of cake mixture. Will looked at him and sighed. Evan at least was coming back home with him and Bathsheba to Herefordshire – probably for good if it suited. Trefor wasn't. He'd be thirteen in a few months time, old enough to start work at the pithead, filling lamps or oiling machines. When he was old enough, he'd go underground like his father. Bathsheba hadn't liked it, wanted to keep him too, but for once Will had put his foot down. So Trefor would stay and Evan go back. As for Megan, nothing was decided yet.

Megan looked at the lines of friends and neighbours in their black cloth coats or best jackets with black armbands and made herself a promise. 'This is my last day here forever.' Her head was aching from Auntie Norrie's attack on it. 'Megan girl, what will people be saying if you go to your mother's funeral looking like that?' Nothing so dreadful, after all, only a dark mulberry coloured felt hat with a wave of hair coming down over her forehead. But Auntie Norrie had whipped off the hat, scraped back Megan's hair into an elastic band from the glass tray on her dressing table that still had some of her own greying hairs clinging to it, clumped on Megan's head her own black go-to-town hat and riveted it with hair pins that almost penetrated the skull. Megan, staring at herself in her aunt's mirror with the silver backing coming away in blisters, saw her mother's face and thought, 'In twenty-five years I'll be dead like she is or ugly like Auntie Norrie is and where's the point of it all? Not here, anyway. Wherever it is, not here.'

Trefor knew he couldn't deal with grieving yet. He'd have to put it away in his mind for a time when he was older. At home the front room smelt of death, the kitchen of the ham that Sarah was boiling because neighbours and cousins would be coming in for tea after the funeral. But now on the hillside he was picking up another smell that was oddly comforting. Because he'd smelt it all his life until the last few months in Herefordshire it took him some time to realise that it was the smell of coal. The warm air carried it from the heaps at the pitheads, from the coal carts rumbling down the valley, from shafts deep underneath the feet of men thudding spadefuls of earth onto his mother's coffin. The earth was a thin skin after all, just enough for burying people in. Under that, coal. Rhondda steam coal, the best in the world. From Cape Town to Vladivostok there'd be ships that got there on Rhondda coal. Explorers cutting through pack ice to the poles, liner passengers across the Atlantic, missionaries to Africa – going nowhere without coal. And the men standing there behind his father, blue marks of coal dust on their faces like tribal scars, missing a shift and bonus money to pay their respects to their friend's wife, were the ones who really owned the coal, practically owned the world. Trefor kept his hands clenched at his sides and drew the coal smell deep into his lungs, glad at least to have come home from exile.

25

Will Thomas, home from the funeral, took to planting the apple trees in the Pleasaunce as if everybody's survival depended on them. He cut squares from the turf with the sharp edge of his spade, dug out slices of red-brown earth until he had twenty square holes in five neat rows. Then Philip came to see and Will had to fill some of them in again because it wasn't what Philip had in mind at all.

'Three in that corner, quite close together. Yellow Ingestrie, Bringewood Pippin, Lemon Pippin. Golds and yellows together. Three Ashmead's Kernel towards the middle. We'll leave some space round them for fritillaries, if they'll grow there.'

He imagined Isabelle's narrow feet and ankles among the white and purple chequered flowers in bright April grass. Some people called them by their other name, Snake's Head.

Where the serpent's tooth is
Shun the tree –

'Five over here – two Early Victorias – they should be the first to flower and people will see them as soon as they come out of the tunnel – then two May Queen for later. We want to draw their eyes in and up.'

To a whole sky of apple blossom, like pink and white cumulus. Sun filtering through it, making patterns on her breasts. He went to get a spade and helped dig holes in the new places. Will took the changes as good humouredly as ever, not understanding in the least but ready to do whatever Philip wanted. On the second day, with the fine autumn weather still holding, they forked up the earth in the bottom of the holes, added well-rotted horse manure. Young Evan brought it over from the paddock where Will's ponies grazed, bent double at the handles of the heavy wooden wheelbarrow.

'Don't work the lad too hard.'

'Good for him, Mr Cordell. Take his mind off things.'

When Evan was away fetching more manure, Will diffidently asked Philip's opinion on the boy's future. Bathsheba's plan was that the boy should go to the village school and help out in the garden on Saturdays and in holidays. Then in four years' time, when he was thirteen, if he still looked like being a steady, hard-working kind of boy...

Philip said, 'He could join you as under-gardener. What a very good idea.'

207

Will blinked, off balance at finding the fruit in his hand before he'd even tugged at it.

'You think Mrs Allegri would...'

'Quite sure she would.'

It had been worrying Philip that there wouldn't be enough hands to keep up the garden. Will worked like two men and the quiet, religious Enoch Pugh had decided to stay on after the others went home and marry Mrs Dane, the widowed woman who kept the village shop. But even though he was designing it to reduce routine work as much as possible, it needed three gardeners at least. Another thing, even more important than the garden – the only times he'd heard Petra laugh were when she was with Evan. Not recently. Not since the night of the storm, and anyway young Evan could hardly be expected to make her laugh with his mother just buried. Still, he must stay for Petra's sake.

'I'll speak to Mrs Allegri tonight. Would you like her to write a note to the schoolmistress for you?'

Two weeks into the autumn term already, the gold and yellow dahlias flaring in Bathsheba's garden in a last blaze of colour before the frosts, the hills blue and misty morning and evening, wood smoke coming up from the village chimneys. Suddenly it seemed urgent to get the apple trees planted, their roots gentled into the ground while there was still some warmth in it. Will shovelled the earth in while Philip held the trees upright in their holes, feeling the life in the thin trunks like blood pulsing in an arm, willing them to survive.

And let them both be happy here. The wish throbbed through his fingers into the tree. Summers sleeping in the shade. Crunch and sweetness of apples in the autumn. All three of us, if possible, but anyway, them.

Will straightened up. 'How you wanted it, Mr Cordell?'

'Yes, Will. How I wanted it.'

In bed at midnight, curled into him with her buttocks into his thighs, hair loose against his chest, Isabelle happily agreed his plan for young Evan.

'But four years is a long time to wait, isn't it?'

'Not for a garden.'

'For anything.'

Her heart beat thirty-five, thirty-six, thirty-seven, thirty-eight years old, lurched on the edge of unimaginable forty. She wriggled round, crushed her mouth against his, open so that his tongue could find its way inside, jerking her body against his, drawing his hand down between her legs. It was only in the last two or three weeks that they'd risked making love under her roof instead of in the garden, always in his room. Mrs Morgan slept only three doors away, her maid Jane almost directly overhead. She'd astonished him by arriving there in the early hours of a September morning two weeks or so after Leon had disappeared, naked under her dressing gown. At first he'd tried to be cautious for her sake, warned that somebody might hear.

'Why not? It's my house, after all.'

The only caution Isabelle observed concerned

Petra. The child slept on the same floor but at the far end of the corridor. Philip knew that, even in their wildest love making, Isabelle was listening for any sound from Petra. Like tonight. They were drowsing again, hand touching hand, when Isabelle went tense and sat up.

'What is it, love?'

'Her.'

Isabelle was out of bed in one movement, tearing her dressing gown off the back of the door. When she opened the door a noise was coming from Petra's end of the corridor. Something between gasps and sobs.

'Coming, darling. I'm coming.'

She ran, but before she got to the end of the corridor the sound had changed into a high wail. Philip, out of bed now, had to fight the urge to run after her, naked as he was. He scrabbled in the damp and tumbled sheets for his pyjamas, put on his dressing gown. It was as well he'd been cautious because by the time he was in the corridor Mrs Morgan's door was open.

'Don't you worry, Mr Cordell, it's only the poor child having nightmares again.'

He hovered outside Petra's bedroom door while Mrs Morgan went in. Surely an old friend of the family could be that concerned at least. He heard Isabelle's low, imploring voice, the occasional murmured remark from Mrs Morgan, the thin screams dying back to sobs, then the sobs to silence. Mrs Morgan came out, saw him there and put her finger on her lips.

'She's asleep now. Her mother's staying with her.'

She shook her head. Three o'clock in the morning, the darkest and coldest time, every fire in the house died down. He went back to bed, pulled the damp sheets round him and lay awake the rest of the night.

In the morning at breakfast the purple shadows under Isabelle's eyes showed she hadn't slept either. When he came in from the garden Mary was in the room, bringing fresh coffee, so he could only ask after Petra as any guest might do.

'I'm letting her sleep in. Mary will take her breakfast up later.'

He sat down and accepted strong coffee. The mail had arrived and there were a pile of letters beside her plate.

'This must be from Marius at Eton.' She read it, smiled, and handed it over to him. 'He seems to be settling in all right.'

Eton.
19 September 1907

My Dear Mother,
I hope you are well. I am well and working hard as you said. Latin is the worst. The food is not bad but my bed is hard. I think they give the worst beds to the new men. There are five new men in my house. One is the son of an Earl so he is a Lord. My gloves are the wrong colour. The earl's son wanted to know if I'd had them made by my kennelman from dead hounds, which they all thought was funny. I know you would not wish me to be laughed at, so I have bought some new gloves and the man in the shop says he would like

211

to be paid by next Saturday, as they don't know me. For the future, it might be best if you write to them and open an account for me so that I don't have to bother you with things like this all the time. I enclose their address. The gloves cost £2 4s 6d as I need several pairs, but it might be best if you send me £5 to cover other things as well.
Your loving son
Marius Allegri

Mary asked if there'd be anything else, was told no and left the room.

Philip said, 'So how is she really?'

She was pretending to read another letter. He moved his chair so that he was facing her across the table. 'Isa, we've got to talk about this. It's five weeks now and it's not getting any better, is it?'

She shook her head.

'Is it that night still?'

'Yes and...'

'And what? Isa, something else has happened, hasn't it?'

'No. It doesn't matter.'

'Isa, for goodness sake.' It was the nearest he'd ever come to shouting at her. 'That child wakes up in the night crying and screaming. Haven't I a right to know why?'

'I took her down to show her where we were going to put the apple trees. I thought while we were down there, I'd try ... you know, your surprise for her.'

He said, understanding suddenly, 'The White Rabbit.'

'I showed her the little cave you'd made for it, said there was somebody inside she might want to meet.'

'Oh no.'

'She must have thought it was Leon waiting for her in there, though how she thought he could curl up in a little space like that... Anyway, in she went on her hands and knees, then this scream. She bumped her head, she was in such a hurry to get out, clung to me and just went on shaking and crying.'

'Did she say anything?'

'Not really. Just kept on about something white and...'

'Tell me.'

'Dead. White and dead. I kept trying to tell her it was just the rabbit from *Alice* but she wouldn't listen. Oh my dear, I'm so sorry.'

'Not your fault. My fault.'

He stared down at the patch of tablecloth round his plate until he knew every thread of linen in it like the veins on the back of his hand, aware of her eyes on him. When he looked up at last tears were running down her cheeks and neck, into the high collar of her blouse.

He said, 'It's not working, is it?'

'Us?'

Her face lurched towards him. He thought for a moment she was going to be sick on the table.

'No, not us. For heaven's sake, not us. I mean Petra and me. I never wanted to stop her loving Leon, whether he's here or not. I just wanted to be part of her childhood.'

He could see more clearly than ever, now it had

failed, how the garden had been planned for the child as much as the woman. When he saw it in his mind there was hardly a part of it that didn't have Petra in it. Petra on a bank picking primroses, muffled up against the cold of March. Petra in June, lips sweet and pink from the juice of strawberries, feet bare in the warm grass. Petra in autumn, running up the steps to show him her handful of hazelnuts. There was one picture even harder than the others to let go. Petra on a long July evening in the blue boat among the waterlilies, so absorbed that she didn't even see the kingfisher darting behind her.

'Give her time.'

'Yes. She needs time, but not with me here.'

'What do you mean?'

He stretched his hand across the table. Hers came out to meet it.

'I'll have to go.'

'No.'

Her fingers closed so tightly on his that it felt like bone grating against bone.

'Not forever, love. I don't mean forever. The garden's here. A couple of weeks from now we'll have done nearly everything that can be done before the first frosts. I'll go back to London, then I can come back here in March when it's waking up again.'

'That's six months. Six whole months.'

'If we're lucky, it may be long enough for the nightmares to stop.'

'Not see you for six months.'

'You could come up to town now and then. I know the house is let, but you've got plenty of friends you could stay with. And now Leon isn't there any more...'

'Even if I come up to London, we couldn't be properly together, could we?'

Carefully plotted chance encounters at concert intervals. Feet pressing under supper tables of friends who knew their secret.

'Losing time. What's worse than losing time? A whole winter.'

She put her elbows on the table, over-turning her coffee cup, sank her head into her hands. The coffee stain spread up the sleeve of her blouse, but she didn't move.

'Darling, you've got so much. Petra, Marius, the garden...'

'Not you, though.'

'You have. Always. Look, we'll see each other in London. And in the spring, I'll come back again.'

'You promise?'

'How in the world could I do anything else?'

Later in the day, with Isabelle dry-eyed and businesslike, they settled that he'd stay until the weekend after next. That would give him time to get the roses and some trees planted and plan with Will what had to be done to keep the garden maintained through the winter.

For those last nine days they were as gentle and strained with each other as visitors in a sick ward. She didn't come to his room at nights. He spent all the shortening daylight hours in the garden with Will. They planted a copse of silver birch trees in the field on the far side of the lily pool and put Isabelle's scarlet dogwood and gold and silver variegated hollies at the edge of it, to stand out against the white trunks in winter. One evening after dinner Isabelle said to him, 'Jane's deserting me as well. She says she'll be sorry to leave me but she's missing London and she thinks this place in winter will give her the willies, as she puts it.'

'Do you want me to drop in at a staff agency for you when I'm in London?'

'No. I thought I might try Megan.'

He stared. 'Megan Thomas as your maid? Isn't she back at home with her father?'

'No. She went home for the funeral and came back. Mrs Morgan's been keeping her tucked away in the kitchen. I know she expected me to send Megan home, but there doesn't really seem any necessity now does there?'

'But when Marius is home on holiday...'

'Oh, I can handle that, I think. She's very neat and quite nicely spoken and Mrs Morgan says she's a quick learner.'

'It's very generous of you, Isa, maybe too generous. Why not think about it a bit more before you ask her?'

'I already have.'

'And?'

'She seemed pleased. Darling, don't look so serious. I'm sure it will work out very nicely, and if it doesn't she can just go back to the kitchen.'

That was Thursday night. On Friday he walked her round the garden one last time, showing her what he and Will had been planting. Later in the dusk he walked round on his own saying goodbyes to the growing things, wondering how

216

many would make it through the winter. With the light going the details of the garden were lost and the grand shapes stood out more than by daylight, the diverted curve of the stream, the rhyming curve of the lavender walk, the long sweep of the lawn down to the bridge and bare earth that would be the iris bed next summer. It looked and felt right against the shape of the hills. He thought 'Whatever happens, there's this at least.'

In the morning he was up as soon as there was enough light in the room to dress by without using the lamp. When he went downstairs in his socks, carrying his boots and his pack, Mary was already in the hall, her hair knotted in an old scarf, carrying out a bucket of ashes from the dining room fire. He put his finger to his lips, leaving her staring, tiptoed to the side door and sat on the bench outside to put on his boots. The air was cold, the grass crisp under his bootsoles. First frost already, but not hard enough to get to the roots of his newly planted things. Soil hoarded warmth as long as it could. His bicycle was in the wood shed, tyres pumped up, chain newly oiled. It was full daylight as he carried it down the steps, pushed it down the fields through two gates to the Hereford road, a few sheep stirring and coughing as he went past. The sun was coming up, a powdering of frost on the last of the blackberries, the hedge maples turning gold. By the time he got to Hereford station it was hot enough for summer again. He propped the bicycle against the wall, bought a ticket and found a post-box for the note he'd written the night before.

Forgive me. I love you both. Take care.

26

Autumn 1907 to 1910

From the early autumn of 1907 to late summer 1910, the stream settled into its new bed. The forget-me-nots Philip had planted along the banks seeded themselves and increased so that, in April, its course was marked by a haze of blue curving across the lawn.

In the same three years Petra Allegri stopped waking the household with screaming night-mares, grew to five foot two and a half by 12 years old and produced 153 pictures in pastel, pencil or watercolour which she kept in a drawer in her bedroom and showed nobody.

The paeony walk matured. Victor Lemoine's glorious Le Printemps, sent especially from Nancy and making what was probably its first appearance in Britain, floated petals the colour of Devonshire cream against its foliage like a water lily on land. Lower and later came a froth of the old-fashioned white cottage paeony, courtesy of Will's garden where they'd been growing time out of mind. (Bathsheba was angry for a week that Will had taken so many of her plants. Will felt honoured they were wanted.)

In three years Evan Thomas learned at the village school in Holdersby to read and write English as easily as Welsh and taught himself to play the Maple Leaf Rag, with variations, on a second-hand clarinet that Philip gave him as a present on his eleventh birthday.

In three years the weeping purple beech didn't do very much except struggle to keep alive. As Philip had feared, the soil didn't suit it.

At Eton, Marius Allegri rowed for his house and could recite the proof of Pythagoras's theorem provided nobody expected him to understand it. For his seventeenth birthday, his mother paid off his accumulated tailor's bill of £207 15s 6d.

In the springs of 1908, 1909 and 1910 the kingfisher and his mate hatched a total of fourteen fledglings, seven of which survived.

Trefor Thomas, working above ground in the lamp room at Penyrheol Colliery, on reaching his fifteenth birthday joined the South Wales Miners' Federation and an up-and-coming organisation called The Plebs' League.

In three years Isabelle went from 34 years old to 37. She experimented with a new French cream that smoothed out wrinkles from round the eyes. Her maid, Megan Thomas, told her she hadn't got wrinkles in any case.

Megan Thomas found her complexion got even better once she was away from the kitchen range and washing-up water. Three times she accompanied Isabelle to London. The third time, a thirty-year-old solicitor's clerk asked Megan, just 17, to marry him. She turned him down.

Will spent a lot of time tying in shoots to the hoops of the apple tunnel and by the third spring when Philip and Isabelle walked hand in hand under it, she came out with petals showered all over her hair. 'Confetti,' he said, then regretted it in case she thought he was trying to persuade her.

Will, amazed to find that his promotion to head gardener brought a substantial pay rise from Isabelle, had spare money in his pocket for the first time in his life. He took Bathsheba to Hereford and bought her a new winter coat and himself six bantam hens and a cockerel from the market.

The foal filled out nicely. His bay colouring, thick black mane and intelligent eye suggested that the father must have had a lot of Welsh cob in him. It was time to break him for saddle or harness, but Will didn't know about training horses, only feeding them, so he grew sleek and easy-going in the old orchard. Will called him Jack the Lad.

The selling price of coal per ton at the pithead fluctuated between ten shillings and nine pence at worst, 11 shillings and ten pence at best. Some of the more radical miners began campaigning for a minimum rate of eight shillings for a seven-hour day underground.

Philip lost half a stone in weight, discovered his first grey hair, made two trips to the Alps and spent a month in the Pontic mountains, where he collected what might possibly be a new variant of oncocyclus but was more probably an unusually pale gatesii Foster. A friend got him a little paid work at Kew Gardens.

27

August 1910

It was the third day of Philip's end-of-summer visit to the garden, after breakfast with sun pouring through the windows of the small drawing room onto a table covered with rhododendron and azalea catalogues. Isabelle and Philip were discussing whether to plant new glades of rhododendrons and azaleas in the little birch wood to the left of the lily pool. The garden liked rhododendrons and the decision had gone in favour, but would make more work than Philip, Will and Enoch Pugh could manage, even with Evan's help at weekends.

Philip said, 'We'll have to get a few of your miners in again.'

'I'm not sure I want to.'

'Why not?'

'I'm having quite enough of them at the moment. The unions think because the price per ton at pithead is threepence up at the moment...' She saw the expression on his face and laughed, a bit shakily. 'I'm sorry. Talking shop.'

'But if it's worrying you...'

'Not worried, no. I'm sure it will get itself sorted out as usual, but... Oh, it's just another thing, I suppose.'

'Petra?'

'Yes.'

His heart plunged.

'I thought she seemed a lot better.'

Not true entirely. Different, though. 'Good afternoon, Mr Cordell,' she'd said to him when he arrived. 'Was your train on time?' If she'd raised her ankle-strap shoe and kicked him on the kneecap she'd have hurt him less.

'Philip, I've taken a decision. I know I should have asked you but ... but you were away and I wasn't sure and... She's thirteen now and we thought she might start after Christmas.'

'Isa, what are you talking about?'

'Cheltenham Ladies.'

'Boarding school?'

'What else can I do? She's growing up. She needs to be with girls of her own age.'

'What does Petra think?'

'She's quite pleased. They've got a Swedish gymnasium, lots of tennis courts and a whole suite of art studios ... and it's not so very far away after all. I think I'll get a motor car, so I could drive over any time and...' She was crying, tears picking up little flecks of face powder as they ran. 'Darling, I don't want her to go away, but what else can I do? Don't look like that.'

He was trying to imagine it. Petra chasing a hockey ball, laughing. Petra at the drawing board. Petra giggling in the dormitory with friends. Only he couldn't imagine it. What was getting in the way was a different scenario altogether. A tall thin house by some London square, the sort he could just afford to rent if he canvassed his friends harder for work. Petra

222

walking home from day school through the falling plane tree leaves of an autumn afternoon, he and Isa watching her from the window.

'If you brought her to London...'

'Where would we live? Besides, she says she doesn't want to go to London.'

'We could find a house. If you wanted, I could have a separate flat on the top floor, or even keep my rooms on and...' She was shaking her head. 'For heavens sake, why not? Isa, he's been gone three years now. Are you going to spend the rest of your life waiting in case he turns up again?'

'You don't understand.'

'I've been talking to a solicitor. No ... not like that, just a friend. The business about desertion...'

'Philip, stop.'

'The point is, desertion comes up quite often in court and...'

'STOP.'

She screamed at him, her whole face distorted, then glanced towards the door and put her clenched hand to her mouth.

'Why? Why can't we even talk about it?'

She got up and turned away from him, muttering something from behind her fist.

'What?'

'I said, wait there.'

He waited, looking out over the garden. Not enough things in flower. Late August was always awkward if you didn't like dahlias, and he didn't. The door opened quietly, catching him by surprise. She was holding two envelopes.

'Read them. You'd better sit down.'

He sat down at the table. One envelope was cheap and white, the other equally cheap and yellowish. One postmark illegible, the other London 2 June, 1910. Both correctly addressed in sprawling block capitals to Mrs L. Allegri, Holders Hope, Herefordshire.

London.
2 May 1910.

Dear Isa,
I hope this doesn't come as too much of a surprise to you. I'm back. A good friend is writing this at my dictation as I have burnt my hand so can't write, or paint of course. I don't suppose you want to see me, but I hope you wouldn't want me to starve. I am in GREAT NEED. If you could find it convenient to send £20 in notes c/o the address below, you would greatly oblige
    Your loving husband
                                        Leon Allegri

'I hope you didn't send any money. It's the most clumsy piece of fraud...'
    'Have you read both of them?'

London.
2 June 1910.

Dear Isa,
Do you want me to starve? I shall never paint again. The nerves in my hands are gone.
    I beg you, if you have any feeling for me, take

224

the key out of the little box on your dressing table (the one with the picture of Dante on the lid), unlock the middle drawer in your bureau where you keep your banknotes and send me £50 to the address below.

If you do this, you will never be troubled again by

Your loving husband

Leon Allegri

She was trembling. He went over and put his arm round her shoulders but she shook it off.

'You can't think it's really him, Isa. It's the oldest confidence trick in the book. A man goes missing and...'

'He's not missing. He just went. There was nothing in the papers so how could anybody know?'

'People gossip, Isa, you know that. And he had friends in London, some of them pretty rum ones. One of his friends is hard up, decides to pretend Leon's come back...'

'He says he's burnt his hands.'

'Of course he would. Whoever it was would have to say that because of the writing.'

'Don't be angry with me. Oh please, don't be angry with me.'

'I'm not angry with you, of course I'm not. Only with whatever heartless blackmailer wrote those letters. I hope to God you didn't send him any money.' She looked away from him. 'You did? Isa...'

'Not the first time, no. Only when the second one came I thought ... you see, how would he know? How would he know about the key and Dante?'

'I dare say Leon talked about it to his friends.'

'Why? Anyway, that box, I've only had it a few years. I don't see how anybody could have known about it but Leon.'

'So you sent the money?' She nodded.

'The whole fifty pounds?'

'Yes.'

'To the care-of address?'

Another nod. He picked up the slip of paper, done in the same sprawling capitals. It was the address of a public house on the Edgware Road.

'Was it collected?'

'I suppose so. I don't know.'

'And you haven't heard any more since?'

'No.' Very quietly.

'Sure, Isa? There's nothing you're not telling me?'

'No.' More firmly.

'Those letters are no proof whatsoever that he's in London, or anywhere else come to that.'

'You think he's dead, don't you?'

He closed his eyes to shut out that stare, took a deep breath.

'Yes. Yes, I do.'

'I don't know how you can be so sure.'

'I'm not sure but... Look, I wasn't going to tell you, but now it's come up... Will you wait here? I won't be long.'

She heard his footsteps going upstairs. He was down again in a few minutes.

'More letters, I'm afraid.'

Two of them, written in copperplate on thick,

expensive paper.

Walbeck and Wells Private Inquiry Agency.
The Strand.
11 February 1908.

Dear Mr Cordell,
Further to our letter of December last, and in pursuance of your esteemed inquiry, I have to inform you that we have still discovered no trace of the subject, Mr Leon Allegri, formerly of Cheyne Walk, London. As we informed you in our previous letter, none of his business or other associates in London appears to have any information as to his whereabouts. Inquiries at embarkation points for the continent, using the photograph which you provided, have had an equally negative result. On our own initiative, and trusting it meets with your approval, we made similar inquiries concerning departures for the United States from the port of Liverpool, but results were similarly negative.

I enclose an account for our services so far.

Yours, awaiting the favour of further instructions,

J. Walbeck

'Why? Why did you do it?'
'I wanted to know.'
She picked up the other letter.

Walbeck and Wells Private Inquiry Agency.
The Strand.
12 January 1909.

Dear Mr Cordell,
Re Mr Leon Allegri.
Thank you for the settlement of our latest
account. As to your query of whether any other
channels of inquiry occur to us, we must in all
honesty confess that we have exhausted all
normal and reasonable methods. As a hunting
man might say, the trail must now be presumed
to have 'gone cold'. We shall, if you wish, be
happy to keep the case on our files and re-open it
should any new field of inquiry present itself.
  Yours obediently

                                          J. Walbeck

She handed them back to him.
  'Is that why you think he's dead?'
  'Yes, mainly.'
  Her eyes went to the block-lettered pages on
the table.
  'It's not him, Isa. It's not. I'll go to that damned
pub – make inquiries.'
  'No! No. If I've been tricked, that's it. Leave it.
Please, please Philip, promise you'll leave it.'
  She was starting to tremble again, so he
promised. They didn't get back to the question of
Petra, so the picture of her walking home from
school through autumn plane trees joined the
other unborn ghosts of her.

28

September 1910

The last day before the village school went back,
Petra and Evan were sitting on the bank in the
old orchard next to the cottage, watching the
horses. Guto and Sonny grazed quietly by the
hedge but Jack the Lad kept coming up and
pushing Evan with his nose, wanting titbits.

Petra said, *'Mae'n geffyl da,* a towel. The horse
is good.'

Evan said, *'Mae'n geffyl trychwantus, mae o hyd
eisiau bwyd.'*

She stared at him until he translated.

'The horse is a fat glutton. He's always after
food.'

She giggled and got him to say the words again,
several times over, repeating them after him. He'd
been unbelieving when, back at the start of the
summer, she'd given up her struggling attempts to
learn to play his clarinet and begged him to teach
her Welsh instead. He couldn't have understood,
even if she could have explained, how speaking or
reading a foreign language fed her need to be
somewhere else – not just visiting but born
somewhere else and someone else so that it could
all come out right next time. Today, aware that
summer was nearly over and school starting soon,
she was hungry to learn as many words as she

could. He humoured her for a while until he shouted suddenly *'Mae'r dyn a'r gefn y ceffyl.* The man rides the horse,' stood up and vaulted off the bank onto the back of Jack the Lad. The horse, astonished, went 'hrrrr' through his nostrils and twisted his head round to see what was happening, but he was too used to human beings in general and Evan in particular to buck or gallop off, so dealt with it the way he dealt with most things, dropping his head to graze. With nothing but a long slide of neck in front of him, Evan yelled, partly with fear, partly with delight at his daring, and twisted his fingers in the only bit of mane he could still reach. Petra laughed and chanted *'O geffyl da, geffyl da, geffyl da.'*

Then Will's voice from the other side of the hedge, 'Evan lad. Where you got to, Evan?'

To Jack the Lad, Will's voice meant food. He went off at a trot, then a canter, towards the gate. Evan shouted stop in Welsh and English, bouncing from one side to the other, hanging desperately to the mane, but it had no effect in either language. Petra followed at a run, shrieking between laughter and fear. At the gate the horse came to a skidding halt, catapulting Evan right over it to land at his uncle's feet. Will stared down at Evan. The horse stared at Will, nervous of having offended him. Petra came at a run.

'Is he hurt? Is he hurt?'

The fear in her voice astonished Will. He took hold of Evan's arm and helped him up.

'Tougher than that he is, Miss Petra. But what did you want to be doing, getting on him like that?'

'It was my fault,' Petra said. 'I dared him to.'

Evan and Will stared at her from the other side of the gate.

'It was his own silly fault to take you up on it. No harm done, if the horse is all right.' Will opened the gate and came through. 'Whoa there. All right, are we? All right and no harm done.'

The gentle chant was as much to soothe Petra as the horse. Evan came and stood beside her, conscious that she'd told a lie for him.

'I'm not hurt. Honest, I'm not. *Diogel ac iach. Diogel ac iach.*'

Will was troubled when the children spoke Welsh, feeling shut out by it.

'Bad manners to talk if people don't know what you're saying, Evan.'

Evan caught Petra's eye, signalling that this was their secret, and instantly repaid his debt.

'Sorry, Uncle Will.'

'We'll be down at the lily pool this morning, raking off the duckweed. I'll get you to go up to the big shed and get out a couple of the wooden rakes for us, and I'll meet you down there when I've done the hens.'

Will lingered, watching the horses. The old bay Sonny was moving stiffly on his short legs and it was a question whether he'd make it through another winter. Will knew that some of his friends would say shoot him now while he's still happy from summer and good grass, don't wait for some wet February morning when he's down in the mud and can't get back on his legs. But the urge of living things to go on living ran through his own blood, deeper than anybody's words.

231

Through to another spring was worth trying for. He was aware of the child standing behind him, also watching the horses.

'How's Trefor, Mr Thomas?'

Even asking about him gave her a little thrill of foreignness because Trefor was a working man now in the other land on the far side of the hills.

'Well enough, thank you Miss Petra.'

The fact was, Trefor was a worry to him again. Two days ago, a letter had arrived from his brother asking, tentatively, whether work might be found for Trefor if he came back to Holders Hope. His father was worried because Trefor was getting into bad company and with the lock-out at Ely Pit at Pen-y-Graig and the possibility of all the men in the Cambrian Combine coming out on strike, there was a lot of wild talk among the young men. Will knew precious little about labour relations and that part of the letter was Greek to him. He and Bathsheba had puzzled over it together and she – willing to have Trefor back again – had been surprised to find her usually gentle husband set against it.

'But he says he might get in trouble back there, Will.'

'There's trouble everywhere if you go looking for it. Besides, it'd unsettle young Evan.'

Will put his foot down very rarely, but once it was down it stayed planted. Between them they concocted a letter wishing everybody well but regretting, which was perfectly true, that there was nobody taking on working lads in a farming area at the start of winter.

'If you'll excuse me, Miss Petra, I'll be getting

back to the hens.'

She gave him a nod and a little smile, but from the look in her eyes her mind was a long way away.

Evan got to the stone-flagged terrace beside the lily pool long before his uncle was likely to arrive. For a while he tried playing ducks and drakes with flat stone chippings, but the water surface was almost covered with duckweed and lily leaves. It struck him that he might as well make a start on the job and try raking in duckweed. He stood on the edge of the flagstones, held the shaft of the rake with both hands, pushed the head out as far as it would go and let it drop into the carpet of bright green weed. The tines sank down. He pulled the rake back in towards him and a great swathe of weed came with it, leaving a track of clear water. Evan yelled with pleasure at finding the stuff so obedient. When he shook it clear from the rake, runnels of water ran back into the pool and little grey shrimp things twitched and hopped across the paving. A green, shivery water smell rose up round him. Seen close to, the mass of duckweed was made up of cushiony bits no bigger than wheat grains, with a clear spongy mass on the underside and little filaments sticking out like insects' antennae. After the first haul he worked methodically, moving a few steps along the edge each time so that a neat slice of clean water opened up between the terrace and the rest of the weed further out. When he came to the point where an alder tree overlapped the edge of the terrace it wasn't so easy. There were clumps of yellow flags there with fleshy green seedpods on thick stems, bulrushes further out. He got one foot in a fork of the alder, the other firmly planted on the flagstones and half-pushed, half-threw the rake out to the patch of duckweed to the side of the bulrushes. He thought at first it must have snagged on the roots of the rushes because when he tried to pull it in it resisted so hard that the shaft nearly jerked out of his hands. He found by accident that if he pushed and pulled the rake instead of dragging all the time, the thing seemed to move. He was getting apprehensive, thinking he might be in trouble if he tore up lily roots, but determined not to be beaten by vegetation. When he saw a streak of yellowish-white in the duckweed he thought at first it might be the inside of a ripped root and his heart lurched. But it wasn't solid enough for that, more of a long streak on the water. It looked like fabric, a piece of old sheet or canvas. It came towards him more quickly on the next tug, but heavier than he expected. It was fabric, yellowish-white and sodden black, vertically striped like stained mattress-ticking but much wider. The rake wavered. He lost the thing, cast out for it again, missing twice, then the tines of the rake caught and tangled. The striped thing rose part way out of the water, trailing duckweed, tipped and rose again. Then the hand came up. It was yellowish too, plumper than a hand should be, fingers spread as if trying to get a grip on the air. Evan yelled, water splashing and rocking, a moorhen in the reeds rattling a reply to his yell. The rake

234

came away with a tearing sound but the hand was still there or at least the fingers of it, stretching up fat and yellow from the rocking water. He dropped the rake on the terrace, ran to a pile of broken flagstones. He picked out the biggest piece he could carry, staggered with it to the pond edge and shied it with all his strength at the fingers. It took six or seven pieces of stone but at last when he looked, trembling and sweating, the fingers and the stripes were gone and there was nothing but a jagged-edged patch of clear water stretching out from the bulrushes. He sat down on the pile of stones and was still there five minutes later when Will arrived, late from stopping to admire his bantams.

'That you calling, Evan boy?' Then, not getting an answer, he took in the clean band of water, the dripping pile of duckweed, the boy's pale and exhausted face. 'You made good start on it, boy, but you don't want to go at a job like that, tire yourself out.'

For the rest of the morning they worked side by side. They didn't say much, but then they never did when they worked together. Every time Evan turned back towards the pool he expected to see the fingers groping for a grip on the air, but there was nothing but frogs and moorhens. If he could have told anybody, he'd have told Will but the sense of wrong done and blame kept him quiet.

29

Marius came to his mother's dressing room on a morning in early September, a few days before he was due back at Eton for his last year before university. He was dressed casually for indoors, light grey trousers, dazzling white shirt, waistcoat in damson coloured brocade, carrying a novel. Isabelle was sitting at her dressing table, hair down, wearing a Japanese silk wrap with iris flowers. Megan stood behind her, pinning a pad of false hair in place with hairpins so that Isabelle's own hair could be tucked round it, giving more height and fullness. When the door opened Megan, well-trained, retreated into the bedroom taking pad and hairpins with her. Isabelle turned.

'Good morning, darling. Did you sleep well?'

Marius perched himself on the end of the dressing table. She swept some pots aside, partly to make room for him, partly to turn their labels away.

Instead of answering he said, in the deep voice that still surprised her, 'I've had a letter from Darronby. He's been discussing things with his father.' Teddy Darronby. Same house and same year as Marius. 'His father says we should all stick together. You know they own a lot of coal mines up near Newcastle.'

'Durham.'

Isabelle had never met Teddy's father, William Darronby MP, but she knew about him. Marius waved away geographical details, intent on having an adult conversation. She put down her nail buffer and gave him all her attention.

'Stick together in what way?'

'As employers. Teddy's father says the south Wales miners are the worst.'

'No darling, they're the best.' She was stung into patriotism. 'The Rhondda miner produces more per shift than in any comparable coalfield. If you're really interested I've got some figures in my desk I could...'

'The worst trouble makers, he means. Teddy's father says the Rhondda pits are full of communists and revolutionaries. He says if the south Wales owners like us don't take a firm line they'll drive all of us out of business.'

That 'like us' was the first acknowledgement he'd ever made that the family business was anything to do with him.

'We've taken a very firm line in the past.'

She still had vivid memories of a strike twelve years before. Her father was still alive then, though only for a few months more. Stomach cancer was eating him and the pain twisting his guts fuelled his ferocity against his striking men. Along with the other owners he'd vowed they should be starved back to work. Unwillingly, he starved along with them, stomach able to keep down nothing but liquids, beef tea in the sickroom in London, mutton broth in the soup kitchens in the mining towns. While it was going on Isabelle read accounts in the papers about the suffering of the miners' wives and children and timidly argued for compromise. He set his jaw and told her that since she was his sole heir she'd have to learn more about the economics of coal mining or his grandchildren would be paupers. So he taught her through endless afternoons with the blind drawn down against the sun. Even now, she couldn't look at a page of accounts without the whiff in her nostrils of beef tea and the opium and brandy mixture he swigged when the pain was intolerable.

Marius said, 'Teddy reckons they're all coming out again. Is that right?'

'So far it's only a lock-out at a Cambrian Combine pit.'

'Will it affect us?'

'If all the men in the Cambrian Combine come out on strike, that's twelve thousand men. It would be bound to affect the rest of us.'

'Couldn't we bring in workers from somewhere else? Teddy's father might let us have some of his.'

'But if most of the pits were on strike the hauliers might come out as well. It's no good having coal sitting around at the pithead. It's only valuable when it's in the docks.'

The old man had taught her thoroughly. Naturally he'd have preferred to pass his life's work on to a son, but like the good engineer he was, he did the best job possible with the materials to hand. She guessed Marius had come in feeling man-of-world, wanting to favour her with his judgement and important contacts, and didn't want him to go away crestfallen.

'I'm glad you're taking an interest, Marius. If you like, I'll show you any letters that come from Mr Gladwyn when you're...'

'Who's he?'

'My manager. Our manager. It might be a good idea for you to meet him when you're home at Christmas.'

She'd have to make sure, though, that Marius didn't try to patronise one of the most experienced pit managers in the Rhondda with Teddy Darronby's second-hand opinions.

He thanked her without enthusiasm, hitched his long legs off her dressing table and went out. She was still smiling when Megan came back from the bedroom to finish her hair.

'You've got clever fingers, Megan.'

Clever in the way they made her hair feel thick and sleek, as if the youth and vigour of Megan's own wonderful hair could be passed on by touch. Clever in making her headaches go away, massaging her forehead, the back of her head behind the ears where the pain coiled itself. When she first tried it, only a few weeks after her sudden promotion from kitchen skivvy to lady's maid, a mad impulse had come into Isabelle's mind to ask 'What did you do exactly, you and my husband?' She'd fought it down then and at other times. In three years, she'd never regretted the decision that had amazed the household. Megan as a maid was near perfection. She learned quickly, never had to be told anything twice and had a passion for clothes, colours, scents that equalled Isabelle's own. They'd pore over ladies' magazines, heads together more like

239

big and little sister than employer and maid, weighing up advertisements for lotions, bath essences, creams. Madame Cross's Beauty Cream 2s 6d and 4s 6d a bottle in plain wrapper. It was Megan who wrote the letters to order them in her neat schoolroom hand, queued for stamps and postal orders at the village shop, spirited the little packages from the tray of post in the hall up to Isabelle's dressing room. Megan gave a last touch of the brush to the shining hair and Isabelle dressed and went down to breakfast. Left to herself, Megan tidied things up. The little spray bottle on the dressing table that held Isabelle's special lily of the valley cologne was nearly empty. She fetched the larger bottle from a cupboard, unscrewed the cap of the spray and started pouring cologne into it through a silver funnel. The door opened.

'Mother, I left my...'

She saw Marius in the mirror but didn't turn.

'She's gone downstairs.'

'I've left my book.'

'It's on the dressing table here.'

Tono-Bungay by H. G. Wells. He came over to the dressing table and stood beside her, but didn't pick up the book.

'Your voice has changed.'

For the rest of the household, the fading of Megan's Welsh accent had been a gradual process. She ignored him, screwing back the cap and the rubber spray bulb covered with pink silk netting. He moved behind her. She'd expected something diffident and clumsy, but the hands that clamped themselves over her stomach knew

240

what they were doing. His long fingers reached down, digging through her skirt into the ridge of her pubic bone. When he felt the lurch of her diaphragm he gave a little chuckle and his fingers dug deeper. Her fingers pumped at the rubber bulb in its covering of slippery silk. She twisted round and blasted him in the eyes with a stinging cloud of lily of the valley. He yelped with pain. 'No. What are you doing?' She went on spraying the back of his fingers, his waistcoat and shirt front. She didn't stop until the spray was empty and they were almost suffocated in the flower smell.

He said, through his fingers, 'You shouldn't have done that.'

He sounded more hurt and puzzled than anything, as if she hadn't been playing fair. Then he went, feeling for the doorknob with one hand, the other still clamped over his eyes. At lunchtime when Isabelle came up to change and brush her hair the room was still full of lily of the valley. Megan said she was sorry, she'd been filling the spray and spilt some. Isabelle told her she should be careful because the cologne was expensive, but she said it without much annoyance. Marius didn't appear at lunch.

30

November 1910

Official Statement from the Home Office, issued on the night of 8 November 1910.

A request was addressed last night by the Chief Constable of Glamorgan to the local military authorities for the assistance of 200 cavalry and two companies of infantry in keeping order in the Cambrian collieries. The Home Secretary, in consultation with Mr Haldane, decided to send instead a contingent of the Metropolitan Police consisting of 70 mounted and 200 foot constables to the district to carry out the instructions of the Chief Constable under their own officers. The force was sent by special train and will arrive in the early evening.

But the front page of the Cardiff paper that carried the Home Office statement added that the cavalry, in the shape of the 18th Hussars, 'all furnished with ball ammunition' had also been despatched to the Rhondda.

Will Thomas never read newspapers. An account of what was happening on the other side of the hills in the Rhondda came to him via Enoch Pugh when the old man was helping him tidy up the birch copse on the far side of the lily pool.

'Bad business, it is. They've brought the blacklegs in and there's men getting killed.'

The second week of November. In the hollows there was still frost on the ground at midday. Will and Enoch were clearing and sawing up dead branches for the woodpile, making a bonfire of the scrubby stuff. Will dropped his branch and stared.

'Killed?'

'Good as. Heads and arms broken and now they're bringing in the mounted soldiers from up north somewhere. Doreen's nephew knows the man runs the signal box at Abergavenny. Had to clear the rails for dozens of horse wagons coming through in the middle of the night.'

'Mrs Allegri wouldn't let them shoot at her people.'

Her kindness was one of the facts of life for Will. She'd given work to him, to Megan, even the boy. She'd turned a blind eye to his horses eating her grass.

'Not up to her, is it? It's the big owners. Round Llwynypia most of the fighting's been so far.'

Will had never heard that name mentioned in connection with his brother's family. It was a relief, because if anything happened to Trefor, Bathsheba would blame him. By the time the sun was down on the hills they'd cut three cartloads of logs and were watching the thin flames of their bonfire wavering in the cold air.

'Another frost tonight.'

Enoch Pugh blew on his ungloved fingertips, his mind on the kitchen down in the village, the brown teapot on the table and a plateful of Doreen's griddle cakes keeping warm by the fire. Will told him not to bother to drag all the way up

243

to the wood shed again. There was only a half load on the cart and he could take it himself. He took his time stowing the logs and walked slowly home with the dog at his heels wondering whether to mention what had been said to Bathsheba. She was onto him before he could get his boots off in the back porch outside the scullery.

'Will, there's a letter.'

He finished taking off his boots and padded in his brown wool socks through the kitchen to the living room. The letter and its envelope were lying on the table in the lamplight. It was addressed to Will but it was Bathsheba's job to open letters, words being among those things that women did better.

'Trefor's been hurt.'

Just one page in his brother's cramped and painstaking handwriting.

Dear Will,

This is to let you know that Trefor had an accident. He went with some of his friends against the blacklegs. We'd told him he had no business with it, but he went without telling us. He got hit on the head and was brought home unconscious. The doctor says he should be all right if we keep him quiet, but the next 2 or 3 days will tell. Will, you know I'd never ask you or Bathsheba for money for myself, but if he comes through he'll need food and caring for. If you could see your way to sending ten bob, I'll pay it back as soon as this lock-out is over. Our love to Bathsheba & Megan & Evan. Tell him to be a good boy and work hard at school.

Bathsheba was watching him. When he looked up she said, 'I went straight down to the shop and sent off a postal order for a pound. I took it out of the egg box.'

She spoke in a fierce whisper, glancing towards the stairs. 'Evan doesn't know.'

Will sat down heavily in his sagging armchair by the fire, pole-axed with guilt and misery. Upstairs, curled up in the nest of blankets he'd once shared with Trefor, Evan jammed his fists into eye sockets crusted with dried tears to stop himself crying again. Bathsheba, bustling around to get his tea and send him upstairs, had forgotten she'd left the letter lying on the mantelpiece, or forgotten that he was now tall enough to see up to the mantelpiece and recognise his father's handwriting. Lying there in the dark he'd been sure that his brother was already dead, seen him lying in the bed back at home with blood running from his smashed skull like yolk from a dropped egg. Then it had come to him that this death was somehow linked with the thing in the lily pool and was his fault. He imagined a drowned head smashing under the stones he'd thrown to sink the thing, or perhaps not even drowned until he'd thrown the stones at it. Now, with the first shock over, he had to decide what to do. The first bit of the decision was easy, get to his brother, alive or dead, and his father. He knew Uncle Will and Auntie Bath wouldn't help because for whatever reasons they were keeping it from him, practically keeping him

245

prisoner. How to get there wasn't difficult either. He and Trefor had discussed it sometimes in the days of homesickness three years ago when their mother was dying. Up and over the hill you could see from the garden and you were in Wales. Then maybe another hill or two, catch a train or a tram if there was one, go on walking if not, and you were home in the Rhondda. Money was the hard part. Enough money and his brother might not die. He had none, not a penny. What he'd earned doing odd jobs in the garden had been spent at the village shop and anyway even if he could call back everything he'd spent on gobstoppers and sherbert sucks and liquorice sticks, there wasn't enough there to put a smashed head back together. He waited and worked it out, listening and smelling normal life going unbelievably on downstairs – the scrape of Will's chair up to the table, smell of steak and kidney pudding, the excited whining of the terrier from the scullery as Will took the plate of scraps out to him. He knew what happened next. Will dozing in the armchair, socks to the fire, the terrier stretched out on the mat. Bathsheba at the sink in the cold kitchen. He stood up, still in his school-going clothes of flannel shirt, knickerbockers, woollen stockings and thin jersey. He rummaged in the pile of clothes beside his bed for the thicker brown jersey Bathsheba had knitted him for gardening, pulled that on as well, then his Norfolk jacket over the top, very tight under the arms and across the shoulders. A woollen scarf and cap and, after some thought, his clarinet unscrewed into three pieces and wrapped in a handkerchief went into the pocket of the jacket. He listened, heard pans still clattering and his uncle's gentle snores and went carefully down the steep staircase, clumsy from all the clothes. In the living room, the terrier woke up and looked at him, but Will didn't. In the kitchen, Bathsheba heard him but didn't turn from the sink.

'You all right, Evan love?'

'Little house up the path, Auntie Bath.'

His boots were just inside the scullery door, alongside Will's. He picked them up and sat down outside to put them on, already aware of cold from the stone step striking up through the seat of his knickerbockers. He walked up the first few yards of path with heavy steps as if really making for the privy, turned off treading more lightly for the gate, then along a path so familiar that his feet went of their own accord even in the dark, across the plank bridge and up the lawn towards the big house. The grass under his bootsoles was already stiffening from frost. There were a lot of lights on in the house. He went slowly at first, then running uphill, faster and faster in the darkness, as if the lighted house were a ship that might sail away before he got what he needed.

31

Isabelle said, 'I wrote to Mr Gladwyn as soon as it started. I said we wouldn't bring in outside labour to our pits whatever the others did.'

'I hope it helps.'

Philip hadn't planned to be there in November but the stories coming out of South Wales had worried him for Isabelle's sake. He'd arrived unannounced from Hereford station on his bicycle just as it was getting dark. Now, washed and changed, he was drinking sherry with her in front of the fire in the small drawing room.

'Goodness knows what will help. I'm scared, honestly scared.'

'You could sell.'

He said it on impulse. He'd been alarmed when he arrived to see the strain in her face, the nervous jerkiness of her movements.

'At the bottom of the market?'

'Why not?'

Isabelle with less money was an attractive thought. He'd be better placed to argue for the house in the London square with the plane trees, the cottage in the Kent apple orchards or any of the other places where they lived together in his fantasies.

'What about Marius? What about here?'

'You could sell this too.'

She looked at him as if he'd kicked a kitten.

'Leave the garden? You don't mean it.'

'Why not? I can make you another garden anywhere.'

'Not like this one. There'll never be another one like this one.'

Her face looked so bleak and stripped that the only thing he could do was put his arms round her and hug her. She pressed her mouth to his, hungry for comfort.

Petra had fallen asleep on her bed over a Welsh grammar and missed Philip's arrival. She woke to find the sky dark outside her window and came downstairs still half-mazed with drowsiness, wondering if she'd missed dinner. Looking for her mother, she opened the door of the little drawing room and saw the two figures in the firelight. She closed the door and left without a sound.

It wasn't so difficult. Evan had done it twice before, but on summer nights, not encumbered by so many layers of clothing. What you did was choose a long stick from the hazel coppice to the side of the house. This took him some time by feel in the dark, but he knew the coppice almost as well as the dormice hibernating there. The next stage was clambering up on the water butt round the corner from the front of the house, then using the drain pipe to help get your feet on the broad stone ledge that ran round the front and sides, just above the ground floor windows. Then wriggle the stick out from under your arm and lean out round the corner, pushing up with the stick, not able to see where it was going but hoping to hear it scraping against the glass of her window. Petra thought at first the sound was rain, hoped it would go on forever, like Noah's Flood only no ark this time. When it turned into a jittery rhythmic tapping she got off the bed and went over to the window.

'Evan?'

She pushed the window up. His voice came to her round the corner of the house.

'Trefor's dying. Have you got any money?'

'Dying?'

'I've got to go to him. He needs money.'

If she'd been less miserable and angry, she might have asked questions. As it was, in a world that didn't make sense to her, this was no worse than anything else.

'Wait at the side door.'

Scarves and gloves went flying as she burrowed in a drawer for the leather-covered box where she kept the money that was given to her at Christmas and birthdays and she didn't have much chance to spend. A staircase went down from her end of the corridor to the back of the house. From there a corridor not much used by the family in winter led to the side door. She hurried along it in the dark, came to the lobby where they kept waterproof coats and walking sticks. He was waiting for her outside.

'What's he dying of?'

'They crushed his head in. He might not die if he can get a doctor and proper food. I've got to go to him.'

It didn't occur to her to ask who *they* were

250

who'd done the crushing.

'I've got some money. Is it enough?' She pushed a handful of notes and silver coins at him. 'It's about seven pounds.'

'Should be enough.' It was an almost unimaginable amount to him. He took it from her, put it in the pocket of his jacket and buttoned it down. 'Thank you.'

They both hesitated, he just outside the door, she inside. She'd come down in her stockinged feet and the cold was striking up through the stone flags.

'How are you getting to him? Are they sending for you?'

'Walking. It can't be far over the hills.'

'I'll come with you.'

'You can't. What would your ma say?'

'She doesn't care about me. She only cares about somebody else. Wait there.'

By the time she was back, a quarter of an hour or so, the first of the tawny owls was hunting, floating its long quavering call over the woods. A sharp phosphorous smell in his nostrils then a flare of light, showing her face, pale as a witch in the hood of her thick coat.

'I brought matches and the candle. And these.' The light died away. She pushed something heavy and knobbled into his hand, a walking stick taken from the cluster of them inside the door. 'Shall I light the candle?'

'Not yet. You'd better follow me.'

A path led down from the side door through the hazel coppice, slippery stone underfoot and dead leaves brushing their sleeves. Evan took the

251

fork that led to the broad sweep of gravel by the front door. The fan-shaped window over the door threw a wash of lamplight down the front steps and over the gravel. The gates to the lane were open. They ran out of the shelter of the hazels, across the patch of light and through the gates. In the lane they walked in silence side by side until Evan stopped at a gap in the bare hedge.

'Climb over.'

He climbed first, then turned to help Petra. While he was doing it he glanced up at the big house and its lighted windows, feeling like an outlaw already, but she didn't give it a single backward look. The first two fields were easy, even in the dark. Petra walked strongly, keeping up with him, saying nothing. On the far side of the second field a broken wooden gate led into a hollow lane, familiar territory to Evan by day because a friend at school came from a farm up the track. Now, with the hedges invisible at the top of the banks, it was a tube of intense darkness. The mud in the lane was too deep for the frost to make any difference. His feet sank into it to his boot tops and made a slurping noise when he pulled them out. Petra's voice from behind him, nervous for the first time.

'Where are you? I can't see you.'

'Hold on.'

He fumbled at the waistband of his breeches, pulled out his shirt tail and let it hang down below the jacket.

'Can you see anything?'

'White?'

'Follow the white.'

After what seemed like a long time they passed the opening to his friend's farm and the sheepdog started barking. He muttered 'Be quiet, Maggie,' glad to have a familiar name to cling to although they were too far away for the dog to hear him. They were now on the far edge of his known territory. There was a different, thinner quality to the darkness now they were climbing out of the valley. Their bodies inside the layers of clothes were warm from climbing, but the air was cold on their faces.

Petra said, 'We could follow the stream up.'

They'd been aware for a while of the sound of running water away to the right. When they got nearer it the ground was wet and spongy, so they kept their distance and followed it by sound. He felt tired, as if they'd been walking in the dark forever, and supposed she did, but she wasn't complaining.

'Rocks.' Underfoot, she meant. Big blocks of them. Then, 'I think it's a house.'

They picked their way over to it, slowed almost to stupefaction by tiredness. One wall, rearing up over them into the dark.

Evan said, 'A ruined house. It could fall over on us.'

Edging away from it, he came up against a lower wall that felt less threatening.

'I think it's a shed or something. Bring the candle over.'

It was a pigsty, more or less intact with a door of warped wooden planks still held to the doorframe by a nail hooked into a staple. There was straw inside, long-dried dung. Petra followed him in with the candle. They scraped some of the cleaner straw into a heap and sat down, side by side.

'Like being in a cave,' Petra said.

Evan didn't answer. The energy that had brought him this far was fading away. His head was bent, arms crossed on his chest, fists pushed into opposite armpits under his jacket.

Petra said, 'What's up?'

'Hand's cold.' Reluctantly.

She grabbed one of his arms and dragged a bare hand out from his armpit. It was mottled red and purple, swollen with cold.

'Haven't you got gloves?'

Petra, drilled from early childhood in wrapping herself up properly before she went out in the cold was wearing thick gloves of holly green wool. She took one off and started working it onto his hand. Her large and square hands had been a grief to her, so different from her mother's or father's. Now she was glad because her glove fitted Evan.

'Other one.' She prised it out, but he resisted. 'All right then, one each.' She clamped both her hands, one gloved and one ungloved round his bare one, kneeling to face him in the straw. He stopped resisting, screwing his face up with the pain of the circulation coming back. Some time later the candle wavered and went out, leaving a smell of hot wax and darkness as solid as a rock face.

She said, 'Is it like this down a mine?'

'Suppose so.'

'Did it happen down a mine? Trefor's head?'

'Course not. It was the owners.'

'Owners?'

'If the miners want more money, the owners call the police and soldiers in to make them go back to work.'

She thought about it. 'My mother's an owner, isn't she?'

It had never been real to her before. She'd known about the coal mines and what a great man her grandfather was, but it was only now that she saw it in terms of ownership.

She said, 'I hate her.'

Saying it was an experiment. It didn't work, quite, because she didn't believe it yet. But it was still an achievement, as if the darkness were a slab of black stone and she'd carved the words on it.

'You can't hate your ma.'

'I do. She made my father unhappy, so he went away.' Evan said nothing. 'I'm going to find him one day. He'll be looking for me too so we'll find each other when I'm about fifteen or sixteen and live in an old palace by the canal in Venice. I'll look after him while he paints.'

After a while he fell asleep, leaning against her. Her nose was running from the cold and she couldn't get at her handkerchief without disturbing him. She could feel from the tightness above her lip a cold-sore forming and a fat splinter from the fence they'd scrambled through throbbed in her wrist. Still, feeling his weight on her, she was closer to being happy than at any time since her father had gone.

Petra was missed first. Now the children were older, dinner was at half past seven but Isabelle

255

didn't make a fetish of punctuality at mealtimes. When they'd finished their soup and still no sign of Petra she began to worry that the child might be ill, told Mary to start serving meat pie while she'd pop upstairs herself to see what was wrong. They heard her feet running downstairs. Marius went on eating. Philip put down his fork and saw from her face as she came in that something was wrong.

'She's not in her room.'

Together he and Isabelle looked in the little drawing room, the library, the big front drawing room. Nobody answered Isabelle's increasingly anxious 'Are you there, darling?' They went out to the terrace, shouted into the darkness. Philip suggested that she might have gone to the Thomas's cottage.

'Without telling us? Why would she do that?'

He went back inside for his boots and overcoat. She wanted to come with him but he told her he'd be quicker on his own. His knock brought Bathsheba to the cottage door, clutching knitting, alarmed.

'Is Petra here?'

That was so unlikely that it took her some time to understand. She asked him inside. Will was still snoring by the fire and Philip, desperately worried now, had to take a tight grip on his patience as he woke up and tried to think where he'd seen the child last.

'Evan will know,' Bathsheba said.

She stood at the bottom of the stairs and called to him to put his clothes on and come down, Mr Cordell was here. No answer. She took three steps up the steep stairs, so that the upper half of

256

her body was inside the loft space.

'Evan, wake up now.' Then, her voice rising close to a scream, 'Will, he's not here.'

32

Philip and Will went back to the house. Isabelle was with them before Philip could get his boots off and the look on his face was enough to tell her.

He said, 'Evan's missing too.'

Megan was standing behind Isabelle and he only remembered when he saw the anxiety on her face that Evan was her brother.

'Have you seen him today? Did he say anything to you about where he was going?'

Megan shook her head. Isabelle put a hand to her face, turned away from all of them.

'What have we done? Oh, what have we done?'

The light came back slowly through the gaps in the pigsty roof. Petra woke stiff-necked to find that Evan had disentangled himself from her and was lying curled up on his side, red bare hand and green woollen hand tucked into his chest. Bladder aching, she crouched her way to the door and went out. The frost had given way to drizzle, softening the outlines of everything except the stark wall and chimney stack. She ducked beneath a heap of tumbled stones to relieve herself, cold fingers fumbling with buttons and elastic. It came

257

to her with a sense of isolation far worse than leaving home that this had been a third day. Normally there were clean knickers waiting by her bed every third day. She'd never in her life worn the same pair into a fourth day before and wondered whether it gave you things. The ruined house was at the top of the tree line. Above it brown bracken stretched to tawny grass, like a mangy lion's pelt. She went back in the pigsty. Evan was awake, arms clasped round his knees.

'We must be nearly there,' she said.

She didn't believe it but she had to stop him looking so hopeless. He stared at her then went outside. She heard a splashing, smelt a urine tang stronger than her own. When she came out he was turned away from her, looking uphill.

He said 'We'd better hurry,' as if she'd been holding them back.

There was a thin line of track leading up from the ruins. They followed it with Evan in the lead, going stiffly and slowly. For Petra, the back of Evan's jacket up ahead was the only solid thing in a world dissolving into drizzle. After a long time he called out something and pointed upwards. She looked and saw that there was only a narrow line of heather left, then nothing but grey sky. 'We're there,' he said and went off up the sheep track at a blundering run. She wanted to run, but couldn't and followed as quickly as she could, thinking of houses down there on the other side of the hill, of Trefor pale and in bed, but saved.

She thought, 'They'll let me stay with them, his family. They'll be grateful to me.'

But when she came up beside Evan his face was

bleak and his voice had tears in it.

'It's not...'

She looked down. The side of the hill they were on sloped down in swathes of heather and dead bracken just like the one they'd climbed, with a few grey stone walls cutting across. In the bottom of the valley a tree or two, then again on the far side to a ridge as high as the one they were standing on, brown bracken, walls, dead heather. Not a building anywhere, not a house or barn even.

'But you said...' Then, seeing the look on his face. 'It must be just over the next hill.'

He said, 'I suppose Trefor's dead by now.'

'My father's dead too.'

She said it because she wanted to share grief with him, but when it came out she knew it was true. Evan was too kind or perhaps too exhausted to remind her about Venetian palaces. Soon after that, without another word, they got up and went on unsteadily downhill.

Philip came back up to the house, around daylight. Isabelle was waiting in the small drawing room, curtains open on the drizzle but lamps still alight, a fug in the room from the fire going all night. Cups of greyish tea, cold and untasted, cluttered the tables. Her hair was coming down and hung round her face in damp wisps. She looked ten years older in a matter of hours, even smelt older, of tears and dried sweat.

'Nothing?'

'Nothing. I've sent a message to the police station to say that they're missing.'

He looked at the chairs by the fire but didn't

dare sit down in case he fell asleep, bone-weary from a night searching barns and ditches. The search party had included almost every man and boy from Holdersby and the neighbouring farms.

'Will's walking along the road to Abergavenny. He thinks Evan may be trying to get home.'

'Yes.'

'You heard about his brother?'

'From Megan, yes.' Her voice was flat and hopeless.

No response. Outside he found Megan sitting on a chair in the hall, looking deathly tired.

'Can you get her to go up to bed?'

'I've tried, Mr Cordell. She won't.'

It was early afternoon before the search ended. A lad on an old black bicycle in an adult raincoat too big for him, belted round the middle with baler twine, wavered into the yard of The Sun and asked for directions to Holders Hope, because they'd found two children over in the next valley. A farmer over Llanthony way came across them walking on a dirt track, dead on their feet with tiredness, reckoning they were walking to the Rhondda. They were safe with his wife in the farm kitchen, drinking broth and having their clothes dried and he'd have brought them home himself only the wheel had come off his cart, so would somebody please come and fetch them. They were brought home in a police brake drawn by two bay cobs, Isabelle on one side, then Petra, then Philip, then Evan. The boy slept for most of the journey, leaning against Philip, but Petra sat bolt upright in between them, answering

Isabelle's anxious questions so reluctantly that in the end they travelled without saying anything. At Holders Hope, Will and Bathsheba were waiting just inside the front door, the first time they had been inside the big house. Bathsheba knelt down and put her arms around Evan. He struggled free, unbuttoned the pocket of his Norfolk jacket and held out a handful of something to Petra.

'No,' she said. 'It's for Trefor.'

Damp notes stuck together and some silver. He wouldn't give up, just stood there, muddy boots planted on a good Turkey carpet, holding out the money. Philip understood first.

'Give it to me. We'll see it gets to him.'

Only then Evan let himself be hustled away and Petra went stiffly upstairs to where Mary was running a bath for her, deep as it would go without overflowing, smelling of lily of the valley, a scent she hated.

Holders Hope
Herefordshire

14 November 1910

Mr S.T. Gladwyn
Penyrheol Colliery, Treorchy,
Glamorgan.

From Mrs L. Allegri.

Dear Mr Gladwyn,
I should be very glad if you would make

enquiries about Trefor Thomas, 15 years old, one of our employees who was injured in the attack by the strikers of Llwynypia Colliery last week.

Please send me news of his condition by telegram and give his family ten pounds ($£10$) for medical and other expenses. Please advise me if further money is likely to be needed.

Penyrheol Colliery,
Treorchy
Glamorgan

15 November 1910

From S.T. Gladwyn
General Manager

Dear Mrs Allegri,
As I informed you in my telegram yesterday, Trefor Thomas is now considered out of danger and expected to make a complete recovery. I have given ten pounds ($£10$) to his father, as requested in your letter of 14 inst.

You should know that the boy Trefor is regarded by many of the other managers here as a young trouble maker who has taken up with some of the older men most to blame for this current disturbance. There is an informal agreement among the managers that any of the men or boys involved in the attack on Llynwnypia who work at other pits will not be taken on again by any of us after the strike is over. It has always been my understanding that decisions on taking on or dispensing with workers are left with me, as being day to day management concerns. You should know that it is my intention to remove Trefor from our pay roll.

Holders Hope
Herefordshire

17 November 1910

Dear Mr Gladwyn,
I acknowledge receipt of yours of 15 inst.
Thank you for seeing Trefor Thomas's family. I confirm that decisions on who you employ are entirely a matter for you and do not seek to interfere.
Yours sincerely,

Mrs. L. Allegri

The strike ended in September 1911, with the miners settling for a cutting price of two shillings and 1.3 pence per ton which they had rejected at the start of the dispute. When Trefor heard the news he walked up the path to the hills on his own, trying to comfort himself as he'd comforted his brother four years ago with the words of prophecy. This time they came from a song one of his friends had written for the strikers a few months before, set to a hymn tune.
The few shall not for ever sway,
The many toil in sorrow.
The powers of hell are strong today
Our kingdom comes tomorrow.

33

Autumn 1910 to summer 1915

Petra started at Cheltenham Ladies College as planned in January 1911. In four years there she learned to speak French proficiently, do quadratic equations and play Chopin on the piano. Her teachers regarded her as dependable and hard-working. She was in trouble on one occasion with a group of other girls for smuggling an abandoned puppy into the dormitory. She was not one of the school beauties but comfortably around the middle rank of looks. Her mid-brown hair was glossy, her body active and quite slim although too broad in the shoulders to be elegant. If anybody asked about her father she said he was dead.

The kingfisher on the lily pool died in 1911 and his mate the year after. The kingfisher's son and his mate successfully reared nine young.

Philip Cordell made long visits to Holders Hope but mostly when Petra was away at school. He went on doing occasional work at Kew, took part in a plant-collecting expedition to China in the summer of 1911 and made two shorter trips to the Caucasus mountains.

Jack the Lad, still unbroken to bit or harness, went on grazing in the old orchard along with

Pont and Guto. Sonny lived through to the spring of 1911 but had to be shot that autumn because his legs were going.

Isabelle turned 40 in 1913 and had a period of depression until Megan persuaded her to go up to London for a shopping trip and the first Chelsea Flower Show. She tried out some new eye cosmetics, spent a shocking amount on summer clothes and even more on orders for roses and rhododendrons. Philip said she shouldn't be allowed loose at Chelsea or any other flower show.

The output of coal from the Rhondda rose to nine and a half million tons a year in 1913. The miners' average wage was around seven shillings per day, rising to eight shillings for the most skilled coalface men.

Trefor Thomas had his lamp stopped in 1910 – the phrase Rhondda miners used for a man thrown out of work from a colliery. After that he took jobs wherever he could get them without moving outside the Rhondda. But his real work was with the Plebs' League. He spent any spare time he had in the League's social club down in Tonypandy or at classes on industrial history or Marxian economics. He saw his brother Evan sometimes at Christmas and Megan not at all.

Evan Thomas left school in 1913 and went to work full time as under gardener to his uncle. He knew Trefor didn't approve, but their elder sister Sarah wouldn't stand for them arguing in the house, especially at Christmas.

Marius went up to Christ Church in 1912 and emerged in 1915 with a mediocre degree, some useful contacts and not quite as many debts as his mother had expected.

The garden grew.

34

Extract from *Gardening Illustrated* July 1915.

Genius Loci in Herefordshire Hills.

If respect for *genius loci*, the Spirit of the Place, is a mark of a fine garden, then there can be few better deserving the description than Mrs Isabelle Allegri's water and woodland garden at Holders Hope, on the far western edge of Herefordshire. Although work on the garden began only eight years ago, its subtleties of planting and respect for the contours of a site make it seem almost part of the natural landscape, or rather what the landscape would be if plants from all over Europe and beyond had chosen to set root there. If a garden could ever be perfect – a possibility which no true gardener may admit – then Holders Hope on an evening in June must come very close to it.

One of the glories is the broad drift of irises at the bottom of the lawn where it meets the stream, graduated in colour from pale lavender to deep purple, sharpened by the blue-green swordlike leaves of *iris pallida dalmatica* and the delicate sibericas. The effect, seen from the terrace, is that of an intense pool of shimmering blue water. At the end of the iris bed, broad steps lead down between borders of paeonies, columbines, geranium ibericum, pale blue anchusa and white oriental poppies to the lily pool, where the kingfisher may be glimpsed on summer evenings.

Where lawn meets woodland, the natural foliage is interspersed with unexpected plantings that have a fairytale effect. The primrose-scented flowers of rambling rose Adelaide d'Orleans hang in clusters from the boughs of native sessile oaks. A native wild rose of China, newly introduced to cultivation in Britain, *Rosa roxburghii*, flaunts its golden stamens in front of a coppice of silver birches. Groups of the stately *lilium giganteum* stand out against the dark edge of the wood. Most striking of all, the Himalayan poppy, *Meconopsis betonicifolia Baileyii* has established itself in cool glades and astonishes with unexpected flashes of purest sapphire blue.

The range of plants owes much to the travels of the garden's designer, Mr Philip Cordell, who was away in London when we visited. In his absence, Holders Hope is maintained by head gardener, Will Thomas.

Kim pushed the photocopied pages back across the grass towards Colin.

'I wish they had people in the photographs.'

He'd been thinking about *Meconopsis betonicifolia Baileyii*. If it really had established itself by 1915 it had disappeared since, or at least he'd found no

267

trace of it.

'And there's nothing about her husband. You'd have thought they'd make some reference to him.'

'It was a garden magazine, not *Hello!*'

'I'll tell you what's really odd about it.'

'Umm?'

'The date. July 1915, for goodness sake. Didn't they know there was a war on?'

35

July 1915

Isabelle was re-reading the magazine piece in the small drawing room when Mary brought in the morning post. She liked the bit about the shimmering pool of irises. Just the effect Philip had wanted. She wondered if he'd seen the magazine in London. She hadn't seen him or even heard from him for nearly three weeks which was unusual but not unprecedented now that he'd taken to travelling again. There was an envelope in his handwriting among the mail but when she picked it the thickness of it made her heart drop. It would only need a sentence to say he'd be with her on Friday evening. The envelope was odd too, coarser than he normally used and scuffed as if it had been a long time in the post.

268

On board ship.
29 June 1915.

Dearest, dearest Isa,
I'm sorry that you should hear from me like this, but I'm afraid there's no help for it. I didn't tell you at the time, but back in the spring – when it was clear this business was going to go on much longer than we'd all expected – I got in touch with a friend of mine about joining a volunteer outfit. Perhaps I should have told you, but I was by no means sure that anything would come of it.

Much to my surprise, things have suddenly started moving fast. I'm afraid I'm not allowed to tell you very much more than that. If anybody should ask about me, please tell him or her that I am away at training camp. I shall be in touch with you as soon as I can, but if you don't hear for a matter of months, or even longer, please, please, try not to worry.

Look after the garden. Did you remember to order more fritillaries for the Pleasaunce? Do get Will to plant them in drifts rather than squares – you know what he's like if left to himself. The best thing is to just throw handfuls around and get him to plant them where they fall. I'll enjoy picturing you under the apple trees, pelting poor Will with fritillary bulbs.

In all seriousness now, I think you should have a talk with Marius. The word in London is that if this thing drags on into next year, they'll be introducing compulsory call up. A lot of lads of around his age are volunteering now to get a chance at the better regiments.

Please give Petra my love. I'm glad she's enjoying lawn tennis. Please take her to Hereford in the holidays and buy her a new racquet from me. I shall be thinking of her, and of you, somewhere in my mind every waking moment.

Oh my darling, I am so very sorry. I'd have given the world for things to have been different for all of us. Who knows, on the other side of this thing they may come out right after all. Above all, keep loving me. I love you with all my heart.

Philip

They were somewhere in the Eastern Mediterranean, Philip knew that much, steaming slowly eastwards with Crete somewhere behind them and Cyprus a long way up ahead. There was no land visible and, with no wind to speak of, the steam from their funnels clung round them so that it was like travelling through the inside a huge pearl – as if destination, purpose, personal identity didn't matter and would never matter again. That was probably just as well because he'd have been hard put to it to answer questions about any of them, beyond that he was sitting on a bit of deck the sailors didn't seem to need for the moment, under a large gun on the port side, reading a guide book to New York and that the labels on the luggage down in his sleeping berth said his name was Hiram P. Jefferson. Even the knowledge that he'd be stopping – only for a day or two – at Cyprus came from what a slick-haired colonel had said back in the second floor office at Whitehall.

'We'll get you as far as Cyprus, old boy, and by

then we'll have sorted something out.'

It had been back in the spring that Philip had made contact with a friend from college days, now a major in a not particularly fashionable regiment. News of heavy fighting in Ypres and the Dardanelles was beginning to come through and it was dawning on even the optimistic that the war might drag on to a second Christmas or even beyond. He'd been at one of his own low points when it seemed to him that all his life had been a mess and a waste. The idea of handing over responsibility for his unsatisfactory life to the war had made a kind of sense to him when nothing much else did. The friend had written back saying he'd see what he could do, but not holding out much hope because of Cordell's advanced age. Forty-two, as it happened. Then everything had gone quiet for two months until, out of the blue, he got a polite note requesting him to present himself at the War Office at 11.30 on a morning in early June. He expected to wait around for hours in room crammed with other would-be volunteers but to his considerable surprise he was shown politely to the lift and told that Colonel Meredith expected him. Even more surprised when the Colonel said 'We gather you're by way of being a bit of an expert on the Pontic mountains.'

An oncocyclus iris, poised like a butterfly on a patch of gravel, darted into his mind.

'Not an expert, exactly. I've been out there four or five times.'

'Good enough.'

Then, having asked for and got a dazed

assurance from Philip that this wouldn't go beyond these four walls, the Colonel stood up, grabbed a wooden pointer from his desk and gave a brusque lecture, prodding his bright new maps like a farmer chivvying cows.

'Dardanelles. Key, absolutely key. Dominate those, get our ships into the sea of Marmara and you've got Constantinople in your pocket. Black Sea ports all open for our Russian allies, we're free to concentrate on beating the Germans out of France and Belgium.'

He looked at Philip as if expecting argument, got none. All Philip was thinking was that it was six hundred miles or more from the beaches of the Dardanelles to the Pontic Mountains, so he had no idea where this was leading.

'Now, things are going very well for us in the Dardanelles, very well,' the Colonel said. 'However, even when things are going well you need to watch your back. And where is our back?' The pointer rapped, tap tap tap, just to the south of the Black Sea on the Pontic mountains. 'There. Enemy brings men up from Anatolia and sneaks up on us over the mountains from the east.'

Philip said, his mind catching up as far as it ever would, 'Difficult country to take an army through.'

The Colonel's eyes gleamed. 'Exactly. Local knowledge, that's what we need.'

Philip thought that if they'd brought him in just to confirm that the Pontic Mountains were mountainous, some of the stories he'd heard about the War Office might even be true. That was before Colonel Meredith dropped his

272

pointer back on the desk, lowered himself into his chair and leaned towards him, voice suddenly quiet, almost intimate.

'Of course, it's not something we could order anybody to take on. Even if you were serving with us, it's not something we could *order* you to take on.'

36

For the first time, Isabelle wished she were labelled 'Cordell's wife,' like a tidy plant with its identity acknowledged and place in the flower bed staked out. Now that she needed desperately to find out all he hadn't told her in his letter – where he was, what he was doing, whether he was in danger – the lack of that label meant she had no standing where it mattered. In the first wild few weeks after his letter arrived she thought about nothing else, hardly eating or sleeping. She wrote to the War Office, first a civil letter asking if they knew where she might address letters to her friend Mr Philip Cordell, believed to be somewhere at sea, then when she got no reply, an angry letter and finally a telegram. This produced two sentences on official notepaper regretting that it was not the practice to give information on personnel to anybody but close family members. She had friends in London to whom her relationship with Philip was an open secret. She wrote to them, asking if they knew anything,

273

begging them to speak to anybody who might help. It puzzled her that the answers came back slowly and her friends seemed almost indifferent to the trouble that was obsessing her, until about a month after she'd received Philip's letter a note came from a friend that shocked her into understanding.

Church Street.
August 17 1915.

Dear Isabelle,
I'm sorry not to have answered. Can hardly write or think. We heard last week that Charles is dead in France. His colonel says he died bravely leading his men – hopes that will be some consolation to us. What the hell do they know about consolation? I'm sorry. Janine.

She remembered Charles as a clumsy but likeable lad with his mother's round face and plump cheeks, liable to blush as red as a geranium when any woman spoke to him. No more than a boy. Not even twenty-one, surely, because he'd been born the year after... He was younger than Marius. The thought of it sent her spinning to the window, then across the hall into the library, then upstairs to his room.

'Marius. Marius, where are you?'

He opened his door and looked out, in shirtsleeves, hair rumpled.

'What's up?'

'What are you doing, darling?'

'Reading some of my confounded law books.

274

Did you want me for something?'

He'd finished at Oxford two months ago. In the autumn he'd start eating his dinners at the Inner Temple, on his way to becoming a barrister.

'No darling. Just wondered where you were, that's all.'

Back in the small drawing room she got out her fountain pen and business notepaper.

Until his mother disturbed him, Marius had been lying on the bed smoking. He picked up the slimmest of his pile of law books and wandered down to the library, intending to put in an hour's reading until lunchtime. It was a room nobody used much, green blinds pulled halfway down to keep the sun from fading the book spines. He read a paragraph, re-read it, wondered whether the law was a good idea after all, lit another cigarette. The door opened and Megan walked in. He'd been keeping his distance from her ever since the incident of the perfume spray. He pretended not to notice her, assuming she'd find whatever she'd come in for and go. Instead, she walked up and stood beside his chair like an equal.

'Enjoy London, did you?'

He'd been up in town for a few days the previous week, looking for rooms.

'Yes thank you.'

He tried to make his tone dismissive but he couldn't keep his eyes from the smooth swell of her breasts under the blue cotton bodice.

'I like London too. I've got quite a lot of friends up there now.'

As if it had anything to do with him. He tore his eyes away from her breasts and looked down at the floor. Slim ankles in sleek white stockings rising out of shoes softer and more elegant than a maid should wear.

'I've got a friend works with the Petersons.'

The family he'd been staying with in London.

'Oh.'

'Says you went out to a party with them. I got a letter from him yesterday.'

He wanted to say something angry about servants' gossip, but from the way she was looking at him he knew there was more to come.

She said, 'I hope it didn't spoil the party, what those girls did.'

Then she seemed to notice something on a little table and, to his relief, stepped away from him. The relief didn't last long.

'Terrible carelessness.' She imitated the little tongue clicking sound the housekeeper made when she found something out of place, picked up something from the table. 'Must have fallen off when somebody was dusting.'

She walked past him towards the door. As she went, she opened her hand and let something flutter down on him. A feather. Not white this time, but grey and bedraggled from a feather duster. By the time he realised what it was, the door had closed behind her.

Petra was down in the Pleasaunce, filling a sack with sphagnum moss. When she had two or three sacks full she'd drive them down in the pony cart to the collection point in the yard of The Sun,

276

where they'd join many more sackfuls collected by the village schoolchildren. Then somebody would take them to Abergavenny and they'd be put on the train for Cardiff. At Cardiff mounds of moss from hundreds of villages would be dried, disinfected, baled up and shipped over to France as wound dressings. To Petra, it seemed like one of those jobs invented to keep children quiet and out of the way – or seventeen-year-old girls from Cheltenham Ladies College come to that. She couldn't imagine the moss doing any good to wounds. She pitied the little fleshy fronds as she tore them up. They were almost un-believably delicate in shape and colouring, shading from bright green at the top to pale rose pink lower down. Progress was slow because she kept stopping to rescue small snails with translucent shells that were clinging to the moss until it occurred to her that it was wrong to be concerned with the lives of snails when men not much older than she was were dying, so she stuffed the handfuls in regardless for a while, snails and all. Then she thought it wasn't the snails' fault and grubbed in the sack to find them, losing more time. Above her and further along the bank Evan cleared brambles with a sickle so that she could get at the moss easily.

'Rabbit.'

He shouted from up on the bank, looking down through a gap in the brambles.

'Yes, I know. It doesn't matter. Just leave it there.'

Even to think of the White Rabbit made her angry. She rubbed the midge bites on her exposed neck. Her hair was ridiculously short. She'd spent some of the summer term in the sanatorium with chickenpox and it had to be cropped for coolness when she was feverish. It was growing again but in thickness rather than length so that it topped her square and serious face with a pale brown thatch, like a Roundhead in a child's illustrated history. Isabelle worried for her sake and sent away for all kinds of shampoos and lotions, but Petra had almost come to like it as far as she liked anything about her appearance.

Evan cleared the last patch of brambles with a few expert swipes and came to kneel beside her, tearing companionably at the moss.

She asked, 'Any news of Trefor?'

'No letters for a while, but Auntie Bath says no news is good news. We're hoping he might be home on leave soon.'

Trefor had joined up almost as soon as the fighting started and was somewhere in France. His letters home were painstakingly copied by his sister Sarah and sent to Will and Bathsheba.

'I've been thinking about him,' Petra said. It was true. She'd thought about him every day when the girls in her dormitory were talking about their brothers in the army and navy. 'He didn't have to join, did he? They need miners as much as they need soldiers.'

'Trefor wasn't a miner. He wanted to be, but after that fight when he got his head broken open, nobody would take him on. They said he was a trouble maker.'

'You should have told me. My mother could

have given him a job.'

He looked at her. 'It was her manager gave him the sack in the first place.' Then hastily, seeing her expression. 'She wouldn't have known anything about it. They leave it all to the managers.'

She turned away, feeling sick from the effort of not showing him her anger. The need to hide her feelings had been there as long as she could remember. Life at boarding school had reinforced it.

'We can't get much more in this sack. Let's take it over and put it in the lane with the other one.'

She stood up. Without needing to discuss it they took the short cut up the bank and into the field, pushing and pulling the sack through a gap in the hedge. They walked across the sheep pasture, sack in his outside hand, inside hand almost touching hers.

He said, 'I'll be seventeen next month. I think I'll join up. If I do it soon enough they might put me in the same regiment as Trefor.'

She felt as if all the wet weight of the moss had been crammed into her chest. They went on in silence but she guessed there was still something he wanted to say. He made several false starts then, 'You remember four years ago, just before Trefor got hurt...?'

It still came to him sometimes in nightmares, the picture of the body sinking under his stones. Now he was going away from the garden, perhaps for a long time, it was only fair to the body to tell somebody else the secret. Petra was the only one who might understand and not

279

blame him. She was waiting for him to go on when they heard a motorbike engine rising to a whine as it tackled the steep pitch of the lane. A man's head appeared above the hedge, leather-cased in a helmet, disappeared as the lane dipped. Then the engine stopped suddenly.

'It's our cottage he's going to,' Evan said. 'It's about Trefor.'

He dropped the sack and ran.

37

Bathsheba was in the garden picking runner beans. After one horrified glance at the oncoming leather helmet she ran inside and called Will. By the time he'd got his boots on, the latch on the garden gate had clicked and leather helmet was walking up the path to the back door.

'Are you the owner of those horses, sir?'

Will didn't recognise the accent. The man came from Worcestershire and was conscious of being outside his own country, so stiff and curt. When he pulled the helmet off, the hair under it was dark and slick with sweat. He had a neat triangle of moustache, like a brown moth perched under his nostrils.

'Horses?'

Being called 'sir' made Will even more confused.

'In the orchard. Grey, roan mare, bay.'

'Nothing wrong with them, is there?'

He'd been down to see them at first daylight as usual, feeding them crusts from his breakfast before starting work. Best crust to Pont, out of habit, with Jack the Lad nuzzling at his pockets, grey one-eyed Guto hanging back, fearful of kicks from the younger horse.

'Can we go down and look at them, sir.'

Will looked at Bathsheba but got no guidance. He was dimly aware of Evan running up the path, white-faced.

'Auntie Bath, is it Trefor?'

She shook her head, lips pressed together. She and Evan stood watching, side by side, as Will and the man walked across the field to the old orchard. Somewhere along the way, from a few formal words that the man said, it sank into Will's amazed mind that he was there on behalf of the War Office and they needed horses.

'For the mines?' he asked, heart sinking. When the man said 'No, in France,' Will went quiet, not understanding at all. Or not letting himself understand. When they got to the gate at the orchard the three horses came shambling up to them, muzzles thrusting at Will's pockets. For once, he pushed them away.

'Guto. Over twenty he is. Only got one eye, see, and can hardly trot, he's so stiff.'

Alarmingly, the man had produced a notebook and pencil from his jacket pocket and was writing.

'Pont's not much better. That's the mare. Might not look so bad now, but she loses condition that fast in winter.'

Will was pleading. Jack the Lad, not used to

281

being ignored, had refused to be pushed away and had his neck over the gate, the whiskers under his chin practically touching the notebook. The man looked up.

'What about this fellow?'

'Just her foal, that is.'

A long way past foalhood, with all a young horse's strength and confidence, Jack the Lad had a gleam on him from the good summer grass. He breathed delicately on the pages of the notebook and registered it as non-edible.

'How old is he?'

'Rising nine, must be.'

The words came reluctantly, with Will feeling like betrayer in saying them.

'Gelded?'

Will nodded. The decision had cost him some regret five springs ago, but you couldn't have old Pont getting pregnant by her own son.

'Broken to saddle or harness?'

A ray of light here at least. Jack the Lad was as innocent of bit or traces as the first horse in Eden.

'Not either.'

'A good looking horse like that. Why not?'

Will said nothing. In spite of his attempts to keep Jack the Lad at a distance his hand had gone automatically to the horse's muzzle, feeling the soft bottom lip nuzzling his wrist, the warm exhalations of breath on his palm. The man looked at them both, wrote some more. Jack made out the words 'bay gelding, 9, 15hh' and his world went cold. When the man asked him for his name and address he gave them like a prisoner in the dock.

'Thank you, Mr Thomas. You'll be hearing from us. Not the two old ones of course, but the bay should be some use.'

Will made a last desperate attempt, the nearest he'd ever get to eloquence. 'But he's not trained to it, sir. He's hardly been outside this field in his life.'

The man looked at him, buttoning his pocket flap over the notebook.

'There are a lot of people having to do things they've never done, Mr Thomas.'

They walked in silence back to the cottage. As the motorbike spluttered away down the lane Bathsheba asked what that was all about.

'Jack the Lad. They want to take Jack the Lad away to France.'

'That's a relief. We thought it was bad news he was coming with, didn't we Evan?'

It was even worse then, knowing that if Bathsheba didn't understand, nobody else would.

38

August 1915

The Aegean off Cape Helles was exactly the effect Philip had wanted in the iris border, intense sapphire-purple out to sea, shading to deep blue, then lighter patches towards the land that were the cool silver-green of iris leaves. He thought of that to take his mind off the heat and the noise of the guns. The land was almost dissolved in the heat haze. You could make out the hilltops on the Gallipoli peninsula, but not the narrow opening to the right of them, leading from the Aegean into the sea of Marmara. The flat area further to the right was the Plain of Troy, where Hector had fought Achilles. Now the Turks had their guns there, firing across the narrow stretch of water to the British positions on the other side. The thumping of the shells had been going on since daylight so that the sea and the land, which looked less solid than the sea, were vibrating with it. To Philip's right, and closer to land, two cruisers like his own were firing at the Turkish guns. In the rare quiet intervals between the big guns you could hear the distant crack of rifle fire from the peninsula. Big push going on there, everybody knew that. He and the sailors had watched the day before as the troopships went past, heat-reddened faces above rows of khaki lining the rails. Once the guns were dealt with, the Navy would sail through the Narrows, up the Sea of Marmara and through the Bosporus into the Black Sea. If that happened, the war might be over in a matter of months. It seemed a reasonable belief that all those troopships, all those guns, would have the Navy through within hours. Only that was also what it had looked like in March when the Dardanelles campaign started, and this was the sixth of August. Whatever the Colonel back in Whitehall had said about things going well in the

284

Dardanelles, once Philip got to Cyprus and beyond it was clear to even to a man of his non-existent military experience that they weren't. He understood it from looks and silences rather than anything said. From the expressions on the sailors' faces when the hospital ships went past, heading westwards. From the silence that fell round the ward room table when a young officer made an unwise joke about visiting the harems in Constantinople. From the way the thin man in the office back in Cyprus hadn't, at the end, been able to meet his eyes.

It had been different at the start of the interview. That was back in July and Philip was still adjusting to being on land after two weeks at sea. They talked over coffee about the situation in the Pontic Mountains. The man assumed that Philip had been told in London what was going on there but seemed only mildly surprised when it turned out that he hadn't.

'We're relying on our Russian allies to keep Johnny Turk occupied in the east while we look after Constantinople. Devilish scrap last winter round Sarikamis and now the Russians are pushing them westwards towards Erzurum inland and Trebizond on the Black Sea coast. That's the Turks' main naval base. We reckon they could have fifty thousand men there. You know both places, I gather.'

'I know Erzurum quite well.' It had been his headquarters on two plant hunting trips. 'I've only spent a day or two in Trebizond.'

'So you're more of a mountain man? The thing is, Cordell, we've got a man in a village not far from Trebizond looking after the coast for us. Tea merchant, his father was an Armenian and you know what they think of the Turks. Sends regular shipments to Constantinople, knows all the boat owners along the coast. But he's not a mountain man, you see. Never been up there at all.'

Philip said, 'I see.' He was beginning to.

'We want to know what's going on up in the mountains. It's one thing our Russian allies telling us what they're doing, Erzurum by the week after next and so forth, but we need to know for sure.'

'So you want me to get up into the mountains and find out if the Russians are winning?'

When he said it, it sounded so crazy he expected the thin man to laugh and say he'd misunderstood. But the man was nodding, a series of quick little bobs over the rim of the water glass, like a bird drinking.

'But if I do find out, how do I let you know?'

'Through our friend. When you, or rather when Mr Hiram P. Jefferson gets to the village, he'll make contact with him. If Mr Jefferson finds any interesting plant specimens in his wanderings through the mountains, he'll naturally hurry back down and entrust them to our friend who'll forward them with an urgent shipment of tea to Constantinople.'

'But Constantinople is...'

'Turkish? Yes, that had not escaped our notice. Don't worry. There will be arrangements to get Mr Jefferson's specimens safely home as soon as possible.'

When Philip said, after only a few seconds,

'How do I get to this place?' the man was obviously pleased at his eagerness, not knowing that when you're through the looking glass, one question is as good as another.

'We'll put you off at Izmit, or as near it as we can get you. We'll give you a corporal to go with you as Mr Jefferson's manservant. A very good man who knows a bit about Johnny Turk. From Izmit, you'll have to make your own way overland to the mouth of the River Sakarya on the Black Sea coast. Our friend will have a boat waiting to take Mr Jefferson and his manservant to the village.'

There was more. A roll of gold Marie Theresa dollars for which Philip duly signed, the address of an outfitter near the waterfront who'd been instructed to supply Mr Jefferson with spare boots, binoculars, a pistol and a good thick overcoat.

'Overcoat?'

It was so hot in the room that even the flies in the window could hardly summon up the energy to buzz.

'I gather it can get pretty cold in the mountains in winter.'

'I'm... I mean, Mr Jefferson will be spending the winter there?'

The man was carefully turning his cup and saucer round on his blotter, as if intent on making a perfect circle.

'It might take a little while to get you out.' Then, hastily, 'But don't worry, there'll be British warships in the Black Sea by Christmas.' That was when he didn't meet Philip's eye.

Philip stayed by the rail most of the afternoon, watching the ships firing at land quivering from vibration and heat haze, smelling the smoke from the guns. It puzzled him that their cruiser was making no attempt to move up and join the ones doing the firing but he assumed it was all part of somebody's plan. The thin man had spoken airily of putting him and Corporal Finch ashore at Izmit. It was at the end of an inlet off the eastern end of the Sea of Marmara and from there it seemed a reasonable enough journey over the hills to the Sakarya River and the Black Sea. The problem was that Izmit was on the enemy's side of the contested Narrows, with at least a hundred miles of Turkish-held sea to sail through before anybody could be put ashore. It was the Navy's job to get him there and he hadn't liked to trouble the remote and preoccupied captain with questions, but he didn't see how it could be done. In late afternoon, with the sun half way down to the sea, Corporal Finch appeared. He was in civilian clothes, light sand-coloured trousers and jacket, white shirt and brown tie, but walked unmistakably like a soldier and stood when he spoke in the stiff way that soldiers called 'at ease' but had nothing easy about it.

'Captain Webster's compliments, sir, and will you join him by the port rail.'

Philip had hoped to spend some of the voyage getting to know Corporal Finch. It looked as if they'd be living for several months at least in enemy territory with nobody but each other to depend on and it would be useful if they liked or at least tolerated each other. But the rigid hierarchy of life on a Royal Navy ship meant they might as well be in different towns. Philip shared a cabin with an officer, while Finch had a hammock with the sailors slung somewhere deep down in the ship. If the two of them happened to run into each other on deck, Finch's arm would twitch towards a salute, then he'd remember that he wasn't in uniform and Philip wasn't really an officer anyway and he'd look unhappy and clamp his arm back at his side.

'Something happening at last then, Finch?'

'Sir?'

The man was ill at ease with the informal tone. Philip sighed and followed him to the other side of the ship. Captain Webster and one of his officers were standing by the rail, silhouetted against the low red sun.

'Your taxi has arrived, Cordell.'

Philip realised that the captain was smiling because he was about to get rid of him. He moved to the rail and looked down. At first he didn't even know what he was seeing. An enormous metal cigar half sunk in the water with a squat iron turret rising from the middle of it, the White Ensign flying from a stubby pole you could hardly call a mast and several sailors in uniform standing beside it, looking up and smiling for all the world as if the thing were a proper ship. From the deck where Philip was standing a new rope ladder with wooden rungs went from a gap where a rail had been taken a long way down to the thing in the water.

'I've sent a man below to bring up your kit,' the

captain said cheerfully. 'Commander Nasmith's ready for you.'

Philip and Finch looked at each other and the corporal gave a great grin, some of the formality of shipboard swept away in his delight.

'I've never been on a submarine, have you sir?'

39

Isabelle's motor car, a black Wolseley, had been standing under tarpaulins in the carriage house most of the summer because petrol was hard to get. On the last Monday in August the man from the next village down the road who understood motors started the engine and drove it out to the sweep of gravel in front of the house. Isabelle stood watching from the steps, swathed in brown dustcoat, chamois leather gloves and straw hat with a driving veil. From one step further up Marius watched impatiently, groaning when the man who understood motors steered too close to the carriage house door and had to reverse.

'I told you you should have let me do it.'

When the car drew up at the bottom of the steps Isabelle waited while the man got out, leaving the engine running, then walked down and took his place in the driver's seat. Marius took the front passenger sear, reluctantly. They'd had an argument over breakfast because he'd wanted to drive but Isabelle wouldn't give in.

'I don't want you arriving tired, darling. We

need you to make a good impression on Mr Gladwyn.'

He'd only grunted at that, not seeing why he should worry about making any kind of impression on a man who was, after all, his mother's employee. But it was an important occasion, when Marius was going to visit Penyrheol colliery for the first time as an adult, so he'd given in, though sulkily.

Isabelle called, above the noise of the engine, 'Has anybody seen Petra?'

Petra, at the side of the carriage house, pushed a brown-wrapped package into Evan's hands.

'Happy birthday.'

She'd seen him at work trimming the Virginia creeper on the side of the carriage house and run back upstairs for his present. The creeper hadn't needed trimming. Evan had given himself an excuse to watch the motor car starting, yearning as much as Marius to be in the driving seat. Even now, only half his attention was on Petra.

'Shall I give your love to Wales?'

He nodded. She ran towards the motor car, still like a schoolgirl on the playing field rather than a young lady of seventeen, weight forward, legs driving from the hip, feet scattering the gravel. Evan waited until the engine sound had died away then undid the clumsy knots in the white kitchen string and peeled back the brown paper. A rectangular case in shining black leather. Inside, silver cylinders and keys in a nest of blue velvet. A new clarinet. The name embossed on the case told him it was one of the best available. He knew from looking in a music shop on a visit to Cardiff how much it must have cost. He snapped the case shut as if the thing might try to escape and stood staring in the direction she had gone.

They stopped on the way to take in petrol for the motor car and glasses of lemonade for themselves. They were all three hot and covered in pale dust from the roads. Marius stood watching the attendant pumping petrol into the tank while Petra paced up and down holding her hat in one hand, running the other through her hair. Still short hair. None of the shampoos and lotions seemed to have made any difference. In fact, looking carefully, it seemed to Isabelle that they'd had a reverse effect and the hair was even shorter than before. Isabelle was going to call her over to ask why, then found she was too scared. Scared of her own daughter. Ridiculous, yet the fear had been growing for some time. Petra was seventeen now. Isabelle had been only a few years older when she'd done something that burst on the family like a grenade, eloping with an artist who was half a foreigner. Nobody had better reason to know the explosive potential of young women. But Petra wasn't like her. Isabelle at Petra's age had hair that streamed all the way down her back, two proposals of marriage from eligible men already rejected, a reputation as a beauty. It wasn't that Petra was ugly. Simply, she didn't seem to care. So what did she care about instead? Painting? Learning languages? Lawn tennis? Surely none of those would account for the intensity she sensed in Petra. It was recognising the intensity but not knowing what it was for that scared her.

Evan showed Will the clarinet when they were packing up their tools after a morning of trimming and weeding in the paeony borders. The paeonies themselves were long faded and their plush seedpods clipped away but the flowers of late summer had taken over from them: white and gold lilies, blue flowered salvias, blue-green cushions of rue frothing into yellow flowers.

Will said, 'Why would Miss Petra be giving you a thing like that?'

'Because she knows I'll be going away. I think it's to take with me.'

This was the first time he'd told his uncle, even indirectly, that the decision was taken and that he was going to volunteer, to try to be with his brother.

'What you done with the little hoe, boy? Is that it on the step down there?'

Fetching it, Evan noticed that the waterlilies were in full flower, white, pink and yellow, almost covering the surface of the pond.

Silas Gladwyn, pit manager, sat at his office desk. Behind him, through the sparkling clean glass of a big window, the winding wheel bringing up the pit cages turned in the sun. The floor to ceiling bookcase to his right was loaded with bound volumes of reports and technical works, Proceedings of the South Wales Institute of Engineers, Returns of Trials of Coal recently made by the Admiralty, accident reports by Her Majesty's Inspector of Mines. The coffee cups were best bone china, fern patterned, kept for the owner's visits. Isabelle finished her coffee, put down the cup on the desk.

'As I see it, it would be very much like being a pupil in a barrister's office. He'd work with you, learn from you then take over the management of Eastside or Victory whenever you thought him ready for it.'

Marius, sitting to the side of them and watching Mr Gladwyn's face, thought, 'He doesn't like it, but there's damn all he can do about it.'

The manager turned his head and gave him a glance, held just a second too long to be polite, that seemed to say, 'Don't be too sure about that.' Then, turning back Isabelle, 'I quite agree with you, Mrs Allegri. There's everything to be said for a young man becoming acquainted with the family business.'

Isabelle, sensing opposition through the politeness, said: 'More than acquainted. Marius wants to be useful and he could be more use here than in France.'

She and Silas Gladwyn respected each other, disagreed from time to time although always stopping short of outright quarrelling. Sometimes he won, sometimes she did, and they'd both learned to recognise the silent moment when one or other of them gave way.

'If it's useful we're talking about, Mrs Allegri, he might help me look after the transportation side of things. Do you know much about railways, Mr Allegri?'

Before Marius could answer, Isabelle said firmly, 'He can learn.'

It had been clear from the moment they arrived that Mr Gladwyn didn't know what to do about Petra. After some embarrassment, he installed her in his secretary's office with her own pot of coffee and a month old copy of *Punch* some visitor had left behind. Petra sipped the coffee and scowled at *Punch*. Then on an impulse, when the secretary was answering the telephone, she stood up and walked out. The corridor outside was covered with brown linoleum that made a tack-tack sound when she walked on it, past rooms where colliery clerks were working shirt-sleeved, perched on high stools. At the end of the corridor, double doors stood open to the pit-head. A steam locomotive pulling empty wagons ground slowly on shining tracks past piles of pit props. She stepped outside, heart lurching at the sight of the great winding wheel, imagining the shaft at the foot of it going down into darkness. She'd have liked to go closer but was scared both of the darkness itself and of annoying the men working there, so turned across the yard and past the clanging repair shop and blacksmith's furnace to the gates. Once through the gates she turned and looked back. There was an arch of wrought iron over them with the words PENYRHEOL COLLIERY 1882. Under it, in smaller letters, her grandfather's name, W Turner. She turned her back on it and saw the rows of houses opposite, as close packed on the hillside as rows of butterfly eggs on a leaf. She jumped back to get out of the way of a tramcar going past then crossed the main road and started walking at random up one of the streets that ran at right angles to it. There was a pavement of brown sandstone slabs, dark and gritty from coaldust, white scrubbed doorsteps leading directly off it, each one a little higher than the one before. The house windows were mostly covered with clean white net curtains. At the top of the street where another road cut across at right angles, Petra stopped and looked down at the valley. There were three pitheads and three sets of chimneys and winding gear directly below her and more than she could count further off, up and down the valley. The big wheels were spinning in the sunshine, a train loaded with coal carts clanking down the valley, white steam rising. There was a buzz that she mistook at first for the blood in her ears pounding from the climb until she realized it was the whole valley humming with the work of cutting darkness into chunks and hauling it out into the light. A woman was walking up the street with a child hanging onto one hand, a bag in the other. It was a string bag, bulging with potatoes and a big leafy cabbage. The woman was bare headed, wearing a black skirt and paisley shawl, looking not much older than Petra herself. On an impulse, when they got near each other Petra said good morning in Welsh. The woman looked startled but replied politely, gave Petra a curious look and walked on. Petra could hear the child asking a shrill question, also in Welsh, and from the way the mother was shushing it, Petra guessed the question was about her and wasn't polite. Still, she didn't mind. She was too full of amazement at having touched even in a small way the life of somebody living in this purposeful place. She thought, 'They all know what they're doing here' and the thought made her both excited and sad. She walked down, crossed the main road and found herself back at the gates with her grandfather's name.

'What in the world did you think you were doing?'

The petrol station again on the way home, late afternoon by now, cups of tea at the place with the petrol pump instead of lemonade. Isabelle was too pleased with the result of the interview with Mr Gladwyn to be angry with Petra, but she'd had a bad shock when she came out and found her missing.

'I told you, just looking.'

The memory of the young woman saying good morning to her was a warm secret, not to be shared. Instead she said, 'Have you ever been inside one of those houses?'

'Of course I have. I remember your grandfather showing me round the first one he had built when I was a lot younger than you are. He was very proud of them.'

'Why didn't he build them bigger?'

Marius made a derisive noise.

Isabelle said, 'They couldn't have fitted everybody in if they'd made them bigger, darling.' Then, laughing, 'You don't think one of them will do for your brother?'

'What?' Marius yelped, spilling tea over his trousers. 'You don't expect me to live in one of those?'

'Of course not. We'll find you rooms with Mr Gladwyn or one of the other managers.'

'Can't I borrow the car and drive over from home?'

'Later perhaps, darling. But there will be a lot to learn at first and the men respect you more if you live on the spot.'

Another of her father's dictums. Petra stared at both of them.

'Why's Marius going to live there?'

'He'll be working, darling.'

'Isn't he going to join the army like Evan and everybody else?'

Marius stood up suddenly, rocking the flimsy table. There was a dark tea stain round his crotch.

'Don't you bloody start attacking me too. I've had enough of it.'

He stamped over to the car, flung the door open and sat down in the front passenger seat, leaving Isabelle too surprised to rebuke him for swearing.

'Petra, could you please try to be a little understanding with your brother. You can surely see he's going through a difficult time.'

'Why? Why should he stay here if everybody else has to go?'

Petra's grey eyes were staring into Isabelle's, like an equal. All through the girl's childhood, those eyes had given Isabelle a pleasurable jolt in the pit of her stomach every time she looked at them because they were so unlike her own, so like somebody else's. Only his had never looked at her in this hard, angry way. It caught her off balance so that she abandoned her carefully worked out defence of how somebody had to stay at home and get the coal out and how Marius was qualified in intelligence and family back-ground to do it. She appealed instead to her daughter as another woman, old enough now to understand.

'Darling, don't blame me. We might already have lost Philip to this awful war. They won't tell me where he is and he could be dead for all I know. You surely don't want me to sit back and let them take Marius as well.'

It was the first time she'd put into words the possibility that Philip might not come back. She expected Petra to look shocked or sorry, but the grey eyes were as angry as ever, lips clamped shut. When they opened at last it was to deliver five words so unexpected that Isabelle's brain wouldn't let them in at first.

'You're good at losing people.'

Stammering, Isabelle asked her what she meant, not wanting an answer, but Petra gave it.

'You lost my father. That didn't seem to worry you so much.'

'Darling, that's wicked. It's just not true. He left me. He left all of us. I waited and waited for him to come back, but he didn't.'

'Waited?'

'Not just waited. Philip spent hundreds of pounds on detectives.'

'Why? He didn't want him back.'

She's guessed, Isabelle thought. Why does it have to be here and now, at this rickety table by a petrol pump? Why not in the garden when he wanted it and they both loved me? In spite of her tiredness and hurt she tried again, trying to push down her fear, making her voice softer.

'Why do you think Philip didn't want him back, darling?'

'Because I saw Mr Cordell hit him. That summer. Just a few days before my father disappeared.'

'Petra darling, you must have imagined it. You were ill that summer, don't you remember? It was a bad dream and you've remembered it as if it happened, poor darling.'

'It wasn't only that.'

'What was it then. What else?'

Petra turned away, looking down at the concrete floor, the dusty hem of her skirt.

'What else? I wish you'd tell me.'

A parp from the car horn. Marius telling them to hurry up. Still without looking at her mother, Petra picked up her plain straw hat, walked over to the Wolseley and settled in the back seat. For the rest of the journey Isabelle drove so furiously that even Marius, who liked speeding, told her to slow down and be careful.

40

July 2001

It was still hot and close at eight o'clock in the evening, with piles of grey cumulus moving slowly in from Wales, the edges glowing gold as the sun slid down behind them. Kim had been restless all day, since reading the magazine piece. Over dinner of eggs and baked beans she told Colin she'd decided to add something to her photo project. She wanted to identify with his help, all the features referred to by the writer in 1915, and photograph them as they looked now.

'Imagine a panel of pictures with captions from that piece, the roses and giant lilies and so on, and now nothing but thistles and brambles. Somebody thought this garden was important enough to die for – actually to die for. And it's just gone as if it never existed.'

He knew the garden hadn't quite gone because it was talking to him, but she was listening to different voices.

'OK, tomorrow we'll take my plan and start going round.'

'Why not this evening? There's at least an hour of light left.'

'OK. Where?'

'The lily pool.'

...a small shady lake where the kingfisher may be

glimpsed on summer evenings. He hadn't dug there since she came up with a possible identity for the bones. He couldn't have explained why and she hadn't asked him. They walked up the field where bullocks dozed under the hedge, too languid from the heat to follow them. There was a sagging barbed wire fence between the bullocks' field and the willows. The place was still shady even though there was no pool to speak of any more. Alders and willows had grown tall and wild mint stayed fresh even in high summer. His excavations by the old stone terrace had made only a small gash in the green.

Kim said, 'Where did the pool go?'

'Silted up. I suppose they had to divert the stream, or partially dam it, to get a decent sized pool. Then when it was neglected the stream just went back to how it was before.'

'Where?'

He pointed to the right, where a swathe of meadowsweet and tall grasses ran between barbed wire fences.

'So how could the bones have got washed down to where you found them? I mean, if she'd had him buried by the gazebo and the stream brought them down, wouldn't they be over where the stream is now?'

He groaned to himself because there seemed to be no getting away from them.

'We don't know they're Allegri's bones. We don't know she buried him up by the gazebo. We don't know she buried him anywhere.'

She was walking round, occasionally looking through her viewfinder but he didn't hear the shutter clicking. So as not to crowd her, he started pulling trails of ivy off the stonework of the little terrace.

'Colin.' She was looking at something by the willows. 'The backpacker's been here.'

'How do you know?'

She pointed at the patch of bare mud.

Footprints, sharp and fresh looking, the imprint of a Vibram sole with the diamond pattern trademark in the middle.

'It doesn't have to be the backpacker,' he said.

'Who else would come here?'

They stared at each other. She said, 'Supposing it's somebody who knows about him.'

'Look, Allegri was born in eighteen hundred and something...'

'1863.'

'OK, that would make him 138 years old if he'd lived and this grieving widow of yours couldn't be more than about ten years younger. Unless she's haunting the place in hiking boots.'

She didn't bother to reply, intent on measuring her own foot against one of the prints.

'I'm size five and it's bigger than that. Come over here.' She made him plant one of his size nines in the mud. 'Smaller than yours. So it could be either a man or a woman.'

'Brilliant, Holmes. So where does that get us?'

'Whoever it was would see you'd been digging.'

'So? Can we leave it before we get eaten alive by mozzies?'

The light was beginning to go, the footprints fading into the general dusk under the trees. They got back under the barbed wire fence and walked down the pasture. At the gateway she stopped and grabbed his arm.

'Did you leave your lamp switched on in your tent?'

'Of course not. It wasn't dark when... Oh God.'

'No, neither did I.'

In the dusk below them, one of the tents was glowing orange from a light inside.

41

Autumn 1915

The men came for Jack the Lad on a Tuesday morning near the start of September. Will was working on his own weeding between the flagstones of the terrace when he saw the six heads coming up the lane – two men's heads in flat khaki caps, four horses' heads. He straightened up, wiped on his corduroy trousers the old kitchen knife he'd been using for grubbing out groundsel seedlings and went into the lane to meet them. Each man rode one horse and led another by ropes attached to the headcollars. One of them, who looked no older than twenty or so, had corporal's stripes on his sleeve. He sat easily but not elegantly on a useful bay cob in his heavy army saddle. When he spoke it was in the local Hereford accent, friendly enough.

'You Mr Thomas, man with a bay gelding?'

Will nodded, his eyes on the horses. The two on

the leading ropes had got their noses down in the grass verge, eating. The second man, riding a grey with its ribs showing like a toast rack, swore and yanked on the rope.

'Where is 'e, then?'

Will gestured with his head, still not able to put what felt like a betrayal into words. The young corporal gave the end of the lead rope he was holding to the other man, slid out of the saddle then handed up the bay cob's reins to him as well, leaving him with all four horses. As Will led the corporal slowly along the garden path between rows of runner beans, he looked back and saw the other man going round and round in a slow swirl of shining heads and backs. There was a squeal, the thwack of a stick, more cursing.

Will found his voice, 'Where you taking them, then?'

'Down to the depot near Abergavenny.'

'Then?'

The corporal shrugged. 'Dunno. On a train to somewhere.'

'He's never even seen a train.' As if that, even now, could save the horse.

Another shrug. 'Most of 'em 'aven't. They'll learn.'

Jack the Lad was grazing with Pont and Guto on the other side of the field under a hawthorn tree with its berries just turning red. He pricked his ears and came ambling towards them. The corporal had a leather headcollar over his shoulder with a rope rolled up in a neat cylinder, army style. He unbuckled it and offered it to Will.

'You like to put it on 'im?'

305

They went through the gate. Will's hands fumbled with the thick new leather and brass buckle while Jack the Lad nuzzled at his pocket as usual. Not expecting this to happen today, Will didn't even have a crust of bread to give him.

'Looks a good one,' the corporal said.

Will wished with all his heart that the horse had one eye like Guro or creaked when he moved like Pont but Jack the Lad stepped out like a race-horse in the parade ring as Will led him out of the far gate and through another field into the lane.

''Old him there, just a minute.'

The corporal walked back up the lane, scrambled into the cob's saddle, took the leading rope of one of the other horses. Will waited by the gate, stroking Jack the Lad's nose, making calming sounds to him. 'Ssssh. Easy now. Easy.' The gelding had seen the other horses, was getting nervous and excited. The corporal came down the lane on the cob, leading the other horse on its near side. When he got level with Will he leaned down from the saddle and held out his right hand for the end of Jack the Lad's headcollar rope. Will hesitated, opened his mouth, closed it then handed over the rope as slowly as if his hand were pushing through water weed. When Jack the Lad felt the tug on the rope he turned his head to Will, as if to ask what was going on. By then the horse on the corporal's other side had started walking off down the lane. The corporal kicked his horse on to keep up with it, jerked on the headcollar rope to make Jack the Lad follow. The bay resisted, rolling his eyes, sweat breaking out along his neck.

'Come on, you bugger.' Still not unkindly, but a stronger jerk on the rope. Jack the Lad backed away, beginning to rear. The rope ran through the corporal's hand and he almost lost it, just grabbing the end of it. 'You bugger,' less kindly now. Jack tried to rear again but the corporal pulled hard on the end of the rope as he got his legs in the air, pulling him down suddenly so that he nearly overbalanced on the deep ruts in the lane. He whinnied, shrill and terrified. Pont's answering whinny came distantly from the meadow.

'He won't go.'

Will was almost beginning to hope, in spite of everything, when the other man and his two horses arrived from up the lane.

'I'll see to the bugger, shall I?'

The corporal nodded, face red and sweating. The other man bunched reins and leading rope into his left hand, lifted his right arm and brought his stick down onto Jack the Lad's rump. The impact sounded like a rifle shot. The horse screamed, terrified and uncomprehending. Will ran forward, protesting, 'You don't need to do that.' But before he could get the words out Jack the Lad was trying to canter away down the lane, with the corporal still hanging onto both head collar ropes and the other horse following at a fast trot. The other man and horse followed closely, so that if Jack the Lad got loose there was no chance of him doubling back. The two riders and five horses reached the end of the lane in a confused bunch, then sorted themselves out and turned for Abergavenny. Jack the Lad still resisted but another two thwacks from the stick sent him in the right direction, heading the group along the road at a hammering trot. Will stood, not moving, until Jack the Lad's tossing, panic-stricken head couldn't be seen above the hedges any more and the sound of hooves had died away. The last he heard was one shrill whinny from a long way along the road, and Pont answering.

Petra heard about it from Evan two days later. They were moss gathering again, this time near the upper reaches of the stream, before it went down into the hazel wood beside the house.

'Didn't you stop them? Didn't anybody try to stop them?'

She'd gone white with shock and anger. Evan knew Petra better than anybody and had become aware over the years of the anger coiled inside her, but it still scared him on the rare occasions when it got loose. She raged at him. 'You should have been there. I should have been there. Why didn't you tell me?'

He'd known she was fond of the horse, as of all animals, but had no idea he'd meant this much to her. Even if she could have explained that her pity and fury were for him because he'd be going soon, as much as for Jack the Lad, Evan wouldn't have believed it. It was all he could do to stop her hiking off to Abergavenny there and then to fetch the horse back. She gave in because he assured her – not knowing if it were true – that Jack the Lad would already have been taken on some-where else.

'I'll find out where then.'

She left Evan with a sack half full of moss and

308

went down to the house to find her mother. Since the argument by the petrol pump the two of them had been on terms of egg-shell politeness with each other. Isabelle was in the small drawing room, writing letters at her desk. When she turned to see Petra in the doorway, face pale and eyes glazed with tears, her heart leapt because the girl had chosen to come to her with whatever was making her unhappy. She could help her, comfort her, be reconciled. But Petra stood stiffly, arms at her side and almost to attention, not letting the tears fall.

'They've taken Jack the Lad away. You've got to get him back.'

Isabelle sighed. The task Petra was putting on her was about the least welcome she could have devised. Getting nowhere with the War Office had become a way of life since Philip went away. To be ordered to go through the same thing all over again filled her with defeat and weariness. Still, because that was what Petra wanted, she made a note of the details and said like one adult to another that she couldn't promise, but she'd see what she could do.

'Now darling, why don't you go upstairs and finish your packing? Mary's put your hockey skirts in the airing cupboard and Mrs Downs has done one of her ginger cakes for your tuck box.'

Petra was going back to Cheltenham next day for the start of the autumn term. When she'd gone upstairs, Isabelle went into the hall and picked up the recently installed telephone. She honestly tried but her heart wasn't in it and after several hours of holding on, getting cut off and being reconnected, she accepted defeat. Next day, she drove Petra to Hereford station with suitcases, tuck box and hockey stick in the back. On the platform, with the train getting up steam, she said, 'I'm sorry about the horse. I did try, but apparently they don't keep records of where they come from.'

'I see.'

Very coldly. Was it her mother or the War Office that Petra didn't believe?

It was time for the autumn tidy-up of the garden. Putting the garden to bed was what Philip called it. In his absence Will went through it conscientiously. From late September he had to do it without the help of Evan, called to join a training camp at Newport. Enoch Pugh wasn't a lot of use once the mornings started getting chill because of his rheumatism so mostly Will had to do it himself, apart from the old terrier curled up asleep under the wheelbarrow. He cleared the dying foliage from the paeony borders and mulched with dry leaf mould, shortened the sappy shoots of climbing roses so that the winter gales wouldn't whip them around or the snow lie heavy and tear them. The iris border needed the persistent couch grass teased out from between the fat rhizomes with the blade of a knife. He worked on through October and into early November, when the leaves had fallen from the apple trees. That gave him the chance to tie back the bare shoots in the tunnel to the orchard. When he made a bonfire of the prunings the column of smoke stood up blue-grey above the valley against a white sky. Next day he cleaned all the gardening tools, oiled the sickle and scythe, wrapped the blades in sacking and propped them against the wall of the toolshed. Back at the cottage he put his gardening boots away under the sink then got out a tin of Cherry Blossom and the pair of shoes he kept for best and polished them till they shone.

The recruiting sergeant was overworked and unimpressed. He worked in a makeshift office in a warehouse near Newport docks, so damp that the bright new recruiting posters kept peeling off the walls.

'How old are you, Mr Thomas.'

'Fifty-two, sir.'

'We're not taking anybody over forty-one.'

'Nothing wrong with me there's not, sir. Never missed a day's work in my life.'

'Know about horses, you say?'

'A bit, sir.'

No use for fighting, of course, but they needed good steady men behind the lines, checking supplies, moving the wagons up.

'Mules?'

They stared at each other. Will knew nothing about mules, neither did the sergeant.

'Are they much different?' asked Will at last.

'Don't suppose so. How old did you say you were?'

'Fifty-two.'

The sergeant cupped his hand to his ear. 'Darned cold's making me deaf. I thought you said forty-two. If it was forty-two, we might get you in.'

Will thought about it, then offered diffidently, 'Forty-two, sir?'

'Forty-two it is.' The sergeant pulled a pad of forms towards him. 'You a married man, Mr Thomas?'

'Yes sir.'

'Discussed this with your wife, have you?'

'Yes sir.'

Even if the sergeant had been able to eavesdrop on the conversation over the fireside between Bathsheba and Will a few nights ago it wouldn't have told him much, because the two of them had a way of understanding each other without more than a few words. When Bathsheba agreed with Will that it didn't seem right sitting around with all this going on, she knew where it was leading. Trefor and Evan were in her mind all the time and although she knew the three of them weren't likely to be together she still hoped that Will might somehow be able to protect them.

'Well, Mr Thomas, the next thing's a medical examination. If you'll go behind those screens over there and take your jacket and shirt off, the doctor will be with you in a minute or two.'

After all that, it was a surprise to Will to find himself back by his own fireside at night, raking off his right best shoes, flexing his toes while Bathsheba fretted about the hole he'd worn in his sock in just one day and hoped it hadn't been like that when the doctor saw him.

'So what did they say to you, then?'

'They're going to let me know.'

The envelope came three weeks later, at the start of December.

42

Christmas 1915/New Year 1916

Cheltenham Ladies College
Sunday 5 December 1915.

Dear Mother,
I've decided I shan't be coming home for Christmas. I've been invited by Auriel Stephens' family (you met Auriel last summer) to stay with them at their house near Manchester over the holidays. They're organising parties and things for poor children in the Manchester slums whose fathers are away fighting and I'll be helping them.

   Miss White says I have to have your written permission because of going away with Auriel's family at the end of term. She's writing to you about it.

   I hope everybody at Holders Hope is well.

   Best wishes from

Petra

Cheltenham Ladies College
4 December 1915

Dear Mrs Allegri,
I believe Petra is writing to ask your permission to spend Christmas with the Stephens family at

their home at Chorlton-cum-Hardy. The school approves of and encourages their 'Christmas Comfort' project and we are pleased that Auriel and her friends are showing concern for those less fortunate than themselves.

I'd like to take this opportunity to say how pleased we've all been with Petra's progress this term, particularly in the fields of domestic science and household management. In this her final year with us, she is developing into a mature and self-possessed young woman who I'm sure will be a comfort and credit to her family.

Yours sincerely

Susan White

Petra's dedication to the homely arts had come as a considerable surprise to her teachers. Through the autumn term she'd applied her formidable determination to mastering plain cooking, hygiene and household budgeting. Gradually the surprise faded to sympathetic understanding. The word among the teachers was that over the long summer holidays Petra must have met a young man. In the nature of events, this hypothetical young man would now be away fighting for his country and she was doing her part by preparing for marriage and home-making on his return. True, she was still young at seventeen but everything was moving faster with the war and there were Cheltenham ladies only a few years out of their schooldays already married to officers no older than they were. True also that, with the Allegri money behind her, Petra wasn't likely to spend much of

314

her own time straining beef broth or making parsley sauce but it was as well to be prepared for the servant problem. A new bride setting up her household once the war was over might find herself training cook-housemaids fresh out of the munitions factories. Altogether, Petra Allegri's judgement and behaviour couldn't be faulted.

'*Comfort to her family*.' Isabelle read the teacher's letter and threw it down on her dressing table. 'Not much comfort to me.'

Angry as well as hurt, she went downstairs to her writing desk and dashed off a formal note to Miss White, giving her permission. The announcement by Will Thomas, later in the day, that he'd joined the army was the last straw. He sent word up to her through the kitchen and the housekeeper that he wanted to speak to her. She assumed it was something to do with the garden and since Will wasn't good with words even at the best of times it took a long time for her to understand what he was trying to tell her.

'But you're too old!' He stared at his feet and said nothing. 'And what am I going to do about the garden?'

He told her, respectfully but in some detail, what would need to be done. He'd got it all straight and orderly in his mind, just as Philip had told him. At the end she said the thing that had been pounding in her mind.

'You're all leaving me. Everybody's leaving me.'

Will left two days later. By then Isabelle had recovered enough to pity Bathsheba, even though the woman's stoicism gave no sign of needing pity. She sent a note down to the cottage letting her know that she'd continue to pay Will's wages as a gardener all the time he was away. By now the idea of Christmas at Holders Hope was intolerable to her. Even Marius had let it be known that he'd only be visiting for a day or two because he was needed at the coal sidings. Isabelle spent a whole morning on the telephone, with increasing impatience. Every hotel in London seemed to be full to the roof with men home on leave. In the end the best she could do was a service flat off Cadogan Square, unexpectedly available for two weeks over Christmas and the New Year, with one bedroom plus a boxroom for a servant. She agreed to the exorbitant rent then sent notes to all her friends in London, accepting their invitations of lunches, dinners, theatre trips 'if you happen to be in town.' It was in her mind that if she spoke to enough people, somebody must have heard some news of Philip.

On December days the Black Sea looked its name, dark as coal cinders under a pale grey sky Philip had taken to walking on the hillside above the village in the hour before the light went, getting air into his lungs to last through another night of wood fire fug and tobacco smoke in the tea merchant's house. If he looked inland, damp slopes of tea plantations or bare hazel bushes ran up to a snowline that was creeping a little lower each day. A muddy track nicked the edge of the snowline then came to a stop. In summer it connected with the Zigana Pass, the old caravan route from Trebizond over the mountains to Erzurum, then on into central Asia. It was the way the Russian allies would come, pushing the Turks northwards to the Black Sea coast, westwards to Constantinople. According to the prediction Philip had been given, they should have been on the Black Sea coast long before winter snows closed the Pontic mountain passes. All through late summer and autumn the American plant hunter Hiram Jefferson and his English manservant Finch had been out in the mountains looking for any sign of the Russian advance. They slept out under rocks, found the occasional goat herd and quizzed him as best they could in sign language and Philip's rudimentary Turkish, spent hours sweeping the rocky landscape with field glasses. Once they had to kick out their cooking fire and dive for cover when a Turkish patrol came puffing up the pass, but the soldiers looked like new recruits, too breathless from marching to notice anything. On another occasion two officers had come on them without warning and shown what turned out to be an entirely innocent interest in their collection of roots and seeds. Philip summoned up enough Turkish to explain himself and answer a question or two about his theoretical home town of New York where everybody was a very rich man like him. Those were the two most exciting incidents in months of nothing to report – not a gun, Russian uniform or as much as a booted foot-print in all the miles of mountains. They'd go down to the village, taking packfuls of plants, bulbs and seeds with them to keep up their cover. Corporal Rob Finch got quite interested and set up a plant press, drying and mounting specimens

317

as neatly as if he'd been at Kew all his life. By the end of October, with the first snows on the Zigana Pass, it was clear that nothing could happen in their part of the world until the spring. While Finch worked with his plant press, Philip sat at the other end of the table by lamplight, carefully encoding the messages that amounted to the same thing – nothing. Still, he wasn't unhappy. Happiness or unhappiness had ceased to mean very much. You were somewhere and you stayed there until something happened, or didn't. He wouldn't have noticed Christmas if Finch hadn't cooked up a small pudding of currants, flour and goatmilk butter, served with a sprig of rosemary instead of holly. It tasted mostly of goat, but they ate it.

43

Isabelle spent the last evening of 1915 with friends, first a revue, then on to a late supper at their flat near Regents Park. There were six of them round the table, her hosts, another couple of their own age, plus a silver-haired man courteous and cautious in his manner, invited so that there shouldn't be an odd number of two men and three women. She looked at the loose folds of skin under his chin, heard his polite 'Do you play bridge, Mrs Allegri?' and thought 'This is what I'm coming to.' It was a subdued supper. At midnight they drank champagne and toasted

318

'Absent friends,' then the women left the men to their port and cigars and went into their hostess's sitting room. At table, Isabelle's relationship with Philip couldn't be acknowledged. But in this soft cave, with its comfortable chairs, dim lamps and small fire glowing in the grate, her friend asked if she'd heard anything.

'I was at Dodie's the night before last,' Isabelle told them. 'You know her husband's at the Admiralty? She wouldn't say openly, but she hinted very strongly it was the Dardanelles.'

Intakes of breath from the other two women. The War Office had only just admitted after eight months of fighting that the Dardanelles campaign was over and a mass evacuation was in progress. Officially, nobody was using the word *failure* yet, but even the War Office couldn't call it a success.

The hostess said, 'He'll be on his way home then. You'll be hearing from him.'

'You think so?'

Isabelle was numb with tiredness after days of running around London looking for scraps of news. Her head drooped forward, bare white neck and shoulders stretched against the kingfisher blue silk of her dress, sapphire eardrops quivering. The other woman guest, who'd never liked Isabelle much, said sweetly, 'Did you ever hear from your husband?' Isabelle's head jerked up.

'No. I never did.'

'You'd have thought after all this time he...'

'I told you, I never heard anything.'

It came out as a near shout, cutting like a razor

319

slash through the cosy atmosphere. The hostess stood up.

'We're all tired. If you'll excuse me, I'll go and see Peters about getting cabs.'

They were horse-drawn cabs, elderly and slow. The silver-haired man insisted on seeing Isabelle to her door on the grounds that no lady should travel alone in a cab through London, especially on New Year's night. But it was a strange new year's night, with the streets mostly empty. Only when they crossed Oxford Circus there was a surge of light and noise, 'Everybody's Doing It' coming out of a doorway, men in khaki and girls in bright dresses spilling onto the pavements.

'They're having a good time at any rate,' the silver-haired man said, without resentment.

When they got to her flat, he waited with her on the doorstep while she found her key.

'Isn't your maid up?'

'I gave her the night off. I expect she's still out celebrating.'

The flat was in darkness, except for a glow from the fire that Megan had banked up before changing and going out. Without bothering to light the gas lamps, Isabelle kicked off her shoes and collapsed shivering into an armchair.

At midnight, Megan was kissing a naval officer in a dance hall off Oxford Circus. Twelve kisses he'd asked for, one for each striking of the clock. By the fifth his tongue was writhing inside her mouth, his body pressed hard against hers. She pushed him away and slipped off among the crowds of entwined couples. 'Should auld acquaintance...'

One hand was grabbed by an army officer, handsome and drunken with his hair flopping over his forehead. There was some competition for the free hand, eventually won by a tall Australian she'd danced with earlier.

'We'll tak a cup o' kindness yet...'

Some of the girls were drunker than the men, stamping and yelling the words out of time without even trying to sing them properly. A man was going round the circle with a champagne bottle, gesturing to people to tip their heads back so that he could pour champagne straight down their throats. The drunken girls gaped their mouths wide and let him pour until champagne ran down their chins and onto their bodices. When he came to Megan she turned her head away. She didn't need to make herself cheap to have men look at her. It was the first time she'd had a chance to wear an evening dress in rose-coloured silk that had been handed down to her by Isabelle, with her hair piled up and pinned with two roses she'd made for herself from a scrap of matching silk and a discreet touch of rouge and lip colouring. The friend she'd arrived with – a lady's maid to one of Isabelle's acquaintances – was simply lost in the first five minutes, not through any wish of Megan's but because of the press of men who wanted to dance with her. They were mostly men in uniform, khaki with a sprinkling of navy blue. It was a surprise at first that they were officers and – except for the ones who got very drunk – treated her like a lady. She could see that the other girls resented it, heard one asking another deliberately

in her hearing 'Who does she think she is?'
Megan simply turned and gave the girl a smile
over her shoulder, letting a captain waltz her
away. As she waltzed, she cast an expert eye over
the other women's dresses. None of them had the
class of Isabelle's dress, but there were things to
learn from them, notably how short the skirts
were. These girls were showing their ankles and
several inches of calf, gleaming in white or grey
silk hose over neat shoes with little Louis heels.
The ones attracting most attention apart from
her were wearing a style of dress she'd read about
but not seen, very full skirts over taffeta
petticoats stiffened with fine wire at the hem so
that skirts and petticoats frothed around their
calves and swung out when men whirled them
round in the dances to show their legs up to the
knee or higher. It was clear they'd spent a lot of
money on their clothes and yet from their talk
they were certainly no ladies. The mystery was
solved for her by the tall Australian.

'Most of them work in the ammunition
factories.'

'Do they get good pay?'

'Thirty bob a week, I heard.'

She misheard over the music and thought he'd
said thirteen bob, but it still sounded like a lot to
her. At two o'clock she allowed a lieutenant to
take her home, avoiding his tentative hands in the
taxicab but allowing him one kiss on the
doorstep before she let herself in and crept
upstairs. Isabelle, lying awake in her own room
heard the door close softly, light steps and a
rustle of silk on the stairs and felt a stab of love

and regret.

'If only Petra...'

Megan lay awake for a long time too, smiling to herself.

Private Will Thomas sat through the turning of the year in a line of wagons in a railway siding somewhere in France along with 24 mules and six horses. They'd been shunted into the siding while it was still light and the latest word was that they wouldn't be moving before daylight. Somewhere ahead and to the right the big guns were pounding, the vibrations of them humming through the ground and along the rail tracks, unsettling the horses. Getting out to France had been all bustle and urgency. The unit he was attached to in England for training had suddenly been ordered to embark at forty-eight hours notice. Within a few weeks of putting on uniform he was crossing the grey and heaving Channel, the first time he'd ever put to sea unless you counted a boat trip out of Weston-Super-Mare on his honeymoon. Once in France all the hurry had evaporated and it was mostly waiting, trying to piece together rumours about what was happening and where they were going. Then Will and a couple more of the older men had been borrowed by another unit who needed help with their horse and mule transports. More waiting – standing by empty wagons for the animals to arrive or else with lines of animals to look after and no train. Then, when animals and wagons had somehow been brought together, waiting as now for the signal to move forwards. The word was that they were delayed because there were a lot of casualties coming down the line. Will sat on a straw bale in the empty wagon and ate a square of chocolate. Chocolate, like sea travel, was one of the new experiences war had brought him. He'd never tasted it until it had arrived in the parcels of Christmas treats for soldiers. When he'd finished it he stood up and went to do his rounds, untethering each mule and horse by lamplight to give it a few gulps of water from a bucket, trying to calm the nervous ones so that they slept a bit. 'Easy boy, easy now.' No Jack the Lad. He'd given up on that as soon as he arrived in France and understood the sheer size of the war. When he thought of home, Jack the Lad was still there under the hawthorn tree along with Pont and Guto, not out here in the dark in some other siding. Walking between wagons, he looked towards the sound of guns and saw shells arcing into the black sky. A horse whinnied and kicked out at the wooden wall of the wagon. He climbed in with her, ran his head along her trembling neck and withers. 'Easy Jenny, easy girl.' Some of the men laughed at him, giving names to them when you weren't with them for more than a day or two but you had to call them something. When she was quieter he went back to the spare wagon, spread a bed of clean straw, wrapped himself in his greatcoat and slept.

44

April 1916

Easter was late in 1916. On the morning of Easter Sunday, April 23, Isabelle stood in the Pleasaunce up to her ankles in grass, listening to the bells ringing from the church tower down in the village. For the first time since Philip had gone away she felt full of strength and optimism, delighting in the garden again. The winter had been a harsh one – torrents of rain in January that flooded the stream and left sheets of mud on the lawn, the worst blizzards anybody could remember at the end of March. Against expectation, everything had come through without much damage. The fritillaries in the long grass of the Pleasaunce were just as they'd wanted them, drifts of almost translucent bells, pure white or chequered purple. The wild Welsh daffodils were almost over but a few of them were still flowering, along with the pale mauve of cuckoo smock. Primroses crowded the bank, the palest of yellows with a hint of green as if they were pulling colour from the moss round their roots. It would be a couple of weeks before most of the apple trees were in flower, but the Early Victoria's were already breaking into pink and white bud, a blackbird in one of them singing a challenge to the church bells. The war would end and Philip would come back. Marius would be safe and Petra would forgive her and love her. Against expectation, Marius had thrown himself into the work of transport manager for the three pits and now spent most of his time in Mr Gladwyn's house in Treorchy, coming to Holders Hope only for the occasional weekend or if he needed to consult Isabelle on business. Mr Gladwyn had been won over. Marius had grasped the complexities of getting coal by rail down the valley and shipped out in a surprisingly short time and had already made some small but profitable improvements. The results were good for the three Allegri pits, good for the Navy's battleships that needed steam coal as fast as it could be got to the docks. Any lingering guilt Isabelle might have felt about Marius being safe faded away. After that dreadful day back in the summer, Petra hadn't said any more about it either. As it happened, Petra hadn't said much about anything, but at least she was there and not arguing. She'd come home for the Easter holidays and behaved politely, if distantly, to her mother. She looked well physically. Her breasts were filling out and she moved with more confidence, shoulders back and looking people in the eye. Hockey and lawn tennis were clearly having some effect at last. Her hair, though, remained uncompromisingly short. She spent some of her own money on a typewriter which arrived by carrier from Hereford and installed it at a small table in the library where she practised on it, day after day. She firmly disregarded her mother's hints that an extra pair of hands would be useful in the garden with Will and Evan away but was often over in the cottage with

Bathsheba. Isabelle supposed Petra was keeping Bathsheba company as a form of war work. There was a lot of kindness in Petra, deep down. If Isabelle were patient she'd perhaps show some of it to her mother. She'd be eighteen this year and would leave school at the end of the summer term. By then, Philip might be back. It had been a bad time through the winter when the men came back from the Dardanelles and there was still no news of him, but it was spring now and things would happen.

'He writes a nice letter, doesn't he?' Bathsheba said.

She kept the letters and cards from all three of them in a drawer of the kitchen table. Will's pile was the smallest. He was even less at ease with written words than with speech so there were only three letters on official soldiers' correspondence forms and one postcard for the five months he'd been away. The card showed the flags of the Allies in bright hand-tinted colours flanking a curly headed child cuddling a bulldog puppy. The printed slogan at the top of the card said *Thinking of Our Dear Ones at Home*. On the other side Will wrote that he had got the socks and the jam, thank you and not to worry because he was all right and keeping busy. Evan's letters made a thicker pile because he wrote every two weeks or so and they hadn't far to travel. To his increasing impatience, he was still stationed at a camp near Cardiff. It was just the luck of the draw that his regiment hadn't been sent overseas yet and were employed guarding the docks and training. He was always hoping his next letter to Auntie Bath would be from France, but meanwhile thank you for the fruitcake. Trefor's letters, from 'somewhere in France' made up the thickest pile and were the ones Bathsheba called nice. Petra read them with a chair drawn up to the kitchen table, Bathsheba standing at the other end of the table kneading dough. Will's old terrier, plumper and lazy now there was nobody to follow round the estate, twitched and grunted on the rag rug in front of the black-leaded range. Trefor's letters surprised her. In writing to his aunt he showed a softer, almost playful side. He said little about the war but a lot about the men serving with him – how one of them had tamed a jackdaw that drank cold tea from a mess tin lid and pecked lice out of the seams of men's shirts, how another could play Italian opera on a tin whistle. 'As for books, we haven't got many, so some of us have formed a reading circle. We'd nearly got to the end of *The Invisible Man* then somebody went and dropped it into the mud in a bit of a panic one night and it was lost. We're now on Ruskin's *Unto this Last* and finding it slower going, though I think it very good.' There was a streak of blue crayon over the next few words. Petra showed it to Bathsheba with a questioning look.

'Oh, you get that with some of them. Mrs Downs says the officers go through them to make sure they're not saying anything they shouldn't.'

Petra scraped at the streak of crayon with her fingernail. 'Although we all know it's a cr....' but after that the next few words were unreadable. It picked up on the next line 'it is an opportunity to

328

talk to men from all over the country I'd never have met otherwise. I'm learning a lot, and when I come home I'm not going to waste it, or let anyone else waste it. I'm due for some leave soon. With luck I may be home around Easter time and if I am I'll come over from Treorchy to see you. Till then, keep cheerful if you can. Your loving nephew, Trefor.'

Petra laid the letter down slowly on the pile with the rest.

'Is he home yet?'

'Not as far as I know. He'd go to his father first, of course.'

Bathsheba's fingers were sticky with dough, so Petra put the letters back in the drawer. She felt odd, as if something important had happened but she didn't know what.

'If you hear anything, will you let me know?'

Bathsheba looked up from the dough.

'From Evan, you mean?'

'From any of them.'

Petra let herself out by the back door and lingered for a long time at the gate before walking slowly up the lawn towards the house. The grass was starred with blue speedwell flowers, hummocked by occasional mole hills. She went up it with long swinging strides, not noticing.

45

There were fritillaries in the Pontic mountains,
looping wiry stems out of the soil as soon as the
snow melted. Further up, great drifts of yellow
azaleas, rhododendron luteum, filled the warming
air with their scent. Further up still, patches of
blue anemone blanda were as startling as
kingfishers against tattered snow. Philip looked
from the anemones to the mountains around the
Zigana Pass, still snow covered, then turned and
looked down over Trebizond and the Black Sea,
blue as the Mediterranean. It was the end of April.
Twelve days earlier the great event of his part of
the war had happened at last. The Russian allies
had taken Trebizond. There were Russian
warships at sea, the sound of heavy guns pounding
the coast to the east beyond Trebizond, reports of
the Turkish army in retreat. Philip and Finch
watched the short battle for Trebizond itself from
the hills. By the time they got down to the village
a party of Russian troops had arrived, tattered and
exhausted from a long winter of campaigning.
They'd been unbelieving at first to find two British
agents in residence but suspicion evaporated with
toasts to victory in throat-blistering local raki and
speeches in good French from the Russian
officers, bad French from Philip. The plan was
that the Russians would press westwards towards
Constantinople, joining up with the other Allied

forces from the Dardanelles. Neither Philip nor the Russians had any knowledge of what had been happening all winter in the rest of the war, but they assumed that such a large force must have managed to get through the Narrows at the Dardanelles by now. Whether Philip and Corporal Finch would be taken off to sea by the British Navy when it arrived or march westwards along the coast with their Russian friends was one of the details that couldn't be settled yet, but it didn't matter either way. Say – being cautious and allowing for delays – they'd be home in about three months, by the end of the summer. There'd be a lot to do in the garden but he could trust Will to have kept it in some sort of order. When he thought of the garden there was always Will there somewhere in the middle distance with his wheelbarrow and terrier at his side. If he got home by late summer he'd be in time to see the leaves change colour and walk in the Pleasaunce with Isabelle, picking sweet Yellow Ingestries and Cowarne Queenings. At some time – while picking apples might be as good a time as any – he'd lay down the law to Isabelle, quite gently but firmly this time. They'd set about dissolving the marriage to Leon, either on grounds of his desertion or his assumed death. He'd have to go to his lawyer in any case as soon as he got back to London, to reclaim and destroy three letters he'd written in a black hour that wouldn't be needed now. Then as soon as the legal business was over, he and Isabelle would marry. Everything seemed simpler, now that the war had come so near to sweeping everything away.

331

Now, with the latest message sent to Constantinople, his duty was done. The decision to see how far he could get towards the Zigana Pass before snow blocked the route was no more than an excuse for a day out, on his own for once because Corporal Finch was suffering from a mild attack of food poisoning. The Russian commander had offered him an escort but he'd refused. The truth was that as the snows receded the old itch had come on him to go off alone and do some botanising. If he settled down with Isabelle it might be a long time before he came back to the Pontic Mountains, if ever. He wanted one more chance to feel his heart jump at the fragile flare of petals from stony ground. Almost certainly too early by several weeks for his favourites, the oncocyclus irises, but there were always surprises with plants. He walked steadily uphill, eyes to the earth.

The day after Easter Monday, Isabelle drove Petra into Hereford to buy things she'd need for going back to school. Petra flatly refused to let her buy a tennis racquet.

'My old one's perfectly all right. Besides, it's only for one term.'

'But you'll be playing tennis sometimes after you leave school, won't you?'

Petra didn't answer. The question of what she'd do when she left school in July was one of the many things they didn't talk about. Isabelle didn't press the point any further, giving only a mental shrug towards Philip. 'Well, I did try to do what you told me.' They didn't talk much on the journey back. As Isabelle guided the car slowly up the lane towards the house, Petra said suddenly,

'Bathsheba's out in her garden.'

'Well she often is, darling.'

'Just standing there.'

That was unusual. Inside or outside, Bathsheba was usually busy at something.

Petra persisted, 'I think she's holding a letter.'

As soon as the car stopped she was out of the door and heading back down the lane.

After the anemone blanda the snow came closer to the track. Philip was surprised to find traces of muddy bootprints on the edge of it, but guessed that some of the Russians might have made an earlier reconnoitre. Once the snow melted they'd flush out any groups of retreating Turks who might have taken refuge in the mountains. If there were any of those, Philip pitied them. Up there in the snow there'd be nothing but mountain hares to eat and they'd have to compete for those with the wolves and birds of prey. The path dipped. Melt water had run into a puddle at the bottom of the dip with a crust of thin ice round the edge. A lot of boot marks here, as if the men had stopped to get their breath. A sound from higher up the track made him turn but he couldn't see anything except curves of snow. Hare, probably. He walked up and out of the dip and it was there at the top of the slope that it happened.

There were a few rocks to the left, with a clear patch of gravelly soil – one of those little freaks of mountains that make warmer and sheltered places. Growing out of the gravel, something that made Philip stop, catch his breath and feel the old lurch of the heart. A pale flame of purest lemon yellow, a few inches above the ground. Iris. Not the strange markings and colours of an oncocyclus. A dwarf form of Juno, almost certainly. Probably the little iris caucasica which he knew flowered early. Not a rarity in itself but amazing to find it here on its own so high up. Moving slowly and carefully, with that familiar feeling that it might take fright and fly away, he left the track and knelt beside it. He probed the soil a little to look at the bulb, then scraped it carefully back into place. There were another three flowering spikes on the gravel patch, two in tight bud, one showing colour. He knelt there for a long time, enjoying them. Then looked up to see a pair of eyes looking at him over a rock. The eyes were dark and scared, in a face roughened by the weather, lips covered with sores, skin flaking away from the nose. Above the face, dark hair flopping over the forehead and a shapeless cap, dark and stained. Philip stood up, believing it to be a Russian soldier from Trebizond, sorry to see the man so scared of him. *'Bonjour, je suis...'* Then remembered that although the Russian officers spoke French, their men didn't. As he stopped, trying to remember the words for 'hello friend' in Russian, the man stood up so that the upper half of his body was visible behind the rock. He was wearing a muddy uniform tunic. Philip noticed that first, then the fact that the man had a rifle levelled at him, resting on the rock. 'No.' Still thinking it was a misunderstanding he took a step forward, gesturing that the man should put the rifle down. He never thought of going for the pistol he always carried in his pocket. The rifle cracked. Philip stood for a moment and fell back towards the track. When his body landed it crushed two of the iris caucasica in bud, just missed the one in flower.

Standing between her rhubarb and the post of the clothes line with the old hessian bag of clothes pegs hitched round it, Bathsheba held out the official letter to Petra.

'They say Will's wounded. He's in hospital.'

It was the oddest of feelings. It had hit Petra as soon as they turned into the lane, even before she noticed Bathsheba in her garden. It was as if her whole mind and body had been held together by some kind of magnetic force and, all of a sudden, somebody had switched it off. That was how she knew with certainty when she saw Bathsheba with the letter that something terrible had happened. She took the letter, read the official phrases, but it made no difference. Bathsheba was saying something.

'...wouldn't have written unless it was bad. Mrs Tibbins' daughter got a letter like that last year and the next thing was a telegram saying he'd died.'

Her face was soft and shapeless with misery and her hand when she passed over the letter was shaking. Petra knew that Bathsheba was begging for comfort, knew too all the things she should be saying to her. But whatever had held her together and might, until a few minutes ago, have made it possible to comfort Bathsheba had been disconnected, like something in the car engine coming apart. She was sure that this feeling – or rather this odd lack of feeling – meant that Will was dead. Until then, she had no idea of what he'd meant to her. He'd always been there around the garden, always kind in his inarticulate way, taking time to show her hedgehogs curled up in leaves, the first of the wild strawberries. His silence and her own had gone happily together. She gave the letter back to Bathsheba, put an arm round her shoulders and held her while she cried silently but couldn't cry herself. After a while Bathsheba blew her nose, said this wasn't getting anything done, was it, and went into the cottage. Petra went up the lane and told her mother 'Will's been wounded.' Isabelle gasped and went straight down the lane without changing her shoes to see Bathsheba, came back and spent a long time on the telephone trying to find somebody who might know more.

'They never tell you anything,' she complained to Petra that evening, tears of grief and frustration running down her face.

It was a familiar cry and Petra made no response to it. She was due back at school in the morning and was calmly getting on with her packing.

46

The train journey was familiar to Petra, from many returns after many holidays. The slow departure from Hereford station, then picking up speed between avenues of hop poles towards the viaduct that hoisted the train high over apple orchards on the approach to Ledbury. Usually a wait at Ledbury, then Newent and on across the wide green Severn Valley. Only this time everything was different. The feeling of being disconnected was still there, as strong as ever, so that she seemed to be looking at herself in the corner of the carriage through somebody else's eyes. Hands obstinately unladylike, square in shape and burnt brown by the sun, resting gloveless on navy blue gabardine skirt. Ankles and insteps in thick brown stockings, toes in sturdy brown brogues. Face, glimpsed in the mirror opposite, pale and serious under the brim of a navy felt hat. As the train slowed down for Gloucester she got her carpet bag off the rack and put it on the seat. On the floor at her feet was the big canvas bag her brother had used for his cricketing gear until he got a better one. She opened the door and dragged it into the corridor, then came back for the carpet bag. There was a moment's panic, because the leather strap that kept the outside window closed was new and stiff and she couldn't unhook it from the brass stud but a new calm voice from outside her head told her there was plenty of time, to take a deep breath and not to be silly. She took a breath. The strap slid up, the window came down and the door opened. A porter was there as soon as she started nudging the cricketing bag through the doorway.

'Cab, miss, or are you changing?'

She passed the carpet bag to him, looked him in the eye. 'Changing.'

As she followed him along the platform she watched the train she'd been on drawing out. All the rest of her luggage was in the guard's van – the trunk with her books, school uniform and pink tea gown in case friends invited her home at weekends, the tuck box with Mrs Downs' special ginger cake. She knew she'd never see them again and felt no regret, just a mild curiosity about what would happen to them.

She took another deep breath. 'What platform does the next train for Cardiff go from?'

There was a restaurant by the Wyndham Arcade in Cardiff that catered especially for soldiers. At teatime it was a crush of khaki, buzzing with talk, hazed with cigarette smoke. The headgear on the tables among the thick white cups or balanced on knees was mostly of the local Welsh Regiment, with a sprinkling of exotics including some Black Watch. The place was even busier than usual because most of those present had just come from a matinee showing of Charles Chaplin's *Charlie at the Bank*. Trefor and Evan Thomas had managed to get two seats together at a table in the corner. The rest of the table was occupied by a group of Royal Engineers, too busy acting out the best moments of the film to each other to take any notice of two brothers talking quietly over their tea and Bovril toast. Trefor was doing most of the talking. Although on leave he was in uniform, with the new second stripe of a full corporal on his tunic sleeve.

'Just stop going on about it. If they say they're not sending you till you're eighteen, just be thankful.'

'When I heard about Uncle Will, I went to Sergeant Rhys and begged him...'

'I know. Begged him to let you get out there and kill a battalion of Huns and win a bloody posthumous VC just because your uncle was too bloody stupid to stay where he was well off. Hope he told you to go away and stop wasting his time.'

Evan started to say something, then stopped. His brother had turned into somebody older and harder. The two stripes didn't help either, seeing that Evan had spent some of the past months learning that privates didn't argue with corporals, or anybody else come to that. Trefor pushed his plate of toast aside half-eaten, pulled out a packet of Waverleys and lit one. When he noticed Evan's longing eyes on it he shrugged and passed the whole packet to him. The smoke from their two cigarettes went up in a double spiral to join the blue-grey cloud overhead.

'Of course, if you'd had the sense you were born with, you wouldn't be in the army,' Trefor said. 'If you'd come home and worked at the pit when I wanted you to, you'd have been a starred trade, couldn't be called up.'

'You don't work at the pit either.'

'Because your precious Mrs Allegri stopped my lamp.'

'She's been quite good to me.'

Trefor made a noise as if he wanted to spit and had only choked it down because of being inside. 'Funny idea of good.' Evan said nothing. 'Well, isn't it? A funny idea of good they've got, all of them.'

A picture came into Evan's mind. The lilies in the pond and, among them, the sodden thing in white and black stripes that had been so reluctant to sink. He looked up, saw his brother's eyes on him and was suddenly quite sure that Trefor knew. One of the Engineers had started singing *'Oh the moon shines bright on Charlie Chaplin, His boots are cracking, for want of blacking...'* The manageress looked their way and his friends shushed him. No singing.

Evan said, without looking up, 'Miss Petra's all right. We're friends, Miss Petra and me.'

'You don't need their friendship.' Trefor caught a waitress's eye, paid and they walked out together and along the arcade. 'Look Evan, when we're both through this, I want you to come home. Dad'll see you get work in one of the pits, you haven't got a bad name like me. I need you there. Once this bloody war's over, whenever that is, then the real battle's just started. We're not going to let them do anything like this to us ever again.'

Evan was still feeling odd in the stomach and the head, trying to come to terms with the fact that Trefor knew, had always known. He was only half listening.

'What battle?'

'The only one that matters, workers' control. You get through this war, learn from it what you bloody can, then you come home, right?'

'Right.'

He'd have said anything. They walked back along the arcade and into St Mary Street. They had most of the evening to spend together until Evan had to report back to barracks and Trefor catch the train to their father's home in Treorchy for his last few days of leave. Later, over a half pint of beer in The Griffin, Evan asked Trefor if he'd heard from Megan. He said no, in a tone that didn't encourage any further conversation on that subject.

There was a park behind the crazy Victorian castle in the centre of the city, with the River Taf running through it. It was a good place to be on a late April evening with people walking dogs and couples strolling in the last of the light. A few people walked alone, including some in uniform who seemed to prefer peace and quiet to the companionship of pubs and cinemas. The figure in the officer's tunic and Sam Browne belt didn't attract much attention. His uniform cap was odd, not immediately identifiable with any of the units stationed near Cardiff and his trousers were unusually badly fitting for an officer's, but then you got all sorts. A couple of people noticed that he walked with a slight shuffle and didn't keep his shoulders back in a soldierly way so assumed the poor man was wounded and convalescent. He lingered by the river until the light was almost gone then walked slowly out of the park towards the lights and crowds. It was nearly nine o'clock by then and a slow khaki tide of men was flowing out of pubs and cafes, moving back towards the barracks. Most of them were cheerful and orderly, but there was some drunken arguing, a scrap in the gutter between a Welsh Regiment man and a civilian broken up by a police constable before any damage was done. The shuffling officer kept his distance from the scrap and everything else as he followed the movement back to barracks. He hesitated at the gate, watched a few soldiers going in then turned off into a side road. It might have been to smoke one more cigarette before going back on duty, but he didn't light up, just stood in the dark out of sight of the sentry. A trio of Black Watch, cheerfully drunken, went past him without noticing and urinated against a wall in competing arcs so close to where he was standing that piss spattered his uniform. He jumped back, with a little gasp of surprise and protest. The three soldiers turned in unison, saw a silhouette in officer's uniform. Arcs dribbled to anti-climax and they started fumbling with trouser buttons and dripping pricks. The one nearest the officer managed it one-handed and snapped a salute at the same time.

'Sorry, sir. Didnae see...'

Something about the way the officer was standing, or perhaps his failure to react to the salute made him stop. He went a step closer. 'Whaur're y' from then?'

The other two moved in beside him, hemming in the officer with the wall behind him.

'That's nivver a soldier.'

One of them put out an arm to take the cap and look at the badge. The officer moved back, shrinking against the wall then, as they came closer, decided to make a run for it. At first he ran towards the lighted barrack entrance at the end of the street with them pounding after him, then unaccountably turned and came running back towards them. The surprise of the manoeuvre and his speed and agility took them by surprise. He was past them, haring for the dark end of the street that they knew was a cul de sac. His cap came off and bowled into the gutter. At the end of the street by a high wooden fence and a rubbish heap they caught up with him, quite certain now he was no kind of soldier. One of them caught him by the chest strap of the belt and dragged him away from the fence. Then he started laughing. The others wanted to know what the joke was.

'It's nae a man at all.'

'Let me go.'

No mistake now. The voice was loud and feminine. They laughed.

'It's a wee hoor dressed up as a soldier.'

He held the belt tighter, dragging her to him and clamped his mouth against hers as the other two cheered him on. She struggled, trying to push him off and he staggered back with a yell of pain.

'Bit me. The wee hoor bit me.'

He threw himself onto her, not even half joking

343

now, and pushed her down on the heap of rubbish. She shouted again and tried to get up, but one of the other men joined in and between them they kept her down. There was something sharp cutting into her back, a hand fumbling at the buttons of her brother's trousers, thrusting between her legs. When she started screaming a hand smelling of beer and piss came down over her mouth. Another hand groped inside her knickers, fingers pushing into her cleft. She drew up her knees and tried to kick but there was another hand grabbing her foot. One of her shoes came off – they'd been far too big for her – then the hand had her by the bare ankle and was pinning it down.

She thought 'People faint' and wondered how you did it.

There was a shout from somewhere. By then she didn't know if it was in her own mind or outside it. Then there was a spasm of pain as the fingers tore themselves from inside her. A noise of disgust or anger, another shout from some-where else, feet running fast. She'd lost any sense of direction and thought there were more people running towards her to hold her down and hurt her, tried to burrow head first deeper into the heap of rubbish as if that would be any protection. A long silence then a voice.

'What are you doing there?'

A different voice in a more familiar accent, but breathless and angry. There was something slimy in her mouth and nostrils. A booted foot pressed against her leg. A flap of something heavy and sour smelling that had been protecting her head was lifted away. She gave a little moan at losing it, turned on her side, legs curled into her stomach, arms clamped to her chest.

'What's happened?'

It was almost completely dark with the only light coming from a lamp standard at the far end of the cul de sac. If she turned her head all she could see was the dark silhouette of a man in uniform. When he knelt down beside her she uncurled a leg and tried to kick him, but without much strength.

'Stop that, I'm trying to help you. Was it a fight?'

She didn't answer.

'Can you hear me?'

She felt an arm thrusting through the rubbish and rolled away from it, pushing herself to her knees. She was beginning to understand that he was nothing to do with the other three soldiers, but couldn't bear to be touched.

'Take my arm if you want it.'

He was sitting back on his heels now, holding out the crook of his arm to her. She had to grab it to get herself upright. The cobbles of the cul de sac were cold under her bare left foot.

'Shoe,' she said.

Although she'd let go of his arm, she felt his shock at the sound of her voice.

'Oh blimey. What is this?'

She said, as if it explained everything, 'My shoe came off.'

He went down on his hands and knees, searched in the rubbish.

'Is this it?'

He gave it to her at arm's length. She had to sit down on the cobbles to put it on and this time he didn't offer his arm to help her up.

'We'd better get you inside.'

She took a step, then another and they went slowly back towards the barracks entrance, he two paces in front. About half way up, where the light from the lamp reached, he turned and looked at her.

'Petra Allegri.' Disgust in his voice. She'd turned her head aside so still didn't know who he was or why he should know her name. It was all part of the unreality. 'You don't know who I am, do you?'

She looked and still didn't recognise him as the pale boy she'd last seen at Holders Hope. He had to tell her.

'Trefor Thomas.'

Even then it took her a while to remember. She nodded, as if finding him there was no more remarkable or unremarkable than anything else.

'I'd just taken Evan back. I came along here for a smoke and I heard...' Then, giving up the effort, he stood and stared at her. Her brother's trousers were still unbuttoned at the fly and the waist. She was holding them up with one hand. The cross strap of the Sam Browne belt was broken, jacket gaping and shirt smeared with all kinds of rubbish. The cap was lost past recovery somewhere in the dark street, her dark hair matted with crushed vegetables. 'What the hell are we going to do?'

Petra said, 'I don't want to go in there.'

She was looking towards the gateway of the barracks. A few soldiers were still staggering inside, laughing and shouting insults to each other for being late. He agreed with her. The idea of walking in there with a young woman – especially this young woman – dressed more or less as an officer was something he couldn't face. Even if they believed him about what had happened, he'd be a laughing stock.

'Where are your clothes?'

'At the station. In the left luggage office.'

He thought of leaving her somewhere while he went to fetch them, but couldn't think where.

'Can you walk all right?'

She nodded. He led her across the street out of the light of the lamp, into another side street that he hoped led in the general direction of the station. He didn't know Cardiff very well but they'd have to keep to the back streets, no choice. Once he'd made the decision not to take her into the barracks he'd be in terrible trouble if the Red Caps or the civilian police saw him. Aiding and abetting an insult to the King's uniform would be the least of it. At first he didn't try to talk to her, just kept a few paces ahead and let her follow. If he'd been less worried and angry he might have been impressed by her stoicism. She didn't once complain or ask him to slow down although the shuffle of her feet behind him sounded like a wounded animal dragging itself along. By the time they came out by some rail sidings and he realised that the station wasn't far away he relaxed enough to wait for her to catch up and asked some questions as they walked.

'What did you think you were doing?'

'I wanted to be sent to the Front.'

'Some game at your school, was it? Some dare?'

'Everybody who matters to me gets killed, so why shouldn't I?'

'Everybody who matters? Your brother's safe enough.'

He'd heard about Marius from his father. It was the talk of the valleys.

'I don't mean him. I mean Will and...'

'Will? My uncle Will?'

She nodded. That puzzled him as much as anything else about it. He thought his uncle would be no more than a paid servant to her.

'Anyway, he's not dead, just wounded.'

No reply. She knew she couldn't make anybody else understand this certainty of death that had come to her.

'Where did you get the uniform?'

'Marius was in the officer training corps at university.'

He whistled, sharp and angry. 'You people. Even when you're dressing up as Sweet Polly Oliver, it has to be an officer.'

'I didn't have any choice.' So far her answers had been quite humble. Now she was angry.

'Did you think you'd just walk in and they'd put you straight on a boat for France? They have medical examinations, for one thing. Strip behind a screen and walk out in front of the medical officer.'

She flinched but didn't answer. No way of explaining to this angry, very grown-up man that when everything in the world had stopped making sense what she'd done was no more peculiar than anything else.

348

He said, 'It's all playing games for people like you, isn't it?' No answer. He felt savage, not so much against her personally as against all privileged ignorance. 'You'll all be swept away soon, you know that?'

She stopped and looked up at him. 'I want to be swept away.'

She said it quite seriously then walked on ahead of him. The station was in sight now. He stayed behind her until she stumbled then felt ashamed of himself, caught up with her and offered her his arm. She didn't take it but let him walk beside her.

'Did they hurt you?'

'A bit. Not much.'

He wanted to ask her if she'd been raped, but didn't know what words to use. He'd been a virgin himself until one not particularly pleasurable episode in a brothel behind a French caff, a few months before.

'Did they ... do anything to you?'

'They pushed me over.'

The cleft between her legs was sore and sticky, chafed by the rough fabric of the trousers. In the next patch of lamplight she glanced down to see if blood was soaking through but couldn't see any.

He said, 'We've got to get you home.'

It was late and there might not be any trains running to Hereford.

'No. I'm not going home.'

She was certain about that if nothing else. He stared at her.

'What about your mother?'

'She won't worry. She thinks I'm at school.'

'What about the school then?'

'I sent them a letter saying I wouldn't be coming back this term.'

'Well, what are you going to do?'

'I don't know.'

'You can't go wandering around Cardiff all night dressed like that.'

'I'll get my clothes.'

When they got near the bright electric lights of the ticket hall he let her go ahead of him. There were quite a few people waiting for the last trains home up the valleys, most of them soldiers, so there was a strong chance of meeting somebody he knew. Luckily, most of them were too drunk or too concerned with their own affairs to take notice of the figure shambling across to the left luggage office. He sat on a bench and wondered what on earth he was going to do with her. He had only three shillings and a few odd pence in his pocket, nothing like enough for a hotel for her even if he had known one that would take in a woman at this time of night. Before he'd come to any decision a woman in a navy blue skirt and jacket walked over and stood beside him, reasonably smart and respectable. She was carrying a carpet bag. It was a second before he realised it was Petra. Her face was pale as paper in the harsh overhead light, the hair over her forehead damp from the handfuls of cold water she'd splashed all over her face. A scent of strong, cheap soap hung round her. She'd washed between her legs over and over again. Only a few spots of blood, but dampness because she

350

couldn't dry herself there on the roller towel hitched high on the wall in the ladies' room and had to use her handkerchief. Now the uniform was gone he could think more clearly about her.

'You'd better come home with me for tonight.'

'Home?'

'Treorchy.'

Goodness knows what his sister would say. She was married now with a child. His father's house was crowded enough as it was. Petra nodded. He left her on the bench and went over to the window for a ticket. Soon after that, the last train for the Rhondda came in. She slept in a corner of the crowded carriage for most of the way up the valley, with him in the opposite corner. It was past midnight by the time they were walking up the street to his home and he was still trying to make sense of it.

'You said everybody who mattered to you got killed.'

She was moving like a sleepwalker. 'My father got killed, you know that. My mother killed him.' He didn't say anything. She went on, 'She and Mr Cordell killed him. We found his body, Evan and I did, then they took it away.'

They walked on in silence between the terraces of houses.

47

July 2001

Colin's tent was the one with the light glowing inside it. He and Kim ran towards it down the tussocky grass. When they were about a hundred metres away from it he put out his hand to stop her.

'Wait there. I'll go and see...'

'Fuck that.'

She ran on past him. He had to put on a burst of speed to catch up. They stopped by the guy rope and saw, against the illuminated orange fabric, the black silhouette of somebody crouching inside.

Colin said loudly, 'Come out of there.'

The silhouette shifted a little but there was no answer. He got down on his knees by the tent flap.

Kim said, 'Wait. Let me get the jack or something from the car.'

'No good. Keys are inside my tent.'

The tent flaps were hanging loose. He pushed head and shoulders inside and smelt cigarette smoke. The lamp shone straight into his eyes, dazzling him. When he shouted a protest the beam shifted.

'Sorry about that.'

The voice wasn't what he expected, neither officialdom nor village yob. It was female and sounded amused. Old fashioned posh, roughened by a lot of cigarettes.

'Who is it?' Kim's voice, from outside.

Even though the lamp wasn't directly in his eyes any more it took some time to adjust. He realised slowly that the figure wasn't crouching but sitting cross-legged, as if she had a right to be there. He started crawling into the tent and felt something hard and knobbly under his hand.

'Oh shit.'

A cackle of laughter. She had white hair and a lined brown face and was sitting at the far end of the tent. Between him and her, on the blue background of his sleeping bag, were the bones – laid out neatly in rows according to size, long thick ones at his end, small fingerbones at hers.

'What are you doing here?' he said.

She looked at him and smiled, showing a line of teeth as white as the bones.

'Just visiting my relatives.'

48

May 1916

It was three weeks before Isabelle found out anything. She wrote to Petra every week at school as usual with news of Holders Hope and Marius and was hurt not to get any replies. Then at last there was some good news to send from Holders Hope.

Wednesday 17 May 1916.

Darling,
Just a line to let you know the happy news – Will Thomas is alive and coming home. We don't know how badly he's been injured because it was an official letter (oh dear, those terribly official letters) but he will be on the way back to England soon – possibly even by the time you're reading this – and will be sent to a military hospital to convalesce. I'll make sure Bathsheba gets wherever it is to see him as soon as she can and will send you the latest news. I do hope you're keeping well, darling, and not working too hard. It would be nice to hear from you.
Your loving mother,

Isabelle

After three days without a reply, Isabelle was puzzled and angry. When the first post on the following Monday still brought no response from Cheltenham, she telephoned the school. There was a silence at the other end of the phone, then a gasp from the secretary and a request to hold on. It wasn't a good line.

'Mrs Allegri?'

The principal's voice.

'What's wrong with my daughter?'

'Petra isn't here, Mrs Allegri. You decided not to send her back after the Easter holidays.'

'What?' She almost dropped the phone. 'It's Petra Allegri we're talking about. My daughter.'

'We were concerned when she didn't arrive

354

back, then we received your letter the day after.'

'Of course she arrived. I put her on the train myself. What letter?'

'Your letter saying you'd decided not to send her back.'

'I never wrote any such letter.'

A pause at the other end of the line, then the beginnings of alarm. 'But if Petra's not with you, Mrs Allegri...'

'I'm coming over. I'll be with you in about two hours.'

It was mid afternoon when she parked in front of the school. Girls in long sleeved white dresses and white stockings were strolling to the tennis courts, chatting and laughing among themselves, swinging racquets. Other women's daughters. Nice, untroublesome daughters. The letter was ready on the principal's desk.

Holders Hope.
Herefordshire.
Tuesday 25 April 1916.

Dear Miss Faithfull,
I have decided not to send my daughter Petra back to school for the summer term.

I am sorry if this causes you any inconvenience.

If there is any money owing, please send me a bill at the above address.

Yours faithfully

Mrs I. Allegri

'Where was the letter posted?'

'My secretary thinks Hereford. She's not sure because there was no reason to keep the envelope.'

Isabelle remembered that she and Petra had arrived in Hereford too early, with half an hour to wait for the train, and that Petra had wandered off for a few minutes. The cruelty of it made her want to yelp like a hurt animal.

'Her friends? Has she written to any of her friends?'

Messengers went flying to library, classrooms and tennis courts. The friends were both appalled and excited, but couldn't help. The principal raised the question of whether it was time to inform the police. Isabelle thought about it and shook her head.

'Not yet. No.'

The principal thought, 'So it is elopement, probably' and knew they'd all have to be watchful because these things always unsettled the more impressionable girls. It never entered Isabelle's mind. She knew this was part of her daughter's war against her and couldn't face the idea of police coming heavy-booted into that. She promised to let the principal know as soon as there was any news and drove home, arriving at Holders Hope bone-tired, well after dark. Her housekeeper, Mrs Morgan, heard the car stopping and met her in the hall.

'You'll be wanting supper, Mrs Allegri. Mr Marius is in the sitting room.'

She hadn't been expecting Marius home, but it was a relief to have him there. She pushed open the door and found him standing on the hearth

rug, a tumbler of whisky and water in his hand.
She started trying to tell him what had happened
but he spoke first, his anger sweeping aside
manners or any reservations about swearing in
front of women.

'I only found out about it this morning.
Mother, what the *hell* are you letting my sister
do?'

49

It wasn't easy to keep anything to yourself in
Treorchy. Still, the Thomas family did manage to
keep it hidden for a surprisingly long time that
their guest was an owner's daughter. Without
actually telling lies, they allowed it to be understood that she was a remote relative visiting from
London – which explained the voice – who'd
been ill – which explained the hair. Petra knew
nothing of this. She'd arrived like a starfish
dropped by some chance into a rockpool, and lay
there calm and placid, stirred occasionally round
her edges by the small warm currents of the
place. It was the other inhabitants of the rockpool who did the scurrying, their lives disrupted
entirely by the dropping in of this unexpected
creature. Sarah, Trefor's elder sister and the
woman of the house now her mother was dead,
had been appalled almost beyond speaking by
Petra's arrival without warning after midnight.
Sarah had left her miner husband and two-year-

old daughter asleep upstairs and come down to make cocoa for her brother's return on the last train, looking forward to a quiet half hour with him over the dying embers of the fire. Sarah was like Trefor both in nature and looks, dark haired and strong featured, inclined to take a serious view of things. She wore her hair in a long thick plait, pinned up on her head by day, down her back at night. She stood by the kitchen range watching that the milk didn't boil over, her mother's old dressing gown over her flannel nightdress, feet in comfortable trodden-down slippers. Being caught unawares like that was one of the things that made her furious when Trefor brought Petra home. They had a whispered conversation in the scullery while Petra sipped cocoa by the fire.

'You might have warned me.'

'How could I?'

'She's got a home to go to.'

'She says she's not going. Anyway, she can't get there tonight.'

'Where's she supposed to sleep then?'

'She'll have my bed.'

'Where will you sleep?'

'The chair in front of the fire.'

'How long is this supposed to go on?'

Trefor didn't have many secrets from Sarah. He wondered whether to tell her that Petra believed her mother guilty of murder. Compromised.

'She doesn't get on well with her mother. I don't think she'll go back.'

'Well, she can't stay here.'

But she did. By the time Trefor caught the train back down to Cardiff at the end of his leave nothing had been decided one way or the other. Petra had begged them not to let her mother know where she was and reluctantly Sarah and her father had agreed not to for a while. The deciding factor was Trefor, who used all his powers of persuasion on Petra's side. Part of it was simple humanity. The more complicated thing, which he admitted to himself, was that Petra was a kind of trophy. Mrs Allegri, as he saw it, had ruined his own working life before it even got started, taken Megan so far away from her family that she hardly ever came home to Treorchy, tried to turn Evan into a fancy gardener when he should be a miner. It was a kind of revenge to see her daughter sitting at their table eating cold mutton and potatoes, washing up at the stone sink in the scullery, playing with his little niece on the rag rug in front of the fire. But the revenge didn't involve cruelty to Petra herself. If she'd shown any sign of unhappiness he'd have taken her straight home. The fact was that she ate mutton and potatoes with as much appetite as if she'd been working down the pit all day, washed up as if she'd been born to it and knew games with bits of string and clothes pegs that kept the child quiet for half an hour at a time. A week after Trefor had gone back, Sarah and Petra were moving around the cramped house almost as easily as sisters, sharing the chores, going together to the shop in the High Street that sold groceries and boots, gossiping. Their talk was always about the family and

359

Treorchy. If Sarah ever tried to nudge it towards Holders Hope, Petra just went dumb. The only exception was her time there with Evan. Sarah watched Petra's face light up as she talked about Evan, his daring with horses, his amazing skill with musical instruments and thought she'd fathomed the mystery of what Petra was doing there. The owner's daughter was in love with Evan. That was what the quarrel with her mother had been about, the only explanation of her flight from luxury to this. Loving her brothers, Sarah found it explicable and liked Petra more because of it. She didn't see how anything could come of it in the end, but with Evan away no harm for the moment.

Just three little matters needed to be settled. The first one was to stop Petra trying to speak Welsh. She knew quite a few words, but her accent made it a strain. If she used it to neighbours their looks of alarm embarrassed Sarah. In the second week, she tackled the problem.

'Would you mind not speaking Welsh with Jenny there? We want her to grow up with English, so as not having trouble at school.'

The second problem was more delicate. Sarah worked round to it by taking more time than usual to count out money on the counter of Short's shop, sighing at the cost of butter and bacon. A few days of this penetrated Petra's starfish calm. Sarah came down from making the beds to find a little pile of notes and coins on the table.

'What's this?'

'It's a bit under ten pounds. I want you to have

it for my food and things.'

Sarah pushed it across the table to her. 'I'm not taking all that. If you want to, you can pay us a bit for your keep every week.'

They settled in the end on five shillings a week for bed, laundry and all meals. Petra counted out ten shillings for the two weeks she'd been there and put the rest away, calculating that she had enough to last nearly through to Christmas, which was further than she wanted to think for the moment.

The third problem was the most delicate of all and Sarah waited until one evening when the family had finished their meal and she and Petra were walking together up a path towards the open hills to get some fresh air after the heat of the kitchen range.

'You feeling better now, after what happened in Cardiff?'

The fact was, Sarah didn't know what had happened in Cardiff. When Trefor had told her about the attack she'd asked outright 'Did they rape her?' and been amazed to hear he didn't know. Now, with the lines of grey slate roofs behind them and a breeze coming off the hills with the scent of gorse on it, she got Petra to talk a little and found she wasn't sure of the answer herself. It took some delicate questioning, and a touch of the directness permitted to a married woman, to find out in the end that the answer was no. She felt relieved for Petra and for Evan. With all that settled, they fell into a routine that depended on the shift patterns of Sarah's husband and father at the pit and if Petra was still

361

an exotic in the rockpool, at least the other inhabitants weren't as disturbed by her as they had been. That was the state of affairs when Petra's mother arrived.

The Wolseley stayed parked outside the manager's office at Penyrheol pit. Isabelle knew there wouldn't be room for it in any of the narrow streets. Marius was parked firmly in his office too because Isabelle knew there'd be no sense to be got out of Petra if the two of them started quarrelling. All the way from Holders Hope, after an early morning start, Marius had gone on asking himself and her what his sister thought she was doing.

'And then the Thomases of all people to choose. Trefor Thomas is one of the biggest trouble makers in the whole of the Rhondda.'

'Are you sure? He's only young.'

'He started young. I suppose she's deliberately chosen the family she knows would do my position here most damage.'

It was a relief to Isabelle to leave him and walk on her own up the steep terraces of houses her father had built. She found the house, stood on the narrow doorstep and knocked on the shining brass knocker. A voice came from inside, not Petra's.

'If that's the man from the Provident Club the money's on the mantelpiece.'

A pause, steps, the door opened and there was Petra in a brown skirt and blue blouse Isabelle didn't recognise. She was holding out some coins, starting to say something. When she saw her mother on the step her jaw dropped.

'What are you doing here?'

'Come to take you home, darling.'

'I'm not going.'

Sarah appeared in the passageway behind her with Jenny hanging on to her skirt. She looked alarmed to see this smartly dressed woman on her step.

'What is it, Petra? Has something happened?'

'It's my mother.'

Somehow, they got themselves into the space that was both kitchen and living room. When Sarah invited Isabelle to sit down and offered tea, she accepted and Sarah and Jenny went to the scullery, leaving mother and daughter alone. She didn't rage at Petra or ask a lot of questions, just sat there and talked gently while Petra stood holding onto the edge of the kitchen table as if afraid she'd be dragged out by force.

'Darling, if I've hurt you in some way I'm very sorry for it, though I don't know how. But please don't punish me like this.'

'You needn't worry. I'm safe here.'

'Safe from what?'

'I'm not going back.'

'Why not?'

'I'm happy here.'

The appalling thing was that, if you disregarded her present tension, she did look as if she'd been happy. Her face and body had filled out a little and her skin was clear. Even her hair had grown a few inches and seemed glossier. She looked at home in what, to Isabelle, was an impossibly crowded and stuffy little room with a jar of rice

363

and a pudding bowl on the table, a child's rag doll flung over the chair, a smell of bacon lingering in the warm air.

'If you're worried about the Thomases, I'll see they're looked after.'

'I'm not worried.'

'What is it then?' Getting no answer, she tried firmness. 'You know you're not of age for another three years? I can insist you come home.'

'How? Call the police and have me arrested?'

'Petra, don't be silly. How could I do anything like that?'

'How then?'

This time, Isabelle had no answer. She stayed there all morning, talked with Sarah then with the Thomas's father when he came home and got nowhere. The Thomases were polite, respectful even, but made it clear that it wasn't their decision. In the end Isabelle was forced to retreat, exhausted and near to tears. In the passage on the way out she tried one last appeal.

'Petra, is there anything I can do or say to make you come home?'

Petra gave her a long and alarmingly adult look, although the words she spoke might have come from a child.

'If you could bring my father home, then I'd come.'

50

June 1916

By mid June the apple blossom was over and small green fruits were forming. The white cottage paeonies were already scattering their petals but the larger flowers of Avalanche were taking over from them just as Philip had hoped, along with the pale pink of Aurore, creamy Stephania with its heart of gold stamens, Marie Jacquin like a water lily on land. Isabelle went slowly down the steps, murmuring their names to herself. She needed soothing. Petra was refusing to answer letters. Marius was furious with both her and Isabelle, demanding retaliation against the Thomas family which she refused to consider. She was carrying a handful of letters which had arrived by the midday post and knew they included another on the subject. Avalanche, Aurore, Stephania, Marie Jacquin. She tried to close her mind and her eyes to a different list of plant names – sow thistle, fat hen, goosegrass, dead nettle, convolvulus. With Will and Evan away and poor Enoch so slow, weeds were making inroads on the borders. She went on down the steps to the little stone seat overlooking the pond. There was one letter addressed in an old-fashioned copperplate hand on a thick vellum envelope with a London postmark.

Lincoln's Inn
12 June 1916

Dear Mrs Allegri,
I am the solicitor of Mr Philip Cordell. There are matters which I should discuss with you and I should be very grateful if you would allow me to call on you at your home whenever is convenient.
    Yours obediently, Wilfred Giles-Shay

She sent a telegram 'COME AT ONCE.' Mr Giles-Shay arrived the following afternoon just after three o'clock by horse cab from Hereford station. In further exchange of telegrams the day before he'd politely refused Isabelle's offer to meet him with the motor car at the station. It was a fine day with the sky over the hills a tight-stretched blue and the last of the hawthorn flowering in the hedges. The swifts were back and she watched them skating the sky in wide looping turns as she waited on the terrace. Some of them swooped so low over her head that she could hear the swish of their wings, like a skate blade on ice. Rees led the solicitor towards her across the terrace. He was a tall man, slightly stooping with greying sideburns. His pin-striped suit and curly brimmed bowler made him look too dark and solid for the brightness of the day. He accepted tea, refused sandwiches, and made conversation about the journey – very pleasant scenery, so refreshing after London until Rees and Mrs Morgan had gone and they had the terrace to themselves.

'Mrs Allegri, I'm sorry to tell you we have news of Mr Cordell.'

'Sorry?'

The whole landscape lurched.

'You should know that when Mr Cordell went away, he made us his legal executors and gave instructions that we were to be informed if anything should happen to him.'

He paused, seeming to need some response from her. She nodded, looking down at her tea. There was a small insect drowning in it, making no attempt to resist. A greenfly. She got it out on her fingernail and watched it.

'I gather you didn't know what kind of mission Mr Cordell was engaged on?'

She shook her head.

'That was also the case with us. We know now he was carrying out very important work on the Caucasus front.'

Runnels of tea had drained away down the dome of her fingernail leaving the insect dry but not moving.

'Last week the War Office heard that Mr Cordell had been killed near Trebizond. They say he was a very brave man and did his duty to the last.'

A leg seemed to be quivering, but perhaps that was just the effect of drying out. Mr Giles-Shay was unnerved by her silence, fearful that she hadn't understood him.

'It seems Mr Cordell was accompanied by another man, a corporal. He survived and found Mr Cordell's body. They buried him there in the mountains. The news of his death came back by

367

a very roundabout way and they only heard about it in London last week.'

The leg had stopped quivering and the insect was nothing but a small green smear on her fingernail. She wiped it off against her dress.

'Should I ... should I call your housekeeper, Mrs Allegri? Is there anybody...?'

She shook her head.

'Philip told you to tell me?'

'Yes. He came to our office a few days before he was due to leave England. He made a will and entrusted us with a package of letters, which were to be given to you by hand in the event of anything happening to him. I have them with me. May I ask if your daughter Petra Allegri is at home?'

'No'.

'Mr Cordell made her the main beneficiary of his will. It is not a large estate, in fact it probably won't amount to more than a few hundred pounds.'

He opened the briefcase, took out a large white envelope and turned it over on the table to show a red wax seal and three signatures across the back flap.

'This was signed and sealed in Mr Cordell's presence on his last visit to our office. He was adamant that in the event of his death it was to be delivered to you with the seal unbroken.'

'Thank you.'

That was his business done. The cab was waiting and he was free to go, only it seemed impossible to go and leave her there.

'Are you going back to London tonight, Mr

Giles-Shay?'

Her voice was very nearly steady. He stuttered that he'd been planning to, ashamed of himself for thinking of timetables. She was ahead of him.

'I believe there's a good train around six. Please don't worry about me.'

He took her hand, assured her truly of his sympathy. On his way out he found Rees and Mrs Morgan hovering in the hall and told them what had happened.

'I'll telegram for Mr Marius,' Rees said. 'He can probably get here by tonight.'

They discussed whether Mrs Morgan should go out to her and decided that she'd want to be left alone for a while.

The sun slid westwards down the sky. Isabelle felt the heat of it on her face and shoulders and as instinctively as any animal looking for shade got up and carried the envelope down the steps to where the apple tunnel led into the Pleasaunce. The grass under the trees was so long that when she lay down in it and turned her face to the side she could see nothing but green. She said to the grass blades: 'I am forty-three years old. Nobody will ever love me again.' Then she thought of the day they'd chosen the apple trees and cried and howled with unbelief until her whole body was shaking. The first thing that reminded her of the thick envelope beside her in the grass was the need to touch something that Philip had touched. She put her lips to the signature that sprawled across the flap in his familiar looping script then tore open the seal, scattering

369

fragments of bright red wax into the grass. She had a hope – a stupid one she knew, but more real than anything else around her – that he'd have put something inside the envelope that would deny what she'd just heard. 'My dearest Isa, Don't believe what anybody tells you. I'm alive my darling. Alive and coming back to you.' She knelt and upended the big envelope onto the flattened patch of grass where she'd been lying. Three envelopes fell out. Two were white ones, normal letter size, addressed in Philip's handwriting simply 'Isabelle' and 'Petra'. The third was a large manila envelope. In capitals on the front – his capitals that she recognised from plant labels – it read FOR THE EYES OF MRS ISABELLE ALLEGRI. She read her letter in the white envelope first.

London
6 June 1915

Darling,
If you're seeing this, then I'm sorry with all my heart for bringing grief to you. If there's a person in the world who was created to be happy, then it's you. I wish so much that things could have gone other ways for all three of us – but even as things are and have been I know that the best of my life is having known you and being allowed to love you.

I don't know where to start writing or where to stop, so I'll only say this. Try for your sake, my sake and Petra's to be happy again one day. Remember our times together not with regret

370

but with the certainty that they were real and all the things that we loved and were kind to and laughed at were real and always will be.

Please give the enclosed to Petra when you think the right time has come. You can guess what's in it. As for the other letter addressed to you, I am sorry to burden you with it. It may be that you never need to use it. I hope so. But if the time does come when you need it, you must show it to whoever you think fit.

That's all, I think. Look after the garden if you can. I planted all my love for you and Petra into it, but I think you guessed that. May everything on earth and above it protect you and make you happy again.

I love you.

P.

Isabelle sat in the grass for a long time before opening the manila envelope. It was hard and resistant in her fingers, tearing raggedly. Inside were two thick sheets of paper covered in Philip's handwriting, smaller and neater than usual.

London.
5 June 1915.

TO WHOM IT MAY CONCERN

This is to state that in July 1907 I killed Mr Leon Allegri at his home of Holders Hope in Herefordshire. I make this statement in sound mind and of my own free will.

The circumstances are as follows. Mr Allegri

believed that I was intimate with his wife, Isabelle. He and I had quarrelled. On the night of his death, he suggested that we should meet in the garden to discuss the matter after his wife and the rest of the household had gone to bed. The garden at Holders Hope was then in the course of construction. There was a pile of stone nearby. Our quarrel resumed, with angry words on both sides. I am not sure who struck the first blow. In any case, I hit Mr Allegri on the jaw. He fell over and struck his head on one of the stones. I believed him to be unconscious and at first intended to fetch help from the house, then realised that he was dead.

Although I had not intended to kill him I knew that the police might not believe this, since our quarrel was well known to the household. I waited for some time to be sure that he was dead then fetched one of the workmen's wheelbarrows from a shed near the house. I loaded Mr Allegri's body into the wheelbarrow, covered it with a tarpaulin and wheeled it across the fields down to the river near the Hereford to Abergavenny Road. I wrapped the body in the tarpaulin, weighted it with stones from the garden and slid it down the bank into a deep part of the river, downstream from the village of Holdersby. If the body had been discovered I think I intended to confess, but I assume it was eventually washed down to the sea or decomposed in the river.

Mrs Allegri spent considerable time and money trying to have him traced. She trusted me as her agent in this and I instructed and paid private investigators both here and abroad on her behalf.

I gave her no hint of what had really happened.

In the circumstances, I cannot have this statement witnessed, but my solicitor, Mr W. Giles-Shay of Lincoln's Inn will recognise my signature. He is not aware of the contents of this.

Signed

Philip Anthony Cordell

She put all three letters in the big envelope and stood up. The sun was low down in the west so the long shadows of brick pillars and rose swags fell across the steps on her way back up. When she got to the bridge two figures came to meet her, Mrs Morgan and Megan, carrying one of her warm cloaks. They wrapped her in the cloak and led her along the path between the lavender bushes, up the steps to the terrace. She kept the envelope with its three letters clamped against her chest.

51

July 2001

'Did she say visiting her relatives?'

Kim's voice, sharp and scared from outside the tent. She was kneeling down, trying to see past Colin. He felt her jolt of surprise when she took in the white-haired woman and the display of bones.

'Oh shit. Trouble.'

'Am I trouble?' The laugh was a crackle rather than a cackle, like paper rustling. 'Why don't you make yourselves comfortable?'

They looked at each other and moved cautiously. It was a tight fit for three so they sat with their backs pressed against the tent, knees drawn up nearly to their chests so as not to disturb the bones. The woman had a sinewy look about her, like a tree root clinging to a precarious piece of earth. Under the wrinkled skin her forehead and jaw were square. Her white hair was cut into a thick cap and her eyes as direct and bright as a child's. She wore a shirt in a blue, white and brown check pattern, denim jeans and walking boots.

'My name's Rosa, by the way.'

'Are you an Allegri?'

Kim asked the question. She sounded angry and although Colin knew it came from nervousness he hoped she wouldn't make things worse.

'Isabelle Allegri was my grandmother.'

Colin took a deep breath. 'The woman the garden was made for?'

'That's right. I've just been reading the article. I hadn't seen it before.'

He noticed that his photocopy of the 1915 piece was on the groundsheet by her foot.

Kim said, 'So Leon Allegri was your grandfather?'

She and Colin looked at each other, then down at the bones and started speaking together.

'I'm sorry, I didn't know when I started...'

'Look, you can't blame Colin. He was only interested in the garden for goodness sake...'

They both stopped. She was looking at them with an odd smile on her face.

'Did you know whose they were?'

Kim started talking again but Colin signed to her to let him do it. He stared into the old woman's bright eyes.

'Not at first, no. I thought they were really old – historical. Then when Kim found out a few days ago about him being killed and the garden being destroyed...'

'So you found out about that, did you? How?'

Kim said, 'There was a maid called Mary. I talked to her granddaughter.'

'They're still gossiping, then?'

Colin said, 'So the bones really are Leon Allegri's?'

'I'm quite sure of it.'

'I honestly didn't intend any disrespect to them. If I'd had any idea...'

She raised a hand to cut off his apologies.

'So why did you come here?'

'I came across that description of the garden when I was doing some research and I was curious to see if there was anything of it left. There was a man named Cordell, Philip Cordell, a plant hunter...' He looked at the puzzled expression on her face and thought he was losing her. 'He's the one who designed the garden. It mentions him in that piece, if you...'

'Yes, I know about Philip Cordell.'

'Did you ever meet him?'

She laughed. 'I'm not that old, even if I look it. He was killed in the war – the First World War, that is.'

Kim said experimentally, 'And your grand-father the painter died trying to save the garden?'

'What?' Rosa stared at Kim. 'Was that what the maid's granddaughter told you?'

'She hadn't got the whole story.'

'She certainly hadn't.'

Rosa wriggled round, reached into a pack behind her and brought out a bottle of Jamesons. She ordered Colin 'Hang onto that,' then leaned forward and started rolling up his sleeping bag, bones and all. Her hands were square and large for the rest of her body. When she'd got the sleeping bag into a neat sausage she turned over the ends to keep the bones from falling out and pushed the bundle into Kim's arms. 'Stow it somewhere, outside if you like. And find us something to drink out of. It may be a long night.'

52

1917

A lot of damage was done through the winter of 1916 and early spring of 1917. Birch scrub crowded the groves of azaleas. Lavender bushes grew woody and split at the joints. Moles rampaged. Isabelle, numbed with misery, looked down occasionally from the terrace and was aware of what was happening, almost welcomed it and did nothing. Until one bright day in April, ten months after she heard that Philip was dead, the urgency of getting away from the house took her across the lawn and down the broad steps to the apple tunnel. Only the tunnel wouldn't let her through. The growth of the previous year had exploded with new green shoots that stuck out at all angles, whipping her in the face when she tried to force a way through. Furious at being denied even this small thing she started grabbing and tearing at the sappy growth, breaking her nails, feeling the stickiness from the flayed apple stems running down her wrists. She was crying, swearing at them. Then a woody spur about the thickness of her finger gave way and fell with a snap, taking a whole swathe of green shoots with it.

'Oh.'

She stumbled and fell on her knees and remembered Philip explaining how you should always make clean cuts otherwise disease and rot would get in. She pictured the tunnel and the whole little orchard on the other side of it, brown leafed and orange mould spotted.

'I'm sorry,' she said to the broken spur. Then she backed out of the tunnel and went at a fast walk up to the tool shed to get Philip's secateurs.

The fight back started from that day. She took to spending all the lengthening spring days in the garden, secateurs or weeding fork in hand. At first she had no very clear idea what she was doing and missed Philip in a very practical way, on top of the ache that was always there. But after the first panic her determination and efficiency started taking over. Enoch, who'd got used to wandering about the garden in his own undirected way, found his working life changed. He was instructed to flatten the molehills and provided with a new mechanical mowing machine with a temperament that became the bane of his life. When the village school broke up in July, Isabelle took on two fourteen-year-old lads as apprentice gardeners and threw them ruthlessly into battle against the couch grass in the iris bed and the riot in the paeony border. By the end of the summer something like order had been restored to the lawns, the lavender walk and most of the borders. But there were failures too. In the lily pool, dull but determined yellow water lilies had taken over from lovely but languorous pinks and whites and they in their turn were losing the battle to duckweed. Isabelle knew it was silting up and returning to the condition of swampy hollow it had been ten years ago. She'd looked for the kingfisher all summer but hadn't seen it. She mentioned it to Will Thomas, when she drove Bathsheba to visit him at a military convalescent hospital in Warwickshire.

'He'll be back,' Will assured her.

He was out of bed by then, allowed to walk round the grounds in his blue hospital uniform. He'd been with a trainload of horses when a stray shell had landed on it. Will's arm had been broken but the worst damage was a broken rib that punctured a lung. Pneumonia set in, then pleurisy. He assured Isabelle he was on the mend now, though he was as thin as a big-boned man could be, with knuckles and wrist bones like scrubbed new potatoes under his hospital-white

378

skin. His eyes were different too, less serene than Isabelle remembered. He comforted her about the garden. He'd be back home with an honourable discharge from the army as soon as the doctors signed him off, then they'd get it the way Mr Cordell would have wanted.

Early May 1917 marked the first year of Petra's arrival in Treorchy, but she was too busy to notice it. Six months before, with the store of money in her carpet bag running out, she'd got herself a job. She was secretary to a solicitor in Treherbert just two train stops up the valley from Treorchy. The money she got meant that she could take a room with a miner's widow in the house next door and relieve the pressure on space in the Thomas's house. She paid three shillings for the room and tea and bread and butter in the morning, another three shillings to Sarah because she still took her evening meal with the family. She enjoyed the work, but enjoyed even more the way it gradually drew her into the life of the valley. She wasn't an object of curiosity any more. The rhythms of the valley became hers. She'd be woken in the morning by the clatter of boot studs down the street as the miners went on shift, travel to work in the train past the coal trucks coming down from the pits at the top of the valley, walk from the station to the office with the smell of coal dust in the air and see, all the way down from Treherbert to Trehafod, plumes of steam rising from the high brick chimneys of the engine houses and the great iron wheels revolving. The speech rhythms became hers as well. Anybody would still know she wasn't Welsh, but the hard edges of English wore off. There were evenings, sitting in front of the fire in the Thomas's cramped little living room, talking over the day's gossip with Sarah while Jenny played on the rag rug and the cat dozed on the back of the chair, when Petra felt happier than she ever had in her life. Sometimes there were letters from Trefor to read. (Though they had to wait to find out from the *South Wales Echo* that he'd been awarded the Military Medal.) Evan, in France now, wrote less frequently, usually with request for jam and socks, and always sent his respects to Petra. Sarah would watch Petra's face when she gave her the letters to read for confirmation of what she'd guessed and smiled inwardly when she didn't find it, concluding that Petra was a close one in some ways. Gradually, Petra's own family came to seem less real than the Thomases. Her mother wrote now and then, hoping she was well, saying how she'd love to see her. On Petra's eighteenth birthday she sent a soft woollen shawl, the kind you might wear over an evening dress to a concert, and a ten pound note. Petra wrote to thank her and said she was well. She tucked the ten pound note away and persuaded Sarah to take the shawl.

For Megan, the spring and summer of 1917 were a season of loss. She'd been patient all through Isabelle's winter of grief and seclusion, believing that softness and colour must surely come back into her working life at some time. But what Isabelle wanted from her wardrobe were plain cotton blouses, skirts that didn't show the dirt too much. Her hair was screwed up into a knot every morning and brushed out with a few quick strokes at night. Her arched feet and elegant ankles spent day after day in woollen stockings and boots while rows of shoes in pearly leather and soft kid sat on their shoe trees in the wardrobe. Megan hated being idle, wasn't trained for it. It was the same with the rest of the staff. Mrs Downs in the kitchen complained that it was all sandwiches, sandwiches with nobody eating proper meals any more. Rees gave up on being a butler almost entirely and spent most of his time on war work, organising the schoolchildren into collecting blackberries and windfall apples to make jam for soldiers and picking up horse chestnuts which, for some reason nobody quite understood, were in demand for the munitions factories. That was about the time that Isabelle and Megan had their serious talk.

It was in Isabelle's dressing room, after a day when she'd been dealing with a bramble crisis in the border. Her hands were reddened and covered in scratches. Megan watched them as Isabelle sat brushing leaves out of her hair until she couldn't stand it any more. She gently grabbed Isabelle's wrists and took the brush away from her.

'What are you doing?'

Not saying anything, Megan took a bottle of glycerine and rosewater off the dressing table and knelt beside Isabelle's chair. She worked on the right hand first, rubbing the slithery flower-smelling liquid into the back of it, pushing down

381

and massaging the skin at the base of the nails then turning it over to do the palm. Her fingers slid in and out between the bases of Isabelle's fingers and the tender web between finger and thumb. After a while Isabelle sighed and closed her eyes.

'Lovely hands you've got still, you should look after them,' Megan said.

She got an emery board out of a drawer and attended to Isabelle's ragged nails, then used the buffer with its tortoiseshell back and pad of yellow chamois leather until they shone as pink as sugared almonds.

'It's time you went, Megan. You've been thinking about it, haven't you?'

'Yes.'

Isabelle hadn't been spying deliberately, but she'd noticed the letters with London postmarks that arrived for Megan.

'I'll help you find a situation, if you like.'

Megan looked at her, defensiveness in her eyes for something she wanted very much.

'My friend Dinah's working in a beauty parlour in Bond Street now. She thinks there's a place for me.'

The place couldn't be kept open for her much longer. She'd been trying to make up her mind for weeks but couldn't bring herself to leave Isabelle.

'Well, you'd better write and tell her you're coming, hadn't you? If you leave on Monday week, say, that will give you time to sort out your things.'

'Monday week?'

Megan's mouth fell open. She'd forgotten how quickly Isabelle could move once she'd made her mind up about something.

'We'll write a reference for you together and go through my wardrobe and sort out some clothes to take with you. Let's say I pay you a month's wages in lieu of notice so you'll have some money to live on in London.'

Megan said, almost wailing, 'But I don't like leaving you.'

'Oh my dear, what is there for you here?' Isabelle put her arm round Megan's shoulders and turned her so that they were both facing the mirror. 'You're beautiful. You'll never be more beautiful and it doesn't last long, so don't waste it.'

She thought 'That's what a mother should say to a daughter.' The formal passing on of beauty. At that moment Megan felt more like a daughter to her than Petra did.

For Evan, the most important event of the whole war happened in early October, 1917. His unit had been sent for regrouping to some French town behind the lines whose name nobody bothered to remember. A battalion of American troops were camped near the town. They were objects of curiosity to the British, many of whom had never met an American before, but there wasn't much chance for fraternising. Until one evening when Evan and a few friends were off duty and wandering in the town square. It was a dim place with the light going, no lamps lit, not even a caff open. The local people had already retired behind firmly shut doors and drawn curtains. Then Evan heard a sound that picked his brain up like somebody hoisting a kitten by the scruff of the neck. It took him a few seconds to identify it as a trumpet, but the noise it made wasn't like any trumpet tone he'd ever heard before. It cut through the dimness and dampness of the closed-down town like an explosion of life. Instinctively, he began walking towards it. One of his friends called out to ask where he was going. He kept walking.

'Evan boyo, it's only some of the Yanks mucking around. Don't you go getting into trouble.'

He went on round the corner and into a side street. There was a bench under a plane tree and a low granite trough beside it with a pipe dribbling water. Two men in the uniform of American private soldiers were sitting on the bench, one with a banjo on his knee. The third man was standing, one foot on the edge of the water trough playing a trumpet, uptilted to the windows of the curtained houses. In the dimness he couldn't make out their faces at all, then realised with a little shock that they were all black. He'd seen black men in Cardiff, but not many. The banjo player was plucking a series of bass notes, the other man beating with the flat of his hand on the bench. The trumpet player was throwing out phrases like spurts of flame and the rhythm of them was like nothing he'd ever heard before. It made the blood pulse in his veins as if it were trying to escape from the regular beating of his heart and join whatever the trumpet was doing. After what seemed like a long time, the

384

trumpeter stopped suddenly, laughed and said something to the men on the bench. His voice was drawling and low in pitch and Evan couldn't make out what he'd said. The man with the banjo gestured towards Evan with his chin and the trumpeter noticed him for the first time.

'Hello, boy.'

Not unfriendly, but not quite friendly either. Defensive. Evan was desperate to get them to talk to him and explain what the trumpet had been doing, but didn't know if they'd understand him.

'You play music, boy?' That from the banjo player.

Evan always carried in his pocket the clarinet that had been Petra's gift, broken into sections and wrapped in a clean yellow duster. The men in his platoon liked him to play things some-times. Conscious of three pairs of eyes on him he unwrapped it and put it together. He thought, Tipperary, might be the safest thing but when he raised the clarinet to his lips what came out was a memory of a wild piano in the back parlour of The Sun at Holdersby. A low and chuckling 'Waaal' from the bench told him that he'd surprised them, then the banjo player started plucking out an accompaniment, the other man clapping the bench in time with him. When he'd finished there was a silence, then the man with the trumpet said, 'Where d'you learn Maple Leaf Rag then, boy?'

'At home.'

'You from England?'

'Wales.'

'That in England?'

'Near it. Where're you from?'

'New Orleans.'

They let him play with them, Maple Leaf Rag again then the tune the trumpeter had been playing, which turned out to be Tiger Rag. They only stopped when an old woman leaned out of the window above them and yelled something in French that unmistakably meant stop it and go away. Back in the square a clock was striking and the three Americans went off at a quick march towards the road out of town that led to their camp. The trumpeter called over his shoulder to Evan, 'Same place tomorrow, OK?'

But the next evening Evan was put on guard duty at the supply tents and the day after that the Americans moved on. He never knew their names or even, at that point, the name of the music they'd been playing but from that evening onwards he had his own war aim. Whenever he was anywhere near an American unit he'd find his way to them for an hour or two with his clarinet in his pocket and Tiger Rag or Darktown Strutters Ball in his head. The rhythms even got into 'Tipperary' and the other men in his platoon complained that it put their singing out. When they asked him what it was meant to be, he didn't know. He had to wait for a chance meeting with a sergeant from Chicago to put a name to it. *Jass.* Or jazz if he liked it better. No problem.

53

Spring and summer of 1918 were a switchback between hope and disappointment. On hope side, some plantings worked even better in their state of semi-neglect than they had through eleven years of care. The yellow roses that Philip had planted as an experiment at the edge of the wood smothered themselves in flowers and merged with the green of the young hazel trees so that it looked at first glance as if a new species had created itself, rose flowered and hazel-leafed. Groves of blue Himalayan poppies, glimpsed through foliage in early mornings looked like distant lakes waiting to be discovered. On the disappointment side, there was something wrong in the iris bed, more leaf than bloom this year; the paeony border had several absentees and slugs munched the delphiniums. Rheumatism caught up with Enoch, who abandoned his struggles with the moles and the mechanical mower and retreated to his own small and obedient garden down in the village. One of the two apprentice lads was only too eager to take on mower and moles, but that left only Isabelle and the other lad to do the weeding and they couldn't keep up with the summer surge of dead nettle and ground ivy, willowherb and ragwort. Things improved after July when Isabelle took on a girl school-leaver and by autumn the michaelmas daisies and sedums were at least able to flower unstrangled. But there was no time in all this for the lily pool. Duckweed covered its diminishing circle of water. Dogwoods and alder pushed roots into the rich mud at the edges. The descendants of the kingfisher had given up in early spring and moved to the river.

All the time, hopes and rumours of peace grew, died and grew again. Sometimes it would be tomorrow, sometimes another lifetime away. When it happened at last in November it took them almost by surprise. It came to Isabelle as she stood on the wet lawn with Will swaddled in coat and scarf beside her, listening to the peal of bells from the church at Holdersby – a disjointed peal because some of the ringers were away in France.

For Trefor and Evan it was waiting in trenches in different parts of France in the unbelievable silence after the guns had stopped, each of them wondering if his brother had come through.

For Petra it was the surprise of the shift patterns being broken, miners' boots clattering on the streets at midday, shouting and cheering at first then a hymn, *Cwm Rhondda*, in men's voices rising up through the narrow streets of houses to the brown hillside and grey coal-smelling sky.

For Megan, it was the shout of the paper boy outside in Bond Street while she was working on a client's eyebrow. *Ugly, coarse and shapeless eyebrows can be transformed into things of beauty.*

Treatment harmless, painless and permanent.
'Armistice. Read all about it.' Her needle
quivered and the client said 'So it's come at last,
then' as if peace were some strange animal that
nobody knew quite what to do with.

54

1919

When Marius pretended to admire the garden,
Isabelle knew for certain that something was on
his mind. Marius couldn't tell a paeony from a
poppy and until now hadn't even tried to hide his
lack of interest.

'It must take a lot of your time, Mama.'

From eight in the morning until the light went.
Then, after a hasty dinner, hours over catalogues
or correspondence with nurseries. Isabelle was
learning that plants wore out just as other things
did and had to be replaced. Luckily, Philip had
kept careful records of his plantings and sources.
It was still a stab to the heart to see his handwriting crammed into the margins of old
catalogues as if he'd written the comments just
the day before, reminders to himself that he
never had time to act on. *No, it's not hardy!* Or
Avoid! Horrible boiled sweet yellow. Or *Out of stock
but promised for next year. Chase up.*

'But it keeps you busy. I mean, you're happy?'

She might have asked him why he thought busy

and happy had anything to do with each other, but she was still trying to adjust to this new version of her son. It seemed as if he was trying to treat her as an old woman. It was all the more disconcerting because Marius, at 26, was so like his father when Isabelle eloped with him that part of her mind felt twenty again and amazed that any human being could look like that.

'I've been thinking that you're taking on too much. It may be time I took some of it off your shoulders.'

'The garden?'

'God, no. The pits, I mean. It doesn't seem reasonable to keep referring things to you, expecting you to read all the reports and make the decisions now I'm there on the spot.'

'My dear Marius, I've been doing that from the time you were nine years old. I hope you're not suggesting I'm getting too old and doddery for it now.'

She was 46.

'Of course I'm not.' He said it automatically, without conviction. 'Only things are changing pretty fast since the war finished, and not for the better. Prices are going down.'

'For the moment, yes. But they'll recover. You've heard they're even thinking of opening a new pit at Fernhill?'

It amused her to tease him, knowing he was the latest in a long line of men to be disconcerted by her head for business. He recovered better than most.

'Gladwyn and I went to a meeting in Cardiff yesterday. The general view is that we might never get back to wartime prices.'

'It goes in cycles, Marius, and as long as demand's holding up...'

'For the moment it is, but the foreign coalfields will be recovering over the next year or two. Unless we increase efficiency and above all get our labour costs down, we're finished.'

She stared down the lawn towards the weeping purple beech. It was one of the disappointments and had hardly grown at all since they'd planted it.

'I mean it, Mama. If the small owners like us are going to survive, we have to work together. Somebody has to take the initiative and, frankly, that's not something you can do part time and from a distance.'

The flat words could have been his grandfather's but they came out of his father's full and curving lips. She'd intended only that Marius should be safe through the war. The last thing she'd expected was that he should become passionate about coal.

'So what are you asking me to do?'

'Hand more decisions over to me. Of course, you'd retain ownership...'

'I certainly would.'

'...so you'd have the final say in anything really important, like amalgamating with other pits...'

'Being bought out you mean? Is this where you're heading – selling to Cambrian or one of the others?'

'Quite the reverse. Expanding. If we act now we could amalgamate with two or three of the other small owners at useful terms for ourselves and be

391

stronger when the big fight comes.'

'What fight?'

He turned to her with the look on his face that Leon had half a lifetime ago when he told her she had only once chance to be happy elope with him now or throw it away forever.

'The fight over labour costs. We've been funking it for the last twenty years.'

They walked up and down the terrace for a long time. Three things were settled. One, he was to represent their pits in any talks with other owners or unions. Two, by mutual agreement, he was to be paid a proper salary with a bonus linked to rising profits. The third point was decided almost casually as they were walking back inside because the air was getting cool.

'I think I might rent a little flat in London, Mama. I have to go up there quite a lot and it will work out cheaper than hotels.'

She was pleased about that, wanting a wider and brighter life for him than dock sidings and committee rooms. It had struck her that neither of her children wanted anything to do with this beauty she and Philip had made and had both, in their different ways, flown away to where the coal came from.

Evan came home to Treorchy in March, Trefor in April. Within ten days of Evan's return – just long enough to do the rounds of friends and relations in the Rhondda and spend most of his accumulated pay on two wild nights saying goodbye to his friends from the regiment in Cardiff – he was working underground at Eastside pit alongside his father. Too many things had changed for him to think of going back to the garden, and anyway it would mean a quarrel with Trefor that might set them apart for the rest of their lives. On his first Saturday afternoon off he auditioned for one of the miners' bands and was accepted, although the bandmaster told him he had a poor sense of rhythm, so for goodness sake, boyo, keep your eye on my baton. Petra still joined the family for evening meals, although quarter of an hour later to give both Evan and his father time to wash the coal dust off in the oval zinc bath in front of the kitchen range.

By accident, Petra was the first one to see Trefor when he came home. She'd just got back from work in Treherbert and was walking up the road from the station when she heard booted feet behind her, and the sound of a man coughing. She turned to see a thin man in a dark suit with a kit bag over his shoulder, bent over and spitting into the gutter. Before she could look away, he straightened up.

'Trefor Thomas.'

His face went red. He came towards her, unsmiling.

'Good evening, Miss Allegri.'

He'd known from Sarah's letters that she was still in Treorchy, but couldn't have expected that she'd be the first person he'd meet. She felt awkward, knowing that his family should have had this right.

'They'll be so glad to see you.'

He saw a tall young woman with hair thicker and glossier than he remembered, the childish square face a little rounded and softened by maturity. She was dressed the way any office girl in the valleys might dress, in white blouse and navy blue skirt and jacket that came from a shop down in Porth. He'd brought her to his home town as somebody rescued, now here she was welcoming him as if she'd lived there all her life. They walked up the road together. Every few steps they'd pass somebody who knew Trefor and called out a welcome. When they were near the Thomas's house, she deliberately fell a few steps back, so as not to complicate his homecoming. Later, when she went next door to join them, Sarah was preparing the welcome home meal, with thick slices of cold ham and pickles, Caerphilly cheese, bottles of beer for the men. They sat round the table together, elbows crushed so close to their sides that if somebody wanted to fork a pickle out of the jar, three people had to move. Soon after the meal she said goodnight and went back next door. She lay awake in the dark and heard Trefor and Evan going up to bed, the murmur of voices and Trefor coughing. She was glad for the family's sake that he was home, but found it hard to look at him without remembering the alley in Cardiff and the tone of his voice when he'd said 'You people.'

In May, Petra got a letter from her mother.

Darling,
Is it too much to hope that you could come home for a day or two for your twenty-first birthday next month? It would be a chance for you to see

Will and Bathsheba. Will asked after you and wants me to send you his regards.

Please do come if you can. There are some quite important things that I want to discuss with you, and I'm sure it would be best to talk about them in your own home. I could come and collect you in the car or meet you at Abergavenny station. Your loving mother,

Isabelle

The letter was in Petra's coat pocket on a Saturday afternoon when she went for a walk with Sarah and Jenny. Petra finished work at midday on a Saturday and it had become a routine to get home, change out of her good working clothes and take one of the paths that led out onto the hillside. On fine days, like this one she'd take the child with her to look at the sheep and wild flowers. That day she persuaded Sarah to go with them because she was looking pale and in need of fresh air. With the brothers home Sarah now had four men to look after in the small house, three of them miners. Jenny went skipping ahead of them and Petra trimmed her usual long strides to Sarah's slower pace. There was a point, going uphill, where the smell of coal dust and smoke from the valley gave way to sweeter air coming down from the hills. The point varied according to the wind and the seasons. Sometimes in winter Petra had walked nearly to the hilltop to find it. Today, with sun warming the hillside, they came to it lower down where a squat rock jutted onto the path and stopped to take in lungfuls of air. Sarah sat down heavily on the rock.

'You heard about Evan last Saturday?'

'What about him?'

'The bandmaster threatened to throw him out for larking around at rehearsal – him and two or three others, but Evan was the ringleader.'

'What happened?'

'Making a mock of the music, he said.'

'I don't suppose he meant any harm.'

Evan hadn't. Simply, at the end of Sousa's 'Washington Post March' Evan and two of the friends he'd initiated into the new music had ripped into the first few bars of 'When the Saints'. The bandmaster wouldn't stand for sacrilege against Sousa.

Sarah sighed. She didn't think her brother was playing fair with Petra and – the gossip in the valley being what it was – it could only be a matter of time before she knew about it. In Sarah's eyes, since Petra had given up so much for Evan, it was only fair to warn her.

'You know he's gone down to Cardiff again today?'

'I didn't know.'

'Spending all his money and back home after midnight. I'd hoped he'd settle when he came home and got work, but...'

Sarah was beginning to suspect that Evan had a girl down in Cardiff If she'd known the truth – that he spent his Saturday nights going round the halls or anywhere else where music was played, hoping to find anybody who spoke the same musical language – it would have puzzled her more than girls.

396

'Perhaps Evan isn't the sort who settles.'

Petra was looking up the hill as she said it, towards Jenny who was trying to get close enough to a sheep to stroke it.

'Do you ever think of going back home?'

'Home?' Petra turned, alarmed. Her mother's letter crackled in her pocket. 'Why, do you want me to go?'

'I don't, that's the truth, but you'll be wanting to get married, won't you? Settle down?'

The sheep lurched to its feet and walked away. Deprived, Jenny started howling.

'Don't worry. I'll get her.'

Petra ran lightly up the track. By the time she came down again, pacifying the child with a twisted barley sugar sweet from the bag in her pocket, Sarah had decided that she'd said as much as was needed about Evan.

'You heard Trefor's got himself a job. With Evans the grocer down in Porth, stacking boxes. Starts Monday.'

'That seems rather...' Petra had been going to say 'rather a waste' but decided against it. '...rather heavy work.'

'Easier than down the pit. Doesn't pay as much, though.'

When they got back to the house, Trefor was working at the table in the living room. He had sheets of paper spread all round him and a cheap fountain pen in hand. His face was paler than when he'd first arrived home and there were dark rings round his eyes. Sarah sighed, a mixture of impatience and concern.

'You said you'd be finished. I'll be needing to

lay that table for tea in a minute.'

'Give me five minutes. I've only got another two to do.'

Sarah took Jenny into the scullery to wash earth off her face and hands. Petra sat down in a chair on the other side of the table, more family now than visitor. She'd never seen anybody so intent. He wrote half a page, then cursed as the pen ran out, dipped the nib into the bottle of Stephens blue-black ink beside him, squeezed and released the lever on the barrel to suck up ink, started writing again. The ink didn't flow. He cursed the pen, shook it, and an arc of blue-black stars splashed over the page he'd just written. Petra felt the disaster of it. If he'd cursed or shouted, she'd have understood. Instead he put down the pen on the tablecloth quite gently, then lay his head down beside it on the splashed page, so weary and defeated it was as if a current running through him had been switched off

'Do you think I could help?'

His head came up and his dark eyes looked at her blankly, as if he'd forgotten she was there.

'Do you know what these are?'

'No.'

'Letters to miners about workers' control.'

'I could type them on the machine in the office.'

'Did you hear what I said, Miss Allegri?'

'Yes.' Then, because he was looking at her in a challenging way and because she wouldn't be again the humiliated girl from that night in Cardiff, she let her voice sound as hard as his. 'Did you hear what *I* said, Mr Thomas?'

Later that evening, in the street outside his house and her lodgings, he handed her a letter to be copied three times to different addresses. When he thanked her, he called her Petra.

17 Talbot Street,
Treorchy.
31 May 1919.

Dear Mother,
Thank you for your letter. I'm glad Will's health is improving. Please give him my very best regards.

I am sorry not to be able to accept your invitation to come and see you on my birthday, but I only have Saturday afternoons and Sundays free and am very busy.

Yours with best wishes,

Petra

55

On the Saturday before Petra's birthday Isabelle drove herself from England into Wales, over the hills from Holders Hope to Treorchy. There were three things on the front passenger seat beside her. A bunch of white dianthus and pink rose buds. A basket of strawberries from Will's and Bathsheba's garden, padded for the journey in their own downy leaves. A flat bag made of red Spanish leather, embossed with a design of grape bunches and vine leaves. The bag contained two letters, one in a white envelope and a thicker one in brown manila. For once Isabelle didn't leave the car parked outside the pit manager's office because she didn't want to risk meeting Marius. He'd hear that she'd been there of course and wouldn't approve but it would be done by then. She found a place to leave the car near the station at Treorchy. Boys, looking longingly, immediately surrounded it. While they stared at the car, she took off her long coat and motoring hat, pinned a little straw hat to her hair and replaced her flat shoes with Louis heels. For the first time for months, she was taking trouble with her appearance. She picked out the biggest boy and gave him a shilling. 'And you'll get another shilling if it's all right when I come back.' He held open the door for her while she collected her things from the passenger seat. She walked up the street past the Railway Hotel to the town centre, the bouquet in one hand, basket of strawberries in the other, leather bag tucked under her arm. She'd imagined that in the long drive over the hills the decision would make itself. She was, after all, so good at decisions. Only, by the time she raised the black enamelled door-knocker of number 17, she still didn't know what to do.

The door was half-opened by a small woman with grey hair. She looked as startled at seeing Isabelle, in her summer hat with her white and pink posy, as if a monster from a fairy tale had arrived on the step and started closing the door again. Isabelle asked, through the narrowing gap 'Does Petra Allegri live here?' Then, more desperately, 'I'm her mother.' The door re-opened halfway and Petra's voice, sharp and alarmed, came down the stairs. 'Who's that?' The grey haired woman stood back, opened the door and said nothing as Isabelle went past her into the narrow hallway and up the stairs. Brown linoleum on the stairs, clean and shiny but worn, making little pocking sounds under her feet. Cream and green wallpaper blurred and suede-textured at hip height where people brushed against it. When she got near the top of the stairs, Petra came out of the room on the right onto the landing. She was wearing a plain blouse of cream coloured cotton and a navy blue skirt, partly unbuttoned at the side.

'I was just changing to go out.'

Isabelle reached upwards with the bouquet.

'Happy birthday, darling.'

Petra took it clumsily, made a shushing motion with her other hand and opened a door behind her. Isabelle followed her into a cube of a room so small that there hardly seemed room for them to stand up together. There was a narrow bed by the wall, a washstand in the corner with an enamel basin and ewer, a chest of drawers in dark wood with a small mirror over it the size of a piece of notepaper. The only trace of individuality were a few books on top of the chest of drawers. Isabelle glanced at them, hoping to see some favourite from Petra's childhood, but they were no help. *The Miners' Next Step* and *Report of the Local Government Board*. Petra dumped the flowers down beside them and Isabelle settled the basket of strawberries tenderly alongside. She kept the leather bag clamped between her elbow and ribs.

'They're from Will and Bathsheba. They were so disappointed you couldn't come home.'

Again, the shushing gesture.

'What is it, darling? Surely I'm allowed to say that.'

Petra pointed to the wall behind the wash stand. 'Mr Dell's asleep. He's a safety officer on night shift.'

'Is there somewhere else we can go and talk?'

'I was going out anyway, with Sarah and Jenny.'

Isabelle had no idea who they were. 'Well, they'll just have to wait. Finish getting changed and we'll go out together.'

She sat on the bed and watched while Petra took off her navy skirt and put on a serviceable grey one. Petra looked healthier cramped in this cell of a room in the most crowded valley in the kingdom than she had at home. Her skin was clear and her hair down past her shoulders, until she twisted it up with a couple of hair pins into an untidy bun.

'We'll have to stop next door and let Sarah know.'

Isabelle waited in the street while Petra knocked on the door of the Thomas's house and said something to the toddler who answered it in a much softer voice than she'd used to her mother.

'Jenny's disappointed, poor thing.'

They walked back through the town. Several people recognised Petra and said hello. Petra didn't stop, as if she didn't want to explain her mother to them. When they got to the car Isabelle gave the boy his second shilling and opened the passenger door for Petra.

'Where are we going?'

'Don't sound so alarmed, darling. I'm not kidnapping you.'

Petra sat stiff and upright in the passenger seat while Isabelle took off her hat and started the car, not bothering to change her shoes. She drove slowly up the valley, through the busy main street of Treherbert and into the open hills. When they were clear of the last of the mines and the houses she parked on a piece of open ground beside some rocks.

'Shall we get out here?'

Isabelle picked up the leather bag from the back seat. The time was here and now, and the decision still not made. 'If I let her read one of them, she might pity me and forgive me. But then, she'll hate him forever. If I give her the other one, perhaps she'll love him but she'll always hate me.'

She walked over to the rocks, hitched herself onto one of them and sat down. Petra crouched down on a lower rock and looked up at her.

'Well?' Petra said. There was fear in her voice as well as impatience.

'Darling, this is going to be difficult for you. There's something I've always intended to tell you...'

She couldn't go on, and now the grey eyes looking up at hers were as scared as a child's and a surge of love and wanting to protect her daughter clamped itself round her chest so that she could hardly breathe, let alone talk. Is it wrong to want her to love me? You wanted what was best for both of us, didn't you. And anyway you're dead and I'm alive so I'm the one left with deciding and oh, it isn't fair...

'Please...'

Almost a wail from Petra. Isabelle pulled the leather bag towards her, scratching its glossy surface on the rock.

'You'd better read.'

For a moment she thought of not looking, letting her hand choose one letter or the other at random. Only the brown one was stiffer and thicker so she'd know. Her hand was in the bag and the two envelopes were nudging her fingers from either side. Her fingers closed on the thinner letter. She pushed it at Petra before she could change her mind.

'It's for you. I haven't read it.'

Then she sat frozen on the rock, staring over Petra's bent head at the valley under its haze of smoke, the winding gear and chimneys.

The noise Petra made was something between a groan and a howl, then she was on her feet. The envelope and sheets of paper slid off her lap to the ground.

'It's not true. Oh it's not true.'

'That Philip's your father? Yes, it is my darling. He loved you very much. He always wanted to tell you only...'

But Petra was running back towards the car. Isabelle slid off the rock and ran after her, stumbling in her Louis heeled shoes.

'Darling, please wait. Wait.'

Petra ran past the car without stopping, onto the road and away downhill. Isabelle followed, losing ground all the time, shouting to Petra to wait until her breath went. Then her ankle turned over and she fell, collapsing face down on the road.

'Oh my darling, please wait for me, oh my darling.'

But when she stood up, Petra wasn't in sight. Her palms were scraped raw and bleeding. One shoe heel had broken. Isabelle took off both shoes and limped slowly back uphill to the car. For a while it was in her mind to drive back down to the town and find Petra, but she knew it would be worse than useless. She went back to the rocks and found the letter still there on the ground. She'd spoken the truth when she told Petra she hadn't read it in the three years it had been in her possession but she read it now.

London.
6 June 1915

My darling daughter Petra,
I've called you that so many times in my mind and it feels strange – though very sweet – to be writing it for the first time. I wish so much that I could have said it to you face to face. Sometimes when you were a little girl playing in the garden I was nearly bursting with wanting to say it. But your mother and I decided it should wait until you were grown up enough to understand. Instead, I tried to say it in a lot of other ways, especially the garden. So many little

405

surprises I put into it that came with invisible labels – for my daughter Petra, with love. Now you know at last, perhaps the labels wont be invisible any more.

Oh my darling, I feel I want to wrap you round with love and protection like a big bird folding you in its wings. Even though I shan't be there for the rest of your life, that love will be. If I'm sure of anything in this world or the next it's that love is never wasted and never goes away.

I love you my darling, for ever and ever.

Your father Philip

Isabelle folded the letter back in its envelope and took it away with her.

56

July 2001

The woman called Rosa poured triple measures and said nothing about adding water so they sipped whiskey neat, Kim grimacing at the smell and taste.

Rosa noticed. 'Not enjoying it?'

'Not much. But you're enjoying it, aren't you?'

Kim didn't mean the drink and, from the way she smiled, Rosa guessed it.

'Am I?'

'Sure you are. We're sort of on trial, aren't we? I mean, you could report us to the police for trespassing or sacrilege or something.'

'Sacrilege? Now, ancestor worship is one thing I haven't tried so far.'

'If you just wanted to talk to us, you could have done it without all this drama.'

'Am I being dramatic? Maybe it's artistic temperament. I suppose it's there in the genes.'

'The Allegri genes?'

'Suppose you just tell me what you've found out.'

Kim looked across at Colin. 'Do we?' He nodded. They both waited for her to go on. 'OK, your grandmother Isabelle marries a famous portrait painter called Leon Allegri. They employ Philip Cordell to make a garden for them, but my guess is that Leon Allegri does a lot of the actual designing. Maybe he thought of it as a present to his wife. I suppose she was beautiful.'

'Yes, she was beautiful.'

'Then, some time between the First and Second World Wars there's a miners' strike and rioting and the miners come here and set fire to things in the garden. He tries to stop them and gets killed. Your grandmother has him buried in the garden and just moves away and lets the whole thing rot until Colin comes to rescue it.'

Rosa took a gulp of whiskey.

'Well,' Kim said. 'Have I got it right?'

'Some of it, yes.'

'So Leon Allegri was killed, here in the garden?'

'Yes.'

'By the miners?'

'No, not by the miners.'

'Who then?'

407

Rosa twisted round and reached into her pack again.

'Something I think you both deserve to see.'

57

Spring 1920

In spring of 1920 Sarah had another child, a boy who weighed just over four pounds at birth. From London, his Aunt Megan sent half a pair of Milanese silk knickers. The form they took when they came out of the envelope at the house in Talbot Street was a postal order for 7s6d, very welcome and proper from the member of the family who was doing well in London. But for Megan it was a setback in the campaign of putting together a spring wardrobe. She thought about it as she lathered rose-smelling soap in a china bowl. Silk knickers fifteen shillings, matching vest thirteen shillings. With luck and good tips she might get there by the end of April. She took a fresh scented towel from a pile on the shelf, wrapped it round the client's upper body and tilted the chair back.

'Now if you'd just put your arm behind your head, Mrs Danby, and keep as still as you can.'

She picked up the little badger-hair brush and lathered the waiting armpit, swathes of coloured silk going through her mind. Ivory, old rose, champagne, lilac, lemon or sky.

'All right, Mrs Danby. I'm trying not to tickle.'

The next thing would be one good dress for the summer. Crêpe morocaine, crêpe de chine, silk georgette, foulard, shantung. Five guineas at least. Weekly wage of £2 a week, plus tips and commission – good admittedly, so good she'd never dared tell her sister that she was making more than half as much as her husband got for his work down the pit. Still, there was her room off Tottenham Court Road to pay for and food sometimes. Her little silver razor cut through the foam, bringing a harvest of fine hairs. Ladies decollete shaving 2s6d. Plus sixpence tip, with luck. It was an annoyance and a mystery to Dinah that Megan made nearly twice as much in tips as she did. Megan sensed the answer but couldn't put it into words without sounding conceited. It was all to do with the unfair mystery of beauty. Beauty was what women came to Madame Merveille's salon to buy, carrying it away in little bowls and bottles or having it stroked and massaged into them. Megan possessed beauty, without vanity but with respect for it. Sensing this, clients paid their tributes like pilgrims at a shrine. Dinah knew in her heart that she couldn't compete. She was pretty of course – Madame Merveille wouldn't have employed her otherwise – but couldn't work the magic. Once she'd accepted that, she and Megan stayed friends. When her client had dressed, tipped and gone Megan went through to the back room where Dinah was spooning pink paste into small glass jars. Madame Merveille's Rose Cream – for motoring and travelling.

'Going out tonight, then?' Megan nodded.

'Same one as last week?'

Another nod. The man was the owner of two shoe factories, widower, late thirties, still quite good looking and devoted to the tango.

'Could do worse. What are you wearing?'

'Bois de rose with the square neck and pleats.'

'You wore that last week.'

'Can't help it.'

'Perhaps he'll take the hint and buy you a new one.'

Dinah usually let a man buy her clothes and take her to bed when she'd been out dancing and had supper with him two or three times and Megan usually didn't. Beauty could say no and be better thought of for it: pretty had to grab its chances. Dinah knew – because Megan had half confided in her – that there had been one serious love affair in her quite recent past that didn't end happily. But for the moment at least she danced, she went to supper, she surely allowed a kiss in the back of the taxicab going home because even beauty had to pay back something, and that seemed to be that. It was a puzzle because Megan freely admitted to being 27 years old – an admission that no power on earth would have wrung out of Dinah – and nothing lasted forever. Dinah threw down her spoon.

'I've got a vibro hair treatment in five minutes and I've got to test the bloody thing. Last time it nearly jolted her right out of the chair.'

Megan took over spooning travel cream. Later, when they were doing the mail orders, she'd send one of the little pots to Holders Hope. Isabelle always wrote grateful little notes in return, hoping Megan was well, giving news of Will and the garden. The little jars of cream and boxes of powder piled up unopened on her dressing table, gathering dust.

Sarah recovered slowly from the difficult birth of the baby so Petra took on as much of the work as she could in the Thomas household. In the evenings when the tea things were cleared away she'd get Jenny to bed while Sarah saw to the baby. Once Jenny's eyes were closed she'd go downstairs and see what copying work Trefor had for her. On Saturday afternoons she'd go down to Short's shop with Sarah to help carry home the groceries. It was those trips that brought home to her that money was getting scarcer in the valley as demand for coal dropped. What showed her first was the bacon. In the good times just after the war the miners ate as well as anybody. Short's slicing machine whizzed in and out of the glistening sides of bacon, carving off pound after pound of thick rashers, moist pink flesh framed in clean white fat. When the bonus money started falling off, people still needed bacon but the cuts had to be cheaper. By the spring of 1920, the rashers were mostly white with pink seams like clouds in an untidy sunset.

One Saturday afternoon, when she and Trefor were waiting together at the tram stop to go down to Porth, Petra told him some of the things she'd been hearing from women waiting at the grocery counter.

'It's the older ones who worry most. They think it's going back to the bad old days before the war when children went hungry. Hope they're wrong but...'

'I don't. I hope they're right.'

She stared at him. 'You want children to go hungry?'

'If it was up to me, there wouldn't be a hungry child in the world. But it isn't up to me or anyone like me. It's up to the owners. Keep cutting back and cutting back the pay until the workers are starving and not fit to work any more, then you know you've got them down as far as they'll go so you let them have a penny or two more so they can work again – and if a few of their children have died while you're doing the cutting back, there's always plenty more where they came from.'

The 'you ... you've ... you're' thumped in her ears. 'Cutting back' made her think of her mother with secateurs. There was nobody else at the tram stop, so she could shout at him.

'*I'm* not part of that. It isn't my fault.'

She saw his eyes change from anger to puzzlement. When he spoke again his voice was low, almost mumbling.

'I'm sorry. I didn't mean you...'

'Say I'm not part of that.'

He nodded, then said formally, like a man withdrawing a motion at a meeting. 'You are not part of that. Not now.'

She said thank you, just as formally. Trefor started coughing. He tried to muffle it in his handkerchief but his whole thin body shook.

412

Petra's anger faded. When he'd finished coughing she asked him, 'What did you mean, hoping they're right about children going hungry?'

'Not children, nobody would want that. What I meant, in the good times with the bonuses coming in, some of the men forgot what it's about. It takes the bad times with the bonuses not coming and wages being cut, to remind some of them there's a war still on. You can think you've got peace, only if it's not a fair peace, it won't last.'

He'd kept the anger out of his voice this time but she could feel it there underneath all the time, like firedamp in the explosive earth under their feet. She knew what it was like to live with anger every day of your life, even if you didn't show it, and felt so close to him that she wished he'd stretch out his hand to her so that she could take it. They sat side by side on the tram journey down the valley. He told her he was transferring to the night boiler shift at Evans' lemonade factory because it would give him more time for trade union affairs in the day. They happened to catch the same tram on the way back and he had a present for her, a second hand copy of Ruskin's *Munera Pulveris*. Seriously flawed as economic theory, he said, but she might find parts of it interesting. She read it in bed at night, listening to the sounds from next door.

58

Summer 1920

It was June before Megan could afford a new dress for dancing. The soft foulard fabric shaped itself round her breasts and ribcage like cream over strawberries. The skirt, tango pleated, swung out when she twirled. It was the shortest she'd ever worn, leaving an expanse of champagne silk stocking from mid calf to shoes. Even more daring was the pattern of orange, emerald and black lines and triangles against a cream background. It was altogether the most exciting garment she'd ever owned. When she was buying it she almost drew back at the last moment, then a rebellious voice in her said that the dress needed her and she needed the dress, so she counted out five guineas in a hurry before she could change her mind. She needed the dress but she wasn't sure for what – certainly not for the owner of the shoe factories who was waiting for her downstairs in a taxicab. For something important that was going to happen. Soon, before the magic of the dress wore off.

'Who's the girl in the swirly dress?'

The man, quite young for an MP but already balding, was twisting round to look over his shoulder at the dance floor, nearly spilling his champagne.

'No idea. What we need is a personal commitment from the minister that if we stand up to them he won't go behind our backs and...'

'Who's the man dancing with her?'

'Don't know him from Adam. We'll have to take losses if we close down for weeks, or months even. The important thing...'

'What does the ass think he's doing?'

'Tangoing, presumably. We want an assurance that if we make a stand...'

'Look old boy, suppose you put it in writing to me and I'll see what I can do. Do you suppose it's worth asking her for a dance?'

The MP's companion gave up. He'd already paid for dinner at the Savoy and it had seemed like a good idea to do some more lobbying at a night spot.

'Well, you'd better go and ask her, hadn't you?'

He looked up at the dance floor. The woman turned, dress swirling round sleek calves.

'What's up, old boy?'

'She reminds me of somebody I knew once.'

'Lucky you. Keep an eye on my bubbly, would you?'

The shoe factory owner had to get quite sharp with the balding young man before he'd take Megan's no for an answer. They watched his unsteady progress back to his own table where another man was waiting for him with an expression of amusement and contempt. It was nearly thirteen years since Megan had first seen the look, but it hadn't changed. The man's eyes met her own and Megan froze with fear remembering a drop of lemonade on a polished boot toe. Beside her, the shoe factory owner was asking if she was all right. Would she like to go outside for some air? Her impulse was to say yes but she got control of her voice, made herself smile. They'd dance again. Wasn't that what he'd like? So they danced, she with more freedom and wildness than ever before, keeping a promise to herself that she'd made when she was 15 years old and come near to breaking tonight. Never be scared again, not of a man or anything else. There was only one man in the world who had threatened her and he'd gone thirteen summers ago. But in the years since she'd seen Marius – since she'd let the feather waft down onto his lap in the library – he'd done something unfair and unexpected. He'd turned into his father.

The MP left soon after Megan had refused to dance with him. Marius sat on his own smoking, making notes on the back of a cigarette packet with a silver propelling pencil of the few possible hints he'd picked up from an expensive evening. The business of lobbying was taking up a lot of his time now, on behalf of a consortium of some of the other smaller pit owners as well as his own family business. He was emerging as a leader, so easily that it surprised him. He was conscious all the time he was writing of Megan dancing only a few tables away. She was unfinished business and that unsettled him. In the past year, he'd been putting right a lot of things. Homes of London friends that had closed their doors while the war was on were opening to him. His mother, absorbed in her garden, was trusting him with more decisions. As for the sister problem, there was nothing he could do about that for the moment except ignore her. Things had been going pretty well until Megan had turned up and the look on her face seemed to him like a deliberate challenge. It took him back to the garden and he was a fumbling boy again, scared of his father, scared of ... not of *her* exactly, but of how much he wanted her. There'd been other women since then, paid for or otherwise. He didn't want or need her in that choking way. But he was scared and he wouldn't stand that. He stubbed out his cigarette and walked over to the table where she was sitting on her own now.

'Are you enjoying yourself, Miss Thomas?'

'Very much thank you, Mr Allegri.'

Perfectly self possessed. She was sitting with silky ankles crossed, light catching the silver buckles of her shoes.

'What are you doing with yourself these days?'

'Working at the salon.'

'Madame Merveille's?'

He remembered the name from bottles on his mother's dressing table. She moved her head up and down.

'Would you care to dance?'

His question surprised him more than it seemed to surprise her.

'No thank you. We're leaving in a moment.'

Her companion was coming back, pushing his way round the edge of the dance floor. When he got to the table she said 'Are we ready then?' making no attempt to introduce Marius. He watched them walking out, heads turning to look at Megan as they went. She moved as confidently as a swan on its own stretch of river.

She stumbled on the dimly lit stairway going out and by the time they got to the pavement in Oxford Street the shoe factory manager was seriously concerned about her. She told him not to worry. Too much dancing, that was why her heart was thumping.

59

That summer, Petra had a new routine for her Saturday afternoon walks up on the hillside. Sarah was too busy with the new baby to go with her and gradually it became accepted that Trefor would be her companion instead. At first it was a matter of practicality. There were things to discuss about the correspondence she was handling for him and on fine days it was easier to do it up on the patches of sheep nibbled grass among the bracken than in the crowded house with the baby crying and Sarah always needing the kitchen table for something else. All summer he'd been shuttling up and down both Rhondda Fawr and Rhondda Fach, liaising with pit lodges all day, then going in to stoke up the boilers at the lemonade factory at night. She watched him wearing himself thin and almost transparent, like the last rim of candle-wax in the holder. His cough was no better in spite of the summer. What was wearing him out worse than the ceaseless work was his own impatience. With nobody else to confide in, because his father wouldn't stand for much discussion of union affairs at home, he got into the habit of bottling it all up until Saturday afternoons with Petra.

There was one particular Saturday when he'd been to a meeting down in Porth and she'd arranged to meet him off the train to save time. As soon as she saw him she knew the meeting hadn't gone well. They walked in silence through the town and up to where the open hillside began, the grass sleek and slithery underfoot. It was a fine afternoon, smelling of bracken and warm earth. Near the top of the hill there was a little grassy depression beside the path, perhaps an old quarry. Gorse grew round the rim, filling the air with a sweet nutty smell. There were some rocks on the floor of it and when you sat down on them you could only see gorse and bracken and blue sky. Trefor leaned back against a rock and wiped a hand over his face.

'Sometimes I wonder ... oh God, sometimes I wonder if we haven't lost before we even start ... if it's ever going to change.'

She'd never heard him like that before, utterly defeated. It scared her – not just for him but for everything else she'd come to care about.

'Do you mean that?'

He didn't answer, just let his head fall sideways against the rock, eyes closed. She sat watching him, turning over something that had been in her mind for months. When he'd been full of nervous energy and pushing himself from one job to the next there'd been no point in talking about it. Now she might have her chance at last, if she took it carefully.

'You need a holiday.'

'Holiday!' He smiled, not angry at least. 'Shall we all go to Porthcawl for the day?'

'I was thinking of Switzerland.'

This brought his eyes open.

'You're going to Switzerland?'

His expression was alarmed, lost. Because she'd come to feel part of his world it hadn't occurred to her that he still saw her as something exotic, liable to run off abroad on the same kind of whim that had brought her there in the first place.

'No, not me. You. I knew somebody who had a cough much worse than yours. His family sent him off to Switzerland for the summer and the mountain air did him so much good that he came back cured.'

She thought at first that the choking sounds he was making were outrage. It took her a while to realise he was laughing, tears pouring down his cheeks, his whole thin body rocking with it. He was trying to say something. 'Oh Miss Allegri, Miss Allegri...' The return to her formal name after months of 'Petra' might have scared her only he wasn't mocking her. He wiped his eyes and started making some kind of sense.

'My dear Miss Allegri, I am deeply moved by your concern for me but I regret that owing to circumstances...'

His cap had fallen out of his pocket while he was laughing. She picked it up and pretended she

420

was going to throw it at him.

'Make sense, Mr Thomas.'

'My dear Petra, it really is kind of you to worry. But you might have noticed I'm not in a position to go travelling for the sake of my health.'

She said quickly, 'I've got some money I don't need, quite a lot of it. Somebody left me some.'

Two hundred and fifty-seven pounds in a bank in Porth, placed in her account when Philip Cordell's solicitor had finally managed to wring the bank's address from her. She'd been horrified to hear that he'd left her all that there was of his money. Only a vague idea – encouraged with the best of motives by the solicitor – that it was against the law to refuse legacies had made her accept it.

'You'll need it one day. You won't stay here all your life.'

'Why not?'

'Sarah thinks you came here because you're in love with my brother.'

'I know she does.'

'Is she right?'

'No. I'm very fond of Evan but...'

'So why?'

'To get away.'

He looked at her for a while, still smiling, then got off and walked away into the bracken. She heard a stream of water hissing on leaves. When he came back some time later he stood behind her and dropped something into her lap. A little posy of hill flowers, mauve scabious, pink centaury, golden vetch, tied with a wiry grass stem.

'What's that for?'

'A thank you.' Then, when she didn't respond, 'I thought girls liked flowers.'

Not wanting to hurt him by saying she didn't, she twitched the posy off her lap, stood up and kissed him full on the lips. It was trampled into a pink and golden mush before they let go of each other.

The next Saturday he said, 'You know I'm not the sort who gets married? Not till we've made the world different. There's so much to do – and children and so on – it wouldn't be fair on them or a wife.'

She said she understood that, and she did. The Saturday after that, on another fine afternoon in the same grassy hollow, they became lovers.

60

One August morning, with business slow because the London season was over and most of Madame Merveille's clients gone to the country, a letter arrived at the salon for Megan.

Dear Miss Thomas,
I have to come to London in the first week in September and thought we might go dancing one evening. Could you drop me a note at my London address? (As above.)

It was signed by a single initial M, looping itself confidently. She threw it in the enamel bucket among empty shampoo bottles and grease-stained blobs of cotton wool.

In August, Evan went without beer and evenings out for two weeks and saved five shillings to buy a dented trumpet he'd seen in the window of Cardash's pawnbroker shop down the valley in Tonypandy. By September he was doing well enough to win third prize and 30 shillings at a brass competition with Handel's Largo arranged for solo trumpet and strictly no messing about with rhythm this time. In Cardiff a few weeks later he met a pub piano player who'd been in London the year before and heard the Original Dixieland Jazz Band. He missed the last train back to Treorchy and spent the night under the billiard table in the back room of the pub, ecstatically drunk on one and a half pints of beer and a lot of music.

In October, Megan got another letter.

Mr Allegri presents his compliments to Miss Thomas and wonders if she would care to join him for dinner and dancing on the occasion of his visit to the Metropolis next week.

They were busier at the salon now so it was covered up quite quickly with used razor blades and hair clippings.

Also in October, Evan lost his job at the pit. No fault of his but, as the pit manager explained to him, the demand for coal was falling and it was only fair that the blow should fall on the men who'd joined most recently. Evan accepted that too happily for his brother.

'The pit ponies get more consideration out of them than men do.'

If he hoped that Evan might turn into a union activist at last, he was disappointed. Evan informed him that he'd been thinking of giving in his notice in any case. He'd pick up odd jobs here and there and try in the longer term to make a living as a musician. Only Petra sympathised, and that had to be outside on the pavement by the lamp post because the Thomas house was still vibrating from the family row.

'In a professional band, you mean?'

'There's the music halls in Cardiff and there'll be pantomimes at Christmas.'

'So you'd have to move away?'

He shrugged, his cigarette smoke spiralling up the cone of gaslight. 'Probably. I can't seem to settle somehow, not after coming back.'

'From the War?'

'From the other place too. I was happy there, with Auntie Bath and Mr Cordell and so on.'

Her face went hard and blank, the way it had done when they were children and he'd committed some casual or accidental cruelty. Like a child making up he touched her arm.

'Don't you want me to go?'

'I'll miss you.'

'But there's Trefor.'

Living as physically close as he did to his brother he was as alive to his mood as an animal in the same burrow. They shared the same bed –

though usually at different times because of shift patterns. Sometimes when Evan got into it, it would be still warm from Trefor's body. He'd sensed that Trefor was – what? Not happier exactly because happiness wasn't a word you'd use easily with Trefor. Something though, and the nearest he could get to it was the feeling he had when he was playing trumpet or clarinet, racing along like when he was a boy on Jack the Lad being run away with and a voice saying go on, go on, the notes will be there when you need them and even if they aren't the grass is soft and deep to fall on, so it won't matter.

'Yes,' she said, 'there's Trefor.'

And what he'd sensed about his brother was there in her voice too.

'Are you going to get married?'

Daughters of owners didn't marry night-shift boilermen from lemonade factories, but then she'd done a lot of other things they didn't do either.

'No. He doesn't want to.'

She sounded quite unworried about it. As children, she'd always been the more nervous one, but now she was going way out beyond him into deep water. He wished he hadn't thought of water.

'If I can ever do anything, you know...'

She gave him a quick kiss on the cheek, turned and went into her lodgings.

On a yellow-grey day in November, with the fog eddying along Bond Street and the electric lights in Madame Merveille's all switched on at mid

425

morning, the florist from a few doors away delivered an orchid for Megan. She unwrapped it from its tissue paper and silver ribbon and gasped as if it were something live that might sting her. She'd seen orchids as corsages and found them shivery, fleshy rather than floral, as if the skin, blood and subcutaneous fat of the women wearing them had somehow worked their way out through silk or satin and writhed into decorations over the collarbone. Dinah gasped too, but from admiration.

'An orchid.' She reached out a coral fingernail to touch it gently. Its petals were gold-ivory, chestnut spotted. Megan was reading the card that came with it: *I'll call for you at your lodgings at eight o'clock this evening.*

'Did you tell him where I live, Dinah?'

'Tall, dark, good looking? Came in yesterday and said he was a family friend?' Dinah was unapologetic. 'Who is he?'

'The son of the woman I told you about, the one I was maid to.'

Dinah whistled, cupped the palm of one hand and bought the other one over to cover it, palm down, as if trapping a butterfly. It was a gesture used in their circle to signify that a girl had made a good catch.

'No Dinah. Not that. It isn't like that.'

Dinah smiled, unconvinced, and went into the back room to pet the orchid and put it in water. She could have it, Megan called after her. She didn't want it. She was concentrating with all her strength on not being afraid. Back in her small room that evening she swept her hair up sideways

426

and pinned it, wafted scent borrowed from the salon. Her winter dress, bought second-hand from a friend it hadn't suited, had a velvet bodice the colour of purple grapes with calf-length skirt in a lighter shade of taffeta. The contrast of the dark velvet against her pale skin could have done with a flower to soften it but it stayed unsoftened because the orchid, swaddled in its tissue paper and silver ribbon, was travelling home on the bus with Dinah.

There was an afternoon towards the end of November when Isabelle knew that almost everything the garden needed for the autumn had been done. She and Will stood by the gazebo, taking stock of the tasks done as the three youngsters from the village swept away wormcasts on the lawn with besom brooms Will had made for them from birch trimmings. He was as industrious as ever, but slower now and Isabelle encouraged him to let the two lads do the hard work His great value to her was as a compendium of Philip's garden wisdom. 'Mr Cordell said this. Mr Cordell wouldn't let me do that, because...' One of the triumphs of the autumn was that the borders were as weed free as they reasonably could be. The girl from the village, Polly, had torn into convolvulus, nightshade and brambles as if they were doing her a personal injury by existing, with Isabelle following humbly in her footsteps. The garden that had so nearly slipped away from her after Philip's death had been brought back again. *Look after the garden if you can.* It wasn't enough but it

427

was all she had and she'd obeyed, as if doing it was a magic spell that would bring back being beautiful and being loved.

'Pity about the lily pond,' Will said.

She looked where he was looking, down the steps to the tangle of undergrowth at the foot of them. Dusk seemed to have come early there and was nudging the bottom step. The gunneras had already collapsed from the frost but alders and dogwood had merged into a thicket that hid the swampy ground and diminished pool. On the far side the silhouettes of the old crack willows stood out against the golden-white sky.

She said, 'I suppose I didn't want to think about it.'

Will nodded. It was, after all, the biggest job left in the garden – too big for the five of them to tackle without more help.

'In the spring, perhaps...'

The last thing left. If you wanted a spell to work, you couldn't neglect any part of it.

She repeated, more firmly, 'In the spring.'

61

July 2001

Colin read first, slowly because it wasn't easy to make out the faded handwriting in the light of the camping lamp. After what seemed like a long time he handed the two pages to Kim without a word. She glanced at the top of the first page.

'Shit. Is this real?'

Rosa nodded. Kim skimmed quickly, reading the occasional phrase aloud as if to convince herself of what she was seeing 'Although I had not intended to kill him I knew that the police might not believe this... Mrs Allegri spent considerable time and money trying to have him traced...' When she came to the end she looked across at Colin as if it were his fault.

'He *murdered* him. Your precious Cordell actually murdered him.'

Rosa leaned over and took the papers from her. 'He says he didn't mean to.'

'Well he would, wouldn't he? So he and Isabelle Allegri are lovers, poor old Leon probably has to pay Cordell through the nose for making the garden to please his wife and all the time they're having it off in the potting shed or wherever.'

Colin said, 'But look, he couldn't...'

'And I don't believe it was an accident. He decoyed Leon down to see how the garden was going, intending all the time to kill him. He and Isabelle probably planned it between them...'

'Kim, remember Isabelle was...'

He glanced towards Rosa.

'Oh don't mind me, dears. I'm not responsible for Grandma Isabelle.'

'You knew?' Kim glared at Rosa, then at Colin. 'Doesn't it bother you, for goodness sake? Or does it make it all right because they made a pretty garden? There were the two of them walking hand in hand among the fucking lilies and roses, thinking how clever they were and

429

knowing all the time that he was rotting under their feet.'

Colin said, 'He'd have had a job.'

'Why?'

'Look, did you take in the rest of the letter, what he says he did with the body? He's quite specific. He puts it in a wheelbarrow, covers it in a tarpaulin, trundles it a kilometre or more to the far side of the village, where he sinks it in the river. So how do Allegri's bones get themselves out of the river, roll themselves back uphill and settle down where we find them in the lily pool?'

'OK, so he was lying about that as well.'

'So whose bones are they then? She says she's sure they're Leon Allegri's.'

'Well how can she be sure? They're just bones, unless we get them DNA tested.'

They were arguing as if she weren't there, until a cough from the end of the tent reminded them.

'Sorry to spoil the debate, but I know they're Leon Allegri's.'

'How? Did Grandma Isabelle make a deathbed confession to you?'

Rosa shook her head.

Colin said, 'So Philip Cordell was lying about the wheelbarrow and the river and so on?'

'Yes.'

'But why, if he was admitting to the murder...' Then, slowly, 'Oh yes, I think I see. He was protecting her.'

Kim said, 'So he knew she'd done it.'

Rosa grinned at him. 'Or *thought* he knew. Ready for a re-fill?'

62

Holders Hope
Herefordshire.
14 March 1921
Mr S.T. Gladwyn.
Penyrheol Colliery

Dear Mr Gladwyn,
I have a plan on hand for my garden and it occurs
to me that it might provide a few weeks' work for
some of our miners who have lost their employment because of the current fall in demand.

The work I have in mind is digging out and
carting away soil from the lily pool. I envisage
that it might occupy six men for around a month,
or longer if necessary.

I should be grateful if you would make inquiries
and send me details of suitable men who are
interested. I'd hope they might be able to start
work before the end of this month.

Yours sincerely,

Mrs I. Allegri

Silas Gladwyn passed the letter across his desk to
Marius.

'I think you should see this.'

Marius glanced and made an impatient noise. 'I

431

do wish she wouldn't...' Then 'Oh God.'

'I agree. It's hardly the best timing, is it?'

'My mother has no idea. I've tried to explain to her, but I'm afraid she's getting hopelessly out of touch.'

'I think I'll suggest that in the light of the strong feelings here, she might postpone her plans.'

'That's putting it mildly. Look, don't worry, I'll deal with this.'

'You're sure? I hate to disoblige Mrs Allegri in any way.'

'Don't worry.' Marius folded up the letter and put it in his pocket. 'Something more important – I've just heard from my friend in the House. He says the balloon will go up in a couple of weeks' time.'

63

On 24 March 1921 the Government gave up the control of the coal industry it had taken during the war and handed it back to the owners.

On 31 March notices were posted at pitheads all over the country setting out the owners' terms for new contracts of employment. A skilled collier's wage would fall from £4-9s-3d to £2-13s-6½d a week. The miners refused to accept the new terms.

On 1 April, the colliery gates were locked against them. Petra, on her way home from work, met Trefor running down the street. His eyes were bright and the skin round his sharp cheekbones glowed as if a candle were shining inside his skull. 'It's started,' he told her. 'It's started.'

Over the next few days, police reinforcements and troops began to arrive in the Rhondda. The regular rhythms of the miners going on and off shift were replaced by the jagged and unpredictable patterns of protest meetings, either official ones called by the Miners' Federation or street corner gatherings of men reacting to the latest rumours. The owners were bringing in blackleg labour from England, from Ireland, from anywhere they could get it. The troops down the valley in Tonypandy had brought a tank with them. They'd driven it through the streets, shouting insults at the women. The navy were being sent in to do the boilermen's jobs and keep the pumps going. Down in London they were running around shit-scared, swearing in special constables so fast they'd run out of truncheons and were issuing them with pick handles, soldiers billeted in tents all over Kensington Gardens. Some of the rumours had truth in them, some didn't but they kept everybody in a state of nervous tension, both wanting and fearing the next development in the crisis. The Thomas household was as disrupted as the rest. Trefor was hardly ever at home and never slept in his bed or anywhere else as far as anybody could tell. Sarah was as strong against the owners as he was and their back kitchen became an unofficial gathering place for the whole street with miners or their wives coming in at all hours.

On the eighth day of the lock-out, a Saturday, Petra took her walk up the hill on her own. She stopped at the usual point to look down over the valley and her whole body went cold with shock at the stillness of it. Every single wheel as far down the valley as she could see was motionless. The only thing moving was a red tram crawling up from Ton Pentre on tracks gleaming in the sun. Petra turned, panicked by the stillness more than any of the rumours in the town and ran back down to Sarah's crowded kitchen. Sarah was on her way out, the baby wrapped in a shawl on her chest, Jenny holding on to her hand.

'Distress fund meeting at the chapel.'

There were about thirty people in the room normally used for Sunday school, most of them women, some young mothers like Sarah, others middle-aged women who'd seen it before. Also a sprinkling of the professional people of the town – the owner of a draper's shop, the librarian, several chapel ministers. Without fuss, they set about the business of running a soup kitchen. The chapel would let them use the hall they were meeting in and the yard outside. Did anybody know where a second-hand boiler might be had? Some money was already coming in. Various chapel congregations had raised £37, the Carlton billiard hall had sent a cheque for £20, a local dramatic group was putting on *She Stoops to Conquer* and had promised the proceeds. They needed to appoint a treasurer at once to keep the books straight. Why not Miss Allegri? It was her education, plus the total respectability of her job with a solicitor. She wanted to refuse, but knew she couldn't back away so Petra Allegri was elected *nem con* as treasurer of the distress fund. At least it made one thing easier. That morning she'd been down to the bank in Porth and drawn out every penny of the legacy, now grown to £269 11s 2d with interest. As treasurer, she could bank it with the rest, duly entered into the account book as an anonymous donation. She felt better for getting rid of that particular burden.

The Monday after that she woke early, around five o'clock, feeling heavy-limbed and sour-stomached and went to the washstand to wipe a cold flannel over her face. The flannel smelt sour too and made her stomach churn so she opened the window and stood breathing in the cool air of an early spring morning, struck again by the terrible silence of the valley. She could hear sparrows quarrelling down in the gutter and the mewing of a buzzard hunting over the open hillside. From her window she could see the tip of the boiler house chimney at Penyrheol Colliery. A few puffs of steam came out of it and she watched them rise slowly into the pale blue sky like clouds in a child's drawing. They were calming to watch and she didn't realise the significance of them until a shout went up. It was a young man's voice, from somewhere near the middle of the quiet town, sharp and angry.

'Fires. They've lit the fires at Penyrheol.'

The town erupted. The door of the Thomas's house next door banged open and Trefor was out in the street, running along under her window shouting, 'Everyone to Penyrheol. Blacklegs in at

Penyrheol.' Their street and all the streets around them were full of the clattering of boots, not the orderly tramp of men going on shift but a gallop like wild horses stampeding down a canyon. One word sounded above the clattering of the boots and turned into a chant 'Blacklegs, blacklegs, blacklegs.' Petra ripped off her nightdress and got into the old clothes she used for housework. From next door she could hear the baby crying and Sarah trying to hush it. When she went out to the street, Evan was just coming out of his front door.

'You stay inside, Petra. Look after Sarah.'

But she knew that Sarah was more than capable of looking after herself. Besides she wasn't the only woman out on the street. Several girls from the houses near them and even a few women carrying babies in shawls were hurrying along with the rest. She fell into step with Evan. At the end of their street they joined a column of people marching along the road to the colliery. Another chant started up in rhythm with the marching: '*Fires out. Fires out. Fires out.*'

By the time Evan and Petra's group got to the colliery a crowd of around a thousand people had built up outside it. She saw the locked gates with PENYRHEOL COLLIERY 1882 in gold letters tarnished by smoke and underneath in smaller letters her grandfather's name, W Turner. Except you couldn't see the whole of the name because some of the letters were blocked off by policemen's helmets. There was a line of about twenty police across the gates, truncheons

436

drawn. They were mostly young men, strangers to the Valley and some of the faces under the helmets were pink and nervous.

'*Fires out. Fires out.*'

She heard her own voice shouting it, Evan beside her. Then the chanting died down and Trefor was standing on a box in front of the gates with his back to the line of policemen and a protective group of miners round him. His voice was hoarse but carried to the back of the crowd. He made no attempt at oratory because the crowd needed no rousing. They all knew the situation, he said. The management had brought in blackleg labour to start the pumps. If they were allowed to get away with it they wouldn't stop at pumping. More blacklegs would be brought in by the trainload to dig the coal and break the protest, at Penyrheol and everywhere else. Only it wasn't going to work because those fires were going out.

'*Out. Out. Out.*'

Some of the men had brought bolt cutters and were trying to get to the chain that kept the gates locked. They were in a struggling knot with some of the police, while the other police tried to keep men from climbing the gates. A nimble boy got nearly to the top with others cheering him on before a policeman grabbed him by the heel and brought him down to a chorus of groans and yells. Inside the colliery yard, near the boiler house, two figures in dark overcoats and trilby hats watched from a distance.

'You all right, Petra?'

Evan had heard her gasp.

437

'Marius. My brother. That's Marius in there.'

'Go home, Petra. Nobody will...'

She joined the chant. *'Fires out. Fires out. Fires out.'*

A cheer from the men at the gates. They'd managed to push the police back and cut the chain and the big gates were being pushed back on their hinges, the front of the crowd running through. Then the forward surge was checked with a sharpness that crushed Petra's breasts against the back of the man in front of her. The triumphant cheer changed to a sound more scaring and angry than anything before, a wild keening that this could be done to them.

'Soldiers. The bastards have got soldiers inside. Bastard, bastard, soldiers.'

They must have been waiting hidden behind the boiler house, because the yard was suddenly full of men in khaki, perhaps a hundred of them with bayonets fixed. Some of them dragged the gates out of the miners' hands and slammed them shut and the rest formed a line on the inside. The howling from the crowd got louder then sank as an officer stepped forward, produced a paper and started reading.

'What's that? Is the bastard giving us a reading from the Bible?'

'Riot Act. He's reading the fucking riot act.'

Part of crowd started singing the 'Red Flag'. Another, more derisively, sang 'I'm Forever Blowing Bubbles'.

Evan said, more urgently, 'Petra, this could get bad. Trefor wouldn't want you to...'

And ere their limbs grew stiff and cold,

Their hearts' blood died its every fold.
'Where is he? Can you see? Is he hurt?'
'I'll go and look. Just stay here, right.'
They fly so high
Nearly reach the sky
'Look, I said stay there. You can't do any good.'
Then raise the scarlet standard high!
Within its shade we'll live or die
The officer rolled up the paper and tucked it away in his tunic. Nobody had heard a word of what he'd been reading.
Fortune's always hiding,
I've searched everywhere,
I'm forever blowing bubbles
'Oh God, they're going to... '
Pretty bubbles in the air.
The singing trailed away. The line of soldiers inside the gates were holding their rifles horizontal at waist level, pointing at the crowd. On a shout of command, the rifle breech bolts clicked back. One voice from the crowd shouted, high and shrill, 'Murdering bastards,' then there was total silence with the line of soldiers inside the gates and the crowd outside facing each other, nobody moving. Petra could feel her heart thumping and tried to calm herself by counting the beats. One, two, three ... eleven, twelve, thirteen. Then with no obvious signal being given the tension that had got to a pitch where it seemed only the crack of a rifle could release it suddenly relaxed a little. There was a murmuring from the crowd at front of the gates, then triumphant cheers. The soldiers and what was left of the line of policemen stood impassively

439

and allowed the gates to be opened a little by the miners, just enough to let three men inside.

'What's happening?'

The question went in hundreds of voices from the back of the crowd to the people by the gates and the reply came back, 'Negotiating. They're negotiating.'

The three men, looking small and shabby in their jackets and caps, walked round the line of soldiers towards the pit buildings and disappeared inside.

'Is Trefor one of them?' Petra asked Evan, her view blocked.

'No. Lodge officers.'

The crowd had gone silent when their representatives walked inside the gates but when minutes passed and nothing happened they started chanting again, but more softly, 'Fires out. Fires out. Fires out.' The chant hissed like a tide against the dark walls of the colliery buildings. Then the three men were walking back out again, saying something to the people nearest the gates. More cheering, spreading throughout the crowd.

'Raking them out. They're raking them out.'

The crowd parted for the soldiers to march out and away down the road, to a chorus of derisive cheers and more singing. The line of police stayed but there was no further attempt to storm the gates. The crowd had a holiday atmosphere about it now, everybody pleased with the victory, seeing it as a sign of a greater one to come. They stayed until word came back from the lodge officers that the last cinder of the boiler room fires had been raked out and not a wisp of steam came out of the chimney, then tramped back into town.

Back in the Thomas's kitchen, Trefor was almost drunk on happiness. Too excited to sit down or stay still for long he ranged round the room repeating 'We beat them. We really beat them,' taking short puffs of a cigarette and gulps of strong tea, getting in the way until Sarah snapped at him for goodness sake to get out or sit down. Petra went out to the scullery with the kettle and stood watching it fill, hands clamped over her breasts that felt bruised and tender. She turned to see Sarah watching her, an odd look on her face.

'Something wrong, Petra?'

'No. Somebody backed into me, that's all.'

She carried the kettle back into the other room and put it on the hob, then went next door to change, already late for work. When she got back in the evening Sarah's face was grim.

'I made him go and lie down. After you left he had a coughing fit so bad he couldn't draw breath.'

Trefor came in soon after that, in waistcoat and shirt sleeves. His face was yellowish, eyes sunken and reaction from the morning had set in.

'We've got a long way to go,' he told Petra. 'We won this time, but there's still a long way to go.'

'We'll win,' she said. Then caught the expression on Sarah's face, standing behind him, that said, 'What do you know about it, after all?' She added, more for Sarah's sake than Trefor's, 'After all, what else is there?'

64

'Gladwyn funked it,' Marius said.

Two weeks after the near-riot at Penyrheol. Through the restaurant windows the horse chestnut trees in Green Park were thick with cones of creamy blossom. Megan was wearing turquoise crêpe de Chine.

'If he and a few others had kept their nerve, it would be all over by now. I begged him to let the soldiers do the job they'd been sent to do. But oh no, it seems he'd had a letter from my dear mother.'

His movements were jerky and nervous. He kept his smoking cigar in the ashtray beside him. He'd sent a telegram the day before. *Arriving London tomorrow. Will collect you for dinner.* A flying visit for some talks at Westminster, he'd told her. He had to be back in Wales by Thursday night.

'Without letting me know, of course. Telling Gladwyn he's not to risk any loss of life. I'm surprised she didn't order him to lay in tea and buns for them as well.'

The waiter arrived to take their plates away. Marius's turbot was almost untouched but he signed impatiently that it should go.

'It's the inconsistency that annoys me. She goes swanning on with her daisies and delphiniums or whatever they are and expects her dividends to come rolling in just the same. When I tackle her

442

about labour costs she even agrees with me. But as soon as it comes to a crisis, she goes behind my back.'

'My brothers were probably in that crowd,' Megan said.

He stared, 'You don't still keep in touch with them, do you?'

'Sometimes.'

She'd put ten shillings aside, ready to send Sarah a postal order. She wasn't a great reader of papers and the first she knew about the dispute was when Dinah told her there were a lot of soldiers in tents in Kensington Gardens, because of the miners.

'I thought you'd broken with all that.'

She shook her head, not caring if she annoyed him. She still didn't know what he wanted from her, apart from the obvious, and since she hadn't given him that there must be something else.

'What about my mother? Do you still write to her?'

'Sometimes, yes.'

'Do you tell her you're seeing me?'

'Why do you want to know?'

Pink and succulent beef arrived. She ate, he smoked.

'I don't care. In fact, I don't care what she does if only she'd trust me and let me get on with things.'

She said, on an impulse, 'I wonder why she doesn't trust you.'

She picked up her claret glass but before she could drink from it his hand came across the table and grabbed her wrist.

443

'What do you mean?'

'Maybe she's remembering the burnt hands.'

'What are you...' Then his face changed and he sat back heavily in his chair.

She smiled like any beautiful woman winning a tiff with her boyfriend, knowing they were attracting attention.

'The letters saying her husband had come back and she should send money for him to go away.'

'She talked to you about that? When?'

'A long time ago.'

'I was just a schoolboy then. I needed money. It didn't do any harm.'

'No. I don't think she minded very much. Not by then.'

'What else did she say to you?'

'We talked about a lot of things.'

Evan's friend Joe knelt on the tumbled coal and tried one last protest.

'Where's the dignity, boyo?'

The word stirred a half-memory for Evan from a long time ago but he ignored it, intent on crushing rebellion.

'If you can eat dignity, keep as much of it as you like.'

By the half open doorway of the coal cellar, Jimmy the trombone player was already smearing his forehead and cheeks with coal dust. After four days in London, sleeping on park benches and scavenging food from dustbins at the back of hotels, it was the best work they'd been offered. The Original Taffieland Jazz Trio. Three sessions nine o'clock, half past ten and midnight, five

444

quid split among the three of them, a pint of beer and maybe something to eat if they were lucky. After three nights of busking theatre queues and getting flung out of pubs they'd struck lucky in a nightclub off Oxford Street. Only there was a condition attached. For the novelty of the thing they had to appear as genuine jazz playing Welsh miners, which was fair enough in one way because all they had were the clothes they were wearing and in caps, jackets and neck scarves they'd have been hard put to look like anything else. Only that wasn't good enough for the management and they'd been sent to the cellars and told to get authentically coal-grimed. Sounds of a foxtrot played by the club's dance band came faintly through the kitchens into the cellar. They filed upstairs and collected their instruments. Evan took a deep breath, holding Petra's clarinet in one hand and the pawn shop trumpet in the other, and led the way between the crowded tables, across the dance floor to the semi-circular podium at the end of the room. Little electric lights on the tables, pink shaded, gave everything a soft glow. There was some laughter from the crowd, but nobody took much notice. The resident musicians, sleek in black ties and dinner jackets, looked at the coal-smeared faces and red neckscarves, whipped their music off the stands with insulting speed and disappeared into a back room. The three of them had agreed on 'Tiger Rag' to start with, Evan on trumpet, nice and loud to let everybody know they were there. They ripped into it and found themselves travelling at about twice their usual speed because Joe was still angry and although the banjo player wasn't supposed to be the man in the driver's seat he was plucking out such a loud percussive bass while threshing his hobnail-booted foot up and down on the hollow podium that all the other two could do was hang on and keep with him. Evan took his first solo at the same breakneck speed and although Jimmy, steady as ever, managed to slow things down, because there was a limit to how much you could hurry trombones, they finished gasping and red-faced while a smattering of applause broke out from the tables. They did 'Barnyard Blues' next, to calm down a bit, then 'Fidgety Feet', with Evan putting his own foot firmly down on Joe's at the start of it, as a reminder not to go galloping off again. By the end of that they were really enjoying themselves and could have gone on half the night with 'Darktown Strutters Ball' if Evan hadn't caught the eye of the manager, signalling to him to wind it up because the dance band wanted the podium back.

They paced themselves better on their second appearance, starting with 'Sensation Rag' and putting in a few things that weren't really jazz, like 'Carry Me Back to Old Virginny' and 'Wyoming Lullaby' because they went well for banjo and clarinet. They were walking back through the tables when Evan felt a tug at his jacket. He turned round and there was a woman smiling at him. She had dark hair coming down in a wave over her forehead and the biggest and darkest eyes he'd ever seen. She wore a dress in a bluey-green colour that clung as close to her full breasts as moss to a rock, with only little thin straps over bare shoulders so smooth it looked as if your fingers would leave tracks on them if they touched. The shock of her beauty hit him first, recognition only after that.

'Megan!'

She was laughing. 'What are you doing here then? How are they at home?'

There was a man in a dinner jacket sitting opposite her. Evan registered that he didn't look pleased, but the surprise of seeing his sister made that an unimportant detail.

'Came down to earn a bit of money.'

'How long have you...?'

'Megan.' The dinner jacketed man, breaking in. 'It's time we went.'

Evan hadn't recognised him at first because he hadn't seen him close to for four years and he'd changed in that time. Anyway, he was the last person in the world you'd expect to see with Megan.

'Mr Marius.'

Marius ignored him, still talking to Megan. 'Have you got the ticket for your cloak? I'll meet you by the reception desk in two minutes.'

He stood up and walked out, brushing past Joe and Jimmy as if they weren't there.

'Are you...?' Appalled now, if only at what Trefor would say if he could see, Evan couldn't put the question directly. 'Are you ... with him?'

'He can wait for a minute. Where are you staying?'

'Nowhere. Can we come and stay with you, Megan?'

It was another way of asking if she was a kept woman of Mr Marius. She hesitated, looking at Joe with his banjo, tall Jimmy with his trombone, thinking of her narrow sliver of a room.

'All of you?'

Jimmy, taking in the situation, told her they'd be all right, find somewhere. Of course she'd want time with her brother.

'Will you let me go ahead of you, Evan. I must...'

He thought, must say goodnight to Mr Marius. He told her they had to play again at midnight.

'Come after that then.'

She took a card and a pencil out of her bag, wrote down her address for him then left, making for the cloakroom. Marius was waiting by reception, frowning and looking at his watch.

'Did you know your brother would be there?'

'Of course not. I thought he was back home in Treorchy.'

He said nothing else in the taxi, didn't try to kiss her and dropped her off outside her lodgings without opening the taxi door for her or waiting to see if she was safely inside. She climbed the dark stairs thinking 'Have I got rid of him? So easily?' And felt just a little stab of regret, as if at having to leave a story before she knew the end of it.

She watched from the window for Evan and saw him coming into the light of the nearest street lamp some time after one o'clock. When she let him into her room he put the trumpet carefully down on the only chair and sat on her bed, still elated from the way things had gone. They spoke in whispers in the dark because she didn't want to light the gas in case the landlord came snooping.

'Do you often go out with Mr Marius?'

'Sometimes, when he's in London.'

'Do you ... like him?'

She shrugged. The smooth shoulders were covered in an old dressing gown now, her hair down and feet in felt slippers.

'He looked mad with you for talking to me.'

'He can't stop me talking to my own brother, can he?'

She started arranging things for the night. Two dusty velvet cushions from the chair, a pillow and a blanket, would make a bed for him on the floor. The lavatory was two floors down, she told him, but for goodness sake don't pull the chain or you'll wake the whole house up. When he got back she was in bed. He took off his boots, waistcoat and jacket and rolled himself in the blanket.

'So how are they really at home?' she said.

'Bad.' For a few hours, galloped away on the back of his wild music, he'd managed not to think about it. 'There's only the few shillings from the Federation coming in, and God knows how long that'll last.'

'What about Trefor? Did he mind you going?'

'Trefor's ill.'

'Sarah said in her letter he had a cough but they hoped he was getting over it.'

'I don't think it's the sort of cough you get over. Like Mum's.'

Even now, he couldn't name it. He heard Megan gasp, then there was silence for a long time. He was afraid she might be crying but couldn't help himself drifting away to sleep. He was most of the way towards unconsciousness when she spoke again.

'What happened to Petra Allegri?'

'She's still there, living next door now and got a job.'

'Sarah thought she was sweet on you.'

'No, it's her and Trefor.'

'Petra Allegri and Trefor! She never is.'

'They both are.'

She tried to ask him more, but he let himself fall into sleep like a man going off the side of a dock.

Evan stayed in London for two weeks more, sleeping on Megan's floor until her landlord found out, then going back to doorways and park benches with Jimmy and Joe. They picked up a few more engagements, managed to send the occasional postal order home and did well playing the queues for Chu Chin Chow until the regular buskers got jealous and threatened to break Joe's banjo. After that Joe said he'd had enough of London and took the guard's van home. The other two limped on for a few days, though a trumpet and trombone duo didn't seem to have the same appeal. When Jimmy was offered work as a bookie's runner Evan advised him to accept. That evening Evan was at the doorway of Megan's lodgings as she came home from work.

He said, 'I'm going back home.'

'Good thing. I've had a letter from Sarah saying he's worse, but Madame won't let me have time off until next week because of the Whitsun rush.'

Megan gave him some money for his fare so he travelled back in a train seat with his trumpet on the luggage rack overhead.

65

'The workers engaged at the Bethesda Chapel Soup Kitchens, Treorchy, are appealing for the loan of a portable boiler for the cooking of food for the duration of the coal strike. At present the volunteer workers are labouring under great disadvantages through there being only a batch of three small boilers. If the request is acceded to, a great saving of coal and labour would be effected. Hundreds of meals are being served daily to children below school age and the little ones are delighted with their "tea party".'

'Tea party!' Petra scrunched the page from the local paper in her hand and looked round the chapel yard with its three cast iron boilers under a makeshift shelter. In a corner of the yard, volunteers were sorting through a pile of potatoes and the smell of the rotten ones hung over everything. A fleshier smell came through the open door from the little room at the back of the chapel where more volunteers were working

451

through a tub of meat donated by a local butcher, mostly pink and quivering lungs but some nutritious pig livers and bullock hearts among the mass.

'Where did they get *tea party* from? I told them we needed another boiler, that's all. And I didn't call it a strike. I said lock-out.'

'As long as we get the boiler,' Sarah said.

She had her baby slung in a shawl at her breast and was trying to get him to take warm water and powdered milk from a teaspoon. Her own milk had dried up weeks ago because of not getting enough to eat and he was sickly, constantly grizzling.

'Sarah. Petra.'

They turned and saw Evan coming across the yard. Petra felt her heart lift but Sarah was too weary and worried to be pleased.

'Where have you sprung from, then? I thought you were in London.'

'I came back.'

'Make our fortune for us then, did you?'

He felt in the pocket of his jacket and passed a few silver and copper coins over. 'Best I could do.'

'You been home yet?'

'No.'

'Petra can walk up with you and take the cart.'

There was a handcart leaning against the wall that had to go back to the butchers. Petra and Evan took one side each of the handle and pulled it up the street between them.

'How's Trefor then?'

'Worse.' Her voice was so low he could hardly

hear it above the iron wheels. 'He had a haemorrhage yesterday and collapsed. We got him to bed. He says he's going to stay alive till the miners have won and after that he doesn't care what happens.'

Neither of them spoke until they were nearly at the butcher's shop, then she said, 'I'm expecting his child.'

'Does he know?'

'No. I can't give him anything else to worry about.'

Evan was out all that evening and got home at about ten, as it was getting dark.

'Is Trefor awake?'

Sarah nodded. Petra was doing accounts on the kitchen table and looked up, alarmed.

'Evan, don't...'

'Don't worry. Just something I need to ask him about.'

Trefor was lying on the old sofa, sheets and blankets thrown back and a chipped enamel bowl beside him. The only light came from the kitchen, through the cracks between door and frame.

Evan sat down carefully on the edge of the sofa.

'Something I heard in the pub tonight, about Mrs Allegri.'

Trefor coughed and spat into the bowl. 'What?'

'Somebody had seen a letter she wrote, asking for men to go and work in her garden.'

'What!'

'She'd written to Gladwyn, wanting men to go and dig out the pond for her.'

'Of all the patronising wickedness. Lock us out from making our livings and...' He started coughing, more violently this time. Evan hurried on, raising his voice enough for Trefor to hear him over the coughing.

'The thing is, some of the men are talking about going over there and doing something, digging up the garden but not in the way she wants. They've even got money to get there. One of them was flashing a ten bob note around. I wondered if you...'

Trefor stopped coughing and levered himself up on his elbow.

'You wondered if I was throwing round some of that Moscow gold we're supposed to have chestfulls of to pay people to ruin that woman's garden?'

Evan glanced next door and signed to Trefor to keep his voice down.

'So you've got nothing to do with it?'

'Nothing, nothing, nothing. No more than I had anything to do with the damage back at your precious garden when we were kids.'

'I never thought you did.'

'Uncle Will did. He never said so, but I knew he thought it.'

'So if you...'

'Do you believe me, Evan?'

'About then or about now?'

'Both.'

It seemed to matter to him more than Evan would have thought likely.

'Yes, I believe you. But how did the people in the pub know about Mrs Allegri's letter and where did the money come from?'

'God knows. Was that all you came in to ask me?'

Evan hesitated. 'Yes. Anything I can get you?'

'Hothouse grapes and peaches. Failing that, a cup of hot water if there's any in the kettle.'

Evan had his hand on the door when Trefor called his name urgently.

'What?'

'Thank you for believing me, that's all.'

The next morning, a Sunday, Petra was on duty at the soup kitchen when the boiler with the crack in it burst at last, scattering hot coals all over the yard. It was half an hour before the children were due there for their midday meal and nobody was badly hurt but the meat and potato broth that had been warming in a huge saucepan on top of it fell and ran away into the dust. Petra helped clear up, to save the bits of meat and potato that were salvageable, to explain to the mothers when they arrived that their children would get only two thirds of the normal ration. Afterwards she gave the treasurer's report to an emergency meeting of the distress committee. Fourteen shillings and threepence, nowhere near enough for a boiler and anyway they needed that money for food. Then she surprised them by saying she was sorry but she wouldn't be in for the next two days. She put a note in the letterbox to the solicitor in Treherbert and, late on Sunday evening, took a train down the valley without telling Sarah or anybody else where she was going.

66

'So you think Isabelle murdered her husband and Philip Cordell knew?' Rosa said.

She shifted, winced and massaged a kneecap. Colin knew he was being forced into the role of defence counsel for Cordell and from the expression on Kim's face she was acting for the prosecution.

'He might not have known for sure, just suspected it. He knew he might be killed in the war so he wrote her that letter in case she needed it – kind of a last present from him.'

'Some present,' Kim said.

'OK, some present. But it was no loss to him, after all. If he was dead they couldn't dig him up from a war cemetery and hang him for murder. But if he took that trouble, that means he had a pretty good idea that Isabelle Allegri had done it.'

'Or both of them together.'

'No, that's where we come back to the business with the wheelbarrow and the river. He thought she'd probably killed him but he didn't know where she'd put the body, so he had to make it up. If he'd known, he'd have put it in the confession – I killed him and I threw his body in the pond. Then they could have come along and found the bones, case all nicely tied up.'

456

Kim asked Rosa, 'Did she use it? Did she show it to the police?' Rosa shook her head. 'I suppose it was because they never got on to her. If you're rich and influential enough, nobody asks you embarrassing things about what you did with your husband.'

Rosa said to Colin, 'Do you agree? Do you think she killed him?'

'I'm sure Cordell didn't. I suppose that means she must have.'

But he conceded it with a terrible sense of loss. If it was true, the almost perfect garden had been poisoned. The woman walking down the steps and smelling the roses, standing on the bridge by the irises, eating golden yellow apples in the little orchard, had deliberately closed a man's eyes and nose and mouth to it all. And the other man, who'd loved her enough to make the garden for her, had known.

He added, almost under his breath, 'But I wish she hadn't.'

And found Rosa looking at him and smiling as if he'd given the right answer.

'Must have? Why?'

'Because he wrote that letter to save her if the truth came out.'

'What so false as truth is?'

'I'm sorry?'

'Don't worry. He thought she'd killed her husband, yes. But he might have been wrong, mightn't he?'

Kim said, 'Surely they'd have talked about it.'

Rosa looked at her, then at Colin and back again.

Kim said to Rosa, 'Yes, I see what you mean.' Then to Colin, 'You wouldn't ask me, would you? If you thought I'd murdered somebody?'

'I don't know. I just don't know.'

Kim said, with certainty, 'You wouldn't. You'd keep it all underground, like the bones.'

'I dug them up, after all.'

'And didn't tell me. I still don't understand what you thought you were doing.'

Whether from the thought of Allegri or the whiskey she was nearer to crying than he'd ever seen her. Rosa rocked forward and put a hand on her arm.

'Maybe he was trying what Philip Cordell would have loved to do – prove her innocent.'

'How?'

'The bones were there in the pond.'

'Yes.'

'And you think Isabelle Allegri knew that? All the time, for fourteen years, she was working in the garden, letting a journalist in to photograph it, she knew her husband's body was rotting under the water lilies?'

'Yes.'

'The lily pool silted up, you know. After the war, when Philip Cordell wasn't there.'

'That would have made it easier for her,' Kim said.

'You'd think so, wouldn't you? It was silting up, the bushes were growing over it. Anything in there would get buried deeper and deeper. You could forget about it.'

'Or try to.'

'Or try to.' Rosa settled back in her place,

shadow crouching on the tent fabric. 'In that case, why does Grandma Isabelle, the murderess, decide to have the pool dug out again, making it nearly certain the bones will be discovered?'

Silence, while they took it in, then Colin said, 'Perhaps she wanted to be...' and Kim cut across, 'How do you know?'

'Because my great uncle told me. Will Thomas.'

'Will Thomas?' Colin made the connection first. 'The gardener?'

'The gardener.'

Kim said, 'But I thought you were an Allegri.'

'My name's Thomas. At least, I was born Thomas. I'm an Allegri *and* a Thomas.'

'You mean, she married her gardener?'

'Grandma Isabelle and Great Uncle Will? Oh dear, I don't think so.'

Kim started to ask something, but Colin cut across.

'You talked to him? You actually talked to Will Thomas about the garden?'

'About the bits that mattered to me. I was a girl of fifteen or sixteen then and he was in his seventies. When it came to anything to do with the garden it was as if he had a notebook in his brain for whatever anybody did or said. I asked him several times over and he was quite certain that in the spring of 1921, Isabelle intended bringing in a group of miners from the collieries she owned to dig out the lily pool. Now why in the world would she have done that if she knew her husband's body was in there?'

Kim said, 'But the miners didn't dig the pool out, did they?'

'No. Isabelle had written a letter, you see. As it turned out, it wasn't the wisest thing in the world, but how was she to know?'

'But they came here?'

'Oh yes, they came.'

67

May 1921

Come for a drive in the country on Monday. I'll call for you quite early, about nine. M.

After the incident with Evan in the nightclub Megan hadn't expected to hear from Marius again. She thought 'I'm winning after all' then wondered how you could know if you were winning when you didn't know what the game was. At nine o'clock on Monday bank holiday morning she was ready and watching from the window when a green open-topped sports car drew up outside. The horn parped. He saw her looking out and made signs to her to hurry and come down. He kept the engine running so didn't get up from the driving seat to meet her, but at least leaned across to open the passenger door.

'Where are we going?'

He didn't answer, concentrating on turning the awkward corner out of her street. They drove through Marylebone and Paddington and took the main road westwards. The bank holiday traffic was already heavy with everything from two seaters like their own to motor charabancs carrying noisy parties to picnic in Burnham Beeches. Megan thought they might be making for Maidenhead and lunch at Skindles but they went on over the bridge, past Reading at a steady thirty. Soon after Oxford he turned down a narrow country road and they had lunch of salmon in aspic and hock at a public house by the river. There was a weir at the bottom of the lawn and peacocks perched on a wooden bridge. Marius was quiet and seemed preoccupied.

She said, experimentally, 'So the strike's nearly settled.'

He'd been staring out of the window, crumbling a bread roll. The look he gave her was startled, even annoyed.

'Where did you hear that?'

They got in the car and drove back up the narrow road, stopping and backing occasionally to let other cars come down because the lunchtime rush was beginning. He cursed under his breath and she thought he was impatient to get back to town, but when they got to the junction with the main road he turned west towards Cheltenham.

'We're going the wrong way,' she said.

He smiled for the first time that day. 'I thought we might drop in on my mother.'

She started protesting that they couldn't get all the way and back in a day, that she had to be at work at eight-thirty sharp Tuesday morning. He ignored her and drove on between the banks of cow parsley that seemed to crowd closer and closer as they went westwards until when she looked back she couldn't see the pale road surface at all, just a foam of white and green closing off the way they'd come.

Something green and feathery-leafed had climbed up the dead oak tree then flung itself down again in showers of white stars, making a kind of vegetable tent over a bench alongside. Petra lay on the bench through most of the afternoon, occasionally sipping water from an old cracked jug she'd found in the porch at the side of the house. When she'd knelt to fill the jug at the pond under the waterfall even the smell of the water had been like a blow because it brought back a picture of Evan with his fife and a girl listening who'd been almost happy for a while because she'd been stupid and lied to. All that was a distraction because she was there to do a job. Sometimes she half dozed on the bench under the green and starry canopy because the afternoon was warm and it had been a hard journey to get there. When she'd left Treorchy on an impulse on the Sunday evening she'd forgotten that it was Whitsun weekend. She slept wrapped in her coat on Cardiff station and the next day it took longer than usual to get to Abergavenny, then another long wait before she could find anybody to take her the last few miles to Holdersby. In the end, she got a seat in a battered old gig delivering a keg of beer to the Sun Inn. She recognised the carter from years ago, but he gave no sign of knowing her. Why should he or anybody else look at a young woman with unwashed hair, skirt stained with meat and potato broth and see Isabelle Allegri's daughter?

At intervals through the afternoon she stood up and looked down the garden. The broad figure of Will Thomas was unmistakable, trimming the edge of the lawn where it met the curving lavender border. There was a terrier with him as usual but not the one she remembered, smaller and whiter. Apart from that, nobody visible. Her mother must be at home because the car was standing on the gravel by the front door. Petra would wait all day and through the night into the next day if necessary. Hunger didn't matter. At first she'd been worried that it would harm the baby but a lot of the mothers who brought their children to the soup kitchen were expecting again so what was the point in worrying? Still, she thought about the baby as she lay in the shade of the starry-flowered thing until it seemed as if she could feel it growing inside her with the same slow and certain rhythm as the plant, connecting itself to the blood pulsing out of her heart and to something in her mind that was hard and curled up on itself like a daffodil bulb, waiting for its explosion of life. She must have dozed more deeply than she'd intended because when she next stood up the shadows of Will and his wheelbarrow were long on the grass and a woman in a blue dress was coming down the steps from the terrace. Isabelle Allegri had come out in the evening to look at her garden.

'Time to stop, Will. You've done wonders.'

'Get it finished tomorrow, with the lads back.'

'I've been looking at the iris bed. I do believe Polly's got every bit of couch grass out of it at last.'

Will put his tools into the wheelbarrow and pushed it away up the lawn. Isabelle walked on down the broad steps between the paeony borders. The roses at the back of the border were growing so vigorously that the ropes and poles were almost hidden, the dark foliage of Félicité Perpétue contrasting with the soft grey-green of Rambling Rector. (She was glad she'd insisted on Rambling Rector, even if Philip had laughed at her for choosing it for its name.) A blackbird had built its nest somewhere in the swags of foliage and was shrilling a warning to keep away. Beyond the roses, the tops of the apple trees in the Pleasaunce were a froth of pink and white blossom. She pushed through the apple tunnel, scattering more blossom, saw the drifts of fritillaries under the trees.

'Just as we wanted them.'

She'd got in the habit of talking to Philip going round the garden. Sometimes, just a few times a year, she could feel the warmth of his arms round her, hear his voice.

If I'm sure of anything, in this world or the next…

Except he hadn't said that, he'd written it, and the person he'd written it to had thrown it away.

'Oh my darling.' Standing under his apple blossom she could almost believe that it might come right in the end with Petra after all. 'At any rate, there's this. It exists. It's beautiful. We made it.'

464

The blackbird was still chattering away in the rose leaves, as if she'd meant it harm.

Once she'd seen Isabelle on her way down the steps, Petra moved quickly down through the hazel thicket to the side door. It opened at a touch and she was inside the narrow corridor that had been familiar once but seemed from another world now with its row of sketches along the white wall and smell of lavender polish. No sound of anybody. She walked as lightly as she could along the corridor and into the front hall. The door to the small drawing room was closed. She opened it a crack and looked inside, then whipped in and shut it behind her. The room was just as she remembered, with the light from the sunset flooding in through the window, giving a copper glow to the big walnut bureau. The middle drawer on the right where her mother always kept money for household expenses slid open as obediently as if it had been waiting for her. Bank notes were stacked at the front of it. She counted out a hundred pounds and put them in her pocket. It came to her that she wanted her mother to know who'd taken the money and why. She grabbed a sheet of headed notepaper from a pigeonhole, looked for something to write with but could only see a pencil with a broken point. She started pulling open other drawers, looking for a knife to sharpen it, getting impatient. When she opened the second drawer from the bottom on the left, the lurch in her chest was the first warning of the trap it held, as if the sight of the handwriting on the white envelope had bypassed

465

her brain and gone straight to the heart muscle. One word, 'Petra.' She clawed the envelope out of the drawer and let it fall on the blotting pad, appalled that it still existed. She'd imagined when she left it on the ground above Treorchy that the wind would blow it away or the sheep piss on it and wash the words out. The fact that Isabelle had picked it up and kept it seemed one more betrayal. There was another envelope under it in the drawer, a larger brown one, addressed in capitals: FOR THE EYES OF MRS ISABELLE ALLEGRI. It was anger that made her open it and read. If it was something they'd wanted kept secret between them at least she could deny them that. She read: TO WHOM IT MAY CONCERN

This is to state that in July 1907 I killed Mr Leon Allegri...

She sat in the chair at the desk and read through the whole thing, slowly and carefully. For a long time she stayed there with the two letters on the blotter in front of her, remembering a dark night with thunder in the distance and rain falling. She felt the squash of mud under her knees as she knelt beside the thing she'd just fallen over, the tautness of skin and flesh yielding under her fingers, wet and slithery like a frog's back. Screams went round and round in her skull, louder all the time, from a terrified child who thought if she could only make enough noise it would blot the thing out. But this time she didn't scream out loud. She said, quite calmly and softly to the two letters on the blotter, 'It wasn't a nightmare. I really knew all the time and you knew I knew.' She got up, leaving the letters where they were, and went through the hall and back along the corridor to the side door, not caring if anybody heard or saw her. Outside, she picked up a rusty coal hammer from beside the coconut mat and felt its satisfying heaviness stretching the muscles of her right arm. It was dusk now with only red and grey rags of cloud left over from the sunset. She crossed a field and scrambled up the bank and through the hedge into the Pleasaunce, the way she'd gone as a child. It brought her to the top of the bank in the corner where there were tumbled blocks of stone lower down, poking out of moss and young brambles. She slid down the bank, let go of the hammer and used both arms at full stretch to grope into the cave under the bank. It was still there, still standing. When she gave a little tug to get its feet loose from the earth it fell into her arms and she drew it out. She laid it carefully across a level piece of stone then raised the coal hammer and brought it down, aiming for waistcoated paunch and the paw holding the watch. The third blow did the job cleanly. She toppled the upper half onto the grass then, to leave no doubt that it had been a deliberate act, picked up the lower half and set it back on its feet in the cave.

Isabelle, walking back up the steps to the terrace, heard the three blows and thought it was a funny time for Will to be chopping wood.

Marius said, somewhere west of Cheltenham, 'Don't you want to see my mother again?'

'Not this way. She's not expecting us.'

467

'It will be a surprise then.'

'I'll lose my job if I'm not in tomorrow morning.'

He drove on with the lowering sun in their eyes, speeding up again towards Hereford, then slowly again along the road to Holders Hope. It was dusk by then and he had to switch the car headlights on. Megan, cold and shivering, watched the moths blundering into them until she couldn't stand it any more, then leaned back and closed her eyes.

'Are you asleep, Megan? We're nearly there now.'

She didn't answer. Then, a minute or so later he said, 'Look!' and jammed on the brakes so that the car skidded to a stop, throwing her forward. 'Look, what's that?' Then 'Oh my God.'

Petra wriggled back through the gap she'd made in the hedge and hesitated, crouched down in the field on the other side. Her mind and body worked well enough if she gave them little bits of instruction, one thing at a time. Drop hammer. Don't need it now. Check money. The whole point of it, after all, getting the money back to Treorchy. Probably couldn't be done tonight, not now it was getting dark. Walk to Abergavenny. A long way and wouldn't the last train be gone? Probably, yes, but walk anyway. She started across the field towards the lane but her feet felt as if they were pushing through sluggish water. Easier to go straight down over the fields. *I loaded Mr Allegri's body into the wheelbarrow, covered it with a tarpaulin and wheeled it across the fields...*

Across the fields, this field where she was standing. The ground under her shoe soles was the same ground that barrow had run over, pressing deep with the weight of the thing under the tarpaulin. She went down on her knees, rocking backwards and forwards, nine years old again and terrified. Her adult mind, contemptuous, told her to get up and go on. Don't think about it. Not the same ground, not the same grass. She went slowly and carefully down the first field, making for the big oak that was just visible as a black shape, knowing the gate to the next field was beside it. But there was something wrong with the shape of the gate, things clumped there, moving. She thought 'Cows, of course.' Then heard the metal fastening of the gate click, a man's voice whispering something she couldn't make out, a low laugh. A match flared and silhouettes of three or four heads stood out. Men wearing caps. Poachers she'd have guessed, but what sort of poachers stopped to light cigarettes? The match had faded now and there were little points of red light in the dark. Then an owl hoot came from the direction of the lane, no owl that ever flew, but a man giving an approximate imitation. It seemed to be a signal that the group by the gate had been waiting for because they started up the field, coming in her direction. She fled back the way she'd come, uphill and through the hedge. She was in the Pleasaunce under the apple trees when she heard shouting from somewhere higher up and the first of the flames came rolling down the border.

469

68

Isabelle saw it from her bedroom window. She'd gone up to get tidy before dinner and was standing with the window open brushing her hair. She thought she heard voices in the garden but knew she must be mistaken because nobody had any reason to be out there in the dark. Then there was a flare of orange flame, near the top of the steps by the paeony border. She opened the window wider and leaned out. Instead of smells of grass and earth a sharp chemical reek caught her by the throat and set her coughing. At the same moment the orange flame surged like a wave. Then there were more flames, by the gazebo, the bridge, the iris bed. She screamed and ran downstairs, through the French windows and out onto the terrace in time to see the lavender border turning into a scimitar slash of fire.

The tops of the apple trees, loaded with leaves and blossoms, looked as unreal as pantomime scenery in the harsh orange light. The fire didn't get to them but ran like a waterfall down both sides of the steps, following the trail of petrol that had been poured over the paeony borders. It ran up the wooden posts and along the ropes of roses. The branches twisted and writhed as they burned, as if they were trying to outpace the fire in a last desperate spurt of growth, thorns and leaves standing out for a few seconds black against red.

From where Petra was crouching under the trees she could hear the sap sizzling and popping as tens of thousands of plant cells exploded and the clack clack warning call of a blackbird, high and useless, its nest a burning ball. The air was full of sparks, saturated with the smell of petrol. Beyond shock or even reason she thought that somehow she'd caused it, that her hatred of Philip Cordell and his garden had summoned up the ropes and waterfalls of fire. She stayed under the trees, waiting for it to break in and burn her along with everything else, her hand on rough tree bark and the ashes of burnt rose trees settling on her hair, watching as ropes parted and dropped in loops of fire onto the blazing borders.

Marius slammed the car to a stop and turned off the engine.

'Go on,' Megan yelled at him. 'It's Holders Hope.'

She stood on the passenger seat and saw gashes of fire high up to the right. He vaulted over the driver's door, ran round and pulled her door open. She toppled and fell against him.

'Across the fields,' he said. 'Lane's probably blocked.'

He took her wrist and half dragged her across the road to a gateway, bundled her over.

'What's happening?'

'Something I was afraid of.'

She couldn't tell if the house itself was burning and she was terrified for Isabelle. There were copses and hedges on their left that hid the flames, but they could see the orange glow in the sky and smell burnt wood. Marius had started at a run and she couldn't keep up with him but before they got to the hedge at the top of the field he slowed down. When she caught up with him she saw he was hobbling.

'Twisted my bloody ankle.'

'We should have stayed in the car.'

'Too late for that now. Can you help me get this gate open?'

It was wired up and it seemed to take forever to get come undone. Halfway up the next field they came above the copse that blocked the view and could see across to Holders Hope. The patches of fire looked less fierce than from the road, mottled red and black now instead of orange flames.

'It's only the garden, not the house,' Marius said.

'But how can a garden catch fire?'

'Anything will catch fire if you try hard enough.'

'Try...? You mean, you think somebody's done that deliberately?'

'I'd heard rumours. That's why I wanted to get down here today to be honest. Only it looks as if we left it too late.'

'But who?'

'The miners, of course. Probably your brothers showed them the way.'

She shouted 'No,' but he was walking ahead of her, still limping.

'Looks as if the worst of it's over now, but we'd better get there and see that Mama's all right.'

From the terrace, Isabelle watched as the flames faded. Once the petrol was eaten up there was nothing much left to feed them. The ashes from burned plants were light, almost insubstantial, and sifted down in flakes on the glowing earth. The heat of the fire didn't penetrate far below the surface before meeting the damp in the soil from the high water table that had made such easy living for the slugs and the snails whose empty and calcified shells now lay by their hundred in the borders, along with the burnt remains of the paeonies and delphiniums they'd fed on. Will stood behind Isabelle, not speaking or moving. When it had started he'd come running up the lane from the cottage and grabbed buckets and watering cans out of the toolshed. Isabelle and Mrs Morgan had to restrain him from rushing down single handed to fight the flames. What could one man do? In any case, the fire itself wasn't the only danger. There'd been men down there, perhaps a dozen or more. From the terrace they'd heard voices, seen black silhouettes against the flames. There'd never been any doubt that the thing had been done deliberately, even before Rees reported that all the cans of petrol they kept for the motor car and mechanical mower had gone.

'They knew what they were doing,' he whispered to Mrs Morgan.

She only nodded, eyes on Isabelle who was standing a little apart from the rest of them.

'I've telephoned the police and the fire brigade,' Rees said. 'But God knows how long it will take them to get here from Hereford.'

'Too late, they're gone now. What about the doctor?'

'Somebody hurt?'

'For her.'

Mrs Morgan nodded towards Isabelle and Rees went back inside. Over to the left, parts of the birch copse were still burning and a Silver Queen holly bush that had resisted so far surrendered suddenly and explosively, bright as a magnesium flare.

Petra watched the flames dying down along the border. The end of the fire, like the beginning of it, was just one more inexplicable thing in a world that had never seemed to accept the responsibility of making sense. She curled up under an apple tree with no plan except getting through the night and starting again in the morning, like any of the thousands of other creatures that had survived the fire.

Down by the giant gunnera leaves at the side of the diminished lily pool the frogs that had dived into the water when the fire started crawled out and settled back in the mud. The blackbird and its mate roosted in an alder bush near a badger sett on a bank just above the gunneras. The badgers had escaped the fire itself, curled in their damp burrows, but the reek of petrol and burning wood unsettled them. A muzzle came up out of the sett. In the darkness, the streak of white on the muzzle was the only thing visible, like the tip of a bulb pushing through the soil. The tip extended itself to a long pale stem and flower bud as the whole head came up and the badger lumbered out to see what was left of the world.

Rees and Mrs Morgan persuaded Isabelle to go inside. She wouldn't go upstairs to bed but they got her to sit down on an armchair in the little drawing room and sip brandy in warm milk. Wouldn't she like a blanket over her? Mrs Morgan asked and hurried upstairs to get one. Left alone, Isabelle saw the letters lying on the blotter and knew at a glance what they were.

'She came with them to burn the garden.' She went to the window and stared out. 'Was it so very terrible what we did? Was that what we deserved?'

She cried, not from anger or even self pity, but for the waste of it.

Megan and Marius came out beside the lily pool. They'd got lost in the fields, had to scramble through hedges and under barbed wire fences. Megan's face was scratched and bleeding, her thin dress torn and smeared with earth. But her mind was clear and somewhere on the dark uphill journey a decision had made itself. Probably Marius had intended them to come out higher up, near the house. When he realised where they were she felt him hesitate so she took the lead, slipping and clambering among the alder trees to get to the terrace at the bottom of the steps. The two lines of glowing ash where the borders had been gave just enough light to see where she was going. He followed, breathing heavily, cursing occasionally as he slipped.

'We can get up this way,' she said and started

up the steps. The stones were hot and some of them had cracked. At the back of the border a rope that had been holding by a few strands parted suddenly and the pole it was attached to shifted sideways.

'Megan, it's too dangerous. Let's go round.'

'Everywhere's dangerous.'

She walked on and heard his footsteps behind her. There was a point where a low wall curved out from the steps, making a stone seat. She sat down on it, moving a can aside, and waited there for him to catch up with her.

She said, 'You knew it was going to happen.'

'I was afraid they were planning something. And they were. Look.' He picked up the can she'd moved. Liquid sloshed inside it and the cap was off. 'Petrol. The place reeks of it.'

'You weren't just afraid it would happen, you knew. You've been deliberately timing it all day, to make sure you arrived when it was too late.'

He put the can back on the seat and wiped his hands on his flannels, looking at her.

'Too late for what?'

'To stop them.'

'Me against a gang of rioting miners?'

'Well, if you were afraid, you could have let the police know.'

'Police? Was that what you wanted then? Let the police know?'

He was giving her his father's look, like somebody experimenting to see how far he could go.

'Why not?'

'You know my dear mother was thinking of

476

getting the pool dug out. Would you want that to happen?'

'Why not? It's her garden.'

'Don't worry. They won't find him now. After this, she'll give up and go away.'

'I don't care. I don't care if they *do* find him. It was you who killed him, not me.'

'You helped me sink him, though.'

'Because you made me. I didn't want to.'

'You could have owned up then, couldn't you? Please Mister Judge, I was two-timing them, Marius and his father. I told both of them I'd meet them in the garden only Marius got there first and his father tried to kill him.'

Megan closed her eyes and heard again Leon's roar from the darkness, then the rain and the panting of Marius running away up the ramp, his father following, both of them scrabbling up there above her while she cried from fear. Then the worse fear. The rush of the stone cart down the ramp, Marius's face in the darkness pale and wet, his breath smelling of sick. 'He's dead. Help me.' She opened her eyes and found him still looking at her.

'I don't care. I'm going up to the house to tell them, the police or somebody else.'

'No.'

He grabbed her wrist as she stood up, trying to force her back down on the bench. The can got knocked over and petrol spilled over both of them, mostly his trousers and blazer. The smell of it made her retch but she managed to twist sideways off the bench and under him, pulling his arm round. He yelled and let go. She kicked

477

out at him as she went, lost a shoe, kicked off the other one and ran up the hot steps in her silk stockings, choking and sobbing. He came limping, five or six steps behind her.

In the Pleasaunce, Petra woke, hearing the pad of running feet. Not far away in the long grass the badger, confused by the smells all round it, decided to give up the search for slugs and get back to its burrow. It made for the border, blundered against the base of the tilted post then, alarmed by the heat of it, turned back into the grass of the Pleasaunce and found a long and unfamiliar route home. The post was nearly burned through and the small collision was enough to set it swaying. It toppled forwards, seemed to hang in the air for a moment then crashed across the border, throwing up a cloud of smouldering ash. The top of it struck the steps, just missing Marius, but fragments of glowing charcoal broke away from it and landed on his clothes. He stumbled on up the steps after Megan without noticing and his movement fanned the small points of fire into flame. Two steps later he felt the heat on his back, twisted round and flapped at it with his hand, still not thinking of it as any more than a distraction. Then he felt the flames spreading up his back and yelled. Megan went on running, near the top of the steps now. The flames leapt round to his stomach and crotch, where most of the petrol had splashed and caught the vapour explosively with a hollow crump, like a fist on a drum. His screams tore into the darkness, high and metallic.

From the top of the steps by the burnt bridge Megan stopped and looked round in time to see a ragged cylinder of fire rolling down the steps with a dark centre to it that she didn't at first realise was Marius. In the Pleasaunce, Petra burrowed into the long sappy grass with her hands over her ears and eyes screwed shut, nine years old again, feeling screams ripping from her own body and the unthinkable thing happening again.

69

Evan found Petra at about ten o'clock the following morning. She was halfway along the road from Holders Hope to Abergavenny, walking slowly but steadily with smears of ash and tear trails all over her face, a blank look in her eyes. He was in a cart lumbering along in the other direction. He'd set out from Treorchy on Monday evening, when the Thomas family realised that nobody had seen Petra since the day before, and arrived at Abergavenny to find the place buzzing with talk. *Miners came, hundreds of them, and burned the house down. Some of the family killed trying to stop them.* Nearly frantic with worry he rushed round the town trying to find any way of getting quickly to Holders Hope, but the best he could do was the cart heading for Hereford, creaking along behind a lazy cob. It was a fine May morning, full of scents and bird song. From his seat beside the driver he saw the figure coming towards them from a long way off, vaulted off the cart and ran ahead of it to meet her.

'Petra, what's happened?'

For a moment she didn't seem to recognise him, then fear replaced the blankness.

'Evan. Is Trefor...?'

'Never mind about Trefor. What's happened at Holders Hope? What's happened to Uncle Will and Auntie Bath and your mother?'

The blank look came back. 'The garden got burned. Did you know Philip Cordell killed my father? I found a letter.' Then, more urgently, 'I've got the money for the boiler. We must get it back to them.'

The cart was alongside by now. He persuaded the driver to stop long enough to get her up beside them. She protested at first that they were going in the wrong direction but gave in when he told her they must find out what had happened at Holders Hope.

The driver dropped them off at the end of the lane. From there, it was obvious that some of the rumours were wrong. The house still stood, pink and glowing in the sunshine. But after a few steps Evan smelt burnt wood and noticed the new deep ruts in the lane, as if a lot of vehicles had been up and down. Bathsheba was out in her garden. Evan ran to her. 'Auntie Bath, are you all right? Is Uncle Will all right?' She grabbed him and hugged him.

'Your uncle's all right. He's just going round the garden with the policemen.' It took her a

480

while to recognise Petra standing at the gate. 'Where did Miss Petra come from? Does she know?'

'Know what?'

'Her poor brother.' Her mouth twisted and tears ran down her cheeks. 'This morning. They got the doctor to him, but he couldn't do anything. His whole body was burned black. Mrs Morgan says he died just before the sun came up.'

Petra was coming towards them. Bathsheba gulped a few words that Evan didn't catch and bolted inside the cottage.

'What's wrong?'

Petra was still quiet and submissive, like a child trying not to get in the way. Evan took her hand.

'I'm sorry. Auntie Bath says your brother's dead.'

He got her to sit down on the bench in the porch, alongside the watering can and the hank of raffia twine. Bathsheba came out with tea in a big willow pattern cup, face full of fear and pity.

'Can you look after her, Auntie Bath? I've got to go up and see what's happening.'

'Your sister's up there.'

The gravel space by the front door was full of vehicles, three motor cars and two gigs. The door itself was open with a couple of men Evan didn't recognise standing beside it. No police visible here at any rate. It was in his mind that he'd have to get Petra away. What they'd do in the long term he had no idea, only that he couldn't stand by and see her arrested. He walked down the steps to the terrace. From there for the first time he could see what had been done to the garden. Streaks and patches of black and grey where the iris bed and the lavender border had been, the gazebo tilted sideways with blackened stems of climbing plants still clinging to it, a smell of burning and petrol over everything. There was a woman standing on the edge of the terrace looking out, wearing a plain dark blue dress. At first he thought it was Isabelle Allegri herself and was going to back away, but the woman had dark hair and when she turned it was Megan. She ran towards him and hugged him more tightly than she ever had when they were children.

'Evan, Evan, Evan.' She was shaking, all her self-possession gone. 'Have you heard?'

'About Marius?'

'I was there. I saw it. I tried to put the flames out but...' He saw both her hands were bandaged.

'Megan, Petra's down there in Uncle Will's cottage. Do you know where the police are? I'd better get her away before...'

'Why? Don't take her away. Isabelle will want to see her. She's asleep upstairs now because the doctor gave her something. Petra's all she's got now.'

'They'll blame her.'

'What for?'

'Bringing the miners here. Starting the fires.'

Megan was staring at him. 'Why should Petra do that?'

'She's ... she's talking odd. She told me Philip Cordell killed her father and she might even be right. I saw Mr Allegri's body, you see ... in the

482

lily pond, a long time ago. So she brought the miners in to burn Cordell's garden.'

Megan was looking at him, shaking her head. He thought it was just in disbelief, despaired of getting her to understand what was happening.

'Look, it was wicked, I know it was wicked, but I can't stand here and see her taken off to prison...'

'She won't be.'

'Megan, just understand...'

'She won't be, because she didn't bring the miners in. Marius did.'

'Marius? Marius! You're mad. Why should Marius of all people...?'

The look in her big dark eyes, ringed with tiredness, silenced him.

'Something I've never told anybody before. I can tell it, now they're both dead.'

They walked side by side along the terrace, close together for a long time.

Down at the birch coppice, Will Thomas and two policemen walked over black and crumbling twigs through what had been the rhododendron glades. He was doing his best, as he always did his best with officials, to give them what they wanted. Show us the damage, they'd said, as if that would do any good. Tell us what was there. He remembered some of their names, William Ewart Gladstone and Duchess of Connaught but mostly he remembered how this one had glowed pink against the early birch foliage, like sunshine through a cat's ear, that one had waxy bells of flowers that smelt of honey, that one was tender and Mr Cordell would get him to throw an old tablecloth over it if it was coming into flower when there was frost in the air. Mr Cordell's name came up so often that one of the policemen said hadn't they better speak to him. Dead in the war, Will told him, and if he'd lived to see this... Then he turned away, not wanting them to see the tears running down his face. 'Oh the waste of it. Oh the wicked, wicked waste of it.' They waited for him to recover, with house martins skimming overhead catching flies that circled in the columns of warm air from the ashes.

70

Megan adjusted the curtains to shut out any chink of light and walked softly across the darkened room. Isabelle's face was no more than a pale oval against the pillows. Her eyes were closed now. They'd been open all the time, Megan was talking, following her movements round the room. While she talked, Megan had tried to calm herself by rearranging the little pots and jars on the dressing table, with their familiar labels and scents, but her bandaged hands were too clumsy.

She said, 'You'll see Petra?'

'Will she see me?'

'I think so. You understand it wasn't her fault, the garden?'

'Yes, but she hates me all the same.'

'She shouldn't.'

A sigh.

'Shall I tell Mrs Morgan to send her up, then?'

'If you like.'

On an impulse, Megan bent down and kissed Isabelle on the forehead.

'Goodbye.'

Isabelle's eyes snapped open. 'Where are you going?'

'Back to London.'

'No.'

'You don't want me here.'

'Don't go.'

'You understand what I've been telling you?'

Isabelle's hands came out from under the covers, found Megan's and closed round them.

'I understand. Don't leave me.'

Petra and Evan were walking up and down the path in Bathsheba's vegetable garden. The scent of parsley hung round them because they brushed against it as they went from radishes to rhubarb, turn and back, time after time. Even when she accepted that Philip Cordell hadn't killed the man she stubbornly called her father, Petra was still angry.

'It was a lie – the wheelbarrow, taking him down to the river.'

'Yes. He didn't know he was in the lily pool all the time.'

And yet, when Petra told him about that passage in Philip Cordell's letter, there'd been a flutter of recognition in his mind. It took him a while to remember the secret journeys in the other direction, up over the fields with barrow loads of water lily roots for the pool. Cordell had simply reversed them.

'Your mother's not a murderer, not even an accomplice. Go up and see her. You don't have to talk to her, just see her.'

'If I do, will you take me back home with you?'

'If that's what you want, yes.'

'Wait for me. Don't leave me.'

71

July 2001

Half past four in the morning. Light from outside was coming in through the tent fabric. The camping lamp had guttered out hours ago. The whiskey bottle was empty and although Rosa had drunk most of it, the husky voice seemed as steady as ever.

'My mother Petra lived to be eighty-four. She never once referred to Philip Cordell as her father.'

Colin said, 'It seems a waste.'

He was weighed down with loss, for Philip and for his garden that would never come back to life now. Rosa Thomas owned the whole place. She'd made that casually clear and he believed her. The angel with the fiery sword had turned out to be an old woman with a pack and walking boots and by the time the sun rose the garden would be closed to them.

Kim said, 'She talked about all this to you?'

'Oh yes. She hated lies, you see, after what had happened. From her point of view she'd spent her childhood being lied to and it wasn't going to happen to her daughter.'

'And what happened after the fire?'

'She went back home to Treorchy. The lock-out was still on. It lasted for another month. Total defeat for the miners, back to work on the employers' terms with wages cut. Grandma sold her pits soon after that. Got out just before the worst of the recession, as it happens. Her business instincts always were sound.'

Kim said, 'What happened to your father?'

'I never knew my father Trefor. He died a week before the lock-out ended, that's months before I was born. I said my mother hated lies but she told one to him. He had a few hours to live. He knew it, they all knew it. Just one thing on his mind – would the miners win? So she knelt down beside the old sofa and told him yes, they'd won. Just telling him wasn't enough, of course. He wanted it all, what the figures were, how the ballot went. She made it up, every last detail and he believed it. But then she had a head for business in her way too. Runs in the family.'

Kim said, 'You'd have thought he'd have been more concerned about her and you.'

'He never knew about me. She never told him.'

'You said she didn't tell lies.'

'She didn't lie. She just didn't tell him. My father Evan wanted her to, but she wouldn't budge.'

'Your father Evan?'

'Don't worry, having two fathers runs in our family. Evan and my mother got married in the chapel in Treorchy when she was seven months pregnant with me.'

'Wasn't there a scandal?'

'They had worse things than that to worry about in the Rhondda in 1921. Anyway, there's more kindness in the world than you'd think sometimes.'

Rosa stretched and reached behind her for her pack. She seemed ready to go but Kim wouldn't let her.

'Were they happy, Evan and your mother?'

'Very. Three children besides me. They didn't stay in Treorchy because there was no work there and anyway Evan was a musician. I shouldn't be surprised if your mother wasn't conceived to his music.'

'My mother!'

'Don't look so shocked. Anybody's mother. Didn't you ever hear of Evan Treorchy and his swinging trumpet? Nearly as popular as Joe Loss for a while.'

'And Isabelle?'

'She and Auntie Megan set up a chain of beauty parlours and a lipstick factory. Turned out to be a lot more profitable than coalmines. That's where most of the family money comes from these days. In fact, that's what we've decided to do with the house in the end – turn it into a training centre for our sales staff.'

Colin thought of the garden made over to grass and evergreens for easy maintenance, an acre of tarmac for sales reps' cars with a few mountain ash staked out to live or die. There was a bitter taste in his mouth from the whiskey.

'So they all just went away and got on with their lives and forgot the garden.'

'All except Great Uncle Will. He stayed in his cottage, tidying up what was left as long as he could. But one old man couldn't keep up that garden, let alone remake it. He died in his vegetable garden one day, just keeled over. I was sorry. I liked Uncle Will.'

So that's that, Colin thought. Philip Cordell and Will Thomas. They made a garden and it went and they went and there was nothing left but a few traces on an overgrown hillside and soon those would be gone too. He shuffled to the tent flap and looked out. More light than dark now, with mist following the course of the river along the valley and coming up in wisps from the trees. He stood up stiffly and began to walk over the fields to the garden. Rosa and Kim were still talking in the tent which was fine by him because he wanted to say his goodbyes on his own. The grass was silver with dew except for green swathes where the cows had walked through it. His own footsteps left a narrower trail. He walked past the crack willows, over the mud of the lily pond and up the steps. He sat down on the top step, looking at the patches they'd cleared and all there was still to do and wouldn't be done now. Sorry Cordell. You and me both.

He'd been there for a while when he saw a movement on the steps below him and there was Rosa walking up, pack on back. Marching orders, he thought. OK, you own the place, but couldn't you have given me these few minutes at least? She climbed up and sat on the step beside him, moving a little cautiously, as if sitting up all night in a tent might have had some effect on her after all. He said nothing.

'Well, could you do it?'

Voice rasping now. She was tired but he felt no pity for her.

'Could I do what?'

'Make it like it was.'

He was furious with her for playing games, the way they'd all played games all along with Cordell's garden.

'Oh yes, with the next ten years of my life and a thousand times as much money as I'm ever likely to have and if it weren't all going under a bloody car park, I could have done it.'

If he hadn't been angry he wouldn't have let himself sound so confident. But it was true. The garden had told him enough now, not to make it exactly as it was – couldn't be done any more than you could roll back a hundred years of history – but enough to put the heart back in it and make it beat.

'Have you got an address?'

'Have I got a what?'

'Do you live somewhere? I can't get people to write letters to a tent.'

'Why should anybody write letters? We've done no harm. We'll pack up and go this morning.'

Fling the tents and Kim's duvet into the back of the VW and off.

'The formalities. I suppose technically you'll be

490

an employee of the company but don't let that worry you. You'll report directly to me and nobody else will interfere. We can probably set it up as a charitable trust.'

'What is this?'

'You'll need to employ people, of course. Do it locally, if you can. I'd like a proposal from you – staff requirements, target dates and so on. Don't look so worried. I expect she'll help you. She seems businesslike.'

'Are you ... are you asking me to take on the garden?'

'You've already started, haven't you? Take this and write me down your address and email.' He wrote them obediently in the little notebook she handed him, still feeling dazed. 'Here's my card. Can you get that proposal to me in a couple of weeks, do you think? We haven't got a lot of time before I go.'

'Go?' He turned and looked at her properly for the first time since she came up the steps. In the daylight she did look frail, tanned skin stretched tight across her cheekbones, bright eyes sunken. 'You mean you're...'

'Yes, a week or two and I'll be going. California. I've got a friend there who's opened a senior citizens' diving school. Total madman, of course, but I like the climate. Only I remembered this place and decided there was some unfinished business to clear up before I went.'

'But you didn't even know the garden.'

'No, but it's been in my mind on and off all my life. Father Evan and Uncle Will talked about it. And then there was the letter.'

'Cordell's so-called confession.'

'No, another one. It is from Cordell though.' She unzipped a flap at the back of her haversack and took out something wrapped in polythene. 'It's addressed to my mother, but I don't know if she even read it. Grandma Isabelle kept it and handed it on to me on my sixteenth birthday. She said it was maybe me it was written for. It's taken me a long time to work out what she meant.'

She unwrapped it and handed it to him. He read with the sun coming up and beginning to warm his back: *My darling daughter Petra, I've called you that so many times in my mind and it feels strange – though very sweet – to be writing it for the first time...*

'You really want me to read this?'

'It goes with the garden.'

So many little surprises I put into it that came with invisible labels – for my daughter Petra, with love... If I'm sure of anything in this world or the next it's that love is never wasted and never goes away.

He read it slowly through again then handed it back to her. They sat side by side, saying nothing, watching mist rise from the tops of the apple trees and small insects going up and down in the air currents from the steps as the sun warmed them. After a while she stood up, stiffly but refusing his help.

'You'll be hearing from me in the next day or two.'

She walked away down the steps, passing Kim on the way up with a wave of the hand. By the time Kim got to him, Rosa was out of sight.

'What's wrong?'

'Nothing. She's just about given me the garden, that's all.'

'Or given the garden you. She's a ruthless lady.'

'But it's what I want.'

'I know. That's why she's ruthless. All those generations of women getting their own way.'

But he was sunk in a kind of practical dream. It had come to him that the autumn planting season was only two months away with a world of work to do. Cordell you bastard, help me. You got me into this, so help me.

'Down in the tent after you'd walked out she asked me if I thought you could do it. I said yes.'

'Does that mean you'll stay and do it with me?'

He'd hardly dared hope that, so wasn't surprised when she shook her head.

'Not stay, no. Too heavy for me. For now at any rate.'

'But you'll come and see us sometimes?'

'Us?'

'Me and the garden.'

'You want me to?'

If I'm sure of anything... But he didn't say it.

'Yes, OK.'

They sat there, tired out and muzzy-headed from the whiskey. He noticed that new bramble tendrils were already shooting out from the border blurring the edges of the steps they'd cleared. No end to it.

493

The publishers hope that this book has given you enjoyable reading. Large Print Books are especially designed to be as easy to see and hold as possible. If you wish a complete list of our books please ask at your local library or write directly to:

Magna Large Print Books
Magna House, Long Preston,
Skipton, North Yorkshire.
BD23 4ND

This Large Print Book for the partially sighted, who cannot read normal print, is published under the auspices of

THE ULVERSCROFT FOUNDATION